Blossom of War

BLOSSOM
of
WAR

MAY WOODWARD

Copyright © 2018 May Woodward

The moral right of the author has been asserted.

Apart from any fair dealing for the purposes of research or private study, or criticism or review, as permitted under the Copyright, Designs and Patents Act 1988, this publication may only be reproduced, stored or transmitted, in any form or by any means, with the prior permission in writing of the publishers, or in the case of reprographic reproduction in accordance with the terms of licences issued by the Copyright Licensing Agency. Enquiries concerning reproduction outside those terms should be sent to the publishers.

Matador
9 Priory Business Park,
Wistow Road, Kibworth Beauchamp,
Leicestershire. LE8 0RX
Tel: 0116 279 2299
Email: books@troubador.co.uk
Web: www.troubador.co.uk/matador
Twitter: @matadorbooks

ISBN 978 1789015 386
British Library Cataloguing in Publication Data.
A catalogue record for this book is available from the British Library.

Typeset in 11pt Minion Pro by Troubador Publishing Ltd, Leicester, UK

Matador is an imprint of Troubador Publishing Ltd

for Karen

Somerlee
Baronets of Eardingstowe

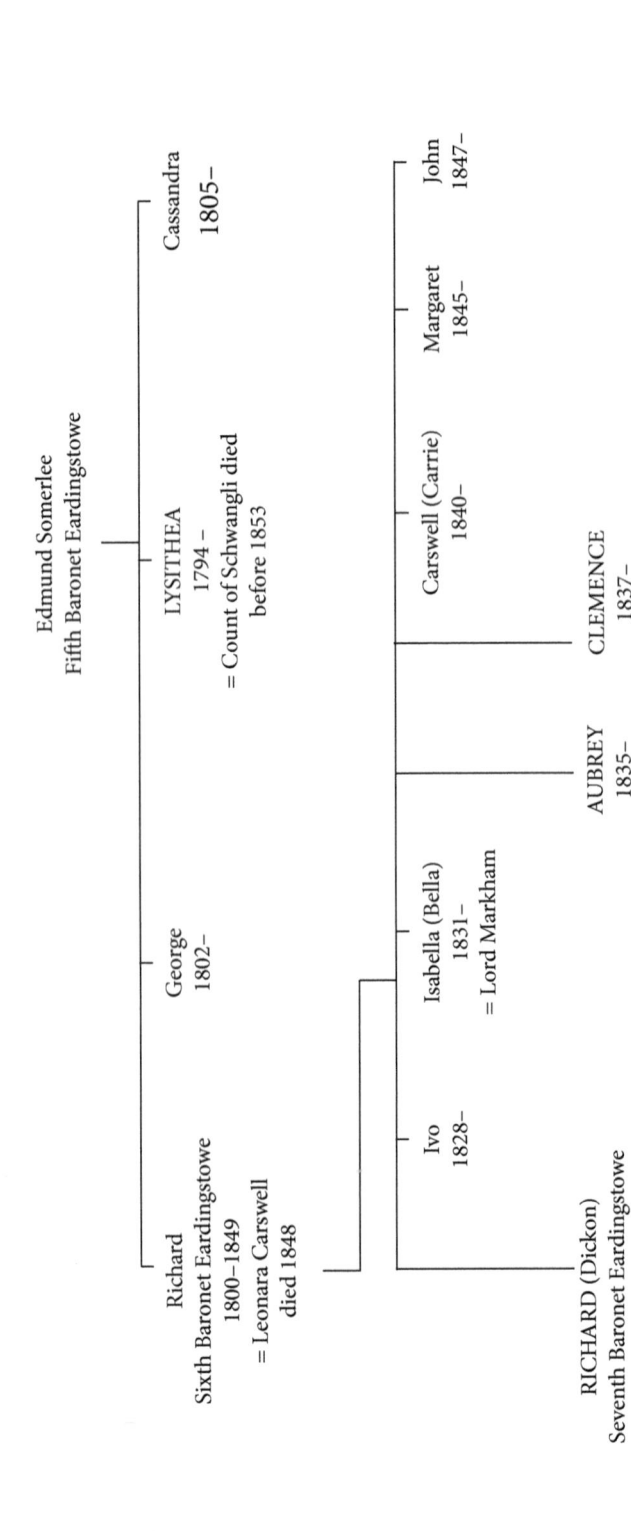

Edmund Somerlee
Fifth Baronet Eardingstowe

- Richard
  Sixth Baronet Eardingstowe
  1800–1849
  = Leonora Carswell
  died 1848
- George
  1802–
- LYSITHEA
  1794 –
  = Count of Schwangli died
  before 1853
- Cassandra
  1805–

Children of Richard and Leonora:
- Ivo
  1828–
- Isabella (Bella)
  1831–
  = Lord Markham
- AUBREY
  1835–
- CLEMENCE
  1837–

RICHARD (Dickon)
Seventh Baronet Eardingstowe
1825–

Children of Lysithea:
- Carswell (Carrie)
  1840–
- Margaret
  1845–
- John
  1847–

AUTHOR'S NOTE

It has never been established who was responsible for the disaster at Balaclava. Nolan is the only one who probably knew the truth, but he died in the engagement. The behaviour of the grotesque crowd on Saupon Hill might have had something to do with it.

'War tourism' was quite common in the 19th Century. I have not invented Lord Raglan's Gallophobic gaffes.

Any reader who regards the Smoky Mountain subplot as farfetched should check out *The Believers* by Adam Lebor. The Aubrey-plot, meanwhile, was inspired by the Tichborne case which gripped mid-Victorian England.

All the characters in this story are fictional apart from the well-known public figures. They include Timmy the Tortoise, the last surviving veteran of the war, who passed away in 2004 at the age of 165.

PROLOGUE
1849

'Let me in! Oh, help me, Miss Honeywell! Let me in… please…'

The girl's small fists hammered the huge front door.

'Don't leave me out here, Miss Honeywell! I'll do whatever you want! But please let me in! *Let me in! Please!*'

Her screams were not answered. From indoors came no sound.

'Miss Honeywell – I cannot breathe! I'm choking!' She took gasping breaths. 'Please hear me – '

Her wails waned into hiccupping sobs. One more time she battered the door. Her nails scratched track-marks in the ancient, brass-studded oak beams. She slumped to her knees – then passed out upon the marble flagstones of the mansion's colonnade.

High above, to the side of the jutting portico, a window snapped open. Out stuck a female head.

'You may come in when you've learned your lesson,' the woman called down. 'Six months, now, you've been moping indoors, Miss Clemence. It's not natural. Learn the hard way, Clemmie. Discipline!'

The governess wasn't finished. Yet she halted – the doorstep drama had an audience.

Two men were striding up the carriage-sweep towards the grand façade of Eardingstowe. Aged in their early twenties, wearing belted Norfolk jackets and leather bluchers, hunting guns were slung over their shoulders.

'What the devil...?' said one. Face down in the porch the unconscious twelve-year old lay, flashing white pantalettes beneath a flouncy frock with its sash tied in a bow. 'Dickon, what the devil's this? That's your sister, isn't it?'

'Yes, it is!' Sir Richard Somerlee raised astonished eyes to where the woman stood framed in the window.

Both men dumped their guns. Across the remainder of the lawn they sprinted.

Slimmer and fitter than the baronet, Lord Brandon Fanshawe got there first. He laid gentle hands on the girl's shoulders, then lifted a wrist and checked for a pulse.

Richard stopped at the base of the colonnade, one foot on the first step. He scowled up at the governess.

'Miss Honeywell! Explain yourself, madam. What have you done to Clemence?'

'Sir Richard.' The female stood tall, chin up, ready to defend herself. 'I thought this might cure Miss Clemmie of this strange affliction...'

'Oh, my God! You foul creature! You could have killed her – '

The baronet's friend looked up.

'She's breathing, Dickon. But her pulse is slow. Shall I carry her inside and send for a doctor?'

'Yes...' Richard heaved a great sigh. 'But the doctor won't be able to help, Fanny.'

The other man cradled and rocked the slip of a thing. His face was horror-struck.

'What on earth is wrong with your sister?'

'We don't know, Fanny.' Richard ran a hand through his thick, fair hair. He glared one more time at the governess – worried, now, that she might be in trouble for this. 'Don't you realise how serious this is, Miss Honeywell?' he snapped. 'Clemence could die if she is forced to go outside the house. She cannot breathe!'

The woman wasn't looking so sure of herself now.

'Sir Richard – I only did what I thought best for the young lady...'

'Yes, and damn near killed her, woman!' Richard flung out an arm towards her. 'Good God, suppose my little brother Aubrey had been here to witness this! I'd have him fretting with nightmares! You know how very close he and Miss Clemmie are. Get out of my sight, Miss Honeywell! I'll speak to you properly later.'

Shoulders heaving, he mounted the steps. He crouched beside his companion and the little one in his arms.

'Clemmie has not been outside the house since Pater died, Fanny. She took his death very badly – coming so soon after Mater's.'

'But that was January!' Lord Brandon Fanshawe gazed around at flowerbeds buzzing with insects, parkland trees in full leaf, sparkling sun, and deep blue sky almost cloudless.

'As I told that blasted governess... tormentress might be a better word for her, Fanny... it isn't that Clemmie doesn't *want* to leave the house. She *cannot*. One step outside and everything starts *spinning*, so she tells us. She says it is as if the whole world is closing in – suffocating her.' The baronet swung his hands together like a trap. 'Sometimes she cannot even *breathe*...' Richard stroked a few strands of hair from Clemence's face. 'I'm going to dismiss that woman for this.'

Brandon looked from Richard to the girl. Her head drooped over Brandon's elbow. Her ringlets, which were the same light blonde as her big brother's hair, dangled on Brandon's knee.

His eyes rose to the time-darkened wood – such a massive portcullis the great front door of Eardingstowe seemed if in front of it you were kneeling – and the scratches so lately grooved there.'

'What does the doctor say?'

'That she is hysterical, of course. And agrees with Miss Honeywell that we should just shut her outside and snap her out of it.'

'That's barbaric, Dickon!' As Clemence began to stir, Brandon caressed her brow with a finger.

'I agree, Fanny,' Richard said. 'But then Dr Moffitt's probably never encountered a case like it before. I don't know anyone who has.' The master of Eardingstowe leaned one arm upon his thigh and gave a nervous cough. 'Clemence was like this once before. Trapped inside for over a year, then. But she recovered, eventually. We prefer to keep it quiet, Brandon. I'm sure I can rely on your discretion, can't I, dear chap? You're my good friend, aren't you? We don't want an affliction like this in the family being broadcast abroad. I mean… well… won't do our reputation much good, will it?'

The other man tutted – sounded very like disgust to Richard. But he had cause to be worried, damn it. The Somerlee family was said to be cursed with mental infirmity. Some tainted ancestors passed on their syphilis; the Somerlees bequeathed their mad-blood. And these little frailties weren't helpful when you were seeking a peerage. *Or maybe they were!* But should he think twice about dismissing Miss Honeywell… a lady in possession of rather damaging inside knowledge…?

Brandon Fanshawe got to his feet. He lifted the limp featherweight. Two blue eyes were struggling to open.

Had the wretched soul been meaning to sup from the cesspool? Oh, Jeannie Mac…

The boy had at first thought the crumpled form, sprawled across his way on the riverbank, was a discarded sack; and then realised it was in fact an old starveling who had expired where he'd fallen.

Och, that was old Jarvis, the lad thought, as he looked closer and recognised the potato-sack cloak. *Someday soon they'll break yer man's legs so we can toss him into the midden-pit and be rid of his stink. With a name like Jarvis I'm guessing he had English blood. Better off without him we are. Why could it not just be the likes of him who die and not those who are really missed, like my ma…?*

The boy listened to the talk of the grown-ups, one of whom was his father. The two men were trying to catch something to eat. But there wasn't much life even in the waterways these days.

'Seamus! I'm offering you a neighbourly warning I am. The Somerlees are for throwing you out – all of ye, childer and all. And then you'll be off to Americay like all the rest.'

'Aye,' the father of the listening youngster said. 'Rather starve in a Yankee wigwam than an Irish hovel, so they would. And eaten by buffaloes if the coffin-ships don't do for 'em. I'll take my chance with our Somerlee landlords, Ruari.'

The boy was gazing upstream towards the waterfall. The cascade strewed spray and ephemeral rainbows as it pounded the rocks. On the bank above its foaming pool an outcrop stood: toadstool rocks piled one upon another as if a giant had abandoned his counting-house long ago.

'You know,' the first man was saying, 'in my travels I passed through Connemara. Saw a pile of dead all stacked like those there rocks, so I did. At least the Irish flies are getting fat. Then this old hag comes creeping up and takes a bite out of one!' The man touched the horseshoe nailed to the nearest tree trunk to ward off witchcraft.

'They say there's food in the towns, Seamus. The Dubliners hide their grain up their arses. Or England maybe? They're supping and farting well enough. And there's good work there.

Talking of Sir Dickon Somerlee, Kilara's phantom landlord. I worked a season in me youth in a mill his family owns. Great, black cavern of a place in that cauldron of the devil they call Manchester. Ah, but the wages...'

The child watched the waters making whirlpools of dead leaves as they were sucked towards the Shannon confluence where this subject-stream paid homage to its overlord.

The Somerlee clan owned the whole caboodle. Everything and everyone hereabouts which the eye could see. Yet never came. Absentee landlords, who from whatever English palatial pile they called home turned families out to starve for want of a shilling they'd never miss…

1853

Four years later

ONE

The soprano finished *Oh, giusto cielo!...Il dolce suono* on a high F natural. Applause broke out. In the change of scene which followed, a vocal murmur hummed around the theatre's auditorium.

'You said you would let me know your answer, Aunt Lizzy. What a fine idea of James's – you and I to go with the hussars when the troops sail!' Clemence gave a tiny thrilled shiver and smiled from behind her fan.

On stage meanwhile, the new scene was set in the castle. Real flame sconces lit up the great hall. Their illumination splayed out over the audience. Diamonds and perspiration were glistening on Lysithea's slender neck and shoulders.

'I really don't know, Clemmie. Dickon, what do you think?' The countess turned to the man sitting on her other side.

'I've told you, Aunt Lizzy,' said Richard. 'I have no objection to your travelling to the war. Can't come to much harm.'

'No! We'll be with Aubrey,' said Clemmie, 'and Captain Swynton.'

'I mean, sister dear, the army won't come to much harm,' Richard said, raising a brow. 'Heaven help the Russkies though. Not that I could stop you doing whatever you want anyway. Well, you'll be seventeen in just two months.'

'You won't be my lord and master any more soon,' said Clemence with a teasing look in her light blue eyes. 'It's James who will tell me what to do.'

'Not even a brave hussar would dare, Clemmie. I feel certain James Swynton will be a meek and dutiful husband to you.'

Clemence laughed.

'Please remember that I followed the drum with Wellington's army.' Lysithea sighed. 'It wasn't all romance, chicken.'

'But you do have some fond memories of the war,' Clemence said. 'Oh, Aunt, the hardships will make it an adventure!'

'We aren't at war yet, sweet one.' Lysithea fanned herself. 'In truth, Clemence, I feel sure it'll be settled without battle. I hope! Poor old Raglan ain't a Wellington.'

'No… could be quite farcical!' Richard said. 'It likely hasn't sunk in that the Iron Duke's dead. The old nincompoop might consult him.'

'Well, I adore a farce,' said Clemence. 'Was Lord Raglan that distinguished gentleman you talked with at the ball last week, Aunt?'

'You mean the one-armed old codger?' Richard said. Clemence fanned hard. She'd tried not to notice the disfigurement. 'If we do go to war, he'll be Field Marshal. Deaf as a post and thinks we're still fighting the Frenchies. It was Boney had his arm of course. Seemed to show a bit of interest in you, Aunt Lizzy, eh?'

'Ah, but you see,' said Clemence, casting her relation a sidelong, admiring look, 'Aunt Lizzy is very beautiful.'

'She's a wealthy widow, Clemmie!' Richard gave a snort of laughter.

'Oh, really, Richard!' said Lysithea.

'Yes, Dickon, that's mean!' Clemence scowled. 'Aunt Lizzy would turn all heads in a room if she hadn't a penny to her name!'

'And you're no better, Clemence!' the countess went on.

'Oh, but it's true, Aunt!'

The stories Clemence had heard about Aunt Lysithea. It was said she'd driven Napoleon wild with desire. Some said she'd been his mistress. In legend there had once been a nymph named Lysithea who in his passion for great Jupiter had turned into a lusting beast. Had a bovine Emperor done so too?

Lysithea turned to her with a serene smile.

'Nothing I say will dissuade you from this adventure you have in mind. And, in a way, maybe it'll do you good, dearest.'

'Aunt, you mean yes? We can go?'

Lysithea said 'aye' with a sound of weary resignation. But what joy. Clemence wafted her fan.

The girl cast her eyes all around the theatre before and behind her: rows of flapping fans, and medals and jewels winked in the dimness. While nothing was happening on the stage, some opera glasses were focussed on the galleries. The Duke of Ardenne's was the notable party here this evening.

She wondered where James was. Somewhere out on the town with his fellow officers. He and her brother Aubrey were in the same regiment, and bosom bows.

'I'll look after him for you, Clemmie, never you fear,' Aubrey had teasingly told her. Shame James did not care for the opera, though, and had declined to come with her instead.

In the stalls, silence fell. Clemence turned back to the stage as the piece resumed.

What did Captain James Swynton care for, she found herself wondering? Would he wish to play duets with her on her beloved keyboards when they were married?

Yet, no... 'Sorry – can't hit a right note,' James had guffawed. But she could tinkle away on the piano if that's what she liked. Himself, he loved a bracing walk in the Broads; fresh air and wind in the hair – except after a repast, of course; preferred to let his dinner settle.

'Oh no.' Clemence had let out a small cry; she hated open spaces, even feared the outdoors sometimes.

'How very odd.' James had raised his brows. He'd beamed, however, and given her hand a little pat. 'You'll love my cook's honey cakes, and marzipan, though.'

They must have something in common, surely? She loved him. This chortling, rather rotund, ruddy-faced soldier who'd swept her off her feet at her début ball. A maidie from deepest Somerset, fresh in town for the season... James Swynton was the only suitor she had known.

'Miss Clemence Somerlee, has anyone told you that you have the loveliest eyes? You're the prettiest girl I've ever seen,' he'd told her during their first dance.

Good gracious – was she really? Whenever she'd looked in her glass, though, she'd still seen no curves where other girls of sixteen had them. Minute breasts and a slender figure. Eyes the colour of an April sky unsure that spring had dawned. And would her moonshine hair ever turn golden blonde?

'Lovely as a dew-kissed rose.' The captain had grinned. 'You will be a beauty, Miss Somerlee. Men will die for you.'

Suddenly, the chandelier they were dancing under had seemed to be radiating fantasy colours from its crystal droplets. She'd blushed as she'd seen herself through this man's eyes. Later, she would tell the birds in their dawn chorus that she'd met the love of her life.

And, she smiled to herself now, hugging herself with the thrill of it – her eldest brother had not been at all pleased with her wayward choice. Richard had had someone else entirely in mind:

'You know Lord Fanshawe's one of my oldest friends?' Richard had urged. 'He'd be a meet match for you, Clem. The

Woodmancote estate's not worth as much as it could be, I suppose. But Fanny's uncle's the Duke of Ardenne. I want to be in the Lords one day. It could help me, Clemmie…'

Dickon might as well have broken wind. His idea of romantic wooing had well and truly put her off Brandon Fanshawe, Dickon's friend who she'd known all her life. *What do you think the women of your family are, Dickon Somerlee – chips to play to make your fortune with?* Oh, yes, no doubt he did, knowing him. At that thought, she'd made a very rude noise with her tongue.

So, James Swynton she'd chosen instead, and fiddlesticks to Richard and the House of Lords. She loved James. She must love James.

When the opera finished, the audience streamed out into the vestibule. Outer garments were collected. Dozens of top hats being decompressed made a pap-pap-pap sound.

The Duke of Ardenne's party came sweeping through. Richard raised his hat to Lady Amathia Consett. Clemence spotted a flickering smile pass between them. The names of the Baronet of Eardingstowe and Ardenne's daughter were being coupled in drawing-room gossip.

Clemence linked arms with Richard as the young lady's velvet and sable cloak swished by.

'You danced three times with Lady Amathia at the Duke of Westminster's ball. It has been noticed, you see.'

'I cannot conceive what you see in the Consetts, Nephew!' said Lysithea. 'We're a much older family.'

'Well, I'd never seen such radiant loveliness!' Richard said. 'Lady Amathia's diamonds must have been worth a thousand pounds. Certainly captured my heart! And being the granddaughter of the richest slave-trading alderman ever to become a duke, she'd be as charming if she were as plain as a mouse! And I'll woo the lady with all my antique charm, Aunt,' he finished, smiling.

Clemence grimaced. She and the Consett girl had been presented at court on the same occasion. Amathia had not endeared herself. Clemence had overheard the flaxen beauty saying to another girl: 'So tedious having to come to the court dressmaker to have one's gown made up. How convenient if one's family was in the trade.' Had her glance fallen upon Clemence whose family owned an…ahem… *cotton mill* in… ahem… *Manchester*? Clemence had a sneaking feeling it had.

More to the point, though, could this woman be trusted with the heart of a beloved brother? Or was Clemence just being the petulant baby sister who resented an intruder stealing Dickon's affections?

Outside, a storm was blowing. The Consetts had to huddle at the foot of the colonnade steps while their carriage drew up and the coachman alighted to put down the step.

A beggar-woman, who had been crouching beneath the corbels of one of the columns, ventured near. She stretched a hand towards the wonderful lady. Amathia slapped her fan across the woman's face and stepped towards the coach.

God in Heaven… how cruel. Clemence hurried down the steps, and out from underneath the awning into the rain.

The creature was cowering behind her pillar. Clemence took a hand from her chinchilla muff and reached for the female's shivering hands. She was no more than thirty, Clemence thought, and drenched from waiting outside the theatre all evening.

'Do you have any trade?' she quickly asked.

'I was a seamstress, miss. Lost my position, though, and cannot get another.'

Clemence read a lot into that. An unwanted child had quickened in her belly. Her employer had discarded her.

She would never work again, and would likely perish in the workhouse, unmissed.

'Listen. I want you to go to Somerlee House in Aldgate,' Clemence told the woman. 'Tell Mrs Weeks Miss Clemmie sent you, and wants you taken on to work in the sewing-room.' She reached into her reticule. 'Here's money for the omnibus fare. And take my handkerchief as proof I sent you.'

She watched until the woman and her astonished face retreated behind the pillars.

Clemence met up with Richard and Lysithea beneath the awning.

'What is all that noise?'

From somewhere in the night, down towards the river, came the sound of trumpet music and cheering voices. Had the opera been so dire, Clemence wondered aloud, that the military had been summoned? Meanwhile, an elderly gentleman close by, his moustache quivering, was asking his lady companion: 'What's to do, d'you suppose, m'dear?'

'What in goodness' name is *this* all about, then?' said Lysithea, turning their attention to a peculiar spectacle unfolding on the other side of the street.

A laughing group of three men pushed to the ground what looked like a great, dark-coated bear. The beast rolled on its side into the gutter. Its tormentors then pelted it with unpleasant things. From the cowardly human way the mincing creature put up paws to feebly protect itself, it was evident there was a person play-acting inside the skin.

Meanwhile, though, Clemence's fiancé, Captain James Swynton was making his way through the crowd.

'I say! Somerlee! Ladies! My dear!' he added when he was at Clemence's side.

'Hello, my dear Captain,' Clemence said as he lifted her gloved fingers to his lips.

'Heard the news, have you?' he asked all three.

'We've been at the theatre all evening,' said Richard. 'Rather mediocre performance of *Lucia di Lammermoor* frankly. I take it you and the rest of the Haymarket have had more entertainment?'

'Been dining at the Travellers! That's where I heard.' One outside leg of the captain's yellow-striped scarlet trousers could be seen beneath his cloak. 'But it's a dashed damp night! Pray come to my cab while you wait for your carriage.'

'Thank you, Captain. So kind,' Richard said, and took his aunt's arm.

The long line of private vehicles was still edging in single file up to the theatre entrance. It would be half an hour before the Somerlee brougham arrived. Clemence and Lysithea put up their hoods, and all four hurried through the wet to where James Swynton had a cabriolet waiting.

'There's been a frightfully unsporting to-do down in the Black Sea,' the captain began as the ladies climbed into the interior and shook rain from cloaks and muffs. 'Turkish navy all blown to pieces by that vodka-soused Czar. Oh yes, indeedy! At a port named Sinope. Seems the Turks were trying to send supplies to their troops fighting the Russians in Asia Minor. The cussed Russkies fired on them in harbour and wiped the lot out! Colossal fire swept the waterfront… burned bodies blown all over the place…'

'Thank you, Captain Swynton,' said Lysithea.

'Well, what was so unsporting,' he continued, 'the Russkies used shells, not cannons. Poor little Turks didn't stand a chance.'

'And where was our navy?' Richard said in disgust. 'It's been out in Constantinople expressly to defend the Ottomans!'

'Still was,' said Swynton. 'Sunning itself and growing plump at the Sultan's table while the Russians did this ghastly deed. I've heard the blighters even put the British flag on their masts to fox those easily-deluded Musselmen. Stap me! I hope I'm there when we teach the rotters a lesson.'

At that point, the little company with the bear swaggered past the cab window… the Russian Bear, of course. All of them, bear included, were singing *'Cheer, boys, Cheer! For country, Mother country! Cheer, boys, Cheer!'*

'So, it is war, then?' Lysithea said.

'I imagine so, Aunt Lizzy,' said Richard. 'If Czar Nicholas gobbles up Turkey, we lose the Black Sea and the trade route to India. And methinks Nicholas will soon be looking westwards towards us!'

Clemence felt a feverish current shivering its way through her veins. Her eyes tracked a firework making an arc above the London chimneystacks. Everyone knew the Home Secretary, Palmerston, had been stewing for battle for months. The newspapers had been clanging on Mars's shield. War had been in the air all summer just as was the scent of honeysuckle and lavender, and at the balls she had attended it had seemed she was dancing to its music. You felt as if you were floating in the clouds. How wonderful to be English, to be alive, how great the time Clemence lived in.

'Well, nothing can have been decided yet,' Lysithea went on. 'The Prime Minister will still favour a diplomatic solution. He was saying as much when I dined with him last week.'

'Bother Aberdeen! Teach the dogs a lesson!' said Richard. 'Else they'll be heading for England next.'

'Dash it, won't be sorry if there is a war, you know!' said James. 'We all have to listen to our paters boasting on about what they all did at Waterloo and so-on… And everyone loves teaching a crowned bully like Nicholas a lesson!'

'But so many might not return home!' Lysithea said. 'What worth an England saved but without the flower of her youth?'

'Ah, but for every drop of English blood spilled, Aunt Lizzy,' said her nephew, 'be sure a blossom flowers in her soil!'

'And spring always follows winter. So, peace follows war, you know!' Captain Swynton chortled. He reached across the space between the seats and took the hand of Clemence who was sitting opposite. 'Our regiment has been ordered to stand by. Don't it make you proud to be a part of history? One of my lot fought at Crécy, you know. Will you come with us, Miss Somerlee?'

A second firework lit up all four people in the carriage. Over near the river, voices could be heard singing *'Cheer, boys, cheer.'* Another pyrotechnic... in its light, cobbles and the dung and straw-strewn rainwater gushing along the centre gutter glistened sulphur-orange and blood-red.

'Plenty of officers' wives are coming, you know,' Swynton went on, eyes brightening. 'And you'll have your brother Aubrey there as well as me to look after you. In fact, we could be married out in the east! Or wherever it is we're heading. Our Colonel's not thought to tell us that much yet! Dash it, Aubs could give you away! Picture it, Miss Somerlee... united, you and I, in a little chapel on the shore of the sunlit Black Sea...'

Really, it was appealing, wasn't it? She had never left England's shore, and whatever dangers, horrors or heartache might be skulking in the field of war, there would be a sea-breeze in her hair, new lands to see.

'As a matter of fact, my aunt and I discussed it,' said Clemence. 'We would love to accompany you, Captain Swynton.'

'Yes... I've given in... against my better judgment!' Lysithea said.

James let out a blissful sigh. As he leaned close, Clemence breathed in his vinous odour. She couldn't help noticing how florid and tubby he looked.

Richard tutted. He lowered his gun. Yet another overweight and unfit victim-to-be had mockingly avoided his aim and flown to safety in the upper boughs.

Rain was pattering the undergrowth. From his host the Earl of Mowbray's kitchen yard wafted the smell of meat being smoked. The sound of fanning wings disturbed the nearby bushes and branches. A constant crack-crack resounded in the woods all around him; he thought the rest of the shooting party must be enjoying better fortune than was he.

Richard had had poor sport all afternoon – had dispatched just the one slow grandfather woodcock. In truth, he was out in the field more for the breeze in his hair. He'd taken a larger dose of laudanum than he'd intended, and it had left him with a thick head. It was not an addiction, of course. No – laudanum just calmed the nerves when you had a cloud on the mind.

He emerged from the tree cover into a clearing. Some of the female house-party guests were gathered there, although most would be in the warmth of the Earl's drawing-room. These doughty ones sat chattering beneath an awning and umbrellas, high tea laid out in the tent on trestle tables. He grimaced at sight of the doughy, creamy viands. He hoped Mrs Dean would be up to her usual low standard when he returned to Eardingstowe, so he could discreetly skip dinner for a few nights and shed the pounds he would have gained.

A young woman waved to him from the tent opening. She stepped towards him with care across the wet grass.

'Frampton, I'll not be continuing with the shoot,' Richard told his loader. 'I believe Lady Amathia desires private talk.' He surrendered his gun, and then returned the approaching lady's smile.

She was as fair as winter aconite. But it was in flattering candlelight that he'd danced with her. In November daylight, he saw how plump she was. How he dreamed of the peerage, high office… if he married her, her father the Duke of Ardenne's influence should get him that.

'Sir Richard. I trust you are enjoying the meet?'

'To be sure, Lady Amathia. Mowbray's renowned for his plentiful game. Unfortunately, my mind has been on other matters today.'

'Of course. You must be yearning for war to be declared. Two whole weeks, now, since that dreadful affair in Sinope, and still the Government dithers. It's quite disgraceful.'

'Yes. But I have pleasanter concerns also.' He made a small, smiling bow. 'A warning, Lady Amathia – you should not venture out into the field; you are looking so lovely this day, you are in danger of being taken for an exotic bird of paradise and shot down.'

Amathia gave a light laugh.

'Come, sir,' she said. 'Let's walk apart together until tea is served.'

He offered her an arm. She slipped through it lace-gloved fingers. Her flowery scent wafted on the air between them.

'May I, Lady Amathia?' Richard pointed out in the path ahead of them a rainwater pool filled with mushy leaves. He bounded across, turned, and held out a hand to her. She laid her fingers in his palm and made the hop to the dry ground. The two stood close, almost touching, and smiled at each other.

'You have prettier manners than your good friend my cousin, Sir Richard,' Amathia said. 'I gather you and my kinsman Lord Brandon Fanshawe were at Brasenose together?'

'And rarely apart since, my lady. He is my goodliest friend.'

'Poor, lonely young man, I always thought. Cousin Brandon barely knew his papa. Mama even less. Sorry little orphan almost before he was breeched. And doesn't have a wonderful brood of siblings like you or I, either. Is family important to you, Sir Richard?'

'Means the world to me, Lady Amathia. I have three grown brothers – Ivo, Aubrey and Carswell – and two sisters, Bella and Clemmie. Once Clemence leaves to get married, only my youngest brother and sister, John and Margaret, will remain at home – they're children still. They're dears! I was left with responsibility for them when our parents passed on.'

'And your home – Eardingstowe? How long has it been in your family?'

'Around two millennia I believe.'

Amathia blinked slowly; corn-coloured lashes covering surprised grey eyes.

'That's a long, long time for a property to be in one family.'

'Indeed, it is.' Richard broke into a laughing smile. 'There is an old family legend that we are the last surviving branch of the royal house of Dumnonia.'

'Gosh!' said Amathia.

'All the world likes to think he is descended from King Arthur. But the Somerlees really are, I think.'

Amathia turned and walked a little further along the path. Over a shoulder from behind her umbrella, she cast a dimpled smile.

'Your brother the cavalryman will be expecting to embark for the war I imagine, Sir Richard? So proud you must be! My own dear brother, being Papa's heir, is not permitted to join the fray. One cannot risk the line dying out.'

'Most sensible,' said Richard. Actually, the Consett line was more like a stump. It began with Consett's sire who had been a borough alderman. Richard recalled Lysithea laughing once, nose in the air: 'When we were fighting alongside Drake, that family would have been paddling our oars.'

'Don't suppose I could leave either seat, either,' said Richard. 'Eardingstowe or the House. My seat is comfortable on the purple cushions for which God designed it.'

'Personally,' Amathia confided, halting and facing him, 'I believe Papa's preference to keep Philoctetes out of the army might have as much to do with the likelihood that Philo would pass out at sight of a Russian bayonet. My brother's a dear boy, Sir Richard, but not the stuff of alabaster memorials!'

A chuckle rumbled up through Richard's insides; she was almost laughing too, looking deep into his eyes.

'My own pater and I were never close, Lady Amathia,' he confided. 'Didn't trust me with the inheritance! "Why do you think I sent you into Parliament?" the pater used to say. "Don't mind you sending the country to the dickens – but keep your meddling paws off Eardingstowe!" Since when was I a troublesome Prince Hal to him? I'm not one for gambling the fortune and debauching the housemaids. Yet once when we quarrelled, he said: "Perhaps I should throw you into the mere for Jenny Greenteeth?"'

'Oh dear, dear me, Sir Richard!' Amathia said. 'And who might Jenny… I'm sorry, I didn't catch the name… be, pray?'

'Jenny Greenteeth. An aquatic damsel who dwells in the Eardingstowe mere, Lady Amathia. The Somerlees are her mortal foes. So, none us cares to take a cooling dip on a summer day.'

Amathia gave a shrill laugh, her face upturned to the speckles of grey light flickering in the overarching branches.

'Have you ever seen this strange creature?'

'Not personally, no. But I've heard many-an odd account from those who claim they have. Pater used to say his favourite hound would never walk the mere path, and would stop there, howling, hackles up.'

'What, pray, does the Eardingstowe estate consist of, Sir Richard?'

'Eighteen thousand acres of grounds and farming land in and around the Quantock hills. There's the house – eighteenth century mostly, but with a medieval wing attached. A chapel – very old, indeed. Some land elsewhere, too – quite a large estate in Ireland. Although that's more trouble than it's worth! I spend most of my time evicting the lazy, grubby tenants when they fall in arrears with their rent!'

'How tiresome!' said Amathia.

'And there's a mill...' his voice wavered just a little; but she had to know sometime that much of his lucre came from the cotton trade. 'Very far away – in some ghastly town in the north. We never go there – just reap the rewards.'

She was still smiling, and he added: 'It makes cotton, does our mill.' Still she smiled, and he felt braver. 'It came to the family through my parents' marriage. My maternal grandfather was a cotton-master by the name of Joshua Carswell. My mater brought more to the Somerlees, my father used to say, than just the Carswells' insipid looks. We're all blond, you see, apart from Aubrey.'

'Pays for your silk cravats though, doesn't it, that little venture in charming Lancashire?' Amathia said. 'You should be proud of it, Sir Richard. All cousin Brandon has on the Fanshawe estate is sheep – lots of them. I see no objection to dipping a finger or two in the steak and ale pie of trade, you know.'

'Yes, but you didn't get called "barrow-boy" and other trade-related epithets at Winchester College I don't suppose, my lady! But you're right... the smog that mill chimney belches out paid for two sisters presented at court, and my brother's commission in a dashed expensive regiment.'

The pair headed deeper into the woodland, away from the sound of the gunshots and keening of the feathered fallen. Richard made out the mounds of badger setts. The soil was only lately overturned, and barely damp from the current rain – had the inhabitants fled from the smell of humans?

'Well, I must say it's all very stirring stuff, this war-fever,' Richard said. 'Fills one with such pride that our brave boys are to be doing God's will – freeing the world from tyrant Nicholas's enslavement.'

'Ah, then pity the poor, weaker sex, Sir Richard,' said Amathia, 'who may only follow the drum from afar!'

'Some women will be travelling with the army, Lady Amathia. My aunt and sister among them. Clemence, of course, accompanies her fiancé.'

'So I heard.' Amathia lifted the hem of her dress. She hopped over a leaf pile. Her look was thoughtful. 'Your aunt…' she went on. 'She has been three years widowed… no children of her own I understand?'

'Yes, that's right. Lizzy's my most dear aunt and godmother.'

'Her late husband was the Juncker von Schwangli – a Swiss aristocrat, yes? He left Lysithea well-provided for I believe?'

Aha, the reason behind her interest in his relation was becoming plain. Richard smothered his unflattering smile.

'As a matter of fact, Schwangli was one of the richest men in Europe. Owned palaces in Geneva, Vienna, Budapest, Pressburg and a castle in Galicia. As you surmise, all these are Lysithea's now.'

'Well, indeed.' A smile lit Amathia's face. That smug, fair, angel face. How could he resist it?

'Lysithea and Clemmie are particularly close. Ever since Mater died they've been bosom bows. Lizzy has been her chaperone, of course, for her début season. In fact,' he scratched his ear as if talking of an unimportant matter, 'I believe Clemmie is to be the main benefactor from Aunt Lizzy's will. Oh, I'm sure I'll get her husband's rosewood cabinet I've always admired. And there might be a jewel or two for my wife should I have the good fortune to find a lady to win my heart. But the bulk of the legacy will be Clemence's.'

Well, he'd shot down two birds after all. This one's face fell with a plunk into the sodden grass.

Richard invited her to take his arm.

'Shall we return to the clearing and sample Mowbray's hospitality, Lady Amathia?'

'Thank you, Sir Richard.' They resumed their walk. She had something very visibly on her mind. Like – how might Amathia remove Clemence from the scene and divert the Schwangli fortune to other channels?

TWO

'Perhaps you might consider the asylum, Sir Richard?'
Who had said that, long, long ago? Was it that horrid governess, Miss Honeywell? Clemence hadn't been meant to hear, of course. Yet she had.

How had it come about? The girl frowned as she tried to remember.

A summer day. She had been alone. Screaming – stumbling through the bracken. She must have been only six or seven. Up in the loneliest reaches of the Quantocks. Nothing but racing clouds and dizzy heights to be seen all the way to the telescopic yonder. Nanny Jude had warned her not to wander far from their picnic, but Clemence had been a little rebel…

Eventually, she'd heard her brothers Dickon and Aubrey calling her across the hillside.

They'd marched her back to Eardingstowe. Everyone angry with her. She'd been imprisoned in the nursery for days as a punishment.

But when her confinement was up…

'Come now and play, Clemmie! It's a lovely day,' Aubrey had been calling to her through the drawing-room windows which overlooked the Crystal Garden.

Yet when she'd tried to…

...it had seemed the heavens had come swooping down. Smothering her. All the horizons tilting on their orbits. She could not keep her balance... as if a sirocco was fuming in from the Quantocks, whirling her round and round and round... Like the world outside was an airless vacuum... sucking... sucking... choking... The girl had found herself gasping for breath – and passing out.

She hadn't been able to step out of doors. The walls of Eardingstowe themselves had become a gaol. As if bolts now barred the great front door.

For almost two years Clemence had lived that hermit existence, a wraith-like face at her bedchamber casement which the estate workers sometimes glimpsed.

During that time, often she would peep at the terrifying gardens, woodland and hills, and would drop the curtain from a trembling hand. What was out there? Why was she afraid of the outdoors?

Oh, they'd tried to cajole her with offers of jellies, ices, whatever she fancied... but she daren't go out. They'd threatened to lock her in an attic where there were spiders and mice... still she couldn't step across that threshold into the fresh air.

The Somerlees kept quiet about it. An aunt, Cassandra – Lysithea's younger sister – was shut away in an asylum. A great-uncle had died there too – he'd tried to shoot the gardener because he'd thought he was Napoleon.

Captain Swynton had not been told any of this. All Clemence had confided to her husband-to-be was that she was not fond of the great outdoors or tight, pressing crowds of people.

She was thinking over these things now as she stood on the shore of the Eardingstowe mere one November evening. Wet leaves blew her way from the parkland trees.

You could make out little below the darkling water. A few waving fronds of weed. Quiet bubbles popping on the surface. How ancient the tarn must be she thought, older than the hall: on the brow above the further bank stood a stone circle and cursus which Clemence's ancestors had raised before the Romans marched the Somerset hills.

Somewhere in the curling mist, sedge and foxtail grasses of the mere, haunted with marsh-lights and calls of moorhens, it was said Jenny Greenteeth lurked. For centuries, the watery creature had been waiting to snatch the Somerlees – her deadly enemies – to their doom in the deep. Who she had been in life no-one now remembered. Some witch one of Clemence's forbears had burned perhaps. Clemence felt rather sorry for Jenny and wished she could reach out a hand of friendship.

Her musings turned to her lost aunt, Cassandra. Clemence recalled that it had been here at the mere-side that Cassie had believed she'd heard the voices of spirits.

There had been no harm in Cassie. Poor old dear. Clemence had even thrilled to hear of the fair folk who Cassandra had claimed she'd ridden about the Eardingstowe lands with while everyone slept.

'One day, Jenny let me into her lair,' Cassandra had once told Clemence. 'I said to her "Aren't you going to keep me, like all the other Somerlees down in your murky halls?" But Jenny said no, she'd let me go, as long as I told you all where I'd been and what I'd seen.'

The household had suffered Cassandra's eccentricities for years.

But then she had prophesied that an elf-prince was coming to destroy the Somerlees. The old baronet, Clemence's father, had finally had enough, and put his sister away in the nuthouse.

But who was mad, really, and who sane? Clemence remembered her father scoring his way through his Irish tenants: 'O'Briens? Not paid rent for six months – out! Flanagans? Not paid for four – out! McFarlands… they're the worst of the lot, damn their hides! Turf them out, out, out! And get tenants in their place who can pay, damn it! What's that you say? Well, I don't believe they are starving! Just their excuse to swindle their landlord, that's all it is!'

Clemence clutched her cloak tight against the wind. Twilight was descending. Rain beginning to fall. She trod the path homeward.

Through the trees ahead of her, the mansion's windows could be made out glowing dusky-gold as the evening lamps were lit. Chimney smoke mingled with the mist. Jackdaws flit and croaked around the stacks, pale Corinthian colonnade and portico.

The first baronet had not had the heart to consign the Norman manor-house and its Tudor lanthorn-tower to dust when he'd built the new house; the one now grew from the other – a gallimaufry of rolling history. And to the west of the house rose the ancient yew which legend said would stand as long as the Somerlees; when it fell, so would the family.

Suddenly, it struck Clemence that in just a few months this would be home no longer.

Not leaving, she told herself. Rather, she was going – by her own choice – to the man she loved. Norfolk would be just as nice, wouldn't it – no wild hills where she could be lost again? And a future filled with James. James's loving embraces. James growing stout and gouty and cantankerous when his infatuation dimmed as she began to grow grey? James's children making her get as plump as Amathia Consett? Daughters growing up to marry Swyntons-to-come? Sons treading the death-soil of some future Waterloo?

The girl gasped and walked faster. She bypassed the house, and continued along the path to St Laurey's, the estate church.

She pushed open the mossy little lichgate and passed into the churchyard.

The small chapel was at least as old as the dwelling which had always stood on the site of the present house. Possibly older. In the legend, St Laurey had lived here as an anchoress.

Clemence stood and stared at the yew whose branches were bowing and creaking in the wind. Around its trunk, men had worshipped before Christ had walked the earth. The tree stood within the yard but had likely grown before the church was raised. The upstart faith attempted to contain the old which it had supplanted. In a storm, the saturnine boughs battered the chapel's south window. In places, the wall was suffering subsidence from the pressure of its antediluvian roots.

The girl stepped through the time-blackened church door.

Clemence had always found comfort in the chapel – the quiet, cool, musty presence of God. She walked the nave without making a sound. Ahead – the plain altar and, above, the Calvary window where was pictured a man lying stretched in agony. On this spot for aeons voices had prayed for deliverance from the Norsemen, the Black Death, Bonaparte.

To the right of the altar, set into a niche in the wall, was the curtained reliquary where were kept certain Somerlee treasures. One was the medallion which St Louis had presented to Rosselin de Somelay. Engraved on it was the earliest depiction of the Somerlee device – the Yew and Quatrefoils. It recalled the miraculous quatrefoils which Rosselin had seen in the sky above the Nile that day in 1250, foretelling a crusader victory. Then there was Father Roland Somerlee's ring – found undamaged among his ashes after Bloody Mary had burned him at the stake.

'I do love James. I do. I do.' Clemence knelt at the altar rail. She fixed her eyes on the altar cross. 'Who could not love a man who thinks she's the prettiest girl he's seen?' *And who isn't the one Dickon insisted you should marry.* The nasty little voice seemed real, sneering in her ear.

She sprang up from her knees, turned her back on the sanctuary, and hurried back along the nave.

Outside, the rain was growing heavier.

Clemence slipped into the house through the garden door. She scurried up the north stairs, along the picture gallery, and into the library. There she sat at the piano, plucking away.

Just getting into her stride she was when she realised she had an unwanted audience. Her fingers clattered on the keys in a chord which sounded like a ship's horn.

'I'm rather glad Beethoven was deaf. You'd have broken his heart.'

Lord Brandon Fanshawe was leaning against the door, arms folded, an amused smile on his face.

'Captain Swynton, I'm glad to say, looks as if he cares more for food than music. How long before they discreetly transfer your betrothed from the Light to the Heavy Brigade, eh, Miss Somerlee?'

Clemence glared, at a loss for anything cutting to say in return. She began to blush.

'James is a finer man than you, Fanny Fanshawe!'

'Oh, absolutely-dootly, Miss Somerlee! How could a dullard like me compare with a dashing hussar?' The young lord put his head on one side, grinning. 'Czar Nicholas is even now trembling, so I hear, in his Winter Palace, knowing the doughty Captain Swynton is soon to face him.'

'While you, Lord Brandon Fanshawe, censure from the soft benches of the Lords! Oh, mea culpa,' went on Clemence. 'You'd not know the way to Westminster if you were asked directions, would you, my lord, since you attend the House so infrequently!'

Lord Fanshawe hid his laughter behind a hand.

'I was in the House only this week, Miss Clemence. And I assure you you'll get your war which you crave so. Bloodshed and gore galore if the mood at Westminster is aught to go by. They'll be hanging Nicholas's carcass from London Bridge by next Christmas. But I'll be going to war, too. Though not, as you surmise, in the field.'

'You'll… be going to the war?'

'Yes, Miss Somerlee, as a war tourist,' he said. 'My uncle the duke has loaned me his yacht, *The Oriflamme*.'

'Well! Journeying all the way to Russia just to watch a fight?' said Clemence. 'Why not visit a boxing booth and save yourself the sea-malaise?'

'Ah, ma'am,' Lord Fanshawe sighed. 'There's naught can compare with charging steeds, flash of steel, blood in your nostrils… We haven't seen a battle since… well, Waterloo I suppose, before you or I was born, my dear. Why – one has to be over fifty to remember a good tussle! And by the time the next comes along I'll as likely be in me bathchair! It should be a marvellous lark. And do you know what, Miss Clemence Somerlee? The hussars will fight all the more bravely for seeing your pretty face cheering them on.'

He waved her out of the piano seat.

'Come, my dear! Let me show you how Beethoven wanted his beautiful melodies to be played.'

'All right, then, arrogant toad! But I don't believe you can play better than me.'

He settled, set aside the sheet-music for the Moonlight Sonata, and took up that for the Waldstein instead.

Clemence seethed as his fingers zoomed over the most difficult bits. His copper-gold hair shone in the candlelight from the ormolu candelabrum which stood on the bureau in the corner.

'I hate you, Fanny Fanshawe!'

She flounced out, his bright laughter following her.

The dressing-room door banged open.

Clemence jumped.

She was seated at her toilet-table. Her maid was uncoiling Clemence's ringlets before bed. Both startled women turned around.

The baronet stood in the doorway, looking thunderous. He got rid of the curtseying servant with a jerk of the head meaning 'be off.'

When she'd gone, Richard slammed shut the door leaving him alone with Clemence. It must be serious. Hardly ever did he come to a female family member's bedchamber.

He advanced a few steps across the rug. Arms folded, he stood before her.

'Just what was the matter with you tonight?' he said. He wasn't angry often. But when he was his fair complexion glowed pink and eyes narrowed to slits.

'I don't know what you mean.' Clemence turned back to the dressing-table. She took up where the abigail had left off. Not easy to wield a brush when you were unaccustomed to doing what maids usually did, and your hand was shaking. In the brief quiet, rain could be heard pattering the window pane.

'You know damn well what I mean!' Richard marched the remaining space between them, seized her shoulder, and forced her to face him. 'You were rude to Fanny all through dinner! If you weren't ignoring him, you were catty. No wonder he retired early in discomfort. I shall apologise to him tomorrow. And I'd like an explanation from you.'

'Dickon – your friend Lord Brandon Fanshawe has teased me since I was in the schoolroom. So, I'm big enough now to pay back some of what I feel I owe.'

'You're not so big that I cannot still take you over my knee and give you a hiding.'

'You were never man enough to do that, Dickon, even when I was naughty enough to deserve it.'

'Listen to me, Clemmie Somerlee! Apart from Fanny being my dearest friend in the world, he's a guest under Eardingstowe's roof! He deserves your respect and courtesy for that alone.'

'Dickon, I was just teasing! Giving as good as I've got. If your friend is too sensitive to appreciate that, then I'm sorry.'

'You're spoilt rotten, missy, you know that?' Richard paced aside. He ran a hand through his hair. 'I always thought Mater and Pater indulged you, second favourite only after their rosy Aubrey. By the time they passed on, it was too late for me to correct their wrongdoing.'

Clemence pulled her brush through her loose hair. How did Robyn do it every night without hurting? Ah, it pained. Or was she yanking in anger?

'I know why you're really upset, Dickon.' She tugged at a stubborn ghost of a ringlet. 'You haven't forgiven me for not marrying Fanny, have you?'

'That's your loss, foolish girl!' Richard snapped.

'Has it occurred to you that I didn't marry Lord Brandon Fanshawe because I don't love him, but I do love Captain Swynton?'

'It occurs to me that you love defying me,' he said.

To Clemence it felt like a slap.

'How dare you!' She flung down the brush and swung to face him. 'James is wonderful, truly lovely. Kind, gentle, adores me, thinks more highly of me than do you, Dickon, says he'd go to war to defend me. And I think he's the darlingest man in the world!'

Richard raised his hands in mock defence.

'I'm not gainsaying you, Clemence.'

'Oh, I think you are, brother dear! I didn't marry the man of your choice and you're angry.'

'Who would blame me? Indulged you, you wayward missy, that's what I did. Should have played the martinet of fairy tales – locked you in your room and forced you to wed Fanny. Soft, that's what I am. Or rather…' A glint came into Richard's eye as he peered around at her. 'Locked you *out* of your room.'

Now that did hurt. Clemence turned to the mirror, hunching her shoulders so that he could not see her pained expression.

'Now, I'm not a cruel man, Clemmie, but I know the worst punishment I could inflict on you – and, by God, right now you merit it.' He stood behind her, hands either side of her elbows as they rested on the dressing-table top, peering over her shoulder at her reflection in the glass. 'That mean governess was right after all, as I recall. Locking you out of the house was the kick up your dainty rear you needed. They heard your screams down at Kilve Beach, you know.'

'You wouldn't do that…would you?' Clemence gripped the chair back.

'Believe me, I thought about it. But, no,' he said. 'What I might have done has no bearing now. You're engaged to that booby, and unless the Czar obliges me by dispatching him to the happy hunting ground, I'm stuck with him.'

He sank into the dressing-room chair, head in hands.

'Clemence, forgive me, that was a cruel thing to say. And I just said I'm not a cruel man!'

'You're the first Somerlee in five hundred years who is not, then,' said Clemence.

He relaxed into a weak smile. Clemence rose and stepped to his side. She laid a hand on his shoulder.

'I'm sorry if you consider I was uncivil, Dickon. I was truly only teasing. But I will apologise to Fanny if you wish.'

He peered out from between the fingers which were stretched across his face.

'You're not as sorry as I am for what I just said to you. It's unforgivable.'

'Dickon, I understand. I goaded you. I was at fault.' She perched upon the wing of the chair, and then kissed the top of his head. 'I'm worried, Dickon, if you want the truth. The man I love is going off to war! Shall I be a widow before I'm even a bride?'

She took his hand in hers. He was almost twice her weight, twelve years older, and had been father and protector to her and her younger siblings since their parents' deaths. And yet he seemed so fragile right then, and watery-eyed after his paroxysm.

'And I'm worried for you, too…' She laid an arm around his shoulders and hugged him. She thought of the girl Richard seemed set on marrying. In her mind she saw Amathia, slapping the beggar-woman. The waif could hide behind her pillar. Where would a man wed to Amathia take refuge?

Five months since the Czar's host had annihilated the Turkish navy in Sinope, Britain's fighting youth set off.

Soon a war fleet was growling along the coastline of the Crimea – a balmy, Black Sea peninsula where the imperial court and Russia's wealthy came for pleasure. Before the summer of 1854 was out, a tranquil waterway called the River Alma would become a Styx bearing away the dead.

THREE

It looked like winking fireflies were dappling the ruddy twilight.

The flamelets and smoky spires spread over the plateau as far as the shadowy peaks on the skyline. They were the lights of bivouac fires which the troopers had lit close to each cluster of tents.

This vast army which was camped in the Crimean uplands came from three allied nations. Over to the west were gathered the French. The girl made out their faraway *Tricoleurs* flapping in the breeze. In the other direction, she could see the Turks at sundown prayer. It was the eerie sound of their muezzin which had brought her over to take a look.

Clemence stood alone, outside the gate of the farmhouse where her party was staying. From the rising, sandy ground you could overlook much of the encampment. Five infantrymen were gathered around the nearest cooking cauldron down to her left. One skinny, wiry fellow was playing a jig on a fiddle.

She breathed in the scents of juniper, cypress and strawberry tree. From the mountains came the cry of wolves. Wheels creaked, a mule's hooves thudded, and men's voices chattered as a wagon grumbled up the mud track from the village. She could hear Aunt Lizzy and the others laughing over their picnic on the farther side of the dunes. Clemence's fiancé James's loud chortle.

Her attention was drawn to the camp. A horseman was thudding a path in her direction. A scarlet cloak was billowing around his shoulders.

'Clemmie…' she heard Lizzy call.

'One moment, Aunt. There's a rider coming. I'll speak to him…'

Clemence drew her shawl tighter around her arms. It was now mid-October and the evening air was turning chilly. She had heard that season followed season within only a few days on this exposed peninsula. Only a few days ago it had still sweltered, and today had been warm until now.

The rider halted his snorting horse beside her. The darkling sun was behind him and made his features dusky. But she recognised one of the Field Marshal's staff officers. The man touched the brow of his forage cap by way of greeting.

'Miss Somerlee! Enjoying the evening air, are ye now?'

'Good evening, Captain Nolan. Yes, and the view of the bay! Inspiring, isn't it?'

From the plateau, the land sloped steeply down to the sea five hundred feet below. Down there on the shore, clusters of pinprick lights marked the little harbour of Balaclava. Further along the coast glowed the golden domes of the great port of Sebastopol's Orthodox churches and cathedral. The war fleet was formed up in a semicircle facing the city's waterfront. At nightfall, the ships looked like black boar poised to pounce.

'But don't let me keep you,' Clemence quickly told the officer. 'I am sure you must have better to do.'

'As a matter of fact, no, I don't.' Captain Louis Edward Nolan leaned down towards her with a creak of leather saddle. Clemence could make out his peering, grey-blue eyes. 'No doubt Lord Raglan will find something for me to do. Tucking the men up in bed perhaps.'

'We, my aunt and I that is, have lately been on Lord Fanshawe's yacht in Sebastopol harbour,' Clemence said in high-pitched discomfort. It wasn't for her to say, of course. But it didn't seem right somehow for him to be criticising the Field Marshal to a civilian. But her brother Aubrey did it. So did her fiancé Captain Swynton… 'Lord F is a dandy fop of whom I am sure you disapprove, Captain Nolan. We were watching the naval engagement. It was, em… most thrilling.'

'Well, I'm sure glad someone's impressed!'

Clemence regarded the Irishman.

'You sound disgruntled, Captain.'

'Begging your pardon, Miss Somerlee, but you did not have the pleasure of four months kicking about in Varna while the Allied high command squabbled over where to head next. We lost more men to cholera than Wellington lost to Boney's bullets.

'Then we hear that Czar Nicholas has aborted his invasion of Turkey's territories – which was the whole reason for the expedition in the first place! So, what do we do,' Nolan said, 'play cribbage with the French and go home? No. Came to duff the Russkies up, we did. Let's give 'em a kick up the arse while we're here, for jolly, what?'

'I'm sorry, Captain, I don't understand.'

Nolan grinned.

'The French are as keen to geld Nicky as we are. So, we thought – let's snatch that charming port Sebastopol! Nicky's gateway to Turkey and mastery of the Black Sea. And 'tis the will of the people, is it not, who cheered us all off? Never mind that the people don't know their arses from their elbows.'

Clemence didn't understand some of his words, but she got the gist.

'So, we can all go home when Sebastopol is captured?'

''Tis the idea… we think! But to tell you truth, Miss Somerlee, I'm not sure anything's decided. Now everyone's seeing action but the cavalry! The Russians who survived the battle of the River Alma fled for Sebastopol. Wouldn't it have made sense for the cavalry to go after them? Put an end to this? If you're in stalemate... it's my belief that you can win a war with a do-or-die cavalry charge.'

'Oh! Gosh...' said Clemence.

'What if it is a charge head first into the darkness and unknown? At least we're free... Do you know old Raglan keeps forgetting we're fighting the Russkies not the Frenchies? I heard him say' – Nolan assumed a plummy accent – '"Plenty of time to engage the Frenchies when we reach more apposite ground. Couldn't risk the cavalry on terrain such as this, what?" And that pompous General Airey reaches over and says: "The *Russians*, My Lord! The Frenchies are on our side this time." By Boney! Wouldn't I like to be there when he and General Saint-Arnaud get together to discuss allied strategy! I'll bet he drops a clanger or two.'

'Yes, I've heard a few gaffes from Lord Raglan, too.' Clemence grimaced. 'We saw the bombardment from the yacht, Captain,' she continued. 'Quite a rude awakening! My betrothed Captain Swynton and I had dined aboard HMS *Queen* as guests of the captain. We met the mascot: a delightful tortoise named Timmy.' Her faint smile faded. 'Well... two mornings later we saw parts of the harbour on fire... could hear the screams from within the city... We felt it was time to leave.

'Just now,' she went on, her gaze focussing on the distant mountain peaks, 'I was listening to that strange rattling sound the wind makes up here and thinking of winter. What hardships will the troops have to face, and what horrors the men in Sebastopol?' She remembered she was talking to a seasoned campaigner who had drunk from Afghan mountain streams and fought through Indian monsoons, and so she shut up.

Nolan's eyes flicked over her. She recognised in his look the restlessness of a fanatic.

'How long will you and the countess be staying?'

'Long enough to be useful, I trust. I'm sure there's something I could do for the troops.'

Nolan's brow shot up.

'Well, there must be some way we could help,' said Clemence. 'Even if it was just letter-writing for those troopers who do not have reading and penmanship.'

'Just about most of them, then!' said Nolan. 'You know, I met a fellow this morning with a black sock over his face. He said it was a hood he'd invented to protect against the hilltop wind. So enthusiastic he was! Said he'd call his little invention a "balaclava." Then he fell over the tent-rope, and I told him putting in two eye holes might improve it somewhat. Well, I must be going.' Nolan turned his mount with impressive grace. Clemence had heard someone say he was supposed to be the best horseman in the army. 'Oh, Miss Somerlee—' he spoke over his shoulder. 'We've heard Prince Menshikov'll be here by dawn. I'd not be getting comfortable if I were you.'

She watched as he went, his horse's hooves kicking up sand.

Captain Swynton came to find her.

'Dashed unpleasant fellow, that – Nolan,' her fiancé said, looking after the departing rider. 'Thinks he should be in command of the whole bally army. Thinks Raglan couldn't command a tea-party. Although,' privately in her ear, 'suppose he has a point there! But, really, I ask you! Who would entrust the fate of Britain's empire to a bog-dwelling Irishman?'

'Well!' said Clemence. 'Wellington didn't look as if he'd ever seen a bog let alone lived in one.'

'No, that's true. Can't think why they didn't appoint Wellington to lead the army on this campaign.'

'It might have something to do with the fact that he died two years ago.'

Captain Swynton rocked with laughter.

'So he did. Ah, how we miss that old ogre! He'd have roared the Russian bear back on the Siberian wind.'

Clemence cast James a quick glance. She thought he was looking better fed than ever. A sudden vision she had of James unhorsed, and puffing an escape with a face like a beetroot oozing juice, evil-eyed Cossacks in easily-gaining pursuit.

And then the thought of Brandon Fanshawe crept behind her shut eyes. His lips curling into a smile. Coppery-gold hair glowing in candlelight. Laughing at her mediocre piano-playing. Perched on the gunwale of the *Oriflamme*, peering at Sebastopol across the bay through opera-glasses, the nankeen of his peg-tops stretched taught.

'Come along, James – you're missing your food. That won't do.' She took his arm and went over the brow at a fast pace.

Brandon Fanshawe was sitting there beneath the branches of a cypress tree, one leg stretched out before him. With him were Aunt Lizzy and Clemence's brother Cornet Aubrey Somerlee.

The group had a picnic spread on the ground, supper laid out on a snowy-white cloth. Lysithea perched on a faldstool beneath a parasol. Clemence settled in the sandy turf between her and Aubrey. Down beside Brandon flopped James.

'Who was that you were talking to?' said Aubrey Somerlee as he went on picking away at the crust of a small veal pie.

'That staff officer of Lord Raglan's, Captain Nolan,' said Clemence.

'Oh, him… trouble, he is,' Aubrey replied.

'Looks like the Russians are coming according to what Captain Nolan has just told Miss Somerlee,' James pointed out.

'Aye, well, we've heard that before too,' said Aubrey. 'I'll believe it when it happens.'

'*Exactement*, my dear Aubs,' said James. 'It shan't spoil our fine dinner, what? Bring us more of those delicious Kherson watermelons we had last night, Wade, there's a good fellow,' he called to his manservant.

Aubrey gave Clemence a quick smile over the pie. He was dark in colouring, unlike the other Somerlee siblings who were fair, and devilish handsome.

There were only two years in age between him and Clemence. She'd always felt closer to him than to any of the rest. To a little girl, Dickon and Ivo had seemed elderly and aloof; she had nothing in common with her sister Bella; and the younger ones were just babies; so, it had always been Clemmie and Aubrey, Aubrey and Clemmie.

'Well, you came a good deal more prepared than the high command, Captain Swynton,' said Brandon Fanshawe, munching away. 'Did you see the landing at Calamita Bay? Frenetic! Soldiers didn't know where they were supposed to be going. Nor did the horses. Or, from what I saw of him, Field Marshal the Lord Raglan! I came prepared, all right,' he went on. 'Wrote ahead and arranged for a Crim-Tartar horse-coper to have some mounts waiting for me.'

'I note you are not in regimentals yourself, Lord Fanshawe – leaving others to do the fighting while you look smugly on!' Clemence said.

He tipped his hat to her with that infuriating smile.

Clemence grabbed a drinking vessel and poured herself wine, slopping a drop or two. And to think she'd have to endure his odious presence for as long as this stupid war lasted. The Russians must wonder what stink was this which the English had brought – ha!

'Not a bad spread, considering!' said James. 'What a pity we cannot get French chefs out here.'

'I agree, Captain. I've always found the French best at everything,' said Lysithea.

'Particularly when they're led by a Corsican, eh, Countess?'

'Do try a garlic tomato, Captain,' Lysithea said without a blink at this nudge on her shady past, handing James the plate.

'*Quel* fine lamb and caper sauce, this, by the way,' said Aubrey. 'I was thinking of dining down in Balaclava with the chaps from the mess. Glad I accepted your invitation instead, James.'

'I'm sure the ladies of Balaclava are not, Aubrey,' said the countess.

'Oh, you do Aubrey an injustice, Aunt!' said Clemence. 'I witnessed his and Dora's tender leave-taking in Portsmouth. I had to wipe my eye! I feel sure he'll be true to her.'

'Didn't you give your Dora something inscribed "Rose", Aubs, ordered two sweethearts ago and only just collected from the jeweller?' James chortled.

'Now, now, James,' said Aubrey. 'Clemmie will tell you I was as faithful as a puppy until I was led astray by you chaps.'

'Oh, I think the hussars have improved you, brother dear,' said Clemence.

'Certainly. You and your fellows have taken Aubrey to your hearts, Captain Swynton. Speaking his w's now like a wegular cavalwyman.' Lysithea laughed.

'Oh, I've always said he was the handsomest of all my brothers.'

'Do you know how to make a fellow blush, Clemmie!' said Aubrey.

'But it's true! What bosom bows the two of us were as youngsters, weren't we, Aubrey? I declare there isn't a nook in Eardingstowe we haven't hidden in together to play pranks on the grown-ups.'

James stroked his whiskers.

'Funny old place, Eardingstowe. What's its history, might I ask?'

'How long have you got?' said Lysithea.

'Oh, it's very, very old,' Clemence said.

'Ah yes, as old as the hills!' Lysithea laughed.

'We had some antiquarians at Eardingstowe the summer before last,' said Clemence. 'From Cambridge. They dug all over the park. My brother Carrie and I helped.'

'Did they unearth any of Eardingstowe's shameful secrets?' asked Fanshawe.

'Yes, they did! They found a skeleton which had had its throat cut! Otherwise they just found weapons and things. Some Viking axes. And musket balls from the Civil War.'

'Well, Eardingstowe's never been peaceful!' said Lysithea.

'Geoffrey de Somelay came over with the Conquest,' said Clemence. 'But he married the local Saxon heiress, and her family had lived there forever. The medieval manorhouse stands on the site of the original Saxon meadhall. The oldest beams are said to date from the eleventh century.'

'Clemence! Always the expert on these things!' said Aubrey.

'And Eardingstowe means "dwelling place," so I believe it must have been our forbears' home, well, since time began.'

'Eardingstowe must have a few ghosts in the back chambers?' James said, taking a sip of wine.

'Yes, we have one or two phantoms as I recall,' said Lysithea. 'Not to mention Jenny Greenteeth.'

'Oh yes, capital! Lurking in the mere, what, to catch a Somerlee and pull him to his doom!'

'Dorothy Somerlee's been seen flitting around St Laurey's churchyard,' Clemence said. 'The first baronet was her son by Charles II. There are those who say, you know, that Charles secretly married her, which would have made their son Alois legitimate and the true heir to the throne! So, my brother Richard must be too, I suppose, since we're the direct descendants! And, oh, you must have admired Gainsborough's Black Beauty, hanging there at the head of the Eardingstowe staircase, Captain Swynton?'

'I most certainly have, my dear.'

'Well, she's our great-grandmother!'

'Her real name was Nkoszana,' said Aubrey. 'Our buccaneering great-grandfather rescued her from a slave ship, bought her freedom, and she became mistress of Eardingstowe and the toast of Georgian society!'

'And don't you think Lizzy looks just a little like her with those ebony locks and plum-dark eyes?'

'If only, Clemmie! You forget that I'm no longer young and my charms fading! But to go on with Eardingstowe's story, don't forget the demon in the chamber.' Lysithea's smile widened. 'Clemence, I imagine, can tell the story better than I can.'

Clemence took a long sip from her second glass of wine.

'We had an ancestor who dabbled in sorcery. Back in the times when they burned witches. Anyway, the silly chap conjured up a demon. Then he couldn't rid Eardingstowe of it. So, what do you suppose he did?' She looked from Lord Fanshawe to Captain Swynton, relishing their wide-eyed attention. 'He trapped the fiend in a chamber in the old hall and sealed it up for ever! On wild nights you can hear it wailing to be set free. But no-one knows where it is… except the present lord of Eardingstowe!'

'What? Dickon?' James exclaimed.

'That's right,' Clemence said. 'And he tells his son and heir on the night of his twenty-first birthday. Takes him there in secret and entrusts him with the key of the demon-chamber.'

'Ah! I recollect the ball at Eardingstowe on the night of Richard's twenty-first birthday,' Fanshawe said. 'Now I think of it, Miss Somerlee, I do recall your pater taking him off somewhere at one point.'

'Might just have been to tell him about Mother Nature, old chap,' James said, then caught Clemence's eye. 'Heirs of great estates must be told about crops and so on, you see, Miss Somerlee.' Aubrey stifled a smile.

'Well, I tried to find the room,' Clemence pressed on. 'I must have tapped at every panel in the medieval great hall, but I've never found it. But you never know... there's always some truth behind these old stories.'

'Oh, absolutely!' Lysithea said as Swynton's manservant arrived to serve the dessert. 'Now, I remember your father's twenty-first, Clemmie, Aubrey. Your Uncle George hid behind the longcase clock so that he could secretly follow our father when he took our brother to the demon-chamber. But George nodded off and missed it.'

'Be rather fun,' Lord Fanshawe said, 'to let the Eardingstowe demon loose... see what damage it could do in today's world.'

'Well, Czar Nicky's as good as that old demon in my estimation!' Captain Swynton said, tucking into the rhubarb tart. 'And at least this is a demon one can fight with rifle and sword.' He turned to his bride-to-be and beamed. 'Miss Somerlee, how about the Czar's head on the Eardingstowe gatepost when we return?'

'Don't promise what you are unlikely to deliver, James,' Aubrey said.

'I was under the impression the Czar has withdrawn from the territories he'd occupied. Why need the war go on?'

'Miss Somerlee! We've not come all this way to sun ourselves on the Crimea's lovely beaches!' said James. 'We cannot allow a bully like Nicholas to sweep all before him. He slices his carving knives over Turkey at his peril. Nicky needs a good thrashing.'

Clemence leaned back against the gnarled bole of the cypress. She listened to the crickets' chirp as James droned on, and Aubrey butted in now and then and argued.

It had been strange, riding through the Crimean country with her betrothed and the army. Everywhere you looked fields of sunflowers and poppies spread into the foothills of the mountains, dotted with grazing goats. War was hard to believe in. She had welcomed their frequent stops at painted homesteads. Householders had offered pastries called *baklava* stuffed with spicy meat and onions, and cups of cherry, pear and peach *kompot* to drink. She had puzzled at this pleasing local hospitality, until Captain Swynton had told her:

'The Crim-Tartars are no friends of the Russkies. I think we'll find our passage through their land quite smooth.'

What about the troopers though? From her comfortable horseback, she'd seen florid, faces damp with sweat as the men mounted inclines. Why – those woollen shakoes the fellows wore blazed in crimson glory on a parade-ground, but – goodness – how inapposite for baking-hot autumn beside the Black Sea.

One youngster had lain sprawled unconscious in the dunes beside their way. Clemence had been about to dismount to go to his aid, when an officer from the company had called out:

'He ain't dead, miss, just fainted, the dainty girlie. Leave him be and let running to catch us up be his punishment!'

The day might come when the soldiers' salted pork ran short, and the dregs in their canteens left thirst unquenched.

She gazed across the bay towards Sebastopol. Streaks of magenta and rust criss-crossed an early evening sky like scars from the talons of a frightened bird of prey. Among them were patches of moribund sunlight which glimmered on the softly shifting dark waves, and then flickered out.

'A beautiful night,' Captain Swynton murmured as he joined her. The pair stood together on the other side of the dune from the picnic party. The chatter of the other three could still be heard from here, beneath the chip-chip-chip of the crickets.

HMS *Agamemnon*, HMS *Queen* and two of the French warships were prowling around the entrance to the port. Grey-black Gargantua blocking out the early stars. Steel steamers. Just think – but forty years it was since Napoleon's navy had fought in wooden vessels.

In less than a half century steam had taken over the world – ruled men's lives as once had the seasons. Now coal drove industry and transport, and even the weapons of war. Would those wheels turn faster and faster until one day there would be firepower to destroy all mankind?

The captain reached into his canteen. He brought out a shiny, oval medallion, and showed it her.

'It's called Our Lady of Kazan. Holy Mother Russia's most sacred icon.' An austere, powerful face stared out at Clemence from the disc which lay in his broad, freckly palm. 'We pursued the Russkies some way after the redoubts fell at Alma. Some chap had dropped this. I spotted it glinting in the sand.'

'I imagine it meant as much to him as a miniature of his own mother would.'

'Absolutely-dootly. Superstitious lot, the Russkies.'

'Perhaps you should send it to the Russian high command. Doesn't seem right to keep something so precious, James.'

'Oh, poppycock!' he laughed as he dropped the pilfered trophy back into his pouch. 'Oh, Clemence Somerlee,' he said as he looked at her. 'How I love and admire you! You made me the happiest of men when you said yes to me!' James clasped her hand in fingers which were still sticky from the chicken drumstick he'd just finished eating. 'When shall it be, my sweet one? The regimental chaplain could wed us, and our marriage night could be beneath a Balaclava moon! Do say it'll be soon?'

Over by the nearest troopers' tent, a man was playing the violin and singing *Cheer, Boys, Cheer.*

James had first proposed to her on a starlit balcony in the month of May, while she'd been loving the wonder of her first season; and the dewy-eyed devotion of a man who was besotted with her. So, it was not turning out quite so magical after all?

Could she blame James? There were worse men than James Swynton out there – rakes and bounders a-plenty. The truth was that James deserved better than her.

'Shouldn't we wait until after the fighting is over, James?'

When James had fallen into a nap later that evening, Clemence climbed the path to the clifftop. There she stood, looking out. When the moonshine had flickered like that on the surface of the Eardingstowe mere, her crazy Aunt Cassie had told her once it was the fairy-folk out dancing. Banished from the daylight by the early Christian priests, they only ventured out by night.

'Aunt Lizzy said I'd find you here!'

She turned to see her brother Aubrey on his way to join her.

Aubrey picked a sprig from the only greenery which was growing near and brought it over.

'Strawberry tree. Doesn't grow well in our cold clime at home but flourishes here.' He plucked a knobbly red berry from the little bough and divided it between them.

'Well… we could try taking a cutting home with us,' she said. 'We've grown more exotic things in our hothouse.'

'Yes… if we ever do see home again.'

'Oh, Aubrey…!'

'Clemence…!' Aubrey caught her by the wrist and turned her to face him. 'Look! You must know that the Russians are heading for Balaclava. They'll be here by dawn, so our scouts are reporting. I know I made light of it earlier. But it is true, Clemmie. We could be in battle tomorrow.'

'It's what you all wanted, isn't it, Aubrey? Throughout those months of inactivity in Varna?'

'Clemmie…' Aubrey looked down at his boots. 'Would you believe I'm frightened? Frightened I might never come back? God knows I never thought it would ever come to this,' he said with almost a cry, dark eyes roving the sky. 'When I joined a fancy regiment, I mean.' He shrugged, and grinned. 'I thought I'd be mincing around in a redcoat and showing off my sword to the ladies.' The smile faded. 'Not facing death in the face...'

'Oh, Aubrey. I don't know what to say to you!' Sure enough, what could she say? I'm sure you'll be safe? Huh – that was utter poppycock. She'd seen the piles of dead at Alma – from a distance, of course; Lizzy hadn't let her go close.

She took hold of his hand as they looked out to sea together. Down below was the fleet of warships. Silver ribbons could be seen trailing those vessels which were in motion.

'I've always loved you best of all my brothers, Aubrey. Maybe I've never told you that?' she said with a small awkward laugh. 'Not just because we're the closest in age. I was always in awe of Dickon, had nothing in common with Ivo, and Carrie pinched and teased me too flaming often! And Johnny is just a baby of course. But you... you've always been there for me. Dependable. Best friend. I can't imagine a world without you,' she finished on a watery smile.

He raised a hand wearing a white gauntlet and rested a finger under her chin. Gently, he kissed her forehead.

'I was just talking to a messmate,' he told her. 'Captain Radlett. Do you know him, Clemmie? We were asking each other whether we think there's an afterlife or not. Two big grown boys. Can you believe it?'

'Oh, I can believe it, Aubrey.'

Clemence looked out over the sea. She picked out in the darkness the domes and fortress walls of Sebastopol around the curve of the coastline. Capturing it was what this war was all about now.

Suddenly, she found herself wondering why. The port was the Czar's principal naval base in the region, yes. Maybe possessing it would give us some strategic advantage in these parts – she really didn't know much about these things, but she supposed it might. But was it really worth the bloodshed she felt sure was to come?

So why, then, were they all still here? She thought of the hysterical newspapers and populace at home baying for war… no, our boys cannot go home without something to show for it. That crowd which had seen them off at Portsmouth with airborne hats, singing Cheer Boys Cheer, would as soon tear them to scarlet ribbons should they limp back without shields having let Johnnie Roosian get the better of them. Like maenads. And the thought made her shiver.

'All that loss of life, Aubrey. Those poor, dead men… English, Russian… and the wives grieving at home. But maybe it'll mean there'll be no more wars after this. Wouldn't that be worth dying for?'

Both cocked an ear as from the city the sound of church and cathedral bells rang out.

'I'll come back, Clemmie. I'll come back… somehow, sometime. I want to give you away at your wedding, don't forget.'

'Here,' Clemence told him, and unfastened something from around her throat.

'Clemmie, this is the locket Mater gave you on your confirmation day,' he said, astonished and dismayed, 'the one with the engraving of St Anne and the Virgin.'

'Take it, Aubrey. Think of me tomorrow. I'll pray for you.'

FOUR

She went out the next morning before her Aunt Lysithea was awake.

Clemence roamed the plateau, keeping well to the edge of things. Her fiancé must be here somewhere. She didn't really want to meet him. For one thing, she'd be a girly getting in the way.

'You! And you!' the girl heard a gingery-moustached sergeant yelling. 'I don't care if the quartermaster is having a lovely dream! Wake the bugger up and get him out here now. In his smalls if needs must!'

The encampment was buzzing with unreadiness despite the advance warnings they were supposed to have had. For days, rumours there had been that the enemy was heading for Balaclava. It looked as if it really was happening, and they'd been caught with their breeches down.

Soldiers were stuffing themselves into uniforms over undergarments and braces. A bearded private of the Wiltshires with an anxious look on his face was sitting on a stool outside a tent, locking and unlocking the barrel of a rifle. A cooking-pot clanged as it was accidentally kicked, and out sizzled a swear-word from the one who'd done it the injury. Chickens and roosters went flurrying and squawking out of the way.

The wind had grown stronger overnight. It was not much short of a gale. All the flags and tent coverings were thwacking against their posts.

Down in the valley the Ninety-Third Highlanders – so she gathered from the men's talk as she passed close by the tents – were facing the Russian onslaught alone… She could hear the rifle-fire above the ruckus. While this wimp of a girl could not face Captain Swynton.

She almost bumped into a man bearing a saddle over his shoulder.

'I'm so sorry!' She backed off. 'I'll get out of your way…'

'You looking for someone, miss?'

'My fiancé, and my brother. I thought I might wish them well before…' *Before you all go out to get killed?*

The private glanced at the men rushing to get ready.

'Wouldn't recommend it, miss. You take yourself off to watch from somewhere safe with the other civvies.' He gave her a sudden grin. 'Give them, and us, a smile with that pretty face, hey? That's the best you can do for us right now.'

She wasn't the only civilian milling around the tents while the soldiery tried to get ready, and not the only blushing maiden to see a trooper in his smalls. One buzzing swarm of "war tourists" as they were known, which Clemence found herself drawn towards the rear of, was heading towards the sound of screams and gunfire which was coming from the valley.

'Where are you all going?' she asked a middle-aged man and his wife.

'The hilltop, dear. Should be an excellent view from there! We understand the Ninety-Third are doing sterling work holding back the Russkies all by themselves!'

'Do join us, dear!' said the wife. 'It sounds marvellous!'

Above the trees ahead of Clemence curled plumes of smoke.

She went where the other people went.

She found herself on the wide, flat escarpment overlooking the valleys. From this place, an awesome view of the mountain peaks spread for miles. A steep, rocky face which looked unclimbable sloped down to the twin valleys where the action was taking place.

The wind was at its fiercest here. She had to clutch her bonnet as she steadied herself and got her bearings.

Along the cliff edge hundreds of onlookers were spreading themselves. It was just such a multitude as you might see out to enjoy the band in the park on a Sunday afternoon: lords and masters, women in bonnets, even a few children and a yapping basset hound on a leash. Up would go a great cheer, or a passionate shout, whenever something dashing happened down below.

A portly gent beckoned to the lone young woman.

'I say, young lady, come observe this fine divertissement, do!'

The man beside him turned to look her way too. Lord Brandon Fanshawe… beneath the brim of his top hat his coppery hair was fluffing in the wind.

'Miss Somerlee!' Lord Fanshawe called. 'Come… you're missing the fight! We've had a deal of excitement already.'

Must she really stand next to *him*? She looked around to see where else she might position herself. But she couldn't snub her big brother's bosom bow, she didn't suppose… Ergo she slipped into the space the two men made for her.

The girl peeped over the escarpment edge.

The high spot where she and the spectators stood was called Saupon Hill. It overlooked two valleys which a ridge known as The Causeway divided. The River Tchernaya's waters could be made out at the head of the valleys, sparkling through the sparse greenery. Along the spine of the ridge spread a series of redoubts which had been in Turkish possession but – she gathered – were no longer.

'Russians evicted the squawking Turkeys first thing this morning,' Lord Fanshawe said with raised voice, one hand clutching his hat.

'Seems Prince Menshikov got most of his army out of Sebastopol before we closed it orf, the crafty devil,' the portly gentleman told her. She could barely hear above the din going on at the foot of the cliff. 'Now he's here to drive us back into the sea! Little he knows!'

Clemence viewed the battlefield. Her own ringlets were blowing across her vision.

The grey-jacketed enemy host was crossing the Causeway from the north into the south valley. They looked like a deluge the colour of smoke. What were the Russians trying to do? Break through to Balaclava to retake it?

'Blasted, clucking Turkeys!' growled the stout gentleman. 'Took fright at the Russkies and scarpered, fluttering their feathers! Russkies hold the Causeway now. But just look at the Highlanders!'

There indeed were the Ninety-Third Highlanders led by Sir Colin Campbell… she'd heard precious else but their name all morning. There… all that stood between the attackers and Balaclava. The scarlet-jacketed Scots were stretched two deep along the southern side of the Causeway, firing at the force which was surging over the ridge above them. The Russian cavalry was being taken by surprise to find them there waiting.

Guarding the village of Kadikoi close by Saupon Hill they had been, someone said, when as the dawn was seeping above the mountain peaks the offensive had come.

'Dashed into this improvised defence, the Highlanders did. The rest of our army was still chomping its morning sausages and doing up its breeches!'

'They've been facing the onslaught for the last twenty minutes,' Brandon Fanshawe shouted. 'Good gracious! There's another one gone down, see!'

Someone among the crowd began singing *'Cheer, boys, cheer, for a new and happy land...'* and soon the rest were joining in.

Clemence couldn't take her eyes off the fallen man who she could just make out through the gun smoke. Even from here, she could see the slimy redness from his chest oozing into the grass.

'Ah, now here's Mr Russell of *The Times!*' Brandon Fanshawe went on as a gruff-looking individual in civilian attire rode by along the escarpment edge. 'I think *The Times's* idea of sending a "special war correspondent" as they call him was a marvellous one, don't you? Gentlemen in London still abed shall not miss out! They'll see it all as if in person through Mr Russell's reportage!'

Hmm... the public right to know? Or the public right to graphic titivation?

The portly gentleman took out a purple fogle and mopped a face shining with sweat.

'By Heaven, young lady,' he bellowed. 'I forgive those Scottish rascals what they did during the Jacobite wars. Why, they're marvellous! Those Russky blighters will not get past this thin, red line.'

Mr Russell halted his horse, cast a glance at the gentleman, took out his reporter's notebook, and scribbled.

Clemence shielded her eyes from the sunlight. Wave after Russian wave came against the line of defenders. Screams of the dying evaporated into the ether like sea spray.

She watched the Scots load and fire. The sound of hundreds of simultaneous gunshots set her ears ringing. What was it they said about the range of Minié rifles which most of the British regiments were using? Whatever... a bullet fired from the Russian flintlocks was much less – Czar Nicholas was paying the price for living in the last century.

Suddenly, one Highlander arched backwards so that his startled face was taking in the sky. Clemence watched his body twist forty-five degrees to his right. He crumpled to the ground, limp and floppy like the rag doll she'd used to play with when she'd dropped it. The soldier lay there twitching in spasms for about half a minute. Then moved no more.

A surge of sickness rose in her throat. She put a hand to her mouth.

The wail of a bagpipe rose above the noise. The Highlanders fired another volley.

Greenly-yellow sulphur-fog smothered the scene, blotting out the sun. Tendril-like coils of smoke crept as far as the plateau where the watchers stood, and into Clemence's eyes, throat and nostrils.

British cavalry was by now galloping into the south valley. Sunlight glanced from the metal surfaces of rifle-barrels and bayonets. A fresh wave of Russians crossing the ridge charged downhill, yelling, to meet the newcomers. Falcons swooped, shrieked and dived overhead as if joining in the fun. A herd of gazelle was fleeing around the flank of the hill into the forest.

'Why, it's quite charming to watch from this vantage,' said Lord Fanshawe as the two forces clashed in the trampled vineyards at the foot of the ridge. 'Like watching the Lilliputians at play.'

The crack-crack-ping of gunfire, clang of striking bayonets, screams and shrill whinnies leaped from the heaving swell below. Clemence pressed her hands over her ears. But she could hear it all still.

Two riders splashed through the ditch which watered the vineyard, one in pursuit of the other. The chaser sliced his bayonet down through the other's skull. Had she felt the impact herself, heard the man's last cry? She took a step or two back from the escarpment edge without realising it.

She'd once hidden in the barn and witnessed two of the hands from the home-farm cut the throat of a swine… seen an arc of blood shoot forth just like that.

Down from the onlookers' left came a clattering rumble as cannons were brought into place.

A shell shot upward, making a whizzing noise. The black projectile described one hot, scarlet arc over the battlefield, and then exploded into sparks over the area where the Russians were densest.

The unhorsed men who were scrambling up the bank of the Causeway were lit up in the white light. The dark-haired glowed violet, the blond tawny… each man shining out just once for an instant of stardom.

'That shell had shrapnel in it,' Clemence's portly neighbour explained. 'Sharp, lethal metal stuff which gets strewn out by the force of the explosion. Just picture one of those pumps your gardener might use to keep your lawns fresh, filled with nails instead of water! Look… see that chappy!'

Clemence watched a screaming Russian private trying to protect his face with his arms.

'Ain't it rousing! Moving, too. Like listening to Beethoven's finest on a glorious summer evening, with the fireworks going off!'

'A concert, sir?' Clemence found her voice to utter.

'Aye…' came out as a blissful sigh.

A symphony, she thought. In the first movement musket oboes roared in counterpoint with rifle flutes, harp chords of clashing swords, and shells trumpeting up the scale, the adagio second movement synthesising all into a homogeny of sound.

The firing of six cannons burst into the allegro third movement. Sparks leaped into the sky. A loose shako sprang with them. The spinning helmet unfurled its plume against the wispy clouds. Back it splashed into the rivulet.

And then the violin section rose in the final movement… wails, screams, cries… leaping one above the other, until falling away into quietness.

'By God, it stirs your blood to listen to it!'

Clemence glared askance at the man standing on her other side.

'There are men dying out there, Fanny Fanshawe, over nothing but a modest little valley!'

'True. I don't forget that poignant reality, Miss Somerlee. But there is such a thing as a noble sacrifice, you know. The widows and orphans of the Battle of Balaclava may take comfort that their loss was in the cause of freedom. Here, Miss Somerlee. Take a look.' He handed Clemence his opera glasses.

Through the magnifying lenses, she could even see the moustaches of the wounded and dying as they crawled across the valley floor… one man with blood streaming from the socket where his eye had been… mothers' sons and children's fathers, other sisters' beloved brothers and other maidens' sweethearts; a tartan kilt bright in the pile of dead; a regimental standard waving through the smoke; a rearing, injured horse… But the Russians were surely in retreat… cavalrymen, hundreds of them, scrambling back towards the Causeway.

They were like floodwaters on the ebb, sucking away the flotsam of what they had destroyed… A dead Kievan's heel was caught in a comrade's stirrups. The charging horse dragged the bumping encumbrance over the litter-field. The cadaver dislodged a heap of other dead which it ploughed into. It went on to smash through the remains of a shattered wagon.

Clemence's gaze returned to the lost shako lying in the stream. The sorry helmet was snared between two large jutting stones, the gushing water tugging to free it.

The bodies of a redcoat and a greycoat swirled by, the arm of one around the other so that they seemed to dance together in a timeless ballet. The fellows' wide-open eyes gazed into the heavens. Comrades without nations in death.

And what was all this for?

Was the Emperor Louis Bonaparte really fretting over an unbridled Russia louring over France's possessions in Africa – *or seeking his famous uncle's glory?* And would victory mean a warm welcome at the Sultan's court in Constantinople for Lord Harry Palmerston? *Or hero-worship to spring him into Downing Street?*

'Fanny! I believe one of the ordnance wagons has been hit. Look!' the portly gentleman called.

'Oh, pooh, just a tinderbox, sir,' said Fanshawe. 'Now, that is what I call an explosion!'

This second bang deadened the world. Even on the distant hilltop, Clemence could feel the ground beneath her feet throb. The Russian arsenal wagon which had been fired on roared into popping flame.

The men who had been manning it were blown airborne. Each figure was starred for a heartbeat, kicking legs and flailing arms, against an orange sky… one man sailed northwards while one of his legs headed west.

The crowd watching on Saupon Hill cheered and clapped.

'By George! They've driven 'em orf! Russkies are falling back, look, over the Causeway! Famous! Bravo the Highlanders! Bravo General Scarlett and the Heavy Brigade!'

'What the dickens is Lucan about?' roared the portly gentleman. 'Look at him – sitting there as if he's at a jaunt in Hyde Park!'

Clemence swung her glasses to see. The Earl of Lucan was in overall command of the cavalry. He was with the Light Brigade – in the north valley, away from the action. The mounted men seemed to be sitting and watching the Russians retreating over the ridge.

'By thunder!' went on Clemence's neighbour. 'The enemy is vulnerable! The Light Brigade is still fresh – could be attacking from the flank! And finish 'em!'

'Aye, you're right, sir!' said someone else. 'Lucan's doing nothing. Again! Know what they called him after he was so bally ineffective at the Battle of the Alma? Lord Look-on!'

'Hah!' The gentleman cupped his lips and barked out: 'Lord Look-on!' Others took up the chant, which became loud enough to carry down the cliff-face. In the valley, the earl shot the hilltop a wintry glare.

The remnants of the Russian cavalry, meanwhile, galloped to the head of the north valley. There, beyond a cypress copse on the bank of the Tchernaya, they gathered to lick their wounds. Between them and the British light cavalry, who rested in the shadow of Saupon Hill, lay a bowl of valley floor. Two barren miles of sand, scree and isolated trees stretched before them, defended on three sides by enemy ordnance.

'Russkies are pretty dashed unassailable behind that battery,' said Portly. 'The Don Cossack that line of defences is called, miss,' he told Clemence, pointing to what looked like a seven-foot-high barricade facing them at the head of the valley. 'Got two dozen great howitzers poking out of it.' He pursed his lips to look impressed. 'Went and had a butchers at it, I did, yesterday evening. Scared the dickens out of me, if you'll pardon my language, miss!' he chuckled.

'Really, sir?'

The morning sun grew hotter.

The girl trained her opera glasses on the scarlet, gold and blue swarm of the Eleventh Hussars. It was one of five regiments which comprised the Light Brigade. There, in the middle of the group, she picked out her brother. Her husband-to-be must be there somewhere too, but his rotund shape eluded her for the moment.

Her brother's words of the night before came back to her. *Would you believe I'm frightened? Frightened I might never come back?*

Now she could see him down there with his fellow hussars, talking with a comrade, tossing back his handsome head in laughter at some jest. How young Aubrey looked, silvery in the sunlight, like the fairy folk their crazy aunt fancied dwelled in the Eardingstowe mere.

The Baronet of Eardingstowe was sitting beside the fire in the lounge of the Carlton Club, reading *The Times*. Rain was drumming on the window glass, and the October daylight was dim.

For the first time ever, a newspaperman was reporting from the theatre of conflict. *The Times's* Mr William Howard Russell would go down in history as the first war correspondent. Russell's eye-witness accounts would bring the nimblest of cavalry manoeuvres and doughty infantry stands into drawing-rooms and parlours a thousand miles away. Richard sipped from a cup of morning chocolate as he digested the latest from the Crimea.

Mr Russell had also had a deal to say which shocked the reading public. Arsenal and food running short; fresh supplies failing to reach the men at the front; cavalry horses not being fed; and oh! what woeful nincompoopiness in the medical corps and quartermaster's division…

Well, Mr Russell's reportage had brought these things before those who needed to know. Parliament was noting the shortcomings. At Westminster's behest, a certain lady with the strange name of Florence was forming a dedicated nursing corps. The real victor of the Crimean War would be journalism.

Not that Russell's contribution had been entirely exemplary, however: he had mistakenly reported the fall of Sebastopol. So perhaps one should not trust everything one read in *The Times*.

'Following the news from the front, old boy?' his party colleague Sir Bertrand asked, settling into the other armchair beside the hearth. 'My nephew's out there with the Buffs. You any relatives fighting?'

'Yes, one brother, and a future brother-in-law. Eleventh Hussars, both. The Earl of Cardigan's regiment.'

'Ah, yes I recall now! The dashing Cornet Aubrey Somerlee,' said the other man. 'Handsomest fellow in the regiment I've heard him called. Darling of all the ladies this last season! Daresay you're damned proud of him, what?'

'Hmmm,' was Richard's response. 'What do you think of the Transport Bill, Bertie? Decided which way you'll vote?'

He'd changed the subject, but not his mood. Aubrey getting his goat was nothing new. Probably went right back to his childhood.

Would to God you'd been the heir, Aubrey my boy… Pater had never actually *said* it in Richard's hearing… but the words had lowered like the shackling heat before a thunderstorm.

What if Aubrey was struck by a Russian bayonet? The silvering scar would be his parlour-game boast fifty years from now. 'See this, m'dears? Ivan gave it me in the Crimea back in '54!' Show it to the ladies at dinner, he would. Especially if it was on the bum.

'Don't let me keep you from the news, old chap,' Sir Bertrand said, gesturing to the broadsheet which lay in Richard's lap. 'I'm going to have a nap. Then I shan't nod off in the House later, ha! ha!'

Richard eased out his belt a notch. Conviviality had been good this season, and his stays felt tight. As he read his 'paper, his fancy bore him from autumnal London to the clean, blustery valley near the Black Sea.

The hoof beats of at least twenty approaching horses could be heard. Clemence wrenched her opera glasses away from the scene below. She craned her neck to see who the newcomers were.

The leader of the group wore a navy frock coat, and a black cocked hat with white and red feather plumes. One empty sleeve was tucked discreetly inside Field Marshal the Lord Raglan's jacket.

He and the members of his staff who were with him drew in their rides close by her spot. Raglan's gaze swept the vista of valley, batteries, river and mountain top which lay before them. He lowered his telescope. His eye fell upon the young woman among the crowd of war tourists.

'Why, Miss Clemence Somerlee! Goodness me. How bold of you to grace us with your charming presence this day. Going to stay and watch us shatter the Corsican monster, eh, young lady?'

'The Czar, Lord Raglan,' sighed a weary General Airey beside him. 'Boney's been dead for thirty years.'

'I know that! I but jest!' Raglan chortled. 'Well, Mr Mapplewell,' he said to the portly gentleman, 'we should be proud of doughty English misses like Clemence Somerlee, what?'

'About ten-thirty by my timepiece, Lord Raglan,' the gentleman replied with a beam. Airey stifled a smile.

'Just so!' said Raglan. 'Ghastly ogres the Frenchies. Always said so.' Perhaps Clemence should tell the auditory-challenged Field Marshal that he and Nicholas should sign a peace treaty. *Splendid idea, what?* he might reply. The power of life and death was hers!

The Field Marshal meanwhile leaned towards his general, looking disgruntled.

'Lucan really ought to have used some initiative, you know, Airey. Could have finished them with a flank attack before they had time to scuttle into their bolthole.'

'Suppose he was waiting for orders, sir,' shouted his second-in-command.

'Orders, eh? I'll give him orders. By Heaven! Now the blackguards are swiping the guns from the redoubts!' Raglan indicated with his overworked, surviving hand.

A Russian detachment could be made out moving along the spine of the Causeway. Four of their men were rolling out a British cannon from one of the captured fortresses. Two more followed bearing a further crate of ordnance. Raglan looked as dismayed as he must have done when he parted with his limb.

'They'll be parading those trophies of war in Paris before the week's out, I'll warrant,' the Field Marshal said in disgust.

'St Petersburg I think you mean, sir.'

'Well, Airey, we can't have this! Propaganda, what? Bad for morale. Our guns paraded before the cheering populace? It'll look like they've had a resounding victory over us!'

'Boney might have had your arm, eh, My Lord,' Airey said, 'but he'll not have your artillery.'

'By God, sir, no! Rider, please,' Raglan snapped his fingers to the adjutants who were waiting to deliver messages. One rode forward. 'Ah, Captain Nolan. Now's your chance to prove your vaunted prowess. You are the best rider in the army, I hear. But then, I am deaf!' Raglan chuckled. 'Well, this is urgent so make haste, man.' He summoned a scribe to dictate his message to. 'Tell Lord Lucan the Light Brigade is to advance to the front and prevent the enemy taking away the guns. Troop horse artillery may accompany. French cavalry is on their left. Immediate.'

'The cavalry, sir, is to ask the enemy to give back the guns?'

'Now, there's no need for sarcasm, Captain!' The Field Marshal gave Captain Louis Edward Nolan a hard look. 'Well? You're an Irishman, ain't you? So, ride like the devil was on your tail!'

Nolan saluted. He turned his horse and rode.

Clemence watched, amazed, as the officer descended the escarpment. Captain Nolan sidestepped his horse down the steep hillside, prancing aside from the streams of scree when he met them, and stepping over straggly vegetation which jutted from the rocks.

'Good Lord! Look at that fellow ride!' exclaimed a bystander. 'Finest rider in the army, they say.'

Down below they had seen him, too. A group of around thirty hussars was gathered at the foot of the cliff, pointing and laughing.

'By God, it's Nolan! You're wasted in the army, man. You should be in Astley's Circus.'

The captain reached the valley floor. He wheeled his mount around once to bask in the applause from his cheering audience up above. Nolan blew them a kiss from his glove. He rode on to where the cavalry commander waited.

'Compliments to you, My Lord. I bring a message from Lord Raglan. His Lordship says the Light Brigade is to advance on the enemy's guns at once.'

The Earl of Lucan eyed the messenger with dislike. Damned, impertinent mick.

'What guns, sir?' Lucan surveyed all around him. From the floor of the valley, he did not enjoy Raglan's Godlike viewpoint. He could not see the summit of the Causeway and its disappearing arsenal.

Nolan flung out an impatient arm.

'There, sir, there is your enemy!'

But where was he pointing? The Causeway… or the Don Cossack Battery, and the Tchernaya at the other end of the valley, where the main Russian force had gathered after its earlier rout? No-one would ever know.

The Earl of Lucan twisted his upper body in the saddle and spied along the valley. A valley defended from both flanks by battery after battery all along its bleak length. And at the further end lay the Don Cossack; it had the firepower to wipe out entire battalions in a single firing.

The earl's eyes narrowed. He looked at the Light Brigade, which was not yet in formation; some men were dismounted, smoking, urinating, jaw-wagging. Lucan turned his eyes to the Earl of Cardigan who was in command of the Light Brigade… a man he loathed with a passion which exceeded that which he had for every Russian and Irishman in the universe combined.

On the clifftop, Clemence lowered her opera glasses. She had observed the Earl of Lucan riding over to the Earl of Cardigan, seen a discourse which ended with Cardigan throwing his arms into the air in bemused outrage. She went on watching, not certain she could be seeing right.

'Lord Raglan!' Clemence called, for the Field Marshal was still close. 'Forgive me, sir, but…'

She was not the only one who had realised something was amiss. At her side, Lord Fanshawe gave a startled cry. Mr Russell stared in astonishment, snapped open his reporter's notebook, and began scribbling. Mr Mapplewell was rubbing his eyes and looking again.

'Lord Raglan… is not the Light Brigade forming into lines, as if for a charge…?'

The baronet stepped out from the porch of the Carlton Club, and into Pall Mall. Rain was blowing westwards. He put up an umbrella.

From somewhere within the curling tendrils of fog which enveloped the street, a disembodied voice called out 'hot chestnuts for sale.' The sounds of coachmen's cries and whip-cracks could be heard, too. This vapour, output of thousands upon thousands of chimneys, was known as a 'London peculiar.' It covered the city throughout the autumn and winter months. The caped and huddled figures who could be made out scurrying through the murk looked like so many stunted hobgoblins.

'Like to share my carriage to the House, old chap?' Sir Bertrand asked, joining him at the roadside.

'Thank you but no, Bertie. I need to call on an infirm relation first. Don't wish to hold you up.'

Richard was meaning to summon a cabriolet instead. Common little vehicles. But he had a mind to call at a nighthouse in the Haymarket instead of going to Parliament; his own carriage, with his Yew and Quatrefoils coat-of-arms painted on the door, was too indiscreet.

'Care for dinner with Grace and me this Saturday?'

'Thanks again, Bertie. But I've already accepted an invitation to Tewksbury's country house-party.'

'Ah!' Sir Bertrand said with a knowing chuckle. 'Dare one say it – seeking plumper game than just pheasant, eh?'

'Yes, Bertie,' Richard said, 'Lady Amathia is to be a guest as well.' Trust Bertie to liken a woman to stodgy food. Private portions as doughy as Mrs Dean's Sally Lunn loaves, indeed?

Once his friend had taken his leave, the baronet hailed a hackney. In a low voice, he gave the Haymarket direction, and then climbed into an interior which was floored with soggy newspaper and reeking of body-odour and dog urine – the ghostly aura left behind of those who had travelled in this space before him. The cab swished out into the roadway, its wheels ploughing up rainwater.

As Bertie had speculated, Richard had decided to make the Duke of Ardenne's daughter an offer of marriage. High connection and influence, the robes of a peer to clad a Somerlee… Amathia's upstart father could bring them all Dickon's way.

Making love to a dainty courtesan this evening he would be, while dreaming of the Consett fortune and patronage soon to be in his bed, in the form of an icicle-hearted woman.

What was happening out at the front right now, he wondered?

FIVE

The Light Brigade was formed up in two sections. Each was two lines deep and stretched across the mile-wide valley from the high ground on the left to the Causeway. In the vanguard – the Seventeenth Lancers, Thirteenth Light Dragoons and Eleventh Hussars. To the rear – the Queen's Own Light Dragoons and King's Royal Irish Hussars.

The crowd looking on from Saupon Hill waited, breathless and hushed. For a long while all that could be heard was the wind, or the jangle of a bit or harness as a horse tossed its head.

Then the wail of bugles broke out, ordering an advance. The front section raised swords and lances. The steady thud of hooves rose as it began to walk its mounts forward. Sunlight flashed from weapons' and helmets' steel surfaces.

At the head rode the Earl of Cardigan. He held his sword out straight before him, as if pointing the way.

'Not to fear,' Field Marshal Raglan announced to the company close by him on the clifftop. 'They're going to right-wheel shortly and assault the Causeway.'

Into a trot sprang the vanguard. Advancing behind them now was the second section. A dust-cloud churned up around the horses' hooves and fetlocks.

Over on the rising ground at the valley-side, the men manning the closest of the Russian batteries had seen them. Figures could be picked out, moving to the fore, pointing. The first cannon-fire hit the valley, boom following light by a fragment of time.

A cry was heard. Forcing a way through the lines towards Cardigan was a lone, galloping rider.

'Egads! That's that Nolan fellow, the one His Lordship sent with the message!' cried Mr Mapplewell. 'What the deuce is he about – dashing to the front like that? After all the glory, is he?'

Captain Louis Edward Nolan's cloak was furling out behind him like a sail, so hard was he riding.

Almost level with the leader, he yelled something. But the absurd aristocrat, sword sticking out before him just like his oft-erect member, took no heed.

At the same instant, a shell was fired from the battery. An orangey-ochre flash.

Suddenly, Nolan jerked as if he'd been yanked across the chest in a rope trap.

The man went crashing to earth, rolling many times before striking a jutting rock. Nolan twitched. And then lay still.

His riderless horse hurtled in a contrary direction, whinnying in its confusion. Three lancers had to swerve. You could almost hear their curses.

'Dear God in his mercy!' breathed Lord Brandon Fanshawe.

At the head of the valley meanwhile, the alarm bugles were sounding. The main body of the Czar's army was rushing into position. Some were scrambling from the river where they had been dipping. The great guns of the Don Cossack were got into place, ready.

'They're not going to turn!' cried Mr Mapplewell. 'By Boney! They're going to charge straight at 'em – right through the Russian guns!'

Clemence's fingers held the opera glasses fast. Clenched so tight that her fingers shook. *My God, they've made a mistake. Holy Jesus, please let them realise…*

The Light Brigade was now in full charge and in roaring voice.

Flashes of sunlight glanced from swords which you had to shield your eyes from. A scarlet cloak billowing, turning inside-out, streaming out like bedlinen taking an airing. A blue shako plume whose feathers were flying out behind with the wind in them. A red plume seeming to interact with it. A grey tail furling out behind. A dark bay mane jouncing beside it. A fierce and screaming face. A face of fear. A face with a handlebar moustache. A face fixed in a snarl.

A thunder of hooves went on and on and made the ears ring.

From the battery on the valley-side, a cannon was pumping out death. Its fire was purplish in colour. You could see its dark-grey nose from the hilltop, swinging to follow the first line of the charge. A flash, a boom, a flash, a boom, a flash, a boom. One man on the edge of the line crying out and falling, then three, then five or six in the centre.

A lancer threw up his arms as blood spurted from his gorge. A dragoon fell sideways. One foot was tangled in his stirrups. His charger continued galloping. The man was hauled along the valley floor. Until he was dislodged, and then kicked aside by another racing horse.

In one nanosecond, the Russians in the battery fired another volley. You could see the grey-coated men raise their musket butts in absolute synchronicity as if each was a clone of the one before him in the line. The explosion came bounding in echo to the onlookers' place. That tingling noise rang in your ear. Like tin cans jangling against each other. Wasn't it called something like that – tinnitus, or something like that? You could feel the tremors in the ground, too.

A hussar swerved and shielded his eyes from the earth and stone-spray which erupted from bullets striking the ground. Shrill cries and startled whinnies tore through the air. Two more dragoons perished.

A cloud of curling grey residue blanked the field.

A moment of quiet. The last of the riders had gone beyond the battery's range. The fogginess faded.

The first of the batteries on the Causeway was now in range of the charging men. The roaring riders faced a fusillade from the other flank.

'Cannons, cannons, everywhere they look. Left, right,' said the reporter, Mr Russell. 'My God! This is a valley of death!'

A man was hurtled, screaming, over his charger's head. He lay face-down in the dust, juddering. His injured horse fell on top. It crushed him lifeless.

One shell whizzed from the Causeway, and another, and another, and a fourth. Clemence covered her ears. She could smell the sulphur now, carried to the hilltop on the wind.

The force of the explosions seized a group of men out of their saddles; one was tossed into the branches of one of the valley's sparse trees; there he hung, swinging like a possum.

Back to the uplands on the left. The second battery had been reached. It fired its cannons. A whinnying horse reared, flinging off its rider. A lancer quivered, blood bubbling from his mouth. Tumbling sideways, he dangled upside-down over the stirrup. The horse went on charging.

Another shell arced over the battlefield leaving a white-orange tail. Just imagine the sun if it was enraged. Engorged and taking over the sky. A boiling orange-yellow heart firing out its mortiferous rays. *Hey, you, earth! You're dead!*

A hussar shot shrieking out of his seat. His sword flew heavenward. Clemence shielded her eyes from the dazzle glancing from the spinning blade.

The cavalry galloped and galloped, thundering on and on deeper into the valley. Plumes of dust wedded with the artillery residue. The smoky blur was closing around the men and beasts of the Light Brigade.

Supernovae flashed and radiated from within the mist whenever a bang went off. A lone wail followed one boom; at the next – multiple screams as comrades rode into forever together; then equine cries as comrades more loyal still followed their masters.

At the head of the valley, the sound of the Don Cossack's great guns started up. To Clemence, the howitzers sounded like the growl of dogs gone wild.

Four shells burst overhead. The toxic stars lit up a vision within the mist for a few heartbeats. An amber-ochre pit of Hell yawned before those looking on… it looked like soldiers of the damned riding through the fiery vale.

The Light Brigade was galloping straight for the Don Cossack's maw.

The stinking sulphur cloud grew thicker. The curtain closed off the scene.

The hilltop crowd went on watching, silent and sombre. Hands were clasped over faces. Field Marshal the Lord Raglan was staring into the valley in horror.

Clemence lowered her glass; it dangled limp from her fingers.

'Did you have a lovely morning, My Lady?' The dull voice of her maid, Vickery, broke in upon Amathia's thoughts. 'A meeting with the handsome baronet perhaps?'

'Just get on with dressing my hair, Vickery.'

Amathia cupped her hands beneath her chin and leaned her elbows on the toilet-table. She peered into the looking-glass. She took up a brooch, turning it over and over, and thought of the man who was emerging as her leading suitor.

Richard Somerlee might only be a baronet... but he was a coming man. Everyone said he'd be holding high office someday soon. His aunt was one of the richest women in Europe. And... there was something else which made him appealing to Amathia. A private smile pricked the corners of her lips. He was Fanny's bosom bow.

She had once had her eye on her cousin Lord Brandon Fanshawe. One of the oldest families in the shire the Fanshawes were, and didn't they know it. Amathia's mind slipped back to a dinner-party one evening two years ago at Woodmancote, the Fanshawe seat. Brandon must have understood the fluttering eyelashes across the table, all right.

But then, as she had been leaving, and he and she had stood together on the step, Brandon had plucked her chin in his fingers, and whispered in her ear:

'Not if you were the last woman alive, Mathy dear!'

Amathia stabbed the back of her hand with the pin of the brooch.

'Oh! My Lady! Have you hurt yourself?'

'Just get on with my hair, Vickery! You're late as it is. And I'm due at Lord Tewksbury's by six!'

Yes, marry Dickon, even if he was only a baronet, why not? And let Brandon see what he had rejected flaunted in his face. Aye, for this could she endure having to rusticate in the wilds of Somerset.

What of Richard's sister, though, who was going to get *everything* one day? Well, Aunt Lizzy's inheritance, anyway. What would Clemence do with Lysithea's fortune? Build a shelter for orphaned rabbits?

Amathia sent the brooch scuttling across the dressing-table surface.

She'd once overheard a snippet of gossip in a drawing-room. *Clemmie Somerlee is not quite right in the head...*

Where was the carriage? Drat that coachman. Amathia stalked the lawn of Kingsmede, her family home, while she waited for her transport.

She gazed beyond the boundary of the park. The mist was thick today, and you could barely make out the Sussex downs. Just round, darker humps against the greyness. Over that way lay Woodmancote, seat of the Fanshawes for generations.

Kingsmede, on the other hand, was so new one of the wings hadn't been finished. Never would be, probably. Amathia cast a critical eye over the house. She watched a vixen slinking from the unfinished section where it must have made its nest.

All those slaves her grandfather had traded for what – this red-brick, turreted monstrosity of a domicile she was ashamed of? And what little of his fortune was left she could picture trickling like sand through the fingers of her only brother. The present duke, Amathia's father, had been eking out a comfortable lifestyle by borrowing against his father's goodly name.

Her stomach rumbled. She wouldn't be eating until eight. And then it would be mouse-sized portions at a society dinner-party. She glanced towards the service wing. Might she pilfer something from the kitchens?

Remembering something made her smile. Feeling peckish one night, she had snuck to the pantry, and availed herself of a veal pie and blancmange. When she'd heard that some wretched scullery maid had taken the blame when the theft was discovered, and lost her situation without a character, naturally that blancmange had not tasted so good after all.

But Amathia had got over it and had come to see the funny side.

'What mischief are you plotting, Mathy? I know that look on your face.'

Amathia's eyes snapped up to the terrace. She had not observed her brother sneaking up or heard his footsteps. He stood at the head of the steps, leaning upon his cane, right leg crossed over the other.

'If you must know, Philo, I was scheming to marry you to a rich heiress.'

'Oh, tol-lol, sissy dear. What'll you do? Lock the poor minx in a tower and force her?'

Maybe it would come to that, and all. Amathia eyed him. Lord Philoctetes Dunkerley, as he was styled until he ascended into the rarefied air of dukedom, was twenty years old. Two months returned from his Grand Tour, he was regarded by the mamas with marriageable daughters as one of the catches of the season. Some girls might find him personable she supposed. What a shame Clemmie Somerlee was already promised to that nonentity of a hussar.

At last, she saw the coach entering the forecourt from the mews.

'If you're not coming to Lord Tewksbury's, Philo,' she said as she swept past him up the steps to the terrace, 'go back indoors, dearest one. The damp air isn't good for your delicate chest.'

'Oh, ha! ha!' sneered the young lord.

The horse was mercifully dead. Wide-open brown eyes stared into equine Heaven.

Clemence clasped a hand to her mouth at sight of the injuries. A sudden squall of wind blew back the beast's black forelock and showered her face with dust.

What had brought Clemence down to this broken place? Didn't remember descending the path… Brandon had been calling her back, hadn't he? *Oh, Heaven… what am I doing… where am I going… is this a dream? Aubrey, where are you…*

Both armies had by now withdrawn from the churned valley floor, of that much she was confident. But what else would she find?

Mounds of the crumpled were scattered everywhere – beasts and men.

One man lay with his leg trapped beneath a dead charger. Something yellowish was oozing from a gash in the soldier's abdominal regions, all over his blue and gold coatee. The tasselled end of his scarlet sash was fluttering in the wind.

Another's head had split like a pumpkin which had dropped onto the floor and smashed, spilling out its juice and goodness. A look of surprise was lighting the man's eyes as he gazed open-mouthed into the clouds.

Clemence knelt in the turf beside the fallen horse. She stroked his nose.

'I hope you're running on the sands of Paradise,' she whispered. These were the true victims of war – the horses. Troopers… well, what had they understood of territorial expansionism in the Black Sea region? They were fighting in the army because it was preferable to starving in the slums whence they came. But still, humans had a choice. Horses did not.

Aubrey, oh, dear God, where are you?

Dear Father in Heaven. All I'm thinking of is Aubrey, Aubrey! My brother is not the only one in need. See the suffering all around.

She unfastened the dead cavalry mount's saddle and tugged off the shabraque from beneath. The saddlecloth was still damp with beast-blood. Embroidered on one corner was the insignia of the Seventeenth Lancers.

'I'm sorry, beauty.' She stroked the donor again. 'This might save a life.'

Close by, she stumbled upon a dragoon who was yet alive. The sound of his groaning had led her to him.

She gasped as she glimpsed his injuries close to. That hole which exposed part of his skull must have been from grape or shrapnel shot out of a shell. His brass helmet was half-dislodged to show it. The black horsehair plume was saturated with his blood.

But there was a bleeding gash in his chest, too. If she could bind his wounds to staunch the haemorrhage… he might survive until he reached the field hospital.

She stepped softly over to the young soldier. He screeched.

'Be easy… sir!' She hadn't a clue what rank he was. Something like twenty-five years old, she thought.

Clemence could feel her heartbeat speeding up. Her knees seemed unstable. But she managed to reach out a hand to touch his face.

'Sorry if I startled you…' She tried to smile. 'I'm making some bandages. Keep still.'

She tore the saddle-blanket into strips. Three times she fumbled. Almost dropped it from fingers she could not keep from trembling. How qualified was she to do something like this? Once, under Nanny's direction, she had bandaged the hand of the boot-boy when he had cut himself!

Those jagged sighs the injured dragoon was letting out were not just an outlet for pain; her man was trying to speak.

'Who are you, miss?' She could just make out the croaky words.

'My name's Clemence Somerlee. My betrothed is out here somewhere…'

'Sorry I shrieked, miss, when you appeared.' A spurt of blood gurgled from his lips. He blew a bubble out of it. 'It's just… I thought you were… well… an angel…'

'Hush! I'm going to bandage your chest.'

He remained silent as she got to work. Those must be the life-threatening injuries tended now. How wobbly were the legs beneath her as she rose. She wiped her brow with a smeary hand.

Clemence stepped back to look over the whole valley. The sun was brighter and hotter now, but the wind no less strong. Her ringlets blew across her vision. What hysteria could have led her to venture down here? Lizzy… where was her aunt?

The contentious earthworks on the summit of the Causeway could not be seen from the battlefield; far away where the river shone, the Russians must be caring for their own wounded; but between them all lay a valley of death strewn with men and horses. Here – a disembodied head with a rictus death-grin. There – half an arm, from the same sundered man she supposed, with the white-gloved hand clutching a sword. Here – a lifeless Cornet Maynard who had been a recent dinner guest. A bayonet was rammed into the sod, the blue and white tassel of the Eleventh Hussars flapping from the hilt.

'Miss Somerlee!'

She looked to see who called her. That dragoon staggering towards her, arm around the shoulder of a bewildered, injured Cossack – she knew him. A friend of her brother's.

'What in God's name are you doing here?'

'Major Pewsy-Hart.' The man was bandaged across the skull, his face pink, shiny and damp, but seemingly able-bodied. 'I was trying to find my brother, and Captain Swynton. Then I stumbled across this poor man. I thought I could help,' she said. She clasped and wrung her hands. 'Major, have you seen James, or Aubrey, or heard of them?'

'Miss Somerlee, we all have our concerns right now! Mine is this chappie,' he nodded to the semiconscious Russian in his charge. 'He's a prisoner but bleeding badly. I'm seeking a surgeon. I saw you bandage that other chap …' He eyed her hopefully.

'Of course, Major.' *Oh God, where will I find the courage to do this? But don't show you're afraid. Don't let him see how much you're shaking.* 'Lay the poor man flat. Find something to use as a bandage. A dead man's sash perhaps. Or a shabraque. That's what I used for the other fellow. I need to get him to a surgeon also.'

She shut her eyes and said a quick prayer before she could bring herself to peep beneath the Cossack's furs. From the longish shape of the chest lesion, she guessed he'd been struck by a bayonet, and it was the major source of blood loss. *Might have been worse...*

'Do you know any Russian, Major?' Clemence looked up at him. 'Me neither.' When the Cossack opened frightened eyes, she smiled and stroked his brow.

'Major?' she asked as she tore the sash he had brought her. 'Is this a silly question? But who won here today?'

Pewsy-Hart turned his eyes skywards and laughed.

'Well, Miss Somerlee, we stormed the Don Cossack battery and took many of their guns. Is that not a victory?'

'I thought you'd all been shot to ribbons!'

'Well, one thing about cannon-fire, Miss Somerlee, is that is doesn't have a brain! You can dodge it, if you've the sense to see what direction it's being fired in. Myself and the chap who was with me – well, we got in close to one of the howitzers, and bunged it up so it couldn't fire anymore.' He gave a low whistle. 'Must have saved a few lives doing that.'

'You know the charge was a mistake, Major? I was nearby when Lord Raglan gave the order to Nolan. You were only meant to stop the Russians taking the guns from the fortresses on the Causeway! Not charge their entire army! They've cut the Light Brigade to pieces.'

Pewsy-Hart hung his head.

'Miss Somerlee, we have been to Hell and back. And no-one will take this victory from us.' He gazed into the sky. 'Cannon-fire everywhere, all around you... slant-eyed faces... slicing swords... bayonets with the sunlight flashing from the steel of the blades... the waters of the Styx flowing in your veins... Ah, I declare they'll be singing of this day a hundred years from now.'

The thud of many galloping hooves was coming near. Clemence and the man turned to look. Seven loose horses raced towards them over the brow. A mixture of hussar and dragoon shabraques… and one with Russian colours. They had gone native – running together as a primeval herd.

Pewsy-Hart gave chase and caught one by the trailing reins. He brought it under control. He helped the first injured man Clemence had tended into the saddle, then mounted behind him.

'I'll take this one to the sawbones, then return,' he called over his shoulder as he set off.

By the time he came back, she had bound the wound of the prisoner. Pewsy-Hart took him too.

'I'll have to leave you to make your own way, Miss Somerlee. On the other side of the pass you'll find a canvas awning which they're using as an improvised first aid point.' He pointed in the direction of the south valley. 'They're treating the injured there before dispatching them on to the field hospitals. Sorry I'm not being a gentleman,' he added with a sour grin, 'but I cannot waste time with this fellow.'

Clemence was left to pick a path through the gruesome battlefield.

She saw the surgeon's tent close by the spot in the ruined vines where the Heavy Brigade had fought. How gentle, now, sounded the ditch-water. A broken rifle, caught in the rocks, disrupted the flow. A dusty forage cap crowned the bush beside the small bridge. In the distance, a firearm could be heard still discharging – someone emptying his gun-carriage. Somewhere, too, the Lord's Prayer was being chanted.

Five men who had perished in an explosion – from the location, most probably the one which had blown up the arsenal and given Lord Fanshawe and Mr Mapplewell such a thrill – spread out from a central point like petals from the corona of a flower. There had not been time for horror to strike their features: each was frozen in his final deed – one man clutching his rifle in the act of reloading.

'Good Lord! Is that you, Miss Somerlee?'

The voice startled her. She had not heeded the approaching hoof beats.

A mounted figure sat there. The gold aglets on the Field Marshal's shoulders glinted in the sunshine. Two staff officers accompanied him.

'What on earth are you doing here, child?' Lord Raglan said.

What am I doing here? That's a good question. Raglan seems more astonished than cross, though.

'I apologise if I shouldn't be here. I just… just wondered if there was something I could do to assist… I found a man alive. Brought him here. Needs help…'

'Well, your concern does you credit.' Raglan's tone softened. 'This is the first aid tent. If you tell one of the orderlies, they'll treat him. But then you must return to your quarters, child. This really isn't any place for you, my dear.' He was about to turn his horse and ride away.

'What were our losses, My Lord?' she asked.

'Early estimates from the sawbones – perhaps as few as two or three thousand. The Frenchies of course have had a catastrophe.'

'You mean the Russkies, My Lord,' said an aide.

'Ah well, Johnny Foreigners are all the same to me! But are you enjoying your stay in the Crimea otherwise, Miss Somerlee?'

'Quite a thrill, My Lord, thank you.'

She'd detected polite contempt in his voice. *Go home and play with your dollies, girlie.*

He's right, isn't he? she thought as she watched the Field Marshal continue on his way. *What might a fragile English rose do for good in this Hell of man's making? Can I do aught to stop it? Or even help…?*

SIX

A barouche drew up in the forecourt of Lord Tewksbury's country house.
Amathia looked on from behind the drawn-back curtain of her dressing-room. She could make out painted on the side door the coat-of-arms depicting a yew tree surmounted by four quatrefoils.

Out stepped the Baronet of Eardingstowe. A light mizzle was in the air, and he put on his top hat. He paused at the base of the steps which led up to the porch and looked up at the façade of the mansion. She got the impression he was marshalling his courage.

Amathia let fall the drape so that he would not see her yet. She was, after all, in her *déshabille*.

'Vickery, lay out the lilac bombazine,' Amathia called to her useless maid. 'No! The gold satin, I think. And no creases this time, if you please. A single crease and you're out without a character, understood?'

'Yes, madam.'

Amathia took one last peep at her suitor down below. Somerlee was by now mounting the steps. She did a little twirl as she stepped away from the window and over to the toilet-table. *Wasn't that what girls in love were supposed to do? Look all dreamy and floaty?*

She sat before the glass and cupped her face.

What was happening out in the Crimea, she wondered? Poor old Major Maudant of the Royal Welch Fusiliers, who had danced with her three times, and taken her in to dinner at Lady Quarmby's ball. She'd not taken much notice of him – then. Didn't have money or property. But maybe she should have. Kate Scobie-Settles was getting on Amathia's damn nerves, gushing on about her captain who'd distinguished himself at the Battle of the Alma.

Amathia dangled first one necklace then another from her fingers.

'Vickery! I don't see the blue pearls. Did you omit to pack them?'

'I'm sorry, madam. You didn't say you wanted them.'

Amathia tutted. She let the inferior stones drop with a clatter.

No, war heroes were all very well to boast of at the dinner-table. Maybe they made decent lovers, too, perhaps... she wouldn't know. But unless your man had land and income... there was no future. Scobie-Settles would not be so smug when Amathia was inviting the ton to her kettledrums, and Scobie-Settles was fobbing her mantuamaker off with promises to settle her bills next year.

Amathia tilted her head to one side, gazing into the looking-glass. She thought of Sir Dickon Somerlee – that fair, solid country gentleman, ever-so-slightly unsure of himself.

What had her father, the duke said?

'They've negro, slave ancestry on one side, you know – the Somerlees. Oh, mostly it's regarded as an eccentricity. Somerlee's great-grandfather, something of a rebel corsair they say, rescued this negro girl from a slave ship, and then married the creature and made her mistress of Eardingstowe! The Black Beauty, toast of Georgian society and all that! All very dashing stuff, straight out of a storybook.

'But taints like that aren't to be lightly dismissed! Polluted blood runs in the veins for generations,' he added, pursing his lips. 'As for old Somerlee, the present baronet's father, he married the daughter of a cotton-master. Well, old Joshua Carswell – rich as Croesus and common as muck – went in bliss to the cotton-fields in the sky believing his girl had married into the aristocracy…'

'Instead of the mere bumpkin gentry,' Amathia had supplied.

'Quite! But the mill came to his daughter's husband, and the Somerlees are fairly rich, I believe. Think he owns land in Ireland, too.'

'Yes… he told me. Some boggy swamp. Dickon's never actually been there. Just evicts the starving tenants when they're making a nuisance!' Amathia had laughed. 'I am rather hopeful, Papa,' she had added, 'that Sir Richard does intend to make an offer. And I'm quite amenable to becoming Lady Amathia Somerlee of Eardingstowe. Although, we might need to keep Richard's unfortunate relatives hidden in the closet, I daresay.'

The duke had glowered.

'Don't forget my grandfather started out as …'

'As if I could!' Amathia had shuddered.

'He's an ambitious cove, you know – Dickon Somerlee,' Consett had continued. 'Probably expects me to get him an earldom. As if I grow the damn things in my hothouses!'

'Really, Papa!' Amathia had said. 'Your language has deteriorated since we lost Mama.'

The duke had wavered in surprise.

'Wouldn't be too difficult to find her again if you really wanted, Amathia. There cannot be that many gaming-houses in Biarritz.'

'Papa! That is something else we don't mention. If anyone enquires, I have lost my mama, and look suitably melancholy over it! Well, now, sir – Richard has the money and ancient lineage; you, Papa, the title and ear of the men who count at court and in Parliament. I truly think this alliance might work.'

Her thoughts returned to the present. At this dreary country house party at Lord Tewksbury's she fully expected the Baronet of Eardingstowe to address her. She picked up one of the discarded necklaces, and let it drop to the woodwork again.

Truth be told, Lady Amathia Consett might have done better for herself than Somerlee. Sir Quincy Dooley. Now, there had been a catch. Amathia'd observed the smouldering desire beneath those grizzled eyebrows when he'd been seated opposite her at a dinner-party. Made his money in banking, ha-ha, having started out as messenger boy no doubt, ha-ha.

But he was wifeless, childless, sixty-eight years old, and had suffered at least one cerebral seizure. So, not long would his bride have to wait before living happily ever after with Dooley's thousands stuffed in her drawers. With his warts, nasal hair and flatulence of the decibels of HMS *Agamemnon's* artillery, Quincy was notwithstanding one of Amathia's most personable beaux.

She'd surprised herself, therefore, in settling upon Dickon Somerlee. He wasn't as rich as Quincy; or especially well-connected; and he was no fool; she'd not be able to work his strings as she could have Quincy's.

But he was Brandon Fanshawe's good friend. The Brandon who had scorned her interest.

Well, now – be as well to look her best for Somerlee, wouldn't it, just in case he was having second thoughts?

'I will have the lilac bombazine after all,' she told Vickery when the maid returned with immaculately pressed gold satin. 'The gold can wait until dinner tomorrow.' *When Sir Richard was most likely to make his overtures.*

A dish of chocolate marzipan had been left on the toilet-table for guests. She plucked and munched one.

'What are you waiting for, fool?' she snapped at the abigail. 'I said fetch the lilac! And I want it properly pressed, mind.'

'Yes, madam!' said the girl, and bustled out.

Amathia sank her teeth into a second chocolate. The light blue eyes and moonshine-pale ringlets of Richard's sister seemed to swim before her vision. What was it about Clemmie Somerlee that always got Amathia's goat? It was more than just the fortune the girl was to inherit, damn her, although that was galling enough.

Amathia pushed the plate of sweetmeats aside. Vickery would have to fetch her some more, now. Well, at least Clemmie Somerlee's presentation gown had had fewer pearls on it than Mathy Consett's – and Amathia was the kind of lass who could count.

While she waited for the lilac dress, Amathia performed a twirl before the cheval-glass in her frillies. She caught a glimpse of white drawers stretched taught across humungous round dumplings, which Dooley had had the bad taste to pat. Like the South Downs following her around. Turning to the front view instead didn't help – the button was fighting for freedom from the blancmange horde. She imagined a ping so loud that the entire dinner table fell silent – what a nightmare.

'Of course your posterior didn't show in your presentation gown, sissy dear,' her brother Philoctetes had suspiciously reassured her. Clemence, blast her, was a twig. But that didn't make her unique. So were most débutantes – with the exception of Pearl Arbroath whose train was still being spread over her enormous proportions by the lord-in-waiting in the anteroom while the rest of her was curtseying before the throne.

'I've told you before, Vickery!' Amathia said. 'Warm your hands before you dress me.'

But as she stepped into the raiment for afternoon tea, and then studied her reflection, her mood lifted. No-one could deny that Amathia was very pretty.

'You're a maiden of summer, Lady Amathia,' one admirer had told her. 'Sunshine, cherries and cream.'

The young woman gripped the post of the first-aid tent for support. It didn't take her long to learn that this stench was the smell blood gives off.Metalic. Like a rusty garden hoe she'd once stumbled across, abandoned in the untended overgrowth where Eardingstowe's Paradise Garden met the wild wood.

At the operating table in front of Clemence, an elderly surgeon was struggling alone. He worked by the light of a single oil lamp hanging from the roof of the tent. She could make out dampness glistening on his brow.

There must be two dozen wounded lying slumped around the floor; among them the pair Clemence had bandaged. One man's face looked like a theatrical mask – one side handsome and normal, the other blown off, with the mouth fixed in a macabre, grinning rictus. Poor soul... but at least he was not her brother. *Heavenly Father, let Aubrey be safe back in Balaclava. James, too... yes, I hope James is well.*

The surgeon glanced up as he cut through torn flesh.

'You'll be the young lady the major mentioned?' he said without surprise.

'Can I do anything, doctor?'

'If you think you can assist, then yes, please...'

Clemence had heard rumours that the quartermaster's department was less than competent. Round lead ball for muskets sent to men who needed the conical bullets for Minié rifles and so on. The rumblings had crept into Mr Russell's newspaper copy. Now Clemence could see that the medical corps, too, was laughable. There was no anaesthetic. The hussar under the surgeon's blade was quivering and wailing.

The girl trod deeper inside the hut, lifting her hem over pools of blood, and took up a sponge and bandage from the doctor's tray.

She began to peel away the ruined coatee from a groaning man's injuries. She dabbed at the congealing ridges of blood, her unsteady hand darting away at each shriek he let out. When she'd cleaned enough to see the source of the haemorrhage, she tried to staunch it.

She struggled to free his canteen from his girdle.

'Here. Drink.'

She held the water-bottle to her soldier's lips. But her dratted hand wouldn't stop shaking. A lot got spilled.

Eventually, he spoke.

'*Kus ma olen? Kes sa oled? Ma olen kohutav valu!*'

So… unknown language… must be one of the other side she was assisting. Well, what did she care?

Clemence had believed she was kneeling in the patient's blood-flow. When she glanced down, the sticky gunge puddling around her knees was not red but brown – from beneath his legs not out of his thorax.

'Doctor,' she called from behind a hand clasped to her mouth, 'I think we have a cholera case. I suggest we move him out, away from the others.'

Outside in the breeze, Clemence pushed back the hair which was clinging to her damp brow. She set a hand to her aching back.

There was Saupon Hill where she and the spectators had stood, darkened now at sundown. Her eyes picked out the path Captain Nolan had taken down its daunting face. Was it really only six hours ago? There jutted each stubby bush which he'd danced his mount around.

'Will you be all right, young lady?' The doctor was strapping some of the injured into a cart to transport them to Balaclava. 'Shall I take you back to Kadikoi?'

'No, doctor – your patients are in more need. I can find my own way,' she said. The surgeon cast her an appreciative smile. He returned to his dray. 'Doctor,' she continued, 'what is to happen to these men? That small hospital in Balaclava cannot cope with all the casualties surely?'

'No, miss. They'll be sent by ship to the field hospital in Scutari on the other side of the Black Sea. Yes, I know,' he added as Clemence must have shown shock, 'it is four days' sailing and many won't survive the journey! God bless you, young lady, though. You've brought them some relief.'

When she and the surgeon had parted company, she took the long track to the village of Kadikoi. Upon the edge of a horse trough she perched, foot sore and weary.

'Clemence! Oh, thank heavens!'

She looked up to see her aunt hurrying towards her.

'I've been worried ever since I could not find you at breakfast!' Lysithea settled beside her. 'Someone said they saw you go down to the valley!'

'Yes, Aunt, I did. Reckless of me, I know. But then, I guess battle makes fools of men, and women, just as drink does!' Clemence sighed. 'I could see the fighting was finished. And I thought of Aubrey. And James. Oh, Aunt Lizzy,' she screwed up eyes hot with tears, 'I never knew there was such suffering...' Lysithea rocked her in her arms, kissing the top of her head. 'You warned me, too. You must have seen this in Spain.'

As she cried in Lysithea's arms, Clemence thought of her mother, dead these seven years.

'Well... I'm proud of you, chicken.' Lysithea stroked Clemence's hair. 'Did you find Aubrey or James?'

Clemence shook her head.

'But I did not search every grisly pile! I take it they did not return with the survivors?'

'No, I have not seen them. But come – return to headquarters with me. News will most likely arrive there first.'

Lysithea led her through rows and rows of soldiers' huts towards the farmhouse where the Field Marshal was quartered.

Whenever Clemence looked up she would see a Highlander, say, sitting outside his tent, bathing a bullet wound on his arm with water from his kettle; or a Buckinghamshire stuffing a hungry mouth with cold, salt pork; and seeming to regard the two gentlewomen with a hostile eye; then a trooper's wife hanging laundry on a rope stretched between tents; two thin children with scabies clinging to her skirts.

At headquarters, the Field Marshal was pacing and fuming. The commander of the Light Brigade stood before him as he faced the music, defiant – helmet under arm.

'You have lost the Light Brigade, sir!'

'I was following the order Lucan gave me!' Cardigan protested.

'You have lost the Light Brigade!'

'Advance on the enemy, Lucan said, dammit.'

'Disgraceful language, sir! There are ladies present.'

As the two decrepit old castles, Raglan and Cardigan, continued to thud each other's outer defences with withered battering-rams, Clemence turned to her aunt.

'Cardigan returned unscathed I see.'

Lysithea laughed without mirth.

'Depends how you define 'unscathed'! He galloped back to Balaclava while the rest of the Light Brigade which had got that far was still in the thick of the fighting. I've already heard hints of cowardice being directed his way. Better, almost, to be lying out there with the dead.'

The two women moved into the next room where General Airey stood briefly unengaged.

'Any news of my nephew, Cornet Somerlee, or Captain Swynton?' Lysithea said.

'I'm sorry, no, Countess. But it will be days before all the dead, injured and prisoners are accounted for. Excuse me.' He edged politely past.

Lysithea and Clemence left the farmhouse. They wandered, arm-in-arm, across the plateau.

Near the encampment of the Westmorlands they halted. Two old sweats were sitting beside a cooking fire, discussing the battle in rough, East End voices. Apart from the gallant Highlanders, most of the infantry had not seen action today. The wound one of these troopers was dressing must be old, from the Battle of the Alma.

The Somerlee ladies stood on a brow overlooking the mountain peaks to the east. You could smell the salt on the wind which was blowing in from the sea.

In the other direction lay the Tchernaya estuary and Sebastopol. Beyond the port on the distant headland rose a grim-looking Russian defence known as the Star Fort. The allied fleet lurked outside the harbour entrance – its ship-shapes black against a violet sea and brilliant bedtime sun.

'Captain Nolan died, Aunt. I saw it,' Clemence said. 'Was he trying to stop the charge when he pushed his way forward like that? Did he know they'd blundered? We'll never know.'

'Or maybe he did know,' Lysithea replied. 'He wanted to prove what cavalry can do – it's well known. He'd even written a book on the subject.'

'You're saying he let the men of the Light Brigade ride to their deaths like that just to make a point? Deliberately misrepresented the instructions Raglan gave him? So the cream of the cavalry lies dead because of braggadocio and deceit?'

'From what I've been hearing – yes. But as you say, Nolan's no longer with us to tell his side of the story. So, we'll never know. At least his body's been brought back so we can bury him.'

If only she knew as much of her brother. Was Aubrey lying dead? Then Clemence might begin to mourn. Was he wounded in one of those abattoirs they called field hospitals? Then she might be with him, holding his hand, wiping fever sweat from his brow. Uncertainty seemed worse even than the finality of death.

Was Aubrey a prisoner on the other side? She and Lysithea could be proactively negotiating release.

Aubrey, always Aubrey. James, too. She must remember her husband-to-be…

'I've been thinking…' Clemence watched four eagles circling the closest blue-green mountain summit. 'I gather they could use some assistance in the hospitals. Do you think I might help…?'

'You? A nurse?' Lysithea laughed tragically. 'You sat with your papa when he was dying! So, you think that makes you qualified?'

'I bandaged two men in the valley! And I helped the doctor in the field hospital. Of course I'm squeamish! I almost gag now just thinking about it. But at least I've not fainted.' A smile broke through the tearful strain. 'And being busy… less time to fret.'

Lysithea smoothed strands of wind-tangled hair back behind Clemence's ear.

'It'll be quite ghastly,' her aunt said. 'That reporter, Russell, has had a lot to say about the state of the hospital at Scutari. So much so that the government has intervened. They're sending over a team of trained nurses led by a Miss Nightingale. I suppose, though, Clemence, you might be better there among the lice and infections… keeping busy, as you say. You will see all the casualties brought in from the battle. You could look for our menfolk there, and I shall continue to seek them here. Although,' Lysithea spoke in a soft voice, 'all I really want is to take you home, my love.'

'Well, we're here, and we cannot leave. Not until we have news of James and Aubrey.' Clemence summoned a smile. 'We might as well make ourselves useful!'

She turned from the mountain-view to look back across the plateau towards headquarters. The first covered wagon had arrived there, bearing dead from the valley.

Someone was approaching, waving to attract their attention.

'It's Lord Fanshawe,' said Lysithea. 'My word, his expression looks bleak.'

The Baronet of Eardingstowe excused himself from the after-dinner company, stepped out of the dining-room, and crossed the tiled hallway.

A beautiful young woman was in the curtained inglenook, seated on a sofa.

'Lady Amathia. Thank you for meeting me,' Richard began. He had passed a note to her maid earlier that day asking Lady Amathia Consett to wait right here at the hour of nine.

The young lady gave a little bow of the head. Always she bore that soft smile on her lips – quite the diplomat at times.

'Yes, Sir Richard. I received the communication you sent me. You wish to speak with me?'

He hemmed.

Back in the dining-room, the gentlemen's merry tones continued. The brandy decanter would be on its second circuit of the table. The hum of female voices and laughter rose from the sitting-room in the other direction. You caught the occasional muffled sound of a footfall coming from the servants' corridor behind the panelling. But otherwise the hall was quiet, with no-one apart from Amathia and him around, and deeply shadowed in those corners like the inglenook which were distant from the few lamps.

'Not very pleasant weather, is it?' said Richard.

'Fine enough for a shooting meet, Sir Richard. Especially for those of us who, by virtue of our gender, may elect to stay within the warmth!' The smile grew wider. 'Pray, what was it you wished to discuss? Or am I just an excuse to leave the table?'

'Oh, you are far too charming to be a mere excuse for anything, Lady Amathia. No-one could take anything but delight in your company.'

'My pleasure, Sir Richard,' said she, on a quick bow of the head. 'Although I imagine you menfolk must be discussing little except the war over your brandy and port. I daresay war-talk might indeed become tedious, even for a gentleman.'

'Ah, yes! Lord Tewksbury was regaling us with the new breed of tomato he's grown in his hothouse,' he said. 'He intends to christen the fruit "Alma" after our recent victory.'

Richard glanced around the cosy-corner. A jardinière stood in the angle, three plants trailing their leaves and shoots over the shelves. A rather faded oval-framed portrait of a very young lady in seventeenth-century dress and hairstyle hung above.

His uncomfortable gaze returned to Amathia. She was as lovely as an icicle. Dazzling to look on perhaps, but you wouldn't want it near your heart.

'I trust you'll be joining us in the drawing-room for the musical recital later?' he asked. 'Madame Lise will be singing.'

'Indeed, Sir Richard. We share a taste for the fine arts, you and I, I believe.'

Richard studied a large seascape hanging by the fireplace in the hall opposite, and admired a Grecian vase standing on the shelf below. His gaze followed the pattern of trailing ivy in the ivory wall panel.

He took a deep breath and launched forth.

'Lady Amathia,' he began. 'I am sure you must guess how much I admire you. Might I entertain the hope that if I asked you to marry me, you would not look with disfavour on my proposal?'

Richard listened to the hooting of the owls outside in the park, and the sound of rain on the glass. If she declined him – oh, would it sting! A man had his pride, dammit. Deuced awkward for his career too; he was hoping her ducal parent's patronage would further it. But in some deep, inner cranny… might he not be a little relieved?

'Sir Richard.' Amathia inclined towards him. 'I am honoured by your regard for me. I can assure you that you will be favourably received if you wish to continue.'

Richard cleared his throat a third time. He pressed on, words rushed, and with none of the panache which had, now and then, enlivened Westminster and withered the odd Whig.

'I should like to remind you, Lady Amathia, that you would be mistress of a considerable estate of great antiquity—'

'Yes, charming, I'm sure. Eardingstowe is not, of course, as extensive as Brancombe Park, but Sir Quincy Dooley's marriage proposal was not as attractive to me in other respects. I have not yet, however, said him nay. I have merely advised that I am considering his offer.' She cast Richard a meaningful look. 'Your late father left a considerable settlement on the younger children, did he not?'

'A small allowance only. Two thousand a year for each.'

'It must mount up, though, among so many?'

'But the estate is healthy enough, I can assure you – can certainly stand trifling expenses like my siblings' allowances…'

'Oh, I was not suggesting otherwise, Sir Richard. You are clearly fond of your relations, and I hope I shall be also. Particularly Clemmie. She and I were presented together, you know – practically sisters already.' The young lady rose from her sofa and extended her hand. 'Indeed, Sir Richard, your suit is most welcome to me.'

Richard went down on one knee. He pressed his lips to her lace mitten.

His eyes moved upwards, taking in gold satin crinoline and cream ribbon, and above the summit of this shining hillside... well, what came into his mind right then was the Causeway at Balaclava as *The Times's* Mr Russell had described the scene... one of its forbidding fortresses fortified with its nine-pounders.

Richard and the lady who was to be his wife emerged into the staircase hall a short while later, her hand resting on his arm.

A footman, clutching a newspaper, was hurrying towards the dining-room where the gentlemen's voices could still be heard.

'I say, you there!' Richard called. 'You look as if you are the bearer of tidings.'

'Indeed, Sir Richard, Lady Amathia.' The man halted and bowed his head. 'News from the front. I am taking the evening newspaper to His Lordship at once. There has been another battle! At Balaclava. Most heroic, it appears. The cavalry fought like courageous lions, it says here.'

'The cavalry? Then my brother would have been involved!' Richard said. 'May I see?' He perused a few paragraphs of the newspaper handed to him.

Great victory! Russians defeated by six hundred of the brave! Well, well, the Eleventh Hussars indeed – James's and Aubrey's regiment. A charge by the Light Brigade into a valley surrounded on three sides by enemy ordnance? Richard shook his head; how these journals exaggerate. Not even Raglan was senile enough to attempt something so reckless. Boney had his arm not his sense.

'I trust it's good news, Sir Richard?' Amathia asked.

'I'm not sure what to make of it,' he said.

Well, whatever the truth behind the story, the casualty numbers were staggering. No names yet. Too early an edition.

SEVEN

Two army horses stood tethered to the gate of the small Orthodox chapel in Kadikoi, cropping the grass around the posts.

The girl's eyes roamed the building before her: a cabin constructed in the shape of a Greek cross, topped with a wooden dome. A streak of blood smeared the step and doorpost... someone injured in the battle must have staggered here to pray.

Clemence drew her shawl around her head and stepped over the threshold of the strange place.

The aroma of incense was as overwhelming as had been the stench of blood in the hospital tent. Her batting eyes took a moment to adjust to the dimness.

A horseshoe lay discarded just inside the door. Sand was scattered and trampled across the tiled mosaic floor. In the aisle gaped one broken window. She could even detect a smell of urine coming from one corner of the vestibule. This House of God must have been getting misused by the soldiery for some time. Yet it remained, and formidably so, a place of worship: around the walls glittered gold-painted icons depicting saints undergoing gruesome martyrdom, or thereafter in glory.

She tiptoed to the shrine where tiny votive flames were burning. Light a candle and pray to the Madonna...? Ah, the ritual might be alien to an Anglican, but the invocation would reach the skies just the same.

Poor James Swynton. Clemence had been there when they'd brought home his portly body in the wagon. What a waste of a young life. One comforting thought when she'd seen his grapeshot-battered remains laid out – he had died believing his Clemence adored him.

What should she ask of the Almighty in this outlandish place of worship? *Let it be yesterday again, Lord, so that none of this need happen? Just take back thirty hours or so, Lord, that's all...?*

No... Man *should* suffer and learn from his mistakes. Were not all atrocities in human history forged from good intentions gone awry?

Clemence took from her reticule a tarnished oval medallion. She held it in the palm of her hand so that it caught the candlelight. Our Lady of Kazan. The eyes of the all-knowing mother gazing out at her in sorrow. James had carried it into battle in his scrip.

For him, it had been no protection. Sure sign that he'd had no business taking so personal a treasure. Some Ivan, or Sasha, or Sergei somewhere was grieving the loss of this.

Clemence enfolded her fingers around it again. She slipped it back into her reticule. She would return it to the Russian high command.

Please, God, at least bring my brother back safe if you had to break my heart over James.

A gust of wind blew in through the broken pane. Some of the little flames swayed or fluttered out and on again.

But you're not sorry he's dead really, are you, minx?

A ground-mist was lying in the hollows of the land. The higher ground seemed to be floating above the silent sea. Distant trees of the parkland, and red-tiled roof of the home farm took form and vanished again as the whiteness drifted.

The baronet sat astride his hunter at the edge of the terrace. Behind him rose the south west range and russet towers of the Duke of Rutland's seat, Belvoir. The company was gathered in the castle's forecourt – steamy-breathed and jolly, mingling before the hunt set out.

The kennelmen were bringing out the hounds. Rooks were circling and cawing overhead – they weren't fools, those feathered fellows; they knew in their tiny minds that a meet meant leftover grub.

Really, Richard's mind kept wandering. *What is happening out in Balaclava? Why doesn't Fanny send a telegram? My little brother Aubrey could be drinking the waters of the Lethe and here am I out for autumn sport!*

He forced his thoughts back to the present. Lady Amathia was walking her dark bay mount through the crowd towards him. She greeted him with a wave of a white-gloved hand.

Richard beckoned over a servant and plucked two steaming goblets from the man's tray.

'How nice to see you again, Lady Amathia. Do try this delicious spiced wine! It quite takes away the chill.'

He smiled as she halted beside him. He handed the lady a cup. The two stood their horses together beneath the boughs of a small pear tree which grew in one corner of the forecourt. Raindrops dripped from the tips of the branches.

'Seeing your gentle sex hunting takes some getting used to, Lady Amathia, Somerset-bred as I am. It is a conservative shire.'

'Oh, hunting is becoming *de rigeur* these days for ladies of the ton, Sir Richard!' She tilted up her chin as she laughed. Her fair hair was gathered in a knot behind her neck. She wore a gentleman's top hat with a womanly veil. 'In our parents' day, I daresay ladies were content to observe the hunt from a phaeton parked a discreet distance away. Now, the boldest of the fair sex are riding fences too.'

As she sipped from the cup, he observed her. A russet-gold leaf meandered down from the tree and lodged on the brim of her hat. It was true that more and more females were taking up the sport of hunting these days – a manly preserve within Richard's own memory! Her dress was like a feminine imitation of a man's hunting garb – dark velvet skirt, boots and white silk gloves. *Good Lord, they'll be taking over Parliament next and giving men the boot – well, cannot say Aristophanes didn't warn us...*

'Do you have any further news from the war, Sir Richard?' She turned her horse so that she was facing him.

'Only from *The Times*. I gather the Russians were driven off from Balaclava. But from my kinfolk and my good friend Lord Fanshawe nothing have I heard!'

'Ah, yes! Your dear aunt and sister. I trust they are finding their trip educational?'

Oh yes, he was sure they must be. Clemence's one letter home had sounded subdued. Had she seen things never meant for feminine attention? Serve her right for demanding to go on this damn-fool vacation.

'The Rutlands' company could be improved on, do you not think?' said Amathia, espying around the chattering groups. 'And the hunt breakfast – second rate, I think. When we are entertaining at Eardingstowe, dear Sir Richard, we shall make our seat the *beau ideal*! We'll be the envy of the ton, do you not agree?'

'Oh, I have every confidence in you, Lady Amathia.'

'But I shan't neglect the first duty of a wife, Sir Richard.' Amathia smiled. She touched his hand. 'That is – to make you the most content of men.'

'This you have already done, sweet lady, by saying 'yes' to me!' said Richard. 'Since you agreed to become my wife, I have been lost in the clouds.'

Amathia laughed.

'Ah, Sir Richard! When your brother Cornet Somerlee returns, we must honour him – our own war hero – with a kettledrum at Eardingstowe. Unless…' she cast her eyes down for a moment. 'Perhaps Aubrey would prefer to lay on entertainment at his own expense? He has such a generous allowance, you were telling me.'

'Not *that* generous!' Richard stroked his hunter's ears. 'No, Aubrey is still dependent on my goodwill for extravagances should he indulge in them. At least, until Uncle George goes to rest.'

Amathia's horse fidgeted, snorting steam, as two other riders passed close by, and the yapping of the hounds rose in pitch. She reached a hand to sooth the beast's ears.

'Your uncle, Sir Richard?'

'Hmm… Aubrey is due an inheritance.'

'Oh? I was not aware.' She fixed her gaze on him. Her eyes were grey, but sometimes, when there was laughter in her face or something had fired her thoughts – there was a greenly hue also.

'Yes. Uncle George is leaving most of his estate to my brother. George is a bachelor, and Aubrey's his favourite nephew, you see. George was at Waterloo – one of Wellington's cavalry officers. Or so he always told us as children. But then I checked the family Bible and noticed he would have been about twelve years old. So, I'm guessing he was a drummer-boy or something like that. But anyway, as you might imagine, he dotes on Aubrey.'

'I see! This legacy would revert to you, one supposes, were Aubrey not to return from the war?'

'I suppose so… I had not thought of it until now.'

Amathia gazed into the forest beyond Richard's shoulder.

Clemence peeped through her netted fingers at the unconscious man twitching in the bed before her.

A lesion yawned in the infantryman's bare ribcage. Like the cave of Erebus where Hades peeped through to the upper world.

It looked like a volcano had gone off in the man's thorax. The scorched landscape and ridges of clotted blood around the crater could have been solidifying lava and molten rock which had come spewing out at the instant of eruption. She was getting to recognise the calderas blasted out of human flesh by shrapnel, grape or canister-shot.

Then she spotted the crawling squatters who had moved in, nibbling away.

'Orderly?' She shrieked to the man who had shown her into the hospital ward.

'I ain't no orderly, miss!' the man laughed. 'I'm Private Bilsborrow of the Dorsets. My colonel thinks this is all I'm good for. Sorry about the stench of pee and blood and maggots and what-not. You gets used to it.'

'Well… private…' she struggled to get out. 'There's a grub on this poor man!'

'Oh, don't 'ee worry about those little gourmets, miss,' said Private Bilsborrow. 'Doing yer man a favour, they are. They eat the infected flesh, see, and the wound'll heal all the sooner.'

'Oh, I see…'

As the battlefield surgeon had warned, it had taken four days to get to the Dardanelles, fretting all the while about her brother who remained missing. A journey she had undertaken by sail along with the wounded. The high command had better uses for its steamships than transporting the no-longer-of-any-use. Some had died before arrival. One with typhoid had been tossed overboard before he was dead. And at Scutari she had found…

'This hospital is a disgrace!'

'Should'a seen it a week ago afore the battle-axe arrived! She's cleaned it up a bit, Miss Florence Nightingale.'

'Oh, that is such an outlandish Christian name!'

'Florence is where she was born, I believe.'

'How fortunate her parents did not visit Wimbledon.'

Clemence took a long, noticing look at her surroundings. The ward was an elongated, tunnel-like room. Lamps hung from its low, arched ceiling, giving off oily light. Some patients lay slumped against the walls for want of bed space. Some were dead. The girl didn't need to bend over them to see that. But there were too few staff to remove them. This young chap likely was not the only private seconded to make up for the lack of personnel.

'Where is your water supply, private, and your linen?'

Private Bilsborrow cackled.

'There's your water, miss.' Pointing to a jug. 'Bandages? That's a laugh! It ain't only bullets and ammunition we ain't getting sent. One trooper's wife ripped orf her petticoat and used that as a bandage.'

'Right! Then turn away, private.'

When the soldier peeped, he caught a glimpse of lacy, beribboned drawers.

'Do this a lot, do you?' he said as Clemence tore her undergarment into strips.

'Two years ago, I was looking forward to my presentation at court!'

The volcano-man, meanwhile, was groaning and stirring into consciousness.

''Ere! What's this la-di-da voice I hear?'

'I am trying to help, private. I'm not a nurse but I've some experience...'

'Grrr!' the man said. 'You be telling Lord Raglan, ma'am, and Lord fucking Palmerston, what sent us into this fucking hell-hole...'

'That is enough, private!'

All three pairs of eyes whipped around at sound of a new voice.

Miss Florence Nightingale needed no introduction. She glared at the invalid, and then turned to Clemence.

'You must be Miss Somerlee?'

The Superintendent of Scutari was a formidable-looking female, though not above average height, just entering her middle years. With chestnut-brown hair and arched eyebrows, she was handsome in a horsy way. She wore a plain, silk gown and lace cap, and was not to be messed with.

'Please finish what you have started,' she told the girl, 'then I'd like a word, if you please.'

'This is what I was laughingly told would be my private office,' Florence Nightingale said of the meagre chamber where she led Clemence. The hospital building had once served as a Turkish barracks. 'For the first two days I had to share this room with a dead Russian officer, until someone thought to remove the poor chap.

'When I got here,' Miss Nightingale went on, 'there were no bed pans, surgical implements, bandages or anaesthetics. Of the latter there still are none. Sir John Hall, the Chief Medical Officer, does not approve of the use of anaesthetic, you see. He belongs to the old school of medicine which believes that a good dose of unrelieved pain facilitates the healing process! The other necessaries I've bought myself from local suppliers. Well! That's my choler vented.'

'I'm sorry to hear of the troubles you've encountered, Miss Nightingale,' Clemence said. 'My brother the baronet is in Parliament as you must know. I will write to him...' If it would do any good. Probably not.

'And what brings you to Scutari, Miss Somerlee?'

Clemence crossed to the window before she answered. She looked out over a choppy harbour. Scutari lay on the eastern bank of the Dardanelles – a narrow channel which connected the Black Sea with the Sea of Marmara and the Aegean. Wars had been fought over this, God's strategic masterpiece. On a clear day, she had been told, you could see the minarets of Constantinople on the far shore.

'Well... I thought I might assist here, Miss Nightingale. I would like to volunteer... if you will have me.'

'I see!'

That sure didn't sound a very enthusiastic take-up. And why should it? Clemence was seventeen years old and had zero training or experience.

But now she had been here for some hours, she thought she maybe could bandage, bed wash, basic things like that. What Aunt Lizzy had said was also true – that she might hear word of her brother from one of the incoming wounded.

'Well... I did observe you tending that fellow back there, Miss Somerlee. You did rather well I suppose.' Florence Nightingale regarded her. 'Do you know that I was a young lady of society once? Yes, does that surprise you? Oh, my family are socially inferior to the Somerlees, but respectable enough to all-but disown me when God called me to nursing. The grisly injuries are naught,' she added with a wry smile. 'Please expect a great deal more of the language you just heard.'

Clemence grimaced.

'Well, yes, if you don't mind, I would like to stay. And I won't be a nuisance. I feel...' she wrung her hands, grappling with the thought, *'responsible.* We sent these men here over a quarrel which is none of their making or understanding.'

'Bosh, Miss Somerlee! Eight months ago, these same men were dancing in the streets, calling for the Czar's head! The people chose to fight this war, not the government. To the people it means cheering over how great their country is. Not a thought do they give about whether it's in their country's better interests, or how prepared we were for it, or that our only experienced military commander is a hard-of-hearing sexagenarian. You owe them no pity. Duty is what I owe, to my God and my country. But whatever your motive, Miss Somerlee, I am sure I will be glad of a willing volunteer.'

'Thank you, Miss Nightingale. I shan't let you down! And it might do me good, too, to be usefully employed at this time.' *And hide from my shame… that I'm not sorry James died.*

'Very well. I shall show you fully around. Come.' Miss Nightingale held out an arm. Clemence laid a hand upon it.

'So, you came from Balaclava?' Florence said as they returned to the ward. 'You could be as useful to me there as here, you know, Miss Somerlee. A murmur – or bellow one daresay – in Lord Raglan's ear… we could use a few more bandages and blankets.'

'Yes, I've already been charged with one message for His Lordship.' Clemence eyed the person on whom she had bestowed part of her frillies.

'You saw the Charge of the Light Brigade?'

'Yes… from Saupon Hill.'

'It was a noble victory in the public imagination,' Miss Nightingale said. 'Brave men charging to their deaths and capturing the Russian guns in spite of the odds. Of course, being the British, we weep more for three hundred dead horses than two hundred dead men.'

'My intended, Captain Swynton, died in the charge. My brother too probably… Eleventh Hussars, both…' Clemence clasped her hands over her face, fighting tears. 'Ah, Miss Nightingale… we don't know what became of my brother, Cornet Aubrey Somerlee! The dead were all brought back in the days which followed, but Aubrey was not among them. Yet when

Prince Menshikov sent a list of his prisoners to Lord Raglan, Aubrey's name was not there either! One of the reasons Aunt Lizzy suggested I come to the hospital was that I might hear word from one of the wounded… one of the Russian wounded maybe.'

'Even so – you might still be better in Balaclava.' Florence Nightingale faced her. 'Here in Scutari you are four days away from any news.'

'No, really! Keep busy and keep the megrims away.' Clemence wiped her eyes.

Each night, Florence Nightingale would inspect the wards. She glided through rows and rows of beds, the beam from her lamp falling on each for a few heartbeats before she passed on. To the patients she looked, by this bleak light, as endearing as the workhouse matron. Few liked this harridan or her stroppy nurses – intruding where females had no business.

'Even being without a tart for five months,' one infantryman grumbled to his neighbour, 'I'd rather shaft me colonel's horse than 'er!'

As the days passed, though, resentment of Florence and her staff became toleration, and then grudging admiration. When the Chief Medical Officer paid the Scutari hospital a rare visit, he was astonished to be told:

'Hope to be back in the trench outside Sebastopol and mended soon, doctor. All new bandages now, changed regular like. And a drop o' brandy to wet a sore mouth. Best thing Parliament done us – sending the lady with the lamp.'

'Drunken harlots!' muttered Sir John Hall. 'What was Lord Aberdeen thinking of?'

The year's first frost had fallen that night. Clemence looked out on a dawn sky streaked with crimson scars, remembering that winter would soon be here. In only weeks the sea crossing could be treacherous. She would get no news from her aunt in Balaclava if the storms swept in and ice bound the harbour.

Somewhere out there in the cold wastes was her brother. Aubrey – the handsome charmer of the family – dead and unclaimed; or in some hospital like this on the enemy side where no-one spoke his language. She went to the ward with a sorry heart.

It was the day the boats brought in the first casualties from the battle of Mount Inkerman. They piled in: too many for the beds… the less grave left to groan on the floor.

'It was Sunday, miss. All the bells of Sebastopol was ringing.' Clemence listened to the prattle of a trooper from the Cambridgeshire's as she unwound the strap from his head. 'Russkies attacked in the mist at dawn… our siege lines outside the city. Up on the slopes of Inkerman in the pines and vineyards. There was buzzards and falcons circling all around!'

'Tell me later, private.' Beneath the bandage lay a crusty, four-day-old gash from a bayonet. It had exposed the cranium. 'Ahh… this needs *cleaning*… and dressing!'

'But we drove 'em back, miss.' A feverish hand pawed her upper arm. 'I was defending the sandbag battery. I'm telling you – there was dead all over the field when I come away. But they died brave, like, and we won the day. My mate Harry fell at Inkerman, bless him.'

'I'm sure it was a brave death.'

The soldier looked bemused.

'Oh, he ain't dead, miss. I mean, he *fell*. His bootlaces was undone. 'Ere! You sound like a lady, miss.'

'Well, I'm not sure about that,' Clemence said, 'but I know Lord Raglan if you want me to tell him where he can stick his bayonet.'

Clemence finished putting on the fresh dressing. She slipped an arm around his shoulder.

'Afraid you might have to wait for a bed. You're not as bad as some,' she said, and then moved on to the next in line.

She could see two of the Nightingale nurses nattering as they leaned against the central arch. One took a furtive swig from a gin bottle which she'd had concealed beneath her apron. Florence's staff were not well-bred ladies: she'd recruited women who were used to dirt and roughness. If Clemence enquired of them the meaning of some new word she'd heard from the men in the ward, they would cackle. 'Ain't you never seen a bull on the back of a cow, miss? Well, folks does it too. That's how we got 'ere. And that's what that word means. Trooper was paying you a compliment saying he'd like to do it to you.'

Eventually, she went to seek out the first ungrateful patient she'd treated on her first day and shook him awake.

'You might have to quit today, private. We're expecting boatloads of casualties from Inkerman. You're well enough, I believe.'

'What would you know, Miss La-di-da never had to scrub for your supper? Bugger-all, like toffee-nosed officers.'

Clemence began to tug at his blanket.

'You're fortunate you don't get a flogging, private.'

'Only ever had one in our battalion that I recall, miss. Chap got a flogging for sleeping with the regimental mascot. Our colonel says, says 'e, "Let that be a lesson to you, my man. No-one but me sleeps with Flossy!"'

Clemence crossed to a bed opposite where a man lay groaning, bending close to hear his words.

'Ada? Is that you?' Troubled grey eyes sought out hers. 'Ada? Thought you was safe back in England, waiting for me.'

By now, Clemence had grown to know that rattling sound in the throat which presaged the end. She laid a hand on the man's brow.

'Yes, my love, it is your Ada. I heard of your injury, my dear one, and hurried here to be with you.'

'You look different, Ada.'

'I've fashioned my hair a new way. But it's your Ada, my love, here to look after you.'

'Gor blimey...!' His head rolled to one side and he fell silent.

Her old enemy pushed himself upright. But for his bandaged thorax, he was able-bodied and lively.

'Ere! Miss Somerlee! Summink you should know, darling. Ada was his pet dog!' he guffawed.

Clemence began to strip the covers from the new dead.

'Miss Somerlee – next time you're sniffing Lord Palmerston's arse, bite him in the balls, eh, until he agrees to send us some decent ammo. Better still...' The doggy diatribe continued.

Clemence hastened to dispose of the blankets before the orderlies could dump a further victim in the same berth.

Outside, she watched the boats bringing in yet more from Inkerman. She had met the sailors often enough now for one of the captains to know her.

'Sorry, miss, I don't bring news of your brother.'

So! Another restless night was to come. Could she bear the sound of those waves all through the hours of darkness...?

She bustled on, helping the orderlies lay out the stretchers on the quay.

'I'm not dead, Clemmie... I told you I'd come home. And I will... one day...'

The girl whipped around to look behind her.

No-one was near. The wind was making a huffing, whistling noise. Sailors in the boat. Orderlies the far end of the jetty. Soldiers... the only ones within speaking distance were lying unconscious on the planks.

Yet she'd heard a voice... somewhere close...

Aunt Cassandra used to claim she'd heard voices like that... And she'd been shut away in a lunatic asylum because of it, poor old dear...

Clemence hurried back to the hospital. Along the corridor the girl ran, knocking a pile of bed pans clattering... up the stairs, into the ward.

She rested a hand on the nearest bedpost. Was that a giggle she heard coming from three Nightingale nurses standing nearby? Did they all snicker at her... patients too? A ballroom miss playing at nursing? A drawing-room poppet wanting a bit of rough? She could almost hear their thoughts...

And, well! Her brother's one of the politicians who started all this... see how she likes it, now she's lost two loved ones of her own... has to watch the common soldiers retch and heave... see the wounds her own people have struck...

EIGHT

She caught sight of the yacht as it was just mooring. A bed pan clattered to the ground as it dropped from her fingers. Down the stairs from the ward she dashed, and out to the end of the jetty. Yes, it was the *Oriflamme*.

Lord Brandon Fanshawe stepped ashore.

He gave a start of surprise to see her, and then smiled a greeting. 'You for certain look like a nurse!'

'Yes. Hard to credit, isn't it, that just two years ago I was in the palace throne room in my presentation gemstones and ostrich feathers!' She forced a smile. 'Florence Nightingale doesn't really approve of charming young gels. I suspect she suffered me to stay because Richard is close to Lord Derby – who might soon be in Downing Street in place of Aberdeen the way this war is being run.' Clemence turned towards the path. 'Come see the place, Brandon! I'll introduce you to Miss Nightingale.'

Her eyes went up to the hospital building on the headland ahead, overlooking the harbour.

What about that bed pan she had just discarded in so unprofessional a way? How patient would Miss Nightingale continue to be? Well, Clemence had a visitor from Balaclava. Nightingale knew how anxious the girl was for news. She'd understand.

And yet… whose had that spectral voice been which Clemence had heard when she'd met the Balaclava boat yesterday…? Where had the words she'd heard come from? Was she losing her mind?

She quickened her pace, as if it was pursuing her from the sea, whatever it was. Brandon was forced to hurry too, calling out to her not to leave him behind.

Clemence halted beneath the awning which flapped over the door, while he caught her up. He was asking if she was all right.

'Yes.. yes…' She glanced his way. He had removed his hat. Hair blowing to and fro over his brow with each shift in the wind direction. A dimple in his cheek when he smiled.

'Do you bring me news?' she asked. *Unlikely. He would have said at once.*

'Of Aubrey?' Brandon turned his gaze seaward. 'I'm afraid not.' He was smiling, though, when he looked back. 'But your aunt has been in contact with the Russians. She's hoping to speak with someone on Prince Menshikov's staff. I'm sure we'll hear something soon. He wasn't among the dead, like old James… I really came to see how you are, Clemmie.'

Could none of them credit her with being capable of looking after herself?

'There are more pressing things to worry about than whether I'm suitably chaperoned, Lord Brandon Fanshawe!'

'Gosh! Sorry…'

Clemence turned indoors. She remembered how she'd almost fainted the first time she had stepped through this portal. She giggled to herself as she saw the effect on Brandon when he followed her in. He stumbled against the doorframe and clapped a hand to his mouth and nose.

'Yes… that's Private Williams you can smell I believe, Fanny. Or maybe Private Godwinson. Survived Inkerman, and the boat journey here both of them, but not the cholera. Goodness, they do go off quickly, don't they?'

'My brother must be a prisoner, mustn't he?' she said. 'If Aubrey wasn't among the dead or the survivors, that's the only possibility, isn't it?'

'Yes, it is. Maybe he was overlooked when the first list of prisoners was drawn up. Mistakes are easily made in war... as we've seen proved!'

Volunteer Nurse Somerlee had come off duty at sunset. She was walking the sandy track along the headland, Lord Fanshawe by her side. The surf could be heard down in the channel of the Dardanelles.

Clemence gazed across the straight towards Constantinople. A brigantine, its sails billowing back and forth, was dipping and rolling its way to port.

How long had she known Brandon Fanshawe? Forever, it seemed. One of Dickon's friends who he'd wanted her to marry. She'd rebelled... *who do you think you are, Dickon Somerlee, ordering me, Clemence the great, about?* So, she'd taken James what-was-his-name instead... *fiddlesticks to you, Dickon...* only to discover that it was the one she'd turned down who she really wanted to walk with.

And now James was never coming back. Was it safe to own, then, that she had not loved him as a sweetheart should? Mistaken for love her pride in the pretty attentions he'd paid her? If so... she and her vanity had done James a wrong. Given encouragement where there should have been none.

You are a traitor, Clemmie!

She swung around at sound of that voice again.

'Clemence? What's wrong?' Brandon stopped and faced her, a startled look in his eyes.

'I... I...' Clemence twisted one way then the other. 'I thought I heard someone calling.'

'I don't think so! There is no-one near.'

She looked from Brandon to the hospital buildings further

down the brow. Nurses and orderlies were going about their business in its precincts. At the jetty in the tiny hamlet, a fishing vessel was mooring. There came words shouted in Turkish as the sailors and stevedores disgorged the cargo.

'No, it was real... I heard it, I know I heard it. Voices, I hear voices!'

Silence of a kind fell. The activity of the hospital, of course, went on uncaringly. A nurse giving someone orders in upper-class tones. Babble of the fishermen down on the quay, and hiss of the waves dragging on the pebbly shore. Cawing of a seabird on his way home to nest for the night. Gate rattling in the wind. But it seemed an unending moment before Brandon stepped closer and laid a hand upon her arm.

'Clemence. What do you mean when you say you hear voices?'

'Nothing! I didn't mean anything. Please forget I said anything, Brandon.'

'Clemence...' Brandon looked into her eyes for a long moment. 'How long have you been toiling on the wards? How many hours? How much rest do you take?'

'I work as long as I'm needed! The casualties never stop coming in, you know,' she said with a strained smile. 'One man dies, two more come in for the same bed! Wounded men, blind men, men without hands, men whose feet have rotted in the dampness of the trenches, men burning with fever... they never stop, never stop, never stop...'

'Clemence!' Brandon's light touch became a grip. He opened and closed his lips several times before he spoke. 'I think it's time you left for England. Me too! Came here as a jolly young blood to enjoy the fun, didn't I? Well, I've grown up now, and want to go home!'

'Aubrey! I cannot leave without my brother... he's out there somewhere... all alone.'

'Let his regiment search for him – it's their duty. And Richard's on his way, you know. He set off when I telegraphed to say Aubrey was missing. *You* cannot do anything.'

No! Men fight wars… women mop up the mess they leave.

Suddenly, Clemence laid her head upon Brandon's shoulder. Her cheek nestled against his. She wanted only to stay there in his arms. Put the past right, forget James, love Fanny. Let her share with him icy December on a foreign clifftop forever.

'Oh, Clemmie!' She felt his fingers stroking the back of her hair. 'I used to tease you, didn't I… Dickon's baby sister!'

The Baronet of Eardingstowe alighted on the Balaclava quayside.

Beyond the white walls and red roofs of the little waterside town he looked, up into the hills where could be heard the distant crack-crack-boom of artillery-fire. As he watched, shellfire lit up the purplish landscape.

'Where does one go to hire a horse?' he asked one of the crew from the ship which had brought him from Constantinople. 'I need to secure transport for myself and my fiancée.'

The fellow shrugged. Too busy unloading.

The dockside was teeming… men in lots of different kinds of uniform… seamen… an Orthodox priest… laden mules… two Turkish soldiers in fez and culottes… all bustling by and leaving the newcomer to fend for himself.

So Amathia might have to walk, might she? His eye tracked the uphill climb one would have to navigate to reach the plateau where the army was camped. He glanced towards the window of the ship's cabin. There his fiancée waited.

What had been in her mind he wondered – accompanying him to the Crimea? Clearly, she was no traveller. She'd been trainsick and had already complained of the noise of the gunfire. And they were only in Balaclava harbour.

In the oily waters which surged and sucked around the legs of the jetty an old rifle floated by. Bits of wood. A horseshoe was caught in the weed which trailed the rudder and keel of a small sailboat. And then... a face-down, deceased person wearing a scarlet-jacketed uniform came floating by.

What way was this to wage war? And Aubrey... infuriating, spendthrift, womanising spoiled pet of both their parents... but Richard's beloved flesh-and-blood for all that. What the dickens had become of him?

Amathia was working at her embroidery in her cabin as she awaited Richard's return. How much longer before they could disembark?

From the small, oval window she could see gaudily-coloured cottages climbing the gradient of the headland. On the brow stood a ruined fortalice; leaden mountains reared against the skyline. The waves glowed hellishly for a few heartbeats as up in the hills an explosion went off.

Aubrey Somerlee not coming back from Balaclava's bloody fields could turn out to be the only real success so far in this blighted campaign. It would mean that Uncle George's legacy would be coming her way instead.

'The *Oriflamme* moors somewhere around here,' Richard told her as he ducked his head under the cabin door. 'But doesn't appear to be in port today. That's as much as I could get out of the stevedores – ignorant crowd.'

Amathia made a noise of annoyance and called to her abigail.

'Vickery, you might as well cease unpacking for the moment and make yourself useful some other way! It doesn't look as if we are going anywhere just yet.'

Richard moved aside to let the maid pass.

'Do you regret, yet, accompanying me on this difficult trip, Lady Amathia?'

'Oh no, Sir Richard! A member of your family has gone missing – soon to be my family. Naturally I'm distressed for you.' As long as they didn't find Richard's sibling, of course. Anyway, she thought the sound of gunfire rather engaging. She fancied a glimpse of these ruffians shooting at each other – although the best had probably passed by now.

She took up her hoop and went on with her stitching.

'That is a very pretty sunflower you are embroidering, Lady Amathia,' Richard observed. 'Perhaps you will have finished it by the time we set sail for home again? I should like to frame and mount it.'

'In a room where it shan't be much on display I trust, Sir Richard? I fear I have very little accomplishment.'

'On the contrary, dear lady. You've only been stitching that same leaf since our stop in Belgrade. Clearly you are a meticulous needleworker.'

So lowly a feminine art, Amathia thought, must remind a male that a woman was his prisoner, sewing away at sacking in a Millbank cell. More fool he: Arachne caught men in her web while they supposed she was only stitching; Queen Matilda stole the Conqueror's crown while he thought her pretty head was bent over her tapestry; and Penelope won a kingdom picking away at her sewing silks.

'Your heart must be aching so, dear Sir Richard.' Amathia cast him a compassionate look. 'I would be heartbroken had my own dear brother Philoctetes gone missing!'

'Yes, I am troubled, Lady Amathia.'

'Are you and Aubrey close, Sir Richard?'

No, he admitted. A decade stood between the brothers, and their lives had flowed in separate courses. But he was fond of the fellow.

'And I'm deuced worried for him, if you'll pardon my language! If Aubrey wasn't killed, what in blazes could have become of him?'

'I'm sure my cousin Lord Fanshawe will have news… good or ill. Better unfavourable news, perhaps, than no news. At least then you… we… might begin to mourn.'

'Yes… yes… quite so, Lady Amathia. Well, Fanny cannot be far.'

'I have not yet had the pleasure of your brother's acquaintance, Sir Richard,' Amathia smiled, 'but anyone dear to you has a place in my heart. And if we should learn the worst, Aubrey shall have a fine marble memorial in St Laurey's! No expense shall we spare!'

'Thank you… dear heart!' His quick smile faded. He set a hand to his brow.

'Not another headache, Sir Richard?' Amathia made to rise and go to him in concern. 'These last few weeks have been such a trial for you! It really is too bad of my cousin not to have sent news more frequently. Perhaps I might fetch you your medicine?'

'So kind, Lady Amathia… I do feel a trifle indisposed again…'

Amathia set down the embroidery frame. She went to fetch the… *medicine…* from his dressing-room. A long, thoughtful look she took at the… *medicine…* in its pretty green bottle, and a long look also at him through the open door while his back was to her.

'Laudanum, Sir Richard?' She'd been surprised the first time she'd caught him taking a few doses of the stuff.

'Yes… it is only for the relief of pain, of course,' he'd assured her. She'd smiled and agreed that laudanum could do one so much good.

But it had set her thinking. Amathia recalled a friend of her father's: poor Sir Hugh was supposed to have succumbed to his gout. But she knew otherwise. A man who took laudanum or opium could not have enough of it… grew to *need* it… unable, finally, to function without it. Such had been Hugh's case. And, for sure, the more dependent was a man on this nectar, the less in control… Until one day over a cliff in his high he would dance.

Amathia would see that Richard got his laudanum with cream and cherries on it. Eventually, he'd be signing whatever banker's draft she presented under his bemused gaze.

She tripped back into the cabin where Richard had taken a seat, a hand propping his sore head. Ah, yes, she'd chosen the right man in Dickon Somerlee.

'Fretting over your poor brother is making you ill, dear Sir Richard.' She stood over him and soothed her soft hand over his brow. 'Here – take your *medicine*.'

Tired, grateful eyes rose to meet hers.

Clemence watched from the end of the quay until Fanny, waving from the stern of the *Oriflamme*, and then his vessel itself, had become just one more among the skittering sparkles of sunlight.

Was it as well Brandon was heading back to Balaclava? The look on his face when she'd mentioned the voices… oh, but how she would miss him until he came calling in his boat again.

He must fear she was going like her Aunt Cassandra. Imagine his infantilising kindness when they put Clemmie away. *Going to live with lots of nice ladies just like you…* Being locked away as a madwoman for the rest of her days? Well, right now, with her world in ruins, this she could face.

'Oh, Brandon, I loved Captain Swynton so, so much! My heart is quite broken!' she'd sobbed. She was upset enough about so many other things right now that hot, hot, authentic tears had come washing down. And Fanny had gathered her in his arms and gone 'there, there.'

He's not yours, treacherous minx. What would he think if he knew how you really feel about your captain's death?

Clemence clenched her fists. The nails cut into the flesh.

That night, on duty in the ward, she saw a man wakeful who had been comatose earlier. She fetched him water.

'Are you Miss Somerlee?' His eyes glittered as the beam from her lamp fell upon his face. 'I've been wanting to speak to you. Something to tell you…'

'Later, private, when the fever has broken.'

'No… listen!' He pawed the edge of his blanket with his one remaining hand. 'I'm in the Queen's Owns. In the charge I was. I've heard about your brother.'

'You know something of Aubrey?' She took hold of the dithering hand.

'His horse has been found, miss… Sparkle… wandering rider-less by the Causeway, he was. Cornet Somerlee's messmate identified him.'

Clemence leaned close.

'Go on… please… if you can…'

'There was a Tartar shepherd what watched the charge from the hillside. Saw a young hussar officer what was a prisoner of a group of Serbs, so he did. Leading him away, bound, they was when yer man saw them.'

'This might have been Aubrey! He could yet be alive!'

'Wouldn't help you, or him, miss. The Russkies is decent enough coves. But the Serbs…'

It was the first hope, though. That was all which mattered. When the boat came tomorrow, Clemence would send word to her aunt.

She gripped the bedstead as the voice spoke her name, booming and fading like cannon-fire, or the waves pounding the sea wall all night long.

'We came as soon as we received your telegram, Fanny,' said the Baronet of Eardingstowe as he strode below deck on the

Oriflamme. Amathia followed close behind. Lord Fanshawe was waiting there in the cabin.

'And we've heard nothing further since that first communication,' Amathia added. 'Really, Brandon! We've had to visit the harbourmaster's office just to find out where your boat was moored! You might have spared Sir Richard's worries. We have been beside ourselves.'

'I had nothing further to report, Amathia,' Lord Fanshawe protested. 'What I told you then is almost as much as I know now! Aubrey did not return from the cavalry charge, and his body has not been found.'

Amathia moved about the floor at a more sedate pace than her fiancé was doing. She ran her fingers through the frilled rim of the antimacassars on the backs of the two window-side easy chairs. She peered at a watercolour depicting the harbour-front at Nice. Her eyes went to the small looking-glass in which she could see her cousin reflected.

Laughable that she'd once set her cap at Fanny Fanshawe. What had she seen in him, Amathia wondered? His land and prosperity, probably. And *that* didn't amount to as much as she'd then naively supposed, now she had a season behind her and had encountered the likes of Sir Quincy Dooley.

'How brown you have grown, Brandon!' she told him. 'Too much sunshine is not a boon, you know.'

She settled in a chair draped in a quilt embroidered with a maritime motif.

A pity Brandon was too cowardly to join a regiment. Wouldn't Amathia love to see him spouting gore as a sword ran through some vital organ? If the stupid Cossacks knew where to aim, of course – the wallet; strike him in the heart or head and nothing would happen because there was naught there.

But, no, on second thoughts – she'd not wish a battlefield martyrdom on Brandon; too quick, easy… and honourable.

Lord Fanshawe spoke to his servant, who was hovering in the doorway which led to the pantry.

'Fetch Sir Richard and Lady Amathia something to drink, would you please, Challoner? What'll you have, Dickon? The local Massandra wine's rather soothing to the nerves. Or might I suggest a glass of Samogon… very fiery vodka. I think you need it, old man.'

'Whatever…'

Amathia kept Brandon in view the whole while. Comely enough, wasn't he, if you liked simpleminded men? But he wasn't married or engaged yet, was he? Come to think of it, Amathia was not the only female whose interest Fanny had spurned. And he a most eligible bachelor for the last four or five seasons. Now why might that be?

'Tell me, though, Brandon.' Amathia inclined towards him. 'Did you actually see the Charge of the Light Brigade?'

Lord Fanshawe nodded.

'And Clemmie and Lizzy did too. We were watching from the hill. That valley is no more than a mile wide, you know! Six hundred men rode in the charge. Over two hundred died.'

'What a lucky fellow you are,' Amathia said. 'For hundreds of years they'll be telling the tale. And you were there, Brandon!'

'It was a mistake!' Fanshawe said. 'A terrible blunder that cost so many lives. And who was at fault? Heaven knows. Raglan blames Cardigan. Cardigan blames Lucan. And they all blame Nolan who can defend himself no longer. As for me, well, I've told Lucan that in my opinion he ought to do the decent – disappear, and never show his face again.'

He turned to Richard.

'I'm sorry for not sending further word, Dickon. I only got the first message off with difficulty. Do you know the telegraph line from London only goes as far as Belgrade? You must send written messages the rest of the…'

'Yes, yes, no need to labour the point!' Richard flopped into a chair and removed his hat.

'My congratulations to you both, by the way,' Brandon said. 'I saw the announcement of your engagement in *The Times*.'

'Thank you, Brandon,' said Amathia. 'My only regret is that my happiness comes along at a time of such great sadness! Clemmie's betrothed dead. Aubrey… Lord only knows.'

'I understand it was you who identified James Swynton, Fanny,' Richard said.

'Yes, when they brought the dead back from the valley. I wished to spare Clemence. Couldn't keep her away, though. She wept over him. Very touching. But Aubrey…' Brandon sighed. 'He was definitely not among the dead. I checked twice. And if he was captured, we ought to have had word from the other side by now.'

'Yes, he'd be worth a ransom,' Richard said. 'Son of a wealthy family. Brother of a Member of Parliament.'

'Lysithea's even spoken to someone on Menshikov's staff. But… nothing. It's as if he's vanished.'

'And while we're grieving and worrying,' Richard said with a gloomy laugh, 'did you know Tennyson's published a poem? *"Forward the Light Brigade! 'Charge for the guns,' he said: Into the Valley of Death rode the Six Hundred."*'

'Yes, well, I'm afraid I've more bad news which will depress you even further,' said Brandon. 'Clemence is volunteering at Scutari, ghastly place. Lysithea even encouraged her.'

'Good Lord! And you didn't think to put a stop to it, Brandon?' said Amathia.

'Even I can't control her, and I'm her brother!' Richard told her.

'Well, I think you'd be wise to bring her away, Dickon,' Brandon went on. 'I saw her seven days ago. She is in dreadful anxiety over Aubrey and working long hours indeed.'

The servant arrived carrying decanter and drinking vessels. Lord Fanshawe waved the man away and took the tray himself. Setting it on the bureau, he poured, and handed Amathia a glass.

'Clemence has heard what might be the first possible news, though. She's sent us word by the boat which takes the wounded to and from Scutari.' Brandon took Richard his wine. He perched on the wing of the seat, an arm resting on the chair back. 'Sparkle's been found alive. And a shepherd watching from the hillside witnessed a group of Serbs leading away a captive hussar. The fellow was bound, apparently… but alive.'

'What? Then yes, this could well have been him!' said Richard, stirring.

'It's a rather vague report, Sir Richard,' Amathia said. 'You must not raise your hopes unduly. It would only lead to disappointment.'

'Yes, you are right. It's an insubstantial rumour. But – it's all we have!'

'And…' said Brandon, 'if the Serbs, the troublemakers of Europe do indeed have him – then God help him.'

NINE

Men who had recovered from their sicknesses and injuries were clambering aboard the Balaclava vessel as Clemence watched from the waterfront; and sailors were loading crates of bullets and rifles to go to the front… or feathers for Lord Raglan's pillow if she was to credit some of the soldiers' ribaldry.

'They're sayin' Sebastopol won't fall this side o' the new year,' the captain told her. 'Most o' these chaps'll not see their loved ones for Christmas, if again. You'd best settle in for a Crimean winter, miss. Why not return to the staff quarters – or better still, England?'

No… she was needed here – she was sure she was.

As the boat headed back out to sea, Clemence was thinking of what he had said of approaching winter. It was raining, and her cloak was blowing all over the place. Only four weeks ago, the sea-breezes had felt wonderful as the land baked under the southern sun.

From somewhere behind the hospital, a muezzin was calling the faithful to noon prayer. How sad was the wailing sound. Would she ever see her brother again?

'Miss...'

The faint voice came from one of the beds she was passing. Clemence went to the shivering man's side.

'Oh! Thank Gawd – you are real, miss! For a moment I thought I was back at Inkerman. Only cockroaches crawling over me, not Cossacks, that's a relief. But the sea. It's so loud! Like it's coming to fetch us away! Maybe one night, when we're all asleep...'

'No, the sea won't take you while I'm here!'

Clemence peeled back the blanket and peeped beneath the bandage. A bullet wound in the thigh. By now, she knew the gangrene which days without treatment wrought. The infection's green, shoot-like tendrils would smother him before dawn.

'I'll look for a surgeon, right away,' she smiled, squeezing his fumbling hand.

She scanned the ward. Not a surgeon in sight.

On her way to the medical store in the yard, Clemence's lamplight fell upon the heap of dead, tossed out like so much refuse.

It looked like a crumpled Hydra – heterogeneous heads, arms and legs sticking out all over the place. No precise Heracles had slain this beast, though: it seemed like the butchery of some incompetent on his first mission.

Clemence pressed her kerchief to her face.

One hand's fingers were trailing in the rivulet of urine and floating excrement which was trickling from the overflowing midden-pit. Another limb jutted out straight as a pikestaff in the rigor of recent death. Here a blue sleeve, there a scarlet one. A gilt button gleamed, gold lace and the plume of a shako. She recognised the uniforms of the Connaught Rangers here, the Coldstream Guards there. A Highlander's tartan sock. A whirlpool of feasting flies had gathered above, revelling in this cornucopia. At least someone was having a party.

We blame you… you! And all your kind, fancy lady. We did what you said – came out to this savage land to fight because you told us the Czar was coming to get us. You lied to us. And one day we're coming to get you. Just like Jenny Greenteeth! We'll get you, we will…

Here a shining blue eye in the mound… there a green or brown one… his last screaming agony crystallised in one man's face… seeming as if they were glaring right out at her.

Amathia sauntered the *Oriflamme's* decks in mounting boredom. When was Sir Richard going to land? She could hear the gunfire and see the plumes of smoke up there in the hills.

'Of course, I'm not happy about what Clemence is doing, Fanny!'

The uptight voice of her husband-to-be came from the on-deck lounge as she passed. Richard's genteel tones had just a smidgen of the West Country in them; 'happy' was almost, but not quite, 'harpy'. Amathia paused and listened to the quarrel going on.

'But at least my sister's safe enough over there with Florence Nightingale!' Richard went on. 'Although knowing Clemence, she'll be telling our future dinner-party guests what an infected boil looks like while they're eating their food! But I'm more concerned about Aubrey right now.'

'Dickon, I'm telling you, there is something wrong, very wrong, with Clemence!' Brandon answered him. 'You need to get her out, and home at once!'

'Why did you not stop her going to Scutari in the first place if you were so damned worried?'

'I have no authority. I'm not her brother! Or her husband! Just a very concerned family friend.'

'I can't just leave Lizzy on her own here to search for Aubrey! Because frankly, Fanny, I cannot see that you have done much.'

'Now, look here, Dickon Somerlee – '

Amathia stepped inside to join them. The pair at once fell silent.

'Forgive me, Sir Richard,' she said, 'I could not help but overhear.' She slipped a hand through his arm. 'Can I help I wonder? I am sure Brandon would not be so concerned for Clemence if there was not good reason. Oh, Florence Nightingale's quite the heroine back home,' Amathia scoffed. 'But I wonder if she's the angel they think? A social climber seeking glory, I suspect. Clemence could be quite corrupted! If she doesn't bring back some virulent disease, she'll bring troopers' language! Why don't you and Lizzy, sir, go to Scutari as Brandon suggests to fetch your sister back? And meanwhile, I could continue the enquiries after Cornet Somerlee.'

'And what makes you think you can…?' Lord Fanshawe swung to face her.

'Please, Brandon!' said Amathia. 'I'm not without connections here myself. Papa knows both Raglan and General Airey.'

'Amathia, you only arrived in the peninsula two days ago!'

Richard raised a hand to cut them both off.

'Lady Amathia could not,' Richard said to Brandon, 'be less successful than *you* have been, Fanny, in *your* efforts to find Aubrey.' Brandon turned away, frowning. 'It is such a kind thing you offer to do, Lady Amathia,' Richard said. 'But I cannot ask it of you.'

'Let me do this for you, dear Sir Richard. Your kinfolk are my kinfolk, remember.' She leaned close to his shoulder. 'Be assured I shall march into Sebastopol if I must to find your brother.'

'Will you be safe here in Balaclava, though?'

'As safe as any woman could be with a ring of battleships to protect her!' Amathia gave him a small, wry smile. 'And Fanny will be staying in Balaclava I assume, and can defend me from the Russian foe, can't you, Brandon?' Brandon did not look her way. She would laugh to herself later.

Richard's strained features relaxed into a weak smile. He raised her hand and kissed it.

'What a loving wife-to-be you are, Amathia.'

'I'll ask everywhere, Sir Richard, I promise.'

She'd see the enquiries after Aubrey were called off. Would tell Raglan and Airey and everyone else that she spoke with Sir Richard's authority. So – if by some miracle this lost Somerlee was alive somewhere, he would never be found. Richard and Lysithea would be on the other side of the Black Sea by then. And who would ever know? As for Fanny Fanshawe – oh, she'd been getting the better of him since she'd shopped him to his nanny for having a runny nose.

Sir John Hall crossed to the window of Miss Nightingale's private study. The latest casualty boat could be seen mooring.

'Oh Lord, not more from Inkerman! We just don't have the beds! Some will have to be sent straight back.' The Chief Medical Officer and Florence Nightingale disliked each other. Privately, he had referred to her as *petticoat imperieuse*. He expected an argument.

Before she could reply, however, something else caught his attention. A fair young woman in a grey cloak was heading along the jetty towards the vessel.

'Is that the Somerlee girl – the Baronet of Eardingstowe's sister?'

Florence Nightingale stepped across to join him.

'Indeed, Sir John. Comely creature, is she not? Not yet eighteen. She meets the boat each day because she's hoping the sailors might bring her news. I allowed her to stay as a volunteer because she seemed sensible. Perhaps I was mistaken! Not for the first time,' Florence added with a rueful smile.

'I hear they're rather an odd genus, the Somerlee family,' said Sir John. 'Did you hear about that Aunt Lysithea of hers? Ran off with Boney or something of the sort! I was in Spain as a junior medical officer at the time. Quite the scandal!'

'Perhaps Lysithea's come to try her luck with our sexagenarian Lord Raglan,' said Florence Nightingale.

'Huh! He wishes!' said the doctor.

He observed the girl out on the waterfront. She spoke with the captain, who shrugged, and shook his head. Clemence buried her face in her hands.

Back along the planks she scurried, the worthy seaman calling after her.

Sir John went to the door of Miss Nightingale's office. He watched, unseen, as the young woman ran in through the hospital porch.

Clemence slid her back down a wall until she was seated on the ground. Arms wrapped around her drawn-up knees, she sobbed. Pressed hands to her ears. *And appeared to be speaking to someone...* But she was alone in the passage, and could have no idea anyone was looking on...

The frowning Sir John retreated without a sound. He returned to Florence's side, and spoke in low tones.

'As I was saying, an odd family, the Somerlees. One doesn't like to heed gossip, of course. But tell me – have you ever heard a rumour? About an aunt of the present baronet who was committed to an asylum? Madness of the female hysteria kind has been known to run in families, you know...'

Clemence peeled back the shivering patient's blanket. At once she dropped it.

'This is not trench fever!' She turned to the orderly who was with her. 'Spots on the chest! Typhoid. Miss Nightingale has said to put any like him into the second ward. Isolate them.'

She stepped back as the man got on with it.

Clemence put a hand to her brow. She heard the orderly coming up behind her… asking if she was all right…

'Yes… I did not sleep much last night.'

She summoned a smile. It was as much an attempt to reassure herself as anyone else. She continued on her way along the ward.

That anecdote which might have been the first news of Aubrey. A captive hussar with a band of Serbs? But nothing had yet come of it. Nothing…

How many hours have I spent in the hospital? When did I last sleep? But busyness relieves the brooding… keeps me moving onward…

She stared at her own hand stretched out in front. The fingers were clawing at the closest bedstead as she gripped it to steady herself. Looked like a pale, trembling spider.

The patient in the bed scrambled to sit up.

'Bajeezus – lookin' fit to pass out, ye are, miss.' A grin overtook his concern. 'Rest on me lap, lass, and ye'll be right again, ye will.'

'No… I'm all right.' Clemence bustled away, through the rows of beds towards the corridor. Were the other nurses watching?

There's nothing wrong with me. I'm tired. I'm frightened for my brother. I feel guilty that I didn't love James.

A wicked wrong, you did, Clemence Somerlee. Who are your people to be fighting the Russians? The Czar's never done a hurt like yours.

Whose was the voice? That Irishman in the bed? No, she was out of his range now.

And you, Clemmie, you sent us into the valley of death… women like you, waving at the troops, baying for glory. It was a way of ridding yourself of me, wasn't it, so you could be free of a man you did not love.

'No, James, I swear that wasn't how it was…' She pressed her forehead against a doorframe.

Well, you took something precious from me, Clemence. My lifeblood. And I'm keeping something dear to you – your brother.

'No, don't punish Aubrey for what I did...'

You'll never know, Clemmie, whether he's alive or dead or what became of him. I'll see you don't. Did you say 'yes' to me because you thought I had money? Then change your mind when you found I did not?

'No, it wasn't like that...'

Private Bilsborrow and his colleague were approaching with the typhoid man on a stretcher. Placing it down, the orderly laid a hand upon her shoulder.

'Ere! You ain't chipper are you, miss?'

She felt a burning sensation in her fingers and palms as they scraped down the bare stones of the wall... and then chilliness as the flagstones struck her cheek.

Clemence tossed in the bed and muttered. At least they'd screened the unconscious girl off at one end of the ward, apart from the soldiers.

'Can you hear me, Clemmie? It is Aunt Lizzy. And Dickon has come also. He's just speaking with Sir John. But he'll be here soon.' No way of knowing if she heard or not. The girl went on mumbling.

Lysithea spoke to the sharp-faced woman who stood beside her.

'My nephew, the baronet, set off from England when we wired him about Cornet Somerlee going missing, Miss Nightingale. He has arrived to face a double tragedy.'

'My Lady!' Florence Nightingale said. 'We have hundreds of incapacitated servicemen from the Battle of Inkerman. Some are yet stacked on stretchers in the yard because we haven't enough beds! Your niece is taking a berth we could use! I had to give her laudanum just to stop her incessant sobbing!'

'Well, Scutari would undermine any constitution, Miss Nightingale,' Lysithea replied.

She glanced about her as she said it. She had been almost unable to credit some of the horrors Clemence had recounted in a letter she'd sent by the boat. If you trod on a cockroach, a legion of her kinfolk would swoop to avenge their auntie's murder.

'My Lady!' Florence sounded displeased. For all her vaunted courage, she was a vain person, jealous of any rival for her place in public glory. 'Before I came, there weren't even any bandages! I had to buy supplies myself!'

'Yes…yes, I'm sorry, Miss Nightingale.' Lysithea looked again at the unquiet dreamer in the bed. 'I'm just so troubled! About my missing nephew, and now my poorly niece!'

'This isn't fever, My Lady.' Miss Nightingale narrowed her eyes. 'Miss Somerlee's behaviour has become… disturbing. The child should be returned to England at once. Forgive me – but she is not of sound mind.'

'This is a breakdown brought on by overwork and worry,' Lysithea replied frostily. 'Yet you are right about one thing. Sir Richard and I will be taking Clemmie home. Heaven knows what else we all might catch otherwise in this dreadful hospital of yours! And now, if you'll excuse me, Miss Nightingale, I must rejoin the baronet.'

She paused by the screen, turning back.

'Goodbye, darling,' she said to Clemence. 'If you can hear me, we're taking you home to Eardingstowe…'

Lysithea stepped out into the ward, aware of the superintendent's glowering eye on her all the while.

In a bed close by, a patient with bandaged ribs grinned, and thrust a hand inside his coverlet.

'You like to see a soldier standing to attention on parade, Countess?'

Lysithea looked bored.

'Yes. But I doubt that's what you have beneath your blanket. More like a wilting snowdrop I imagine.'

She swept on her way through rows of appreciative cackles.

TEN

After looking in on his unconscious sister, Richard wandered outdoors. He stood by the harbour wall overlooking the water.

Discharged patients were crowding into the Balaclava boat. Richard listened to one group of three singing a ballad called 'Battle of the Alma', while a fourth played the Irish pipe.

One of the seamen who were loading up the craft was gazing up into the firmament.

'Might have to postpone this trip. Goin' to be a storm.'

'I suppose you know this through sailors' lore – some esoteric sign in the welkin, my man?'

'Ooh yes, sir. Big, black cloud on the horizon.'

'Quite. Well, I expect Sir John can accommodate us until tomorrow.'

His aunt came to stand beside Richard.

'What a restless sea,' Lysithea said. 'So massive and mighty! Can break you with one wave. Destroy a kingdom with a savage tide. Doesn't it make you fear the Almighty, Richard?'

'Indeed. Fearful, truly.' He'd not considered it until now. Richard treated his God like one of his tenants to be visited in his dwelling once a week, told he was doing a splendid job, and given a modicum extra when times were hard. 'I've never thought of God as cruel, Aunt Lizzy. Man, yes…'

'What could be crueller than the loss of a brother in a military catastrophe?'

'God did not order the Light Brigade into the valley.'

'Many would disagree, Dickon. Are we not fighting for England and St George?'

She was right, bless her.

'I thought we were supposed to be fighting for England's freedom.' Richard smiled bleakly. 'To get our country back from the Czar's clutches. Although I'm not aware he ever had it! Think I'm letting worry overwhelm me, Aunt. Worry over Aubrey. And over Clemmie. This isn't just a fever, is it?'

'No, it's some kind of breakdown.'

Richard nodded.

'That's what I mean! I can't help remembering those times when Clemence was confined to the house and couldn't go out. And then I remember Aunt Cassie too. Lysithea – tell me truly… do you think Clemence might be… *mad*?'

Lysithea slowly shook her head.

'But then,' she said, 'if you want me to be truthful… I don't think Cassandra is either. Fey, perhaps, would be a better label. But tell that to your mad doctors!' She slipped a hand through his arm. 'But anyway… let's talk of something cheerful, hey? Like your approaching very grand nuptials in Westminster! Quite the wedding of the season, I think. Royals, and half the peers of the realm to be present. What an occasion for the Somerlees!'

'Yes… and it's something else which pricks me with concern if I'm honest, Lizzy. Oh, not the expense and all. Consett's paying for most of that—'

'Well, if second thoughts you're having…'

'I didn't say that, Aunt Lizzy!' Richard laughed without mirth. 'Call the marriage off, eh? Be sued for breach of promise, shamed as a bounder for the rest of my days, and Consett condemn my career to the waves?'

'Well, I'm your godmother, Richard, as well as your aunt. May I give you my advice?' The countess moved to face him. She cupped both hands around his face. 'You're standing at the crossroads of your life! And I've never believed she was the right wife for you.'

'Oh, yes, I know! When we were fighting alongside Drake, the Consetts were paddling our oars!'

'It's not that! I'm not convinced you love Amathia, or she you.'

'Love? Oh, fiddlesticks, Auntie! I'm after glory and power, that's all. The ear of a Peer! And I imagine she only wants to marry me for my ancient lineage or some such. I'd be very surprised if Amathia turned out to be the kind of wife who bathes my sore bunions of an evening. Nor can I see her weeping over my bloody corpse as Clemmie did her James. Practical people don't marry for love, Lizzy.'

'I think she'll hurt you, Nephew!'

Richard shuffled his feet at that, feeling uncomfortable. He turned his eyes towards the shore. Waves were starting to crash against the sea wall, spewing up seven-foot high showers of spray.

He thought back to his interview with the Duke of Ardenne at Kingsmede when he'd asked for permission to address Lady Amathia. Richard had feared Consett might tell him a piffling baronet would not do for a duke's child. But, no – Ardenne's face had brightened. In fact, he'd shaken Richard's whole body with his handclasp.

'Take her, Somerlee, with my blessing! Anything I can do to help with the arrangements, dear chap, you've only to ask!'

Hmm… the duke had stopped short of offering to throw in his gilded Worcester dinner-service as an additional incentive.

Well… just as long as Richard got what he was really seeking from the Consett connection… Meanwhile, though, Lysithea had not finished.

'I don't believe Amathia loves you, Richard. I don't think she even respects you! Thinks you're beneath her… daughter of a Peer of the Realm, and you a mere baronet.'

'Aunt Lizzy, Amathia and I understand each other!'

'Please be careful, Dickon. I don't want to see you hurt. I don't want to see Eardingstowe hurt – I'm a Somerlee born and bred too.'

Richard put an arm around Lysithea's shoulder and walked with her a little way.

'Come along, Auntie dear. This storm looks as if it's going to be bad. Seems we'll have to stay in Scutari, and do without our silk coverlets, for one night further at least.'

Both clutched their hats as they returned along the harbour-front towards the hospital.

Amathia witnessed the storm from the other side of the Black Sea. Her room was in the eaves of the farmhouse where she was staying, high on the headland. The distant golden domes and reddish roofs of Sebastopol were darkling under a bruising-purple sky.

By late afternoon, the wind was rattling the window glass. Rain even trespassed down the chimney flues and made the hearth flames hiss.

A typhoon which uprooted trees. She watched the dark shape of a cypress somersaulting across the harbour-front. From the branches of a thorn which grew below her window a nest was ripped away; before Amathia's eyes, it was shredded into a thousand twigs which went scattering far and wide.

Over by the allied encampment, she discerned a train of three wagons with billowing tarpaulins; one almost got tugged off the track.

Could she make out the siege towers too in the dusk? Yes... sinister Gargantuas standing out blackly against the evening mountains, between the allied lines and the beleaguered city.

She knew the names of some: the closest Russian-held one – that was the Malakoff. Semi-circular, turret-like construction with ordnance on its platform. When its guns fired, the whole structure from platform to base lit up, and you could feel the vibration from the spot where she now looked on. It stood silent, now, as night fell.

The wagons which she could make out, though, were heading for the half-raised Lancaster battery which the British were building to attack another Russian post, known as the Great Redan.

Earlier that day, she'd had an audience with the Earl of Cardigan, the Somerlee boy's regimental commander. Word would get around the camp, of course. The sad-eyed beauty searching for her kinsman. How fetching. Richard, she hoped, would get to hear.

'I very much fear that Sir Richard is resigned to his brother's loss,' Amathia had said. She had dabbed an eye with a lace handkerchief. 'We don't believe anything will be gained, My Lord Earl, by your continued enquiries.'

'Lady Amathia, the Eleventh Hussars will not abandon one of their own...'

'Yes, we know you have been diligent, Lord Cardigan, and the Somerlee family is grateful. But Sir Richard fears that it is time to face up to the worst. Cornet Somerlee is clearly lying dead and unidentified in some lonely place, and, sadly, must probably remain so.'

'Not necessarily!' Cardigan protested. 'He could be a prisoner, but unconscious and unknown to his captors due to some injury. Only today we had word of a band of Serbian mercenaries in the area who might well be those who were seen with the captive

British officer! Tomorrow morning, I was intending to send one of my most trusted staff on a quest to learn more...'

'Lord Cardigan! The family wish to begin to mourn! Those were Sir Richard's words to me before he left for Scutari. And they cannot begin the grieving process if you persist in raising, and then dashing, their hopes!'

'Ah! Yes... I take the point, Lady Amathia...'

'These are Sir Richard's express wishes, Lord Cardigan.'

'Well... I suppose if that is the case...'

'Lord Brandon Fanshawe,' Amathia continued, 'does not share Sir Richard's feelings in this matter...' More dabbing at the gushing waterworks – nice touch. One thing Cardigan could never, ever resist was a womanly face. 'Might I suggest, therefore, My Lord, that you call off the search discreetly, without alerting Lord Fanshawe... ?'

So, wherever you are, Aubrey Somerlee, you will stay.

And anyway – is Aubrey's lot now so very dire? Poor, sweet hussar. He is one of the Six Hundred who rode into the Valley of Death, who will be lauded in Valhalla for all time, immortalised like constellations of the ancient heroes. Of this boy-soldiers dream; would have yearned for when he played at battles in the gardens.

As she watched, a small sailboat smashed against the sea wall, sundering wreckage to the four winds. Rollers swelled like mountain crests and crashed upon the shore as if the whole Crystal Palace had tumbled in a million shards of glass.

Amathia lay down her head that night just as the chimneystack took off on an adventure of its own.

In the morning – among the upturned boats they would find amputated limbs which had been dumped in the harbour for want of better disposal.

In the trenches and flimsy awnings outside Sebastopol, men would freeze to death that winter because all the new tents being brought in had sunk along with the supply ships, and cavalry mounts would eat each others' tails for their hay had gone to the deep.

By daylight, Amathia beheld the devastation.

The war ploughed on for eight months more.

A Mr Fenton arrived in the Crimea with his contraption and took what would be the first ever photographs from a war zone. From home also donated by a concerned public came knitted Balaclava hoods and Fortnum hampers, which were often the only rations the soldiery got; *The Times* dug in for a wearisome trench campaign against incompetence and bureaucracy.

Prince Menshikov mounted a surprise winter assault on the coastal fortress of Eupatoria. But Omar Pasha and the Turks held fast and righted their disgrace at Balaclava. This time it was the Russians who went scuttling in bloody retreat.

Far away in St Petersburg, Czar Nicholas heard of the rout, clutched his broken heart, and fell dead.

In June, the British attacked the Great Redan. Wave upon wave of infantry charged and tried to scale the V-shaped slopes of the humungous tower.

From the platform, the defenders poured molten lead… men were swept screaming, like so many ants as a kettle of bubbling water was emptied onto them. Thousands of their blackened and swollen cadavers lay bursting and popping on the plain beneath a pulsating sun. On the summit of the Redan waved Our Lady of Kazan's banner.

This failure to capture the Russian stronghold was Raglan's final act. The Field Marshal was said to have been carried off by dysentery, but – who knows? Maybe the *The Times's* merciless onslaught did do for the old fellow in the end.

But while the British were lamenting their defeat – the French had seized the Malakoff. And were soon pouring into the city.

Within days, Sebastopol was a holocaust. Churches, houses, hospitals – all were alight. In the garrison, a young Russian lieutenant named Leo Tolstoy faced the falling firebombs of the enemy attack. He would one day recall all this in his great prose.

From afar, the township looked like a mushroom of smoke – popping and banging as armouries caught fire and exploded. The Russian fleet, too, was blown up; its ghostly masts would be seen rising from the waters for a hundred years.

The victors took many prizes – the greatest, perhaps, the bell from the Orthodox cathedral. It would cross a continent to find a new home in Windsor Castle, where it hangs still, and tolls for the passing of a monarch.

1857

Two years later

ELEVEN

Lord Aberdeen's Government had fallen in the two years since Russia's surrender; Viscount Palmerston was now in power. Meanwhile, the power-looms of Carswell's cotton mill went on weaving, and its mules spun the Somerlees diurnally richer. The steam engine chug-chug-gurgled, and the chimney belched while India mutinied.

The baronet looked up as his butler announced his solicitor.

'Flitcroft, Mr Boscawen and I would like a brandy,' Richard said from behind his study desk. 'How is Mrs Boscawen?' he asked his visitor and listened politely to the reply until the butler had left the room. 'I've just been reading about that gallant Dr Livingstone,' Richard said, tapping the newspaper which lay open before him. 'Stunning waterfall he's discovered in darkest Africa. Stirred me, Mr Boscawen! I've a fancy for some intrepid exploration myself. Thought I might mount an expedition to find my constituency.'

Richard folded the newspaper, took up a letter and glanced through it.

'Anything you wish to bring to my attention in your correspondence, sir?' asked Mr Boscawen.

'Well, I was wondering what to do about our Irish estate,' the baronet said with an irked tut. 'More bother than it's worth, you know. Yet another letter here from the agent about troublesome tenants.'

'I don't suppose you've actually been there, have you, sir?'

'Of course not.' Richard glanced up at the other man. 'Not even sure where Kilara is exactly. Limerick, I believe. But it's trouble – like that whole windswept isle! Good Lord, Boscawen, if they aren't starving, they're making a nuisance of themselves following that O'Donnell rebel! "Just evict 'em, man!" I tell the agent. God! I'd like to be rid of this damned millstone around my neck. Not worth my worry! I'm not convinced the income I get from the rents makes it worthwhile.'

'Would you like me to see about selling it, sir?'

'Well… maybe someday, if it starts running at a loss.'

'We'd get a better price selling the estate while it's at least profitable!'

'Yes, that's true…' Richard ran a hand through his hair. 'Ah, but my father put a lot of work into the devilish place. It feels a bit traitorous to abandon it. For the moment it's bringing in a profit – just. So, let's leave it for now.'

Richard turned to a new problem. He lifted another sheaf from the bundle of correspondence on his desk.

'Sad – this business with Uncle George. Shot to death by the rebel sepoys in the massacre on the bank of the Ganges! What a way to go!'

'Daresay he would have wanted to die in India, Sir Richard. He'd been an army man all his life. Loved India. Pity it didn't love him.'

'George never married as you know, but he had a mistress. She was with him in Cawnpore throughout the siege. She got thrown down the well along with the rest of the captured women and children.'

'Aye, very sad,' said Mr Boscawen.

'For Uncle George, I daresay. Not for India. I believe this mutiny affair has finally convinced the P.M. that the East India Company cannot run the place. Going to make India a Crown Protectorate, I believe. In everyone's better interests if they do.

'Well, anyway… this missive I have here is from the old chap's solicitor!' Richard peered short-sightedly at the letter to check the details. 'George never changed his will after Aubrey vanished. Always held out hope his favourite nephew would come home one day. I didn't realise George's estate was worth quite so much, though. Ten thousand pounds George was sitting his comfortable backside on out in the swamps and monsoons. But should Aubrey predecease him and leave no heirs, well, the will clearly makes me the principal beneficiary instead.'

The solicitor read it through while savouring his fine brandy. Richard relaxed back in his chair, hands clasped over his stomach.

'I assume you have no news or you'd have pre-empted me with it.'

Mr Boscawen shook his head.

'It seems your brother has indeed disappeared without trace. All prisoners the Russians took at Balaclava have been accounted for and returned. No trace of Aubrey Somerlee. There was the story which Miss Clemence heard. So, I've followed this lead too – contacted the Turkish Embassy since our friends the Serbs are reluctant subjects of that august nation. No word there either.'

Richard drained his glass. He looked at the man sitting opposite.

'Might we reasonably infer that Aubrey is not coming back?' he said in a quiet voice.

'I'll not stop enquiring, of course.' Boscawen sat up straight. 'But,' he said in sombre tones, 'I'm becoming less hopeful as the months… years… pass. Three years now, is it not? The legacy which George Somerlee has left will, in the meantime, go to

Aubrey. However, it will come to you when your brother is declared legally dead. But that will take some years yet.'

Richard rose. He went to the window overlooking the terrace and parterres.

Raindrops glistened on the rims of the marble flower-urns. Branches swayed, and grass rippled in a strong breeze. Three peahens and a cock were picking their way over the wet lawn. Beds of flowering convolvulus, coralberry and dendromecon led down to the shore of Jenny Greenteeth's lair.

Richard's gaze moved to St Laurey's and the great tree. Heaven knew how old the yew was. Older than both chapel and house. At the May Day Festival that year, more than twenty villagers and estate-folk had joined hands to dance around its twisted girth. It shook sorry arms in the gale of Somerlee disasters; its dark green needles and red berries shone in Somerlee glory. He could only just picture the juvenile Aubrey climbing those formidable limbs. His brother's face and form were fading from Richard's memory.

None of what Boscawen was telling him made Richard easy. The law was such a tricky old thing. But then, so was Boscawen. A dangerous man, really. He was privy to much that Richard would prefer to keep quiet. He gave the notary a broad smile.

'Would you and Mrs Boscawen care to come for dinner with Lady Amathia and me on Wednesday?'

Clemence breathed in the mossy scent of the trees as she moved among them and listened to the breeze soughing through the lofty leaves. They were all old friends: copper beech, grey alder, silver lime, sorrel with its starry white blossoms, violet willow, and the dark blaze of the flame tree. Sunlight winked in the overhead net of branches. Calls of woodcocks and doves roamed the glade. The ferns still dripped after the rain.

The waters of a half-moon-shaped pond gleamed ahead, half-hidden from Clemence's view behind a palisade of tall sedge. An ornamental walkway known as the Tea Bridge crossed the small pool. Pink and orange petals from the waterside shrubbery fluttered to the surface. Two little grebes glided by, sundering into ripples the reflection of the miniature pagoda on the far shore.

The Paradise Garden this spot in the Eardingstowe grounds was known. In buzzing summertime. Or in owl-haunted snowdrifts. Never changing, only revolving with the wandering stars.

Yet something had gone from Eardingstowe. Innocence? Goodness?

The young woman halted beside the yellow wood tree. It had always been a favourite. She loved the perfume of the gold-dotted, white flowers, and held a bough to her nose.

The war was over now. Or so she believed. Sometimes in her thoughts it was hard to disentangle happening from nightmare.

Would she one day tell her grandchildren she'd met the celebrated Florence Nightingale, and looked on while the Light Brigade charged to its death? Maybe not... because the memories were already too clouded. Her illness... a rolling sea-vessel on the journey home... it was all just a blur of garish mises-en-scènes... with just an occasional nice image, like the sunshine lighting Fanny's hair as it fluffed in the upland breeze.

She watched one of the water birds waddling ashore and start preening. The surface splashed as a frog jumped from the depths onto the bank.

Somewhere in her foggy past was that September day when the news came to Somerset that Sebastopol had fallen. Fireworks had lit the countryside for miles around. St Laurey's tower had shone golden, then violet. A victory beacon had licked the black sky on the heights of Will's Neck. Oh, yes – and Richard and the Consett woman had got married. A propitious time for one happy couple.

But the wedding ball at Eardingstowe...? Almost two years ago. A warm, starry night... the essence of mown grass blowing in through the French windows. An orchestra playing in the gallery overlooking the great hall, and the guests dancing. Bare-shouldered ladies wearing dizzy-coloured crinolines? Gentlemen in evening dress and regimental uniform? Convivial chatter all around, all around, all around.

And yet... someone had been *sobbing*. And voices... yes, she recalled those voices screaming, wailing... in her head... four corners of the hall, rafters, everywhere... The demon in the chamber crying to be let out?

Goodness, no, it must have been *her*, Clemence. Must have been... she called to mind the soreness in her throat and chest. An ache you only get from abandoned weeping.

Aubrey, Aubrey, how can they be so cruel – dancing when my brother has never come home...? Didn't she see Aubrey – standing on the bank of the mere in the dark? A blood-smeared hussar, looking sad... forever shut out... unable to come and join the party...

Eyes...eyes... all around the great hall... staring at her? Alarmed faces. Turned up as she huddled on the grand stairwell and gripped the banister....

And then... Richard sweeping through aghast onlookers, grasping her by the arm, steering her upstairs... could not remember any more.

Clemence began to make her way home. She reached the ha-ha. The narrow ditch separated the outer grounds from the parterres, lawns and house, and was crossed by a miniature wooden bridge. A wet August it had been; twigs and sedge were dashing along a channel full of rainwater. Around the posts grew white-bloomed clematis, and silver and gold oat grass which, with the sunlit raindrops caught up in it, looked like a spread fan adorned with a cascade of miniature diamonds.

She mounted the walkway. Before her spread the gardens; the small, round, white-stoned Temple of Victory stood on the house side of the ditch; sunlight struck the pinnacles of its columns and cupola looking, too, like tiny gemstones.

Wasn't there supposed to be madness in the family? It was one of the Somerlee legends she had grown up with. And it scared her… when she thought of what had happened the night of the wedding ball… the bits she could get her head around, that was. Such a scene she must have been making there on the stairwell that she'd brought the whole dance to a standstill. And made Richard and Amathia very embarrassed indeed. There might have been even worse which she couldn't remember. Had she flashed her drawers to the assembly as her brother dragged her away?

Her grandfather's brother had gone away with the fairies… nearly threw himself over the Cheddar Gorge once… had to be confined for life like poor Aunt Cassie, so some aged gardener had once told Clemence in her youth. But the old rogue had been trying to scare her, surely?

The Somerlees could not really be cursed, could they? Brandon Fanshawe had been Dickon's friend for years. They'd been at Brasenose together. Fanny couldn't think the Somerlees were tainted or he wouldn't be Dickon's bosom bow, would he?

I love Brandon. I know that now.

Well, she was free for him. James Swynton's death was the blood-soaked tragedy which could bring them together.

Clemence wandered among the flowerbeds. Pink, white and red roses, and some which seemed a combination of all three shades – the colour of sugar, Clemence thought. Lavender, marigold, apple blossom, buttery delphiniums and irises the colour of blue flames – all nodding their heads in the perfumed air. Hovering bees were everywhere. Roving lovers who would leave the flowers weeping in the autumn rain but be back to break hearts anew when June came again.

A sun-shadow slunk over the house as Clemence approached the path which led to the garden door. There was a Lady Somerlee ruling here nowadays, and Eardingstowe was hers; Lady *Amathia* Somerlee as she insisted on styling herself, because she had been of higher rank than her husband before her marriage.

She doesn't want me under her roof though, that's plain. And who could blame Amathia in her delicate condition? Cannot have the gestating Baronet of Eardingstowe exposed to a nutcase raving all over the place.

'The Consetts are broke, sweetheart,' Lysithea had once told Clemence. 'The duke's been living on borrowed money for years. Oh, they've kept it quiet. But I have ways of finding these things out.'

So, now Dickon was shackled to grasping, feckless in-laws. Lord Philo Dunkerley, the duke-in-waiting, would willingly spend the Exchequer on a shooting party or inamorata's fine tastes. He and Amathia between them could drag Richard to the depths of the mere sooner than Jenny Greenteeth ever could.

'Oh, Miss Somerlee! *Quel* darling gown! You must give me the address of your mantuamaker.'

Clemence smiled at the gushing stranger who had stepped in front of her.

'Why thank you, my dear!' She tapped the woman's arm with her fan. 'And you are looking even more radiant than when I last saw you at the opera! Was it seven months ago? Goodness!' Which was as good a guess as any. 'And so delightful to see you here.'

'What? Miss the wedding of the year, Miss Somerlee? Who would dare?' the woman enthused.

'You must come to tea at Somerlee House sometime...' Clemence managed over her shoulder as she edged past.

She had been to Buckingham Palace before – not least for her presentation. But had there ever been *crowds* and *crowds* like these here tonight to celebrate Princess Vicky's happy occasion? How did they share all the air for heaven's sake?

Descending the grand staircase meanwhile were Lord and Lady Palmerston. Clemence nodded to the glamorous Prime Minister and his vivacious Lady Emily as they drew level. Clemence couldn't hear what they were saying. One almighty gallimaufry of yattering and blaring orchestra music was going on.

A blue porcelain vase which stood in a niche was winking critical eyelets. Ivory statues, humungous portraits of dead monarchs... far-seeing eyes following, following, following your every step...

A male figure, his back to her, was standing at the head of the stairs. Gold-braided, cornflower-blue coatee. And red trousers with yellow stripe... The hussar's hair gleamed, glossy and dark brown. A pretty girl gazed up into his face. He was making her laugh.

Aubrey... she whispered her lost brother's name.

The hussar turned around. A stranger was looking at her in surprise.

Clemence stumbled against the balustrade.

'For pity's sake, Lysithea, get her to a seat before she makes a fool of us!' came Amathia's voice from behind her.

The ladies' crinolines whirling around the South Drawing-Room all blurred into a mélange of colours. Like watching a fairground dobby going around and around when you were a bit queasy from eating too much ice-cream, Clemence thought. Heat from hundreds of sweating bodies, and thousands of candles in chandeliers and candelabra was making a steamy swamp of the great chamber.

Clemence let her aunt and sister-in-law lead her to one of the side chairs, where matrons and wallflowers sat out the measures they had no partners for.

Some of the people gathered nearby were cooing a little ditty.

'God save the Prince and Bride! God keep their lands allied!'

Clemence had heard the townsfolk, who'd gone out into the January snow to see the passing bridal carriages, chanting it too. The Prussian royal marriage seemed popular.

'Princess Vicky and Prince Frederick are a sober and serious-minded pair,' Lysithea was telling her in a low, laughing voice. 'Well-suited to each other. I cannot imagine they will be giving many gay revels such as this at the Stadtschloss in Berlin!'

'We all likely lost someone in the Crimea, dear Aunt-in-law,' said Amathia. She had taken the seat on Lysithea's other side. Clemence couldn't help noticing how quickly Amathia had cosied up to the rich relation. 'It's peace we want! And our Queen's daughter marrying the heir to the throne of the most warlike nation in Europe should mean that. Should the Russian Bear roar again, we'll have the iron Prussians on our side!'

Clemence could make out the ivory-gowned, dumpy little figure of the Queen seated on the dais. Beside Victoria stood her stout husband in the dress uniform of Aubrey's regiment. Prince Albert was its Colonel-in-Chief. Grey and tired he was looking these days.

Clemence turned her gaze back to the waltzing pairs. Among them she spotted her sister. That wasn't her husband Isabella was dancing with. Odd chap, Lord Markham. Preferred the company of members of his own sex to that of his pretty, lively young wife. And didn't seem to care that she'd flirted with half the household cavalry. Lady Markham was becoming a bit of a scandal, and an embarrassment to her family at Eardingstowe.

Meanwhile, a young man was approaching the corner where Clemence was sitting. In front of her he halted. Her heart skipped a beat. Someone was asking *her* onto the dance-floor?

'Miss O'Driscoll? Might I have the pleasure of the next?'

Clemence hid behind the quivering feathers of her fan as the young man led out the eighteen-year old who had been seated beside her.

No-one wanted to dance with Clemence. Three waltzes and a polka had gone by and no-one had asked for her hand.

She gave a small gasp. Brandon Fanshawe had just entered the ballroom. He wore a blue sash beneath his evening coat. Clemence watched him move through the press of people in her direction.

Then a nuisance of intruders crossed her view, and she lost sight of him. They took their time, edging towards the dance-floor; and pausing to utter inanities:

'My dear Maria! Even more blooming than when we saw you at the Beauforts' Hunt.'

When the obstacles were gone, Clemence found herself looking up into Lord Fanshawe's face.

'Miss Somerlee! How wonderful to see you here tonight. May I join you?'

He flicked his coat-tail and took the vacant place. An arm resting on the chair back, he leaned towards her. On her other side, Aunt Lizzy and Amathia had their heads together in private talk.

'You look in good health, my dear,' he said. 'I hope this means we'll be seeing more of you this coming season? We have missed you.'

Clemence flapped a small foehn with her fan. It was true she had not been much in society these last two years. Her illness had taken a lot of getting over.

'I'm very, very well indeed thank you, Lord Fanshawe.' She cast him a sidelong look. Brandon had lost the tan he had acquired in the south. When he'd stood by her side on the hilltop, tiny pale creases had radiated from the corners of his eyes from having narrowed them against the sun.

'And putting the Crimea behind you, I hope?' he went on.

'Well, that I'm not sure of! Do you believe that inglorious war did any good, Lord Fanshawe?'

'Certainly! Had we lost, we'd be sitting here tonight supping vodka and that revolting black salty stuff Ivan thinks such a delicacy!' He laughed and tapped his knee. 'There was a time in man's remote past, you know, when he had to fight to survive. The tribe over the hill would take all the game otherwise, and leave you starving. I'm convinced, you know, that our periodic hankering for war every forty years or so is a throwback to all that. Ten thousand years of civilisation hasn't changed our species much. Perhaps Mr Darwin should reconsider his theories before he publishes this much-talked-about forthcoming book of his!'

'We'll watch our sons marching against some new aggressor, then?'

'Exactly! To learn the same truth you and I did.'

'Actually,' she continued, 'I'm hoping to do something useful with the money my father left me. It's mine now I've turned twenty-one. Something to benefit those who lost so much in the war as I did, I mean.'

'The Crimea made a few stout hearts quail,' he said. 'What have you in mind?'

'I was thinking, perhaps, of a convalescent home for the war wounded.'

'Indeed! A most worthy enterprise.' He regarded her, head on one side. 'Might you consider marriage again though someday, Miss Somerlee?' *Oh, yes. Ask me, just ask me, Brandon.* 'Captain Swynton left you heartbroken, I know. But he would not want you to shrivel into old maidenhood for his sake.'

'Oh, I am not intending to remain a bitter spinster, dear as James was to me. But we shouldn't be remembering the war tonight!' she pressed on. The Prussian Prince was just at that moment dancing by, a hand clasping the waist of his bride, Princess Vicky, who was wearing a dress of magenta-coloured silk. 'We should be thinking of marriage and blessing our happy couple.'

'Indeed! And another happy couple too, I hope.' He cast a look at her askance.

How heavenly sounded this present polka that the band was playing. She would remember it forever as the tune which was playing when Fanny asked her to marry him.

He took her hand in his. She felt as if she could have taken wing to dance.

'Miss Somerlee. Clemence. Would you be a maid of honour at my wedding?'

'A… *maid of honour*?'

'I've asked Dickon to be my groomsman. Phyllis and I want all our dearest friends around us at our special time.' He turned fully to face her. 'We shared so much, you and me, in the Crimea!'

'Phyllis?'

'Miss Phyllis Guilfoyle!' He sounded surprised. 'Has Dickon not told you, then? We're to be married next month!'

'No, my brother has not given me this news.'

'Ah, well, perhaps he feared you were not yet over your broken heart and talk of someone else's nuptials might have been hard to bear.'

'Yes… I suppose he must have…'

She clenched her fingers around her fan so tightly, they blanched.

'I wish you – and Miss Guilfoyle – every happiness.'

'Thank you, Miss Somerlee! Clemence. And now…' Lord Brandon Fanshawe offered her his arm. 'Would you favour me with a dance?'

TWELVE

'Are you ready to receive little Miss Caroline, My Lady?' asked the nursery-maid.

'Not yet... allow me another half an hour please.'

The mistress of Eardingstowe swung back and forth in her rocking-chair and sulked after the girl had gone again. Amathia tugged her shawl around her goosepimply arms. They mustn't have updated the Eardingstowe heating system, whatever it consisted of, since the Dark Ages.

The small room where she found herself, on Eardingstowe's first floor, was known as Lady Clémence's Sitting-Room after Dickon's and Clemmie's grandmother, Lysithea's mother. She had been a refugee from the Revolution, some sort of distant cousin of Louis XVI. The furnishings might have come from old Versailles: Louis Quatorze chairs and sofa, a Van Der Meer painting, Sèvres porcelain.

Not family heirlooms, of course. Even a Somerlee woman would not have been insane enough to rescue her ottoman from her burning château. Lady Clémence must have acquired these objects from auction houses after her exile from her native land.

Amathia's eyes moved to the view outdoors – looking southwards towards the village. It was early spring. Patches of stubborn, greyish snow which had fallen a week since were dotted around. In the willow coppice just beyond the walled garden, she could make out four or five labourers clearing the undergrowth with hedging-hooks.

The Quantock Hills and a ring of trees enclosed most of the grounds. If you walked the track which led from the mere to the edge of the woodland, you would see amber eyes and shadows slinking through the bracken and ferns: a guard regiment of badgers, tawny owls and wild ponies. And this feral place was to be home for the rest of her days?

Amathia rose from her chair. She dawdled out into the North Lobby and Picture Gallery.

It didn't bother her if the nursery-maid was unable to find her again. Each day Amathia was obliged to spend time with the infant ... *her* child... her *child*. Richard's *fungus* more like which had grown inside her from his poisoned seed – that's what it was.

Now, four months on from her lying-in, she could not distinguish between birthing depression and Eardingstowe depression. The one blurred into the other.

It was not that she regretted her choice of husband precisely, no. She had a fair chance of Aunt Lysithea's fortune coming her way. But that was but a bubble right now; and she was, meantime, having to endure her growing dislike of Dickon and his home.

A pity the baby wasn't a boy. Not that she thought boys were superior to girls; but as mother of the baronet-in-waiting she would have wielded power – over Dickon, Eardingstowe, the master-to-come. Instead, she had it all to do again.

She did not turn into the nursery wing. She could hear the crying voice of Eardingstowe's newest resident coming from there. Amathia went instead down the south stairs, ambled along the Lower Gallery, and came upon her lord and master's study. The door was ajar. Amathia could see him in there, with his solicitor.

What was that pair discussing? Her father's finances perhaps? That thought made her uneasy. Richard had returned from Kingsmede two days ago in a right mood about that. It seemed some of the bills from the sumptuous Westminster wedding had ended up on Richard's desk after all.

Well, no-one had ever told him the Consetts were rich. He was the one who'd assumed that. Despite all the hints which Fanny and Lizzy had no doubt dropped.

'Strange how the duke's penury hasn't prevented your brother doing the Grand Tour or running a hunting stable,' Richard had said to her during a heated exchange earlier that day.

The Little Drawing-Room, where she eventually settled, was one of Eardingstowe's loveliest chambers: Amathia rather liked it compared with the rest of the house. The painted columns were in the Roman style; the ivory of its ceiling sculptured into a pattern of quatrefoils and pendants. Frescoes in the gold-bordered wall panels depicted scenes from mythology: she gazed up at the yellow-tressed Sun wooing the maiden Leucothoe on the Aegean shore.

Amathia didn't stay long though. She had just heard Richard taking leave of his visitor, and his footsteps heading this way. In the mood to meet him she was not. Instead, she slipped out through the garden door, and followed the path which led past the yew and church wall.

Glancing up at the house, she could see lamplight glowing behind her sister-in-law's shut drapes. Amathia intended to have that room fumigated once she'd finally got rid of Clemence.

Clemence was in her bedchamber most hours. Amathia didn't believe she'd seen the woman since yesterday. Clemence, indeed, hardly went outside at all except to pray on her bony knees in St Laurey's. Not even that, now, for over a week.

Now, what could be wrong with that headcase – more wrong than usual, that was?

Richard took up *The Times*, which had been left on his favourite armchair in the lounge of the Carlton Club as he liked it.

Let's see what's on the business page.

SMOKY MOUNTAIN SHARES SOARING

The Smoky Mountain gold mine continues to grow from strength to strength, our reporter Mr Hughes writes.

The mine, in the Transvaal province of South Africa, was opened in 1855 after the discovery of the gold seam. Since then, vast quantities of the precious mineral have been extracted.

The Smoky Mountain Company, which controls all share stock in the mine, has seen its own profits double in the last quarter. Sir Roger Cormorant, Director of Smoky Mountain, said:

'The output from the mine has been quite overwhelming. It has exceeded even my expectations. Smoky Mountain has made a terrific boost to the economy of the Transvaal, created employment for hundreds, as well as attracting investors from as far as Iceland and South America. Today I'm meeting three Swiss financiers with a view to funding further underground exploration.'

Yesterday, Her Majesty the Queen was seen sporting a necklace of Smoky Mountain gold at a royal drawing-room at Windsor Castle...

Richard read, engrossed, until a party colleague came and joined him. Richard put the newspaper aside.

Later, as he was returning home to Somerset on the Great Western Railway, he went back to the story about the gold mine. What a good read. Took his mind off having to apologise to his wife for the ding-dong they'd had.

'I'm sorry for the way I behaved on Monday, Amathia. It was dreadful of me. Your father's ill. However much I don't get on with the fellow, he is your flesh and blood. Please accept my apology.'

'Perhaps a good night's sleep would do you good, sir?'

Amathia turned away from him in the fourposter bed, on her side, concealing her face. Would he take the hint and clear off?

But no – Richard perched on the edge of the mattress. Still, if he was depressed about money, he shouldn't be in the mood for anything else. She didn't mind him *sleeping* beside her, as long as that was all he did. At least he didn't snore. And with his extra padding he was plenty snug. *And* Eardingstowe by night was rather creepy. She kept dreaming Jenny Greenteeth was sneaking in through the casement.

Why had he married her, she wondered? Wanted to be a duke's son-in-law, didn't he, and his clodhopping, bumpkin self supping cider in the gracious halls of the House of Lords one day.

And now it sounded as if his row with her father had brought on a seizure.

'I noticed no sign of ill-health,' Richard had reported in surprise when the telegram from her brother had arrived that evening. 'Fellow was shouting like a street-vendor when I saw him last. Huge purple face… pumping veins. Thought he looked in very rude health! Although I know his doctor's been warning him for years to cut down on the brandy and sweet puddings.'

Suddenly, she thought she loved her dear papa very much. If he died, she would blame Dickon. She and her noble sire had never been close, true; she could call to mind no affection from him, ever. But she wanted to see him if he was dying. He must, after all, be leaving some kind of will.

'I've ordered the carriage for mid-morning,' she told her husband. 'I must visit my poor father if he is so ill.'

'I don't know why you didn't go straight away. I'd have let you have the carriage.'

'It would have come to grief in the dark on the roads whose upkeep you, as Justice of the Peace, have sadly neglected.'

'Very drole, my dear!'

He grunted his way into bed and turned his shoulders away. The pair lay in silence, backs to each other, for a long while.

Moonlight slunk through gaps in the drapes and fell shimmering on the faded satin of the Provençal quilt. You could see the criss-crossing bars of the lattice reflected in it. Whiteness shone too on the blackened oak of the bedframe. The fourposter in Eardingstowe's master bedroom was two hundred years old. The posts were carved into a pattern of coiling yew needles and quatrefoils. Richard, Lizzy, Clemmie and the others had all been born in it. Conceived too one must suppose.

'Richard,' Amathia said. 'What is the matter with your sister? Is she ill?'

'No, not ill… I don't think.' The baronet fell silent again.

Amathia did a bit more probing.

'Clemence has not left the house for three weeks, sir. The servants are gossiping… and shut up when I come upon them. Clearly, they see me as an outsider not to be trusted with family secrets! But you must learn to trust me, Richard. I'm your wife.'

Richard heaved himself into an upright position, bracing his back against the propped-up pillow. He twiddled his fingers and opened and shut his lips several times before speaking.

'Clemence has been like this once or twice before. Last time was when our father died. If she goes outside she… well… she cannot *breathe*… almost suffocates… passes out.' He fiddled with the tasselled edging of the quilt. 'I've consulted a few doctors about this matter – discreetly, of course. But the only explanation they can give is hysteria… or madness,' he concluded on a bit of a choke. 'And then, of course,' Richard continued, 'I think back to her breakdown when Aubrey went missing.'

Amathia reached across the space of goose-down mattress which lay between them. She took hold of his hand.

'So, it is upheaval and tragedy which affect her, then?' she said in soft, worried tones. 'But why now? The war has been over for more than two years.'

'I cannot imagine, Amathia! I have not quarrelled with her or said anything to upset her... nothing I can think of, anyway.'

'And nor I, Richard.'

'I get so concerned, Amathia, when anyone mentions madness.' His hand, still clasped in hers, felt a little damp. 'You know we have an aunt in Dwellan House? And I believe there was a great-uncle too...'

'Maybe Clemence is only hysterical, Richard. A notorious female affliction! Some might say it is her continued unmarried state which has brought this on!' He didn't seem to notice her flippancy, being deep in thought.

Richard sighed.

'Ah, well, my dear...' A smile crept across his face as it slowly swivelled around to her.

Amathia knew that look. She couldn't dignify it by calling it *lust*. Lust was what he might feel for some dairy woman or Haymarket doxy. No, what crossed Richard's features when he was in the mood for taking his conjugal rights was a kind of contempt, as if he blamed Amathia for the discomfort in his undergarments. What went through *her* mind meanwhile when he was doing his stuff was the soon-to-be-dead-and-damned surging up the Great Redan's slippy, sloping V, and – oh, you happy Roosians – blasting the invader to smithereens. When he'd done, she would picture the citadel and smoking harbour of Sebastopol in ruins.

'I don't enjoy this any more than you, Amathia....'

'We already have a child, sir. Healthy, as far as I'm aware.'

'But – in case it has escaped your notice, dear – the wrong sex!'

THIRTEEN

Richard settled into his Carlton chair another evening in March. He picked up his copy of *The Times* and turned to the business page.

LORD MAKES A MINT FROM SMOKY MOUNTAIN
Lord Hubert Spuffington spoke publicly yesterday of the success of his share venture in the Smoky Mountain Mine Company. Lord Spuffington was one of the earliest investors in the South African mine.

Richard bristled at the name Lord Spuffington. A long-time foe of his, and rival for cabinet post should Derby ever get into Downing Street.

'I've never been a fellow for the stock market, really,' said His Lordship. 'I'm a racing man. But my cousin lives out in the Cape and knew all about Smoky Mountain from the start. He persuaded me I should take a look at the mine. I'm jolly glad I did. I've just received my first returns and I've made a fourfold profit! I'm quite overwhelmed.'

Smoky Mountain Company Director, Sir Roger Cormorant, said:

'I'm delighted for Lord Hubert, and of course for Smoky Mountain.'

As new gold seams continue to be found in the mine in Transvaal, South Africa, the price of shares in the company has risen to five pounds and is expected to rise still further. The mine was first discovered by Boer farmer Piet...'

Richard slapped the newspaper down and took a long drink.

At Westminster the next day, he spotted Lord Spuffington alighting from his carriage. The two men curtly nodded to each other and exchanged insincere greetings. Spuffington was showing no sign of his new prosperity. Same frock coat and black silk waistcoat he'd been sporting for two seasons. But then he always was a parsimonious bounder.

Strolling through St Stephen's Hall towards the Central Lobby, Richard asked a colleague:

'What do you think of this gold mine in South Africa, Mr Anstruther?'

'Which gold mine would that be, old boy?'

'Smoky Mountain. It was in *The Times*.'

Mr Anstruther pursed his lips and shook his head.

'Must have missed it. Good investment is it, what?'

Richard felt a surge of jealousy.

'Oh, not really, Mr Anstruther. Nothing worth investing in. Just a story about a nasty accident in the mine, that's all.'

He barely listened to the debate in the Chamber that day. He returned home to Somerlee House in Aldgate, deep in thought.

A few evenings later, as Richard was entering Covent Garden Theatre, a fellow was arguing with the box office clerk.

'I say, this is dashed inconvenient, you know. Why, my man came by only this morning to reserve my ticket. My name's Sir Roger Cormorant. Please check again.'

'I'm sorry, sir, I really do not have a reservation in that name.'

'How deuced perplexing! The only performance of *Nozze di Figaro* this season and I miss it because of this theatre's bumbling incompetence!'

As the harassed clerk struggled for his livelihood, Richard stepped across.

'I say,' he ventured, removing his hat, 'I could not help but overhear your predicament, sir. In fact, I have a spare ticket. My wife is unable to attend due to an indisposition.' She was nothing of the sort. She was far away in Eardingstowe and the other ticket had been meant for his courtesan, who had not yet arrived and would be sent packing when she did. 'Perhaps you would be my guest, sir?'

'Well!' said the man. His rugged face lit up with astonished delight. 'How generous of you, sir! I don't believe we've had the pleasure of prior acquaintance.'

'Richard Somerlee, Baronet of Eardingstowe.' He inclined his head.

'Why, I know of you, sir. One of the few members of Derby's party who speaks sense in my opinion.'

'Oh, really, sir?' said Richard, who didn't often get such compliments.

'Why, yes! I was most impressed with how you spoke against the Education Bill. You were quite right, sir! How can a poor man feed his family if he has to send his little ones to school instead of putting them to work in the mills and factories? Outrageous piece of legislation in my opinion!'

'Pleased to meet you, indeed! And I, sir, am Roger Cormorant.' Cormorant held out a hand. The two men clasped and shook. 'I have a little mining company you've probably never heard of. Named Smoky Mountain…'

Inside his gloves, Richard's palms were sticky with excitement.

'I believe I read something in *The Times* recently,' he said. 'But come, sir, let us divest ourselves of coat and canes; and since you clearly love opera as much as I do, pray accompany me afterwards to Bertolini's for supper where we may discuss the performance …'

The two men left the restaurant in the early hours of the morning, both a little worse for drink.

'I am rather interested in buying shares in your mine, Sir Roger.' Richard signalled to the doorman to summon them a cabriolet.

'Delighted to do business with you, sir,' said Cormorant.

Not long into their conversation, Richard had learned that his new acquaintance was a Winchester old boy like himself. Tough, Richard thought, beneath his elegant manners and greying moustache; as if he had struggled through hardships to get where he was. A pale cicatrix dignified one cheek – relict of some honourable duel in Cormorant's past, perhaps? Richard admired that.

'I shall make a small investment to begin with. See what sort of return I get. If I see a handsome enough profit, I shall increase my outlay.'

'Clearly you are a man of sound financial sense, sir.' Cormorant beamed.

Ought Richard to consult his man of business first, though? Oh, fiddlesticks. Even if this gold mine was to collapse in a flash flood tomorrow, he would only have lost a thousand pounds or so. He'd lost more than that in a single night at Crockford's. And if Smoky Mountain truly was the cornucopia *The Times* would have him believe… well, it might just make him rich…

Amathia piled apple scones and lemon curd onto her breakfast plate. She was dressed all in black – her father had passed away a month earlier.

She paused before taking her seat at the dining-table, looking from the window.

Eardingstowe's informal dining-room stood on the upper floor. This was the closest point in the house to the chapel. In a high wind, the yew tree's boughs would rap the glass. The old needled monster was making a creaking noise even now when nothing but a gentle spring zephyr was wafting through its limbs. When the yew fell, so went the aphorism, so would the Somerlees? Wouldn't Amathia love to take out an axe… ooh, choppy, choppy, chop in her dreams!

'Good gracious, Dickon. What has your sister been doing?'

Eating his breakfast and reading the newspaper, Richard glanced up.

'Clemence,' she went on, 'was in here, the sitting-room and the Little Drawing-Room not long ago collecting all the blooms from the vases. Now they appear to be floating on the lake.'

'Good Lord,' mused Richard. 'I haven't done that since my boyhood.'

'Ah, then it is some pagan ritual practiced here since the world was young? Now, why does that not surprise me?'

'I suppose it is,' said Richard. 'On the first of April we make offerings to Jenny Greenteeth. Give her blossoms to say sorry for whatever wrong we did her in days of yore. In truth, though,' he added, smiling, 'I believe she's hated the Somerlees for so long, I doubt a few fresh flowers will move her watery heart.' He munched his Sally Lunn loaf, cheese and pickle. 'I see you don't believe in Jenny,' he said with raised brow. 'Out there in the Long Gallery – the portrait you are so taken with? Rupert Somerlee?'

Amathia glanced door-wards. Yes, she knew the one he meant. Rather a nice picture. The youth with flaxen ringlets, Prussian-blue satin doublet and Van Dyke collar was one of Eardingstowe's few charms, she thought.

'Now! Rupert was walking the bank one day, when he saw a lovely maiden sitting on the islet in the middle of the lake, singing and beckoning to him. Rupert swam out towards her. He was not seen again.'

Oh, stuff and nonsense. These tales were meant to frighten children. With Clemence they had clearly succeeded. And if Jenny *was* real, well... Amathia felt she had an ally of sorts in this fugacious damsel who haunted the mere – mutual distaste for the family who lived in Eardingstowe.

Amathia kept glancing up at her husband as she nibbled her breakfast. The Somerlees had been here for as long as the Quantocks and expected to remain until the winds wore away those same hills. The Somerlees never had to tighten their belts. Or fear the executioner's axe of the bankruptcy court. Or lie awake at Kingsmede aware that your father was going to the dickens, fretting over whether all this would be gone by new year, and yourself and your siblings in the workhouse. Richard and his family might be uncouth bumpkins, but they had so much... so much!

'I am so looking forward to visiting Manchester,' Amathia remarked. 'I do hope to see this charming mill of yours.' Hit him where it hurts – with the sordid origin of his present comfort. Richard shot her a wintry look.

'But we really must discuss Clemence's future, Dickon,' she pressed on.

'Is there anything to discuss? There's no reason why she cannot remain at Eardingstowe. A spinster aunt has her uses,' he said, stroking the head of a Welsh terrier which had come padding to his side. 'She's always been good with our youngest siblings, Margaret and John – adores them, you know.'

'Indulges them, you mean.'

'Still – she's cheaper than a hired nanny and governess.'

'But she isn't stable, Dickon, this you cannot deny,' his wife insisted. 'She should be married. She has an income, still only twenty-one, fair enough in an elfish kind of way... I daresay there must be some middle-class merchant type person looking to advance socially, who would welcome the connection with the Somerlees and Consetts, and who is not too fastidious in his tastes.'

Richard grunted, and took up his newspaper once more.

'This I shall leave in your capable hands, my dear. It is what females excel in.'

A footman entered with a pot of fresh hot chocolate. As it was being set on the silver stand, Amathia rose from the table and stepped back to the window.

A mallard with a retinue of yellow youngsters was passing on the mere, leaving a wake of shining V's radiating out across the surface. The further bank looked like one cream and golden blur, spread with daffodils in full bloom. Richard's youngest sister and brother, Margaret and John, could be seen tripping, giggling, along the shore, scattering further flowery tributes.

'I suppose it's too much to hope that Clemence went *outside* to give Jenny her dues?' said the mistress. 'I expect she diverted one of the domestics from his or her more pressing duties to make that floral display on the lake.'

'I imagine so,' Richard said.

'Why don't you just push her out and shut the door on her? She'd soon snap out of this silliness.'

'Because she'd die!' he replied in thumping tones. 'She stops breathing, Amathia! Don't imagine that crude attempt at a cure wasn't tried in the past.'

'Then she should most definitely be married, Dickon. That will stop her moping. I shall consider some suitable candidates.'

'Some sham duke on the verge of bankruptcy perhaps?' He went on staring at the print.

She felt the sting as if she'd been slapped.

Well, my ignoble baronet... she narrowed her eyes. *Now you mention it, I believe I know just the man.*

What woke Clemence?

It must be the dead of night. The house lay silent around her, the moon high above the casement.

An unnatural kind of light was flickering on her coverlet. Moonbeams didn't flit like that. Rather, the orange tongues leaped and pranced.

The young woman sprang upright, staring towards the curtains.

Out from her bed, her bare toes padded across the rug and floorboards.

Holy God, it seemed to be in the village. One of the cottages must be alight. How many times had Dickon, curse him, been told that old thatch was a hazard?

What are you thinking, Clemence Somerlee? Here was she – looking on, shaking her head over her brother's failings as a landlord? Lives might be lost.

She grabbed a shawl. Sprinted from the room. Scurried down the north stars. Into the passage which separated Richard's study from the great hall. He'd dumped a pair of black leather bluchers outside the door: Clemence slipped her little feet inside, and then galumphed in them across the tiles.

Her hand was on the three great locks across the main exit when it hit her: God... she couldn't go.

She was stuck inside and couldn't leave.

What can I do? How can I get help? Why am I so useless... useless?

She'd roused two of the dogs; they bounded about her, yapping; but no-one else was yet stirring that she could hear.

One glance up the grand stairwell. No, Richard would not show himself. He had left for London in the afternoon. Flitcroft and the male servants were far away on the topmost floor and attics. No time was there to reach them.

Clemence stared at the massive front door again. The butler barred it every night. She knew how to unfasten the bolts. At least in theory. In practice, the fastenings were stiff and old. To reach the topmost one, she had to drag a pier chair across the vestibule, then stand on the velvet upholstery in Richard's outdoor footwear.

No time to think what she was doing... one fraction of a second, that was all which flashed by, and... Swung the master's boot at the great portcullis. Open it yawned. In flooded the night air.

Clemence retched as if she was going to heave up her dinner. Frog-sounds in her windpipe.

It was like a vortex spinning around and around and around... sucking her down into oblivion. All colours blurring... like all those scattered, jumbled-up bits when you look inside a kaleidoscope.

Barking dogs... parkland trees... the flamelight flickering through the trees... timbered beams and sculptured, plaster ceiling of the great hall... Sir Alois Somerlee's framed painting gleaming in the nightlight... gargoyle banister heads of the grand stairwell with their toothy mouths gaping... Jacobean screen... eight-day clock... hanging lanterns... longsword... fireguard...

Where was she? Cold beneath hands and cheek. The tiles of the vestibule. Had she passed out? Paws of one of the dogs pressing upon her spine. He licked her ear, and that woke her properly.

She could, now, hear calls and slamming doors in the far parts of the house.

But there was still no time. She must get out.

Beside her lay the chair – upturned, on its side. It had tumbled down with her. Its clattering must be what had roused the sleepers upstairs.

Had she knocked her head on the floor? The dull pain had just become manifest.

Clemence eased the dog off. She heaved herself onto her back so that she was facing the door. The black void beyond seemed to rush towards her. As if it was going to smother her in its suffocating folds.

Sucking out all the air which there was in Eardingstowe. Squashing, squeezing – as if the walls were closing in and crushing her. Clemence choked, retched; wetness spotted the hands which she clasped to her mouth.

No, she would not turn back. If she was to die… might as well be in the attempt to save others.

She swung her legs around. Rose to her feet stage by stage. One huge lungful of the remaining oxygen. Then she lunged across the threshold.

FOURTEEN

A footman carrying a drinks tray was weaving a path through the guests. The assembly was gathered in Eardingstowe's Great Drawing-Room before going in to dinner.

The baronet took two glasses and handed one to the man he was talking to.

'Any thoughts on how it might affect you, eh, Dickon?' Lord Tewksbury asked. 'Probably weren't expecting it, were you – Palmerston down over that Conspiracy to Murder Bill?'

'No. I'd not have thought Pam would tumble.'

'But he has. And Derby is in the ascendancy, eh? Well, who'd have thought it? Suppose you're hoping for office, what? You've been one of his stalwarts.'

'Yes… could be the biggest squabble since the Repeal of the Corn Laws!'

'Oh, you get all the bluster in the Commons, my dear chap,' said His Lordship. 'Rarely much excitement in the Lords.'

'Yes, the House can be lively,' Richard mused.

Still, he'd settle for snoozing in the Lords if it meant a peerage.

Richard was moving gradually from dinner-party guest to guest, sipping his wine as he went. A smattering of Whigs was among the company as well as Derby's followers. Never hurt a chap to be sensible.

Through the open door which led into the passage he could see the State Dining-Room done up in splendour. It was only used for formal entertaining. For daily eating, the family used the more modest dining-room on the first floor.

As this was a special occasion, a small orchestra had been engaged to play during the meal. The drawing-room windows had been thrown wide open to show off the beautiful Crystal Garden whose parterres and walkways were lit with multi-coloured Chinese lanterns.

His wife was talking with the wives of two men he was keen to get on his side, he was glad to see.

His sister, however, stood alone by the Jacobean fire-screen. Clemence still wouldn't go near the window – because the glass was open, he assumed. She also kept her back to the people in the room. But at least she'd made an effort to look well, in a lime-green silk crinoline and ivory-lace fichu and wearing their mother's daisy-chain pearls.

'Thank you for turning out so prettily, Clemence,' he murmured in her ear. 'I understand Viscount Van Schalten has been asking who you are.'

'Has he?'

Yes... who's the freak who looks as if she hasn't been out of doors for a year?

'Van Schalten's a distant cousin of Derby's. And quite a handsome chap, wouldn't you say? Considered quite a catch I'm told,' Richard went on. 'You have more admirers than you think, Clemmie. You really look quite personable when you try.'

'Thank your wife,' she replied. 'My dress and hair are the work of her mantuamaker and coiffeuse.'

'Please be polite, won't you? There're a lot of people here tonight who might just put in that good word I need with Derby.'

'You know I don't like crowds.'

'Just try and be pleasant,' he muttered, around a smile which he was forcing out for a passing junior minister. 'And anyway, I thought your heroism of last week might have shaken you out of this nonsense.'

Clemence raised wide eyes to him.

'I reacted in a dangerous situation – that is all. We can all be heroes in a crisis, Dickon!'

'Just so.' He took a few sips from his glass. 'Actually, I haven't really had a chance to thank you yet, have I? Getting to Constable Shankly's house and rousing him like that? You probably saved Bob Shiner, and his wife and children. He's a good carter. I'd have been sorry to lose him.'

'At least it's forced you to do something about those cottages, Dickon!'

'Yes, you're right, Clemence. Too busy thinking of Parliament these days. Neglecting my duties at home. I stand rebuked.'

Still, he thought, she must be getting over her icky spell, whatever she believed to the contrary. Gazing out of doors now and then, wasn't she? Her little adventure on the night of the fire probably had been the kick up the rear she needed. So, everyone was a winner; Shiner got a new cottage, and Richard got back a marriageable sister.

'Well, anyway, you do look nice, dear.'

'Your wife outshines us all of course,' Clemence sighed. 'Even in her mourning black, Mathy must be one of the most charming women here tonight. You're quite envied, you know, Richard.'

'Am I?' He took a gulp of wine.

'Well, you are happy in your marriage, aren't you?'

'Do I not look the picture of happiness, and health?'

'No, Dickon. You're putting on weight. You ought to be careful. You won't be a young man much longer.'

'Poppycock, woman! The pater ate birdseed like you, was as thin as a stick like you, and the consumption bore him off before he saw a half century! I think marriage and fatherhood agree with me.' He finished his drink in two mouthfuls, and then clattered the vessel onto a passing footman's tray. The way she eyed him, though! 'God, Clemence, sometimes I wonder if you can see into my mind, do you know that? Our remote ancestress St Laurey was supposed to have the second-sight, you know. I wonder sometimes whether you possess just a smidgen, maybe?'

Before she could answer, however, Clemence drew in a sharp breath. She was looking beyond his shoulder. He turned to see. Lord Fanshawe had just entered, arm-in-arm with his bride.

'Look well, don't they?' Richard said. 'Just returned from their honeymoon in Venice. I once entertained hopes of you and Fanny, you know,' Richard went on. 'Yes, I did indeed! But you knew your mind, of course. You couldn't have known your chosen one would fall in the biggest military disaster this side of Actium.'

'Oh, you can be tactless, Dickon! And what's more – how could I care for someone like Fanny Fanshawe who used to pull my ringlets? In fact, I quite resent him!'

Good Lord, he'd touched a nerve there. He was about to retort that, really woman, how can you expect to marry for love these days… what romantic nonsense! What about your duty to me, the brother who's clothed and fed you all these years, and so on, and so on… But, actually, he ended up having a quiet chuckle to himself. Sometimes you could read females like books.

'Ah, well.' He glanced over at the newlyweds. Fanny was introducing his lady to Lord Tewksbury. 'What do you think of Phyllis? Lovely, isn't she?'

Blisteringly winsome the former Miss Guilfoyle was. White rosebuds in her Grecian coil of dark brown ringlets.

'I don't yet know Miss Guilfoyle well – Lady Fanshawe, I mean – but she is truly handsome. I trust she makes Fanny as happy as Amathia has made you,' Clemence added with a sly glint in her eye. And he'd thought she'd left her spirit in Balaclava.

Flitcroft arrived to announce dinner was served. The party began to make moves. The Duke of Beaufort as the highest-ranked guest would be leading the company into the dining-room. Which gentleman-guest had Amathia paired her with, Clemence wondered?

'Dickon, who will be accompanying me to dinner?'

It might be Brandon Fanshawe! Or some other charming, handsome young fellow.

'I believe you are with Colonel Cumberpatch. Talk to him about the Crimea, my dear. He so regrets he wasn't able to take part since his leg was shot off at Waterloo. But his grandson died at Lucknow – so India's probably a topic of conversation to avoid.'

Richard gasped when he opened his first statement from the Smoky Mountain Mining Company. The modest five pounds' worth of shares he had purchased to test the water had returned a profit of twenty.

He sent, at last, for his notary.

'Mr Boscawen, I wish to invest in this company, Smoky Mountain. A gold mine in South Africa. I know the Director, Sir Roger Cormorant. I had dinner with him after the opera recently – most splendid company, he was. He's a Wykehamist like me. We tested each other on our notions; he caught me out a few times! Anyway, the company's quite sound, I assure you. Open up an investment portfolio, would you? I will commence with one thousand pounds' worth of shares.'

'But, Sir Richard!' The solicitor was taken aback. 'I have never heard of this company!'

'Then you obviously don't read your *Times* very thoroughly.' Richard showed him the two editions with the relevant articles.

'Well!' spluttered Boscawen. 'I thought I did read my *Times*, but clearly I skipped on these days. I cannot argue with the wisdom of *The Times* of course.'

'As you see, Lord Spuffington had no qualms about investing in the company. And has done very well for himself out of it so far by the look of things.'

'I know you and he are not close, Sir Richard, but I am acquainted with Lord Hubert's man-at-law. I am rather surprised he did not mention this venture to me.'

'Professional loyalty, man! Surely you see that? I would not expect you to blab about my financial affairs to every other man-at-law in the shire!'

'No! Naturally. That makes sense…'

'You will make the purchase then?'

'Of course, sir.'

Clemence gazed across a waterway teeming with ornate barges. The water their prows were ploughing before them was making cascades of shimmering sunshine.

Some were almost like little houseboats, festooned with trellis vines and flower-garlands. The people on board were waving to those on shore. Men wearing boater-hats. Women all in white from hem to lacy parasol. All of fashionable society was gathered at the Henley Regatta.

I guess Dickon was right, she thought. It took an almost tragedy to cure her of her latest bout of strangeness. Her kick up the rear as he'd so delicately put it. Whatever ailed her didn't have a name. Terror of the outdoors? Fresh air sickness?

'Clemmie! We're about to start the picnic!'

Her sister-in-law was hailing her. Amathia was seated beneath a parasol in the shade of the willows, Richard beside her. They had a luncheon spread out on a cloth. The children, Margaret and John, and baby Caroline were here too, playing with the nurse.

'I'm not hungry yet, Mathy. You start without me. I want to look at the boats from the bridge first...'

'Don't wander too far,' Richard called.

Bless them. They thought her tetched, of course. Everyone who'd ever seen her when she was confined to the house thought so. And treated her as such. By *don't wander too far*, they meant, *don't be doing anything to show up the family, strange one*.

Well, she was well and truly outdoors now, and meant to stay.

The day after the dinner-party, she had looked on the view from the library. The coralberries were in full bloom. She could see as far as the hills. That was where she should be. Not moping in here, letting her broken heart freeze into ice, making dirges out of Bach's livelier sonatas on the ivory.

Clemence wandered down to the waterside through the many picnicking groups. Laughter and song was all around. As was the scent of lavender and buzz of bees. The field was covered with white campion, elderflower and meadowsweet. Children playing with balloons and hoops.

It was the height of the London season. Dickon and Mathy must be hopeful they could yet find her a match. The eligible partis they were introducing her to, though, at the balls and kettledrums they were attending were increasingly less wealthy, connected or youthful. Clemence's desirability was ebbing as she gathered dust on the shelf, and rumours of her instability spread.

Sunbeams were dazzling Clemence... swelled the water sparkles into glowing moons... cast into bronze all the trees and folk on the far bank, and the fancy vessels as past they glided...

In all that strange light, her brother Aubrey's features seemed to smile from behind the pole of the passing punt. James was sitting beside the gunwale, trailing a hand in the ripples. Captain Nolan perched in the prow. He waved to her. *We are leaving. Don't miss the boat. The boat of no-return…*

Would they let her go? If she slipped into that beckoning water? Drift into a cool, timeless republic?

The sound of a lady's gay, silvery laugh snapped her mind back to the present.

'You look pensive, dear coz.'

Clemence looked up to see a young, male figure perched astride a magnificent chestnut hunter.

Amathia's brother, Philoctetes Consett, Duke of Ardenne, wore a hat with a black silk band, belted Norfolk jacket and peg-top trousers. He was twenty-four years old, had come into his dukedom on the death of his father five months ago.

'Do I not get a greeting?' Philoctetes asked, patting his horse's neck. 'Some commonplace at least? Like, how are you enjoying the meet, Philo?'

The sunlight was behind both horse and rider and was for a moment blinding. She shielded her eyes.

'I don't suppose you are here for the races, being in mourning, Your Grace?' Clemence asked at last.

'Philo, please! We're kinfolk by marriage, you and I.' He pushed back his hat, beaming down at her. 'And I'm here to enjoy the fine day and charming company, as are all. Jolly warm weather, what?' He took out a bright red fogle and wiped his brow.

She turned her eyes back to the ambling water-traffic. A young man in a straw hat poled along a skiff, and sang to the object of his fancy who was sitting opposite:

With sorrow, deep sorrow, my bosom is laden,
All day I go mourning in search of my love;
Ye echoes, oh, tell me, where is the sweet maiden?
"She sleeps, 'neath the green turf down by the ash grove."

The girl in the pretty craft looked about four years Clemence's junior. She felt her age. The years were speeding by and old-maidenhood looming.

'Do you hunt, Miss Somerlee?' the Duke of Ardenne asked. 'Shall we see you at the Quorn?'

'No, I don't hunt, Philo. I don't care for chasing and killing God's creatures.'

The duke fondled his chestnut's ears.

'Hear that, Miniver? You're one of God's creatures! But you love the chase, don't you, my boy? Quite grumpy, aren't you, through the tedious summer months?'

'Gosh, the hunt can be a riot, you know, Miss Somerlee,' he went on. 'You know those pigs' bladders you can get which make a rude noise when you sit on them? Bluebely Baxter and I took one to the Duke of Beaufort's last year. We sneaked it onto quite a few saddles, including the Countess of Bedingfield's. And Lord Palmerston's! Actually, Bluebely and I haven't been invited to Badminton this year.'

'I'm sure I cannot imagine why, Your Grace... Philo.' Clemence found herself returning his smile. He was trying to cheer her up, bless him. It was more than Dickon and Mathy had managed.

Philoctetes was not really handsome – cheeks a little florid, eyes rather small, more flesh on him than was good in a young man; but his eyes were a lighter grey than his sister's, and his hair a sunnier blond. His dukedom and unmarried status, of course, would hide the grossest of disfigurements and basest of vices. The world must look lit with rainbows from on board Miniver.

'Lady Quarmby's giving a kettledrum next Tuesday,' the duke said. 'It sounds tedious – a few écarté and poker tables, and some German lady singing to the Quarmby girls' mediocre accompaniment. But I should grace the occasion if you were present, cousin Clemence. Why – I could take pleasure in a trip to the dentist in your company, dear lady!'

Clemence eyed the young aristocrat – claiming the right of family connection to call her cousin; and likely not just hunting the furry-eared fellows of the field. She could almost hear him swaggering to his cronies in the Travellers: *I've had m' leg over that frigid Somerlee bitch, my bucks; can anyone better that, hey?* But he was at least smiling with her. His were the friendliest features here.

Clemence stroked his handsome animal's nose. Miniver nodded and stretched his head towards her, blowing into her ear.

'I take it you ride even if you don't hunt?' the duke asked.

'Oh, yes, I'm very fond of horses. They are such good listeners. Understand me the way men never do.'

The duke smiled, teasingly.

'I don't let many other than meself astride Minnie. Worth the stars to me, he is. But for you, Miss Somerlee, if you'd care to take him out…'

'Thank you, Philo! I would like this.'

'Then Minnie shall be yours. I'll fetch my groom and have Minnie fitted with a ladies' saddle.'

Miniver dipped his head to the slush-pool hard by the jetty, sniffed, snorted and blew more slime over her dress. Even the creatures of the field were laughing at her. But she found herself laughing too.

'Minnie likes you,' the young duke said. 'I expect all animals do. You have a way with them, I can tell.'

'I often find them better company, I must admit,' Clemence said. 'I look after my lost brother's warhorse, you know. Sparkle. He's retired to our stables.'

'I see. You have had a difficult few years, haven't you? Not knowing what happened to your brother – oh, that must be tragic for you, Miss Somerlee! Or may I call you Clemence? Such a lovely name, which so suits you.'

'Clemmie, if you like, Philo.' She gave Miniver's neck a stroke. 'I was named after my grandmother, who almost died on the guillotine. She got a stay of execution with a few hours to spare.'

'Courageous lady! I've no doubt you take after her.'

'I wish I did. But I'm not sure I do,' she replied. 'I was thinking about Aubrey just before you joined me a moment ago. I keep thinking I see him, you see...'

'Oh, that's part of the normal grieving process, my dear!'

'Is it?' Miniver blew into her ear. She nuzzled his nose with hers. 'Will you be joining us for the picnic, Philo?' she asked shyly. 'As long as you are not too partial to mushroom vol-au-vents, because my little brother and sister will have all but finished them off by now.'

'I don't much care for the company of my trying sister, truth be told, Clemmie,' he smiled. 'I don't envy you, living with Mathy. Surely you don't intend to remain at Eardingstowe for ever? Such a waste! You're a beautiful young woman with your whole life ahead of you.'

'At the moment I can't afford to leave!' she said.

She'd once had fantasies of never marrying, running a school perhaps, for similar-minded young girls, leading a single woman's war against mankind. That dream had gone plop, as dreams like that usually did. The allowance her father had left her, she'd learned, would barely keep her in stockings.

As for her noble vision of a convalescent home... well, let's just say she had rather underestimated how much capital it would involve. A girl's governess was somewhat neglectful in teaching her about such things as financial management; although she could press flowers very nicely.

'Why don't you borrow against your expectations?' Amathia had suggested.

Yes, she supposed she could. But, oh, that seemed so like taking advantage of Aunt Lizzy. She'd wanted to achieve something for herself for once in her life.

Anyway, much as she and her sister-in-law didn't get on too well, Eardingstowe was Clemmie's home, which she loved more than anyone did, even Richard probably. And she loved her little sister and brother, Margaret and John. *And* the only motherly attention baby Caroline received was from her Aunt Clemence.

'Well… I promised you a ride, Clemence.' The duke nodded towards the closest trees. 'There's quite a good run on the other side of that small wood. Half an hour should show you just what Minnie can do.' He removed his hat and inclined towards her. 'After that – would you join me on the bridge to watch the next race?'

She looked at him, really seeing him for the first time. A bounder who was trying to take advantage of a vulnerable young woman. Maybe even after marrying her because he knew the countess intended to leave her money to her. Stranger things had happened. A smile pricked the corners of her lips. He could hardly make her opinion of men lower than it already was whatever he did. And she might, just might, have some fun through it herself…

FIFTEEN

Richard turned around on the spot, gazing up into the rafters of Eardingstowe's old wing. Sunbeams slinked through gaps in the shutters. The roof timbers had grown dark with the smoke from thousands of fires over many centuries.

This, the oldest part of the house, was not much used these days apart from storage and servant accommodation. At one end of the great hall, the floor rose into a dais where once had stood the high table. In the opposite wall gaped three arches which led to the buttery and kitchen. The newel stair wound into darkness in the south-western corner.

On the floor above were the great chamber, where the medieval lord had slept, the closet where he'd prayed, and a solar where his lady retreated. Here too was found one of Eardingstowe's treasures – the stained-glass oriel window. And finally – the long gallery where the ghost of Clovis Somerlee was said to walk; Richard had heard the strange footfall himself and felt the cold spots. The boards yet bore the stain of Clovis's blood – spilled when he was suspected of turning traitor to his fellow Gunpowder Plotters.

At least three monarchs had dined here – the family still owned a chalice Elizabeth had given as a gift, and a gold filigree brooch set with an amethyst which Queen Philippa of Hainault had bestowed upon her Somerlee hosts.

This present structure dated from Saxon times. But as a dwelling-place Eardingstowe went back, back into the miasma of pre-recorded history. Roman mosaics had been found beneath the newel stair. When Richard closed his eyes, and shut his ears to the cooing of pigeons, flutter of bats' wings and scratching of rodents' claws, he could almost hear the laughter of the housecarls at the dining boards before they'd ridden to face the Norman invader.

Why had the old hall fallen into neglect? It was a breathtaking place.

Richard's wife didn't care for it much. That was one reason, he supposed. Just as well Amathia kept away – she'd give Clovis and the other spectres the fright of their deaths.

Stormed at with shot and shell, boldly they rode and well, into the jaws of Death…

Richard struck his fist on the stone arch framing the entrance to the newel stair. Somewhere in the vaulting, a startled pigeon's wings fanned.

How many among the jealous nobility and gentry married for love? No, you entered the sacred bonds of matrimony for wide acres and sparkling coronets, or just a father-in-law who might advance your career. Remember Richard's old pater who'd wed Richard's mother for a cotton empire? Dickon, Clemmie, Aubrey and all owed the breath in their lungs to Joshua Carswell's mucky mill.

His finger traced the chain of worn quatrefoils cut into the stone.

Still, Richard's parents had been together for over twenty years with no major upsets; if Somerlee had been unfaithful to her, it was his secret. Perhaps that was a kind of love.

But Richard – he was bound to a woman he was growing to hate, and all for nothing.

His glacial bedchamber couplings with the Handmaiden of Boreas, God of the Cold North Wind had yielded only one girl so far – sweet enough little thing, bless her, but useless for a title and estate which needed an heir. If he failed to produce a male heir, the estate should pass to one of his younger brothers. But Ivo was interested in nothing except his career in the church. Aubrey was gone, of course. Which still left young Carswell and little John. Even so, the uncertainty made Richard uneasy. He'd breathe sounder if he had sons of his own.

Naturally, any bride might have had the misfortune to be barren. Couldn't hold that against Mathy Consett. That was just good or ill luck.

But her family turning out to be all but broke; and not having the clout he'd thought they did was not. The duke had deceived him. Mathy had. That was a god-damned wrong he had been done. 'No-one ever told you the Consetts were rich...' Maybe not, but they'd let him *assume* it. Yes, they had.

Richard strode under the central arch at the lower end of the hall, passed the old buttery and kitchen passage, and through the ancient doorway which led into what was now Eardingstowe's new wing – in days of yore it had been a courtyard egress.

He stalked the entrance-hall, dumped his outdoor Norfolk jacket on the pier table, and paused beside the grand staircase. He looked up at the life-sized, gilt-framed portrait which hung there. The first baronet, Sir Alois Somerlee, in early Georgian dress, was frowning down at him as if to say 'what are you doing with my inheritance, you young shaver?'

In his study, Richard kicked off his bluchers, poured a brandy, plumped down in the chair behind the desk, and stuck up his feet.

This was his place more than any other. A masculine preserve like the gunroom. Atmosphere of cigar fumes. Nothing floral or delicate. Hunting scene in the painting above the fireplace.

The baronet's old pointer slumbering by the flames. It was the master's hideaway where he could retreat after a hearty repast, undo tight buttons and belch without fear of female frowns.

Down by his side was a chiffonier. In a cache he kept his supply of narcotics. Just for medicinal reasons – if he came home from Westminster, say, with a bellyache whose aetiology was Whig. There was no harm in laudanum. Nanny Jude used to prescribe it for a tickly cough or sore thumb.

But the more and more you took of the stuff, the otherwise black and white world became a fantastical phantasmagoria. You felt as if the glorious final movement of a symphony was playing in your skull. You could stand in the House and blast Palmerston into a supernova. Shrivel Whigs into nothingness in the blackness of space.

It was several hours before Richard went to the sitting-room. There, from the ottoman, his wife was directing operations for that evening's dinner-party. As he walked in, the housekeeper was facing a tongue-lashing.

'I won't listen to your excuses, Mrs Kirkbride. Don't you realise the Earl of Derby is to be a guest? Sir Richard's career is at stake. We must have the Sèvres porcelain! If one piece is missing from the set, then you must send to Taunton for a replacement before tonight.'

The minion went away on her forlorn hope mission.

Richard poured a brandy. Oh dear, it would be his third of the day, and it was only mid-afternoon.

'I take it, earthenware excepted, you have everything under control for this evening?'

'Absolutely!' said Amathia. 'The menu will be Potage Printanier followed by Herring Roes à la Varsovie, and Veal à la Bourgeoise.'

'Well, we'll not poison the Prime Minister.'

'I'm determined this evening is to be a success,' said Amathia. 'It is a pity we are so in the wilds here, so remote from civilisation.' An expression of distaste crossed her face as she looked from the window towards the hills. 'Well, we might not be able to change Eardingstowe's unfortunate provincial setting, but we can make it tolerably fashionable. I mean to see all of high society at our kettledrums in the years to come. And as your star rises, darling, we can afford to build a new country seat in a more apposite spot.'

'Indeed, my dear. I already hear you talked of as one of the most gracious of society hostesses.'

'One does one's best with limited resources, considering Eardingstowe is so backward and, well… please don't be hurt, dearest, but… *shabby*.'

'Ah, well, it has taken a battering in two millennia of history.'

He stood behind her, looking down at her floral décolletage, chemisette, and morning cap with its long lace lappets over the ears. Caroline's birth had taken its toll on her looks. He could see for himself, with his inexpert male eye, what exertions her maid must be undergoing to lace her corset. She'd need an Iron-Maiden let alone corsets before she was forty. Gratifying thought. Serve her right for her rudeness about Eardingstowe.

'While we are on the subject of my star rising,' he told her, 'I've been in discussions with Mr Boscawen, my man-of-business. There really seems little chance my brother Aubrey will be found alive. Boscawen's going to start proceedings to have him declared legally dead. Then Uncle George's legacy will come to us.'

'Hmm… now that would be useful extra income,' Amathia said. 'Eardingstowe has inadequate guest accommodation. We could build a new wing… have the old hall demolished. Oh, Dickon, I have such plans!'

Richard flapped out his coat-tail and sat beside her.

'There's something else I want to talk to you about, Amathia. Your brother intends to speak to me this evening before dinner, I understand,' he said. 'He wants permission to court Clemence. But I'm not sure it's a good idea.'

Amathia gave a light laugh.

'Clemence is twenty-one! She can decide for herself. Even if she was still your responsibility, she defied you once before. Became engaged to Swynton just because you wanted Fanny Fanshawe.'

'She's older and wiser now.'

'She's feeble-minded! Wandering in her wits. You needn't take my word for that. No less an authority than Florence Nightingale believes it.'

'Well, if you are right,' he said with an acidic smile, 'then she will be malleable. She'll do as I say as she did not when she had her wits about her.'

Her eyes turned to him.

'Why would you wish to withhold your consent, anyway? You spent all that money presenting your sisters at court in the hope that one of them would marry into the aristocracy!'

'I happen to think your brother's a nincompoop.'

'As a matter of fact, so do I. But why should that stop you, or Clemence?' Amathia raised an eyebrow. 'I'd have thought you'd welcome the prospect of a blue-blooded in-law you imagine you can get the better of!'

'Am I really so mercenary as to wish my gentle sister on the likes of him? I do have a heart, God-damn-it, a soul! And you know damned well there's no money with that god-damned title. She'd be a duchess who had to launder her own gowns! And no, I'm not going to apologise for my language.'

In the dangerous silence which followed, the clock ticked on, sounding unbearably loud. Out on the bank of the mere, a peacock called; a hen answered from a distance. Amathia turned her head as the sound of a woman's skirt rustled in the doorway.

'If you please, madam, the dining table is now prepared, and awaiting your inspection.'

'Thank you, Mrs Kirkbride. I shall be along shortly.'

Richard's second statement from the Smoky Mountain Company was a blur of strange figures which he could make nothing of. He showed it to Mr Boscawen. The notary stared in astonishment.

'I have to say I believe you were right, sir! These figures mean a profit of seven thousand pounds!' He handed the document back, eyebrows still raised. 'I took the liberty of checking the company out – obtained a copy of its annual report. Perfectly sound to my professional eye. I'm just surprised I've not heard of anyone else investing apart from you and Spuffington.'

'It does not astound me, Boscawen! Gold mines abroad – risky business. Stick to solid, English companies. That's the way most of these dullards think. No imagination. And that's going to be to my advantage.'

Richard met Roger Cormorant for supper one evening.

'My treat, sir,' Richard told him as the two men settled at table. 'We'll have a bottle of Château St Emilion,' he told the waiter, 'and I recommend the Dover Sole,' he said to his companion.

'I take it you were pleased with your share returns,' Cormorant said, tucking in his napkin.

'Most satisfied! In fact, I have a proposition, Sir Roger, which I will tell you over dinner.'

They ate their entrée and listened to the orchestra. Richard drank half a glass of wine. He eyed the older man.

'You do not seem to be attracting many investors,' Richard said. 'Lord Spuffington is the only one I know of beside myself.'

'Yes. I am rather disappointed. More publicity is needed perhaps.'

'That is what my idea involves, Sir Roger. I have many contacts in the government and society. Publicity in newspapers is – forgive me – not the route forward. It is too much like advertising. The nasty word 'trade'. Personal contact however – that is the way to proceed. The upper and middle classes will buy a product because the Duchess of Somewhere recommends it, but not if some dirty little costermonger advertises it.'

'I see your thinking, Sir Richard. I like your style. And you talk sense.'

Richard leaned across the table. He looked the other man in the eye.

'What I'd like to suggest, therefore, is that I become a kind of unofficial agent for you. I persuade my friends and colleagues what a strong investment I've made… they'll be keen as mustard, believe me. They, in turn, will spread the word among their own circle of acquaintance. We can form a discreet network.'

'Ingenious!' Cormorant sipped his wine. 'Keep my name secret, perhaps? I'll be the puppet-master behind the scenes, you the public face of the company. Yes…' The man's grey eyes gleamed. 'The mystique will be part of the attraction! But I'm waiting for the *coup de grâce*, Sir Richard. You would expend much time and effort on this. What would your expected remuneration be?'

Richard sat back, clasping his fingers over his dinner jacket.

'I want part ownership of the company.' He fixed his companion with a shrewd look. 'Fifty per cent ownership.'

Sir Roger dabbed his lips with his napkin and eyed him right back.

'Twenty-five.'

Richard leaned forward again.

'Forty per cent.'

The waiter arrived with the fish course. Cormorant ignored him. He gave Richard a faint smile.

'You're a hard man to do business with, Somerlee, but, by God, I don't think I'll rue the day. You've a deal.'

As Richard left the restaurant later, he put up his collar. A moon peeped now and then from behind the clouds. The night had grown chilly, and rain was on the way. The first overtures of autumn.

Ever so slightly tipsy, he raised his cane and summoned a cabriolet. He was smiling to himself as he climbed inside. The future looked good.

1859

Six months later

SIXTEEN

A blizzard was blowing through the city streets as dusk fell. Around the church lichgates shivered the homeless who had gathered there in the hope of a bite to eat. Every roof, fence, gate and pane were buried beneath bluey-whiteness. The dome of St Paul's rising above them all was a grey blur.

The wheels of a gold-painted brougham crunched to a standstill in a quiet sideroad. A coachman perched on top plumed the air with steamy breath.

Three passengers peered from the glass to see the cause of the halt.

A plain box of a coffin was being hurried across their path. There came the sound of a woman's sobbing.

Inside the coach, the Duke of Ardenne removed his top hat as the dead one and his shabby attendants passed.

'Bless us! Looks like we've another epidemic on our hands!' Philoctetes said.

Clemence could just make out the funeral procession through the thick, fast snowflakes. The crying they could hear came from a creature all in rags who was following behind the box. The coffin must carry her husband and wage-earner, Clemence thought. She watched the bearers pile it onto a cart which already held others, stacked like crates.

A weeping daughter came behind the first woman. A second was keening in Irish. The sound of the mourning-song made Clemence uneasy. She thought of the malnourished tenants who her father, and now her brother too, had turned out into the cold for want of a few pennies' rent.

'You've seen many dead then, Philo?' asked Lysithea.

'Aye! It's an old friend back calling! King Cholera,' the duke said. 'Took a whole family out two days ago from one of the cottages on the estate. All caught it from each other.'

'Yes, I've seen it too,' said Clemence. 'I was delivering food to the village only yesterday. I nursed two I found there with the fever.'

'Oh, Lord! And breathed in the miasma I suppose,' sighed Aunt Lysithea. 'Oh, you and your kind heart, Clemence!'

'Well, I think you're noble, Miss Somerlee,' said the duke.

'Thank you, Philo.'

'And as for airborne infection, Countess,' Philo went on, 'do you know there's quite a modish notion in the medical fraternity that infection is waterborne, not bred through poisonous miasma as we've always believed?'

He rapped on the roof with his cane and called to the driver.

'Alston – see if we cannot find another route to Apsley House. A backstreet if you must. We don't have all night.'

The Ardenne brougham lurched around and retreated the way it had come. Clemence kept her head turned and eyes on the wake, until Lysithea pulled down the blind.

The Queen was to be a guest at the ball they were on their way to so a smattering of snow would stop no-one.

A dance given by the Wellingtons to rejoice for the birth of Victoria's first grandchild… new arrival in Berlin's royal palace for the new year of 1859. Born with an arm crippled after a traumatic and protracted labour, and probably mildly brain-damaged although no-one knew it then – little Wilhelm of Prussia held the future of a continent in his frail baby fingers. A truly winter prince.

Was that shellfire which Clemence thought she could see above the towering cream façade and Corinthian portico of Apsley House? No – a pyrotechnic. Someone was letting off fireworks. Bulbs of light burst in the sky, then passed away in showers of winking silver and violet starlets.

Clemence clutched the blind of the coach window she was peeping out from. As the fireworks went off, her fingers looked as if they were alight with white fire.

'All right, darling?' Lysithea touched her hand.

'The fireworks. They remind me of the shells in the war.'

The young duke laughed.

'I should hope not, Clemence! To the Queen, young Wilhelm is her first bonny grandson. To our two nations England and Prussia – he is supposed to be a beacon of hope and lasting peace! Or so we're told.' Philo raised a teasing eyebrow. 'Don't Wellington's little place evoke kindlier memories than gunfire in the Crimea? It ain't so many years since your début season. Didn't you attend the Waterloo Banquet here that year? Sissy did.'

'Yes... I think so...' said Clemence. 'You seem to remember my début season better than I do, Philo. I didn't believe I'd made much of an impression, really...'

'Ah, no, you had more admirers than you credited, dearest,' Lysithea put in. 'But you had eyes only for your hussar captain!'

'Indeed! And did not notice any other – such as me,' the duke said. 'I was in the throne room the day you were presented, cousin Clemmie. You and sissy was up on the same day. Thought you was a stunner then! And you had a prettier dress than Amathia.' He put his head on one side and smiled at Clemence. 'Quite stole my heart.'

'Your heart, maybe. Not your nose, though, if you'd whiffed my sore feet that night!' she said. 'Standing about in pinching shoes, waiting to be called into the royal presence! In a rather itchy, once-occasion dress which cost enough to feed half the poor of London!'

'You wouldn't have believed you had sore feet, sweet one. Ravishing you looked! I still call to mind that Yew and Quatrefoil stitched on your bodice in all those thousands of diamonds and pink pearls. And that legend picked out in sapphires on the train. What did it say, pray?'

'"*Tempestibus hiemis defendimus*" – the family motto,' supplied the countess.

'Quite,' said the duke.

'And then I was perspiring, too, beneath so many petticoats! Which ladies are not supposed to mention! And unable to visit the water closet!' Clemence gave a shrill giggle. 'You know, Philo, I have become quite foul-mouthed since the two of us became friends! Anyway, what was your court presentation like, Aunt Lizzy?'

'You make me feel my age by mentioning it, chicken!' Lysithea laughed. 'My father said we could have ransomed half the prisoners taken at Trafalgar with what we spent on my dress. I was presented to old Queen Charlotte. The girl before me passed wind as she curtseyed.'

'Imagine going down in history as the débutante who passed wind in front of the Queen,' Philo remarked.

'That's nothing to the thrill Isabella had, though,' said Lysithea. 'When my other niece, Lady Markham, was presented, a crowd of Chartists pelted the carriages with eggs. Yelling "death to the aristocracy!" and such. Bella dined out on the story for months.'

'Hah!' Philo laughed. 'And the lower orders are soon running to us when they want to be kept safe from foreign oppression, and shelter from the winter wind.'

'Undeniably,' said Lysithea. 'That's what the Somerlee motto means of course, Philo. "We shelter you from storms of winter."'

'Does it? Afraid I spent most of my school days smoking behind the sheds,' Philoctetes bragged.

Clemence kept her eyes on the carriages pulling up in the forecourt of Apsley House, and their descending occupants. Blurry forms wrapped against the weather, one and all. You glimpsed their features in firelight as they passed along the colonnade where two torches burned. Now and then – someone she could name.

To be honest, she didn't feel so very well. Nor had the Wellingtons' ball seemed frightfully appealing when Philoctetes had invited her and her aunt to accompany him to it. But Fanny Fanshawe would be there.

Alston the coachman swung open the door. In blew the snow.

'Ready, Clemence?' Lysithea slipped an arm around her shoulder. 'You look very pretty, you know.'

Clemence gave her hand to the coachman and stepped out.

'Do you intend to spend much time in the Lords, Your Grace?' asked Lord Tewksbury over dinner later that evening. He had been a friend of Clemence's father and had accompanied her into the dining-hall.

'Expertise to dabble in politics I don't possess, old fellow!' replied Philoctetes, who had been placed opposite at the table with the elderly Lady Croombe. 'I shall leave the tedious stuff to you chaps in the know. Just spoke to young Kennilworth, you know, who's just come into his title. He asked me what I think of that bounder Mr Lincoln. Should bring back slavery in this country, what, and get some of these good-for-nothing mouchers off the streets. His opinion, not mine! That's the type you're getting in the Lords nowadays, Tewksbury! So, I'll stay well away, methinks!'

Tewksbury gave a harrumphing kind of cough.

'Well, if you do consider attending the Lords, Your Grace, would you be Whig or Tory, do you think?'

'My dear Tewksbury, I believe a wig is something one wears.'

'So do I!' said Tewksbury with a grimace. 'Very wearing.'

That was Philo's second glass of wine. Clemence was keeping watch as she moved a few pieces of fish around her plate to make it look as if she was eating her meal. And his voice was growing louder. Well, if he could damn well please himself, why not she? She waved an empty drinking vessel in the direction of one of the dozens of wigged footmen who were waiting at table.

The gentleman sitting on the other side of Lady Croombe, meanwhile, was talking about the grand opening of the new clock and bell tower they'd built for the Houses of Parliament. He was wondering if His Grace and Miss Somerlee would care to join the party he was getting up to welcome "Big Ben" to the city's landscape.

Clemence sipped and sipped. The clack of cutlery and voices of hundreds of diners was going on all around. The orchestra was playing *Wiener Karneval*.

She cast her gaze the length of the long, long hall. Cerise-coloured wall-hangings, gold-sculptured ceiling, paneling and painting frames. Two Siberian porphyry candelabra stood each a third of the way along the dining-board, which was spread with a white, white cloth, festoons of winter flora, and set with a Meissen porcelain dinner service. Chandelier whose eight points and droplets seemed to engorge as you looked on, like ice crystals hanging from the eaves as the morning sun rose.

Her chaperone, Lysithea, was remote from her, thank Heavens – sitting two silver épergnes away; she could do without Lizzy's worried eye on her. And the overfed sparrow that held half the world in her diminutive talons was a squat, ivory and royal blue splotch in the far, far distance.

'What is your taste in art, Miss Somerlee?' Tewksbury asked after a few mouthfuls of Salmon Coulibiac. 'Only reason I ask… I'm thinking of bidding for a Frith when it is auctioned next month.'

'Oh, I much prefer the Pre-Raphaelites, Your Lordship. And Ingres, and Delacroix, and the coming man Monsieur Manet. Frith paints crowds. Vulgar, and quite threatening, I think. Those great Frenchmen paint mankind as he should be – baring his soul.'

'And in the buff,' said the duke.

Lady Croombe turned from speaking to the person on her other side.

'I believe the countess has just returned from Austria, Miss Somerlee? I trust she found the Emperor well?'

'Oh yes… keeping well as ever, the dear fellow,' Clemence said.

'Myself and Lord Croombe have been travelling on the continent too. But, oh dear, we did find Venice and Sardinia in revolutionary ferment when we stopped there! So much talk of throwing off the Austrian yoke and you cannot imagine what! Did you know, Miss Somerlee…'

Clemence kept one ear open while her eye strayed elsewhere.

Lord Brandon Fanshawe was sitting on the opposite side of the table from her, about six places away.

Clemence's second glass of wine was half finished by now.

Between where she and Brandon sat was one of the branched candelabra. Its sixteen points of light appeared to be reproducing themselves as she tried to blink them into focus… and Mr Darwin, bless him, was right: the new generation was brighter and unspotted. So, this was what being tipsy was like? Hey… she could see what her late Uncle George had seen in it after all.

''Tis a fine vintage, eh, Miss Somerlee?' The duke was waving his own glass towards her.

'I wonder if you are quite well, Miss Somerlee?' came Lord Tewksbury's distant, tinny voice.

'Miss Somerlee is flourishing, sir, flourishing!' Philo shared with her a wicked smile.

The sound of the twittering and music kept booming loud, and then fading. The room and all the creatures in it had become in her eyes a blurry Arctic blizzard haunted with spots of feverish colour. Must be fire somewhere... she was starting to grow warm and feel unwell. Oh, to be out, alone, in the snowstorm...

For the first time Brandon Fanshawe did catch her eye. He at once looked the other way. Lady Croombe was talking about the weather to someone else. Rather loudly.

'...discussed it at length, haven't I, Miss Somerlee?' She focussed on Philoctetes who'd just spoken, and the ghostly doppelganger sitting beside him. 'With your admirable brother Sir Richard?'

She blinked from one Philo to the other.

'Our possible nuptials, Miss Somerlee...?' Philo supplied.

'Are congratulations in order, then, Miss Somerlee?' asked Tewksbury.

'Oh... oh...' Clemence glanced at Fanny again. 'Oh... yes, My Lord! I do very much hope so—'

'Well! There you are, Your Grace!' said Tewksbury, and got on with his dinner.

Lady Croombe was starry-eyed.

'Did I hear correctly, Miss Somerlee? You intend to accept the duke's offer? Oh, how very charming! A wedding! At Westminster, I am sure.'

'Absolutely,' said Philo, eyeing Clemence with a gleaming smile. 'No expense will be spared for this loveliest of brides.'

Lady Croombe returned to her other interlocutor.

'What splendid news I have just heard! Miss Somerlee has...'

Said yes to Philo. So it seemed. With a roomful of witnesses.

She stumbled to her feet. A footman rushed to draw back Miss Somerlee's seat. She stuck a hand on the tabletop. Stop the damn thing rocking so. Wait for the uneven floor to steady itself.

'You are leaving us, Miss Somerlee?' asked His Lordship.

'Do excuse me, Lord Tewksbury…'

Bumped into a chair on her way out…

'I'm so sorry…' Clemence mumbled to its occupant. 'I think I am unwell. I need a little air…'

A lull seemed to fall in the talking. Then started up again, even louder.

She caught an eye here and there which quickly glanced away. Far away at the head of the table, the mousy head of the Queen was straining to see what was going on.

Clemence threw Brandon Fanshawe one final look over her shoulder. He caught her eye… blinked heavily in what looked like embarrassment… and turned his attention to his plate.

See, you fool – I landed a duke. You and your wife will have to call me Your Grace. And go behind me when we go into dinner. So will Amathia – ha, Lizzy too!

She was relieved to reach the nude, marble statue of Napoleon which guarded the stairwell and way out. Two footmen flanked the main entrance, staring unseeingly straight ahead. One opened it for her.

Oh, how wonderful felt the wind.

She held up her face to the blizzard. Flakes melting on her outstretched tongue.

Philoctetes Consett was a scoundrel. And the thought of his sweaty hand inside her drawers made Clemence shudder.

But why not marry Philo, indeed? She would endure his slobbering intimacy twice a week, maybe, when the duty of begetting an heir pressed on him. Would he trouble her otherwise? Hah! Not as long as there were dancing-houses in the Haymarket.

And there was something else, too. The Consetts were Brandon Fanshawe's cousins. His Sussex home Woodmancote neighboured the Consett seat, Kingsmede. They should meet often… At church. Out riding. As guests at Woodmancote…

Oh, what were they all thinking of her back there in Apsley House? Snickering behind their feathered fans? Footmen whispering… passing the word right down to the scullery maids? Clemence couldn't help laughing to herself.

Good Lord, and the tattle that there would be among the ton… how delicious!

My dear, what's this I hear about that Somerlee woman? Engaged to the Duke of Ardenne? Ensnared the poor duke through dark arts – that's all I can surmise. Bewitched, the Somerlees are.

She should be locked away! Of course, the duke's so young and gauche – can he really know what he's doing?

Oh, I'm not so certain, Harriet. I hear he's a bounder! Do you know he danced with my Lucy three times at our ball but failed to make any overtures of marriage to the poor gal? But they're not old blood of course, the Consetts – one can always tell a yahoo dressed in gentleman's weeds.

Clemence began to walk, out of the courtyard gates, away from the light and music of the Duke of Wellington's seat. She'd reclaimed her otter-fur mantle on the way out, but on her hands wore nothing but black lace fingerless mittens, and on her feet satin dancing-shoes. She wound the cloak's edge and lining around her goosepimply arms.

Wheels came crunching through the snow towards her. A Hansom slowed and halted. Down leaned the driver.

'You all right, madam?'

'Yes… yes… don't fear for me. I just need some time alone. To think…'

She glimpsed the fellow's doubtful frown in the light of the cab's lamp. He hesitated. *Go away, just leave me alone.* She only thought the words... but she must have looked fierce: the cabman cracked his whip and travelled onward as fast as he could.

On she carried ... into Piccadilly now. Dancing-shoes kept skidding on the ice where the snow had been cleared. Never been alone in the city before.

She made for one lamp, then the next – only way to pick your path along a pitch-dark London street. You would see quicksilver snowflakes slipping slantwise into the fuzzy aureoles of light – then vanishing again into the blackness.

Past the walking woman rumbled a cart. The horse pulling it snorted a plume of steaming dragon-breath. A tarpaulin covered the vehicle. She could not see the cargo. More poor men's coffins? She had seen whole battalions fall to cholera's celerity in the Crimea: a youthful trooper hallooing louche ballads at breakfast, sweating and febrile come noonday, and laid out by evensong.

She heard the bells ringing ten p.m... footsteps coming close... a beat policeman approaching... *cross the street... avoid him... avoid everyone...*

Did that shadow move? There – in the black ginnel between those two buildings? What if it did? Shadows cannot harm us. Wraiths... that is what shadows are. Ghosts from Balaclava... Aubrey's ghost, James's, all the war dead... *why are you here, safe and well, when we are lost...?*

A flash of silver blade. She let out one startled shriek. Then the form was gone again into the alley.

He'd reached for her windpipe. Cut her throat?

Her hand flew up. Was there blood? *You have your wish, Aubrey, James...*

Where was the blood? Shouldn't a sliced artery be pumping like a burst pipe all over cobbles, wall, her lemon satin crinoline?

No blood… but something had changed, something gone from her neck…

Clemence laughed. Her jewels! Of course. Her necklace was worth more to the shadow someone than her life.

The lamplights seemed to be swaying in her vision. As if they were at a light-ball of their own and doing a sashaying little dance. Or gliding like a ghost-ship slipping into the mist…

But she knew where she was. Recognised St James's Music Hall in Regent Street right before her… came to a concert here once with Aunt Lizzy…

Lord, what were these warm and chilly shivers? Prickling all over… *So hot. An inferno! So thirsty…*

The snowy ground came hurtling up to her.

SEVENTEEN

To these angry waves you are just another bit of flotsam to be battered and tossed and flung wherever their current wills... you have no strength to swim yourself free! You swallow the saltwater as each tsunami overwhelms you! It is just chance if you surface... sometimes the rollers heave you to the world above. Gasp the air – before the waters suck you down again.

I am not alone in the ocean. Others are near and struggling. I feel their hands grab for me... can make out their sea-bruised features in the greenly gloom...

Dear Lord, save us!

Some vanish and do not reappear. Don't let that happen... fight against it, Clemmie... Another man alongside me... I don't know him... yet we cling to each other; but, Ah... over us washes the surf... my friend is gone – spinning, spinning, down, down into the deep.

'Mater?'

Isn't that my mother beckoning me from the Paradise Garden on the far side of the Eardingstowe ha-ha? But she's been dead almost ten years...! How can she be here?

No, it is not my mama. My brother Ivo, rather – he's an ordained vicar now, I remember, and he's coming towards me wearing his clerical robes and dog collar.

Ivo fingers my face. Heavens – his touch is chillier even than the brine! Why, this seawater is not cold at all… but strangely warm.

Another hand strokes my brow. I reach out for this new, friendly limb. I know him now… my brother Richard.

Clemence's eyes fluttered into semi-wakefulness. Leaping firelight filled her vision… *so sore.* In her ears was the sound of sleet rattling against window-glass.

She blinked, and blinked, until her painful sight was able to take in more images. The fire she could see was that in the hearth of her bedroom in Somerlee House, and she was in her own bed there. Her lemon-papered walls and peach-coloured curtains.

Toy Noah's Ark with its dinky wooden animals sitting on the bureau – childhood memento she'd been too reluctant to part with; copy of Danby's *View of the Avon Gorge* hanging on the wall opposite her bed; above it, a framed Daguerreotype of her aunt and Lizzy's late husband the count; Clemence's set of cartes-de-visites spread on the occasional table; watercolour miniatures of her brothers and sisters.

Why… she could barely open her mouth. How incredibly parched she was. When did she last drink?

She turned her aching head on the pillow.

Her sister-in-law was seated by her bedside. And Dickon was perched at the foot.

She saw fatigue in Richard's features. No, not tiredness. He looked as if he had been crying.

Amathia lifted Clemence's hand between both of hers.

'Welcome home, sister dear.'

'I have been ill?' Clemence struggled to croak out the words.

'Oh, a little.' It looked as though Richard's smile took valiant effort. 'Just a wee touch of the cholera. It's the season.'

Her head lolled onto one side.

'We thought we'd lost you!' Amathia pressed her hand tighter. 'Your brother Ivo even gave you last rites.'

'Yes... I think I saw him do it... must have been semi-conscious, I suppose...'

Richard rose, came close and stooped to kiss Clemence's brow... her brother's lips were warm... must have been the fever-inferno which had made the dream-touch seem so cold.

'I'm off to tell Ivo you're back – he's hardly been off his knees, praying. And a message to Aunt Lizzy too – she's spent days by your bedside... she's only retired now to sleep.'

Richard slunk away with bowed head and sluggish gait. Now was not the time to be telling Clemence that four servants had taken the sickness from her; so had Clemence's and Richard's little sister and brother Margaret and John, and they would not be coming back from the sea.

When Richard had gone from the sickroom, Amathia went down to the morning-room. There her brother was waiting, an elbow leaning on the mantelpiece.

'She's very, very weak still,' Amathia told him. 'She'll be a while mending. But out of the woods, I think. Thank the Lord,' she said on a sigh of relief.

'Thank the Lord, indeed!'

'But anyway – well done you, Philo! You managed to charm Clemence. Sounds as if she was quite taken with your pretty attentions at the regatta and the ball.'

The Duke of Ardenne blew out a pleasurable mouthful of cigar smoke.

'Wasn't all pretend, you know, Mathy! She is quite a taking little thing.'

'If you like the milksop type, I suppose! But, then, your taste in women isn't very refined, Philo. Clemence is probably an improvement on the bride you would have chosen otherwise!'

A female servant's voice was heard outside the door. Her footsteps passed quickly by along the corridor. Amathia gave a small gasp. Must not forget this was a Somerlee house. Aldgate had been the easiest place to bring Clemence the night she'd fallen poorly. Loyal bondsmen might be listening at every chink.

Amathia dropped her voice to a murmur.

'Go back to your bachelor hovel, Philo. I'll meet you there in an hour.'

They continued the conversation in the duke's rooms in Mayfair.

'Unless you're adamant you want a big white wedding at Westminster, Philo, then we could have you and Clemmie joined in holy matrimony in just a few days' time, by special licence.' Amathia laid a hand upon his shoulder. 'She needn't even leave her sickroom.'

'I could have done without the flux Lysithea's legacy nearly flowed in on!'

'Really, Philo! If the cholera had carried Clemmie off, she'd have taken her inheritance with her! Look, all we need is the services of some ambitious but penurious clergyman. You could offer him the vacant living on the Ardenne estate, and he shall be evermore grateful to you! No doubt you can think of a couple of persons you could do similar favours for who would act as witnesses?'

Philo raised his eyebrows.

'All sounds rather shady and underhand, Mathy!'

'But perfectly legitimate! Think of all the people who heard her profess her desire to marry you at the ball, Philoctetes – inebriated though she was? No-one would ever believe she was forced against her will!'

'And if she does threaten to make a scene?'

Amathia went to the window-seat and draped herself there. Outside, the storm had not let up. Like teardrops on a human face, the sleet was meandering down the glass to softly settle in the rim of the pane. She could make out the hexagons, octagons and many-pointed stars which formed the crystals. Some had fiery hearts where they caught the light from the lamp which stood on the sill.

'Clemence is a sick woman,' Amathia said. 'Has been since she returned from the war. Maybe even before that... We'd have no trouble from Clemmie if she's shut away in an asylum.'

'If only it was that easy to have someone inconvenient put away! Our loony bins would be overflowing, sissy dear!'

Amathia faced him.

'Dozens can testify to her crazed behaviour on the night of the Wellingtons' ball, from the Queen down to the cabriolet driver and policeman who found her unconscious in the snow!

'It is my understanding, Philo, that the consent of three separate medical personnel is needed for a person to be certified insane. Our papa did a lot – an awful lot – for our Dr Neave, did he not? Dr Neave will do as he's told, I'm sure. Then there's that fool John Hall who was out in the Crimea. That's two for a start. And what of Florence Nightingale herself – greatest heroine of our age? Her opinion will be considered sound, I'm certain of it.'

'What about Lysithea? She might exclude Clemence from her will just to spite me... I know I would!'

'Lizzy's getting on in years. What do you reckon? Sixty-six or seven or so? And I've heard – from Dickon – that Lysithea's been seeing a physician about heart murmurs.'

Philoctetes tossed his spent cigar into the hearth.

'By Jove, sissy, I didn't realise just how little you cared for the family who feed you!' The duke gave a low laugh. 'Papa might have ended up in Newgate as a debtor if it hadn't been for Dickon, you know...'

'I know that! But you think Richard acts out of Christian charity? Or for love of me and thee? Oh, no, Philo! He was after

Papa's title and the money he assumed went with it. I'll never forget the look of anger on Richard's face when he learned there was no money.

'You remember that day Richard raged at Papa, accused him of trickery, hoodwinking him and Heaven knows what else? And it was only two days after that vicious confrontation that our father collapsed and passed away!' Amathia wiped away tears with a shaking hand. 'I blame Richard, Philoctetes, just as surely as if he'd struck a dagger in Papa's heart.'

'Steady on, sissy.'

'Well, I'm angry, Philo! I've tried to be a fond wife to Dickon. Heaven knows I've tried! But he's treated me with nothing but coldness! I've not had one kind word from him or loving look! I've given him love, tenderness, devotion, winning smiles… but I receive, at best, cordial indifference. And yet – just see the affection in those same eyes when he is with Clemmie or Lizzy – even, on one ghastly occasion, his *whore!* Oh, Philoctetes, I'm so miserable!'

'I say, Amathia!' Philoctetes gave an uncomfortable chuckle. 'Can't say Dickon and I have exactly hit if off either, but aren't you, well, overdoing it, what?'

'Oh, yes, of course! One more hysterical, irrational female, aren't I?' Amathia said. 'I don't expect you to believe that a member of your sex could be less than perfect.'

'Now, look here, Amathia…'

'You want the Schwangli legacy, don't you? Well, we can have it, Philo.' Amathia wiped away the last of her tears and smiled. 'To be sure, we shan't have a better opportunity than now – while Clemence is befuddled still, and Richard and the rest of the family, Lizzy included, are distraught over the youngsters' deaths…'

A little gold fetter! Clemence gazes at a ring slipping onto her finger… at Philo smiling down from her bedside, holding her hand… at the young, pale vicar with the prayer book, who looks as if he could do with a good square meal. Are they truly married, then? She is too exhausted to say much. That tide of death which so nearly claimed her is still not far away.

A Black Maria is waiting at the gate of Somerlee House. This man is a warder leading her away to Newgate!

No, that is an undertaker's wagon she can see, down there in the wet street. Someone in the household has died.

But she, however, is going to her bridal chaise… isn't she? Willingly, too. More readily than the thousands of bartered brides through the ages whose raped wombs the aristocracy gestated in. She hasn't been forced. Said 'yay' to Philo of her own will. She's chosen Philoctetes Consett… hasn't she?

1862

Three years later

EIGHTEEN

The passenger called out to the driver to halt the coach.

The large house ahead was half-hidden behind a grove of mature elms and limes. The carriage-sweep leading to the forecourt twisted and turned, and the hummocky ground helped to keep the building out of sight from the lane. The sun shone from behind the grey-tiled roof, and most of the frontage lay in shadow.

Built, perhaps, for some prosperous merchant, alderman or banker circa 1750, and now in other hands. Noisy rooks had colonised the three chimneystacks and gables of the dormer windows. Ivy was creeping over its great chamber.

Most folk who had no business with Dwellan House stayed well away. A lunatic asylum was a place to fear – like a crossroads or gallows tree.

'Drive on,' the visitor called to his coachman.

As the wheels drew him closer, Lord Brandon Fanshawe saw the outbuildings. Former stable-blocks had been converted into patient accommodation. High walls to the rear of each must contain the airing courts.

The superintendent of the asylum came out into the porch as the conveyance neared, to greet a distinguished and titled caller. Brandon alighted beside the steps which led to the house's gabled entrance.

His eyes rose. A look of horror spread across his face. Dr Warburton followed the direction of Brandon's look, above the façade and mullioned windows, to the battlements of the roof.

A woman could be seen pacing there. Her mane of black hair and white nightgown streamed behind her in the wind. In one hand she waved a flambeau. She let out a lupine howl and appeared about to apply the torch to something flammable.

'Good God, man, don't just stand there! Do something!' Brandon cried.

Dr Warburton scowled up at the spectacular figure.

'That's Cora. She only plays her ridiculous Mrs Rochester joke when someone she fancies is due to visit. She must have heard you were coming, My Lord. Take it as a compliment!'

In her room, Clemence took up notepaper, ink and pen.

> "Fifteenth of March, 1862. To my dear husband Philoctetes, Third Duke of Ardenne."

The first of many pauses; her eyes moved to the framed lithograph of his profile which stood on her desk. She only wrote as often as she did because he was good for disgorging vitriol to. Quite an emetic, indeed.

How could she despise Philo? Philo was not the shadowy genius manipulating the shutters and light beams which made the wonder of the magic lantern show. Philoctetes, God rot him, was as much a victim of Amathia's machinations – he'd been pressured to marry where he did not wish.

Little in Clemence's life was certain anymore. Maybe she was to spend the rest of her days within these walls. Or maybe the Russians would invade and free her and all the other inmates. But one thing was sure, definite, ultimate, absolute, unchanging as leaf-fall in autumn – she hated her sister-in-law.

"It is a lovely spring day and I am sad that I am indoors," she wrote.

Ah, yes, cheerless indeed. She gazed around a boudoir brooding under yellowy dimness. The drape was covering the casement, although it was broad daylight. She had not been outside for over three years. Even looking on the hospital grounds from the safe side of the glass gave her collywobbles. But now she peeled back the curtain and managed a peek.

High in the ivy of the building's east wing, her window overlooked Dwellan's parkland. Sunlight sliced through the branches of the elms and limes which stood sentinel at the boundary. Shy rabbits bounded from the spinney onto the bank of the lawn, and back into the shadows. A fan formation of birds was crossing the Quantocks and summit of Will's Neck.

"How well you looked when I saw you most recently, Philo dear. I trust you enjoyed your stay in Marienbad? The mountain air favours you. I so look forward to your next visit."

In fact, that was true. Anything to break the monotony of her days. But when had her husband last called? The month just gone? No – she recalled staff and inmates had been dragging a pine tree into the entrance hall; Philo had slipped in the scuffled snow which had come in too and grumbled about it. Must have been December, then.

'I'm afraid we have Prince Albert to blame for this inconvenience,' she had told him. 'Since he started bringing in a tree at Windsor and decorating it for the festive season, all of fashionable society feels the need to ape this German custom. "Stuff and nonsense, this new fuss over Christmas!" my Uncle

George used to say. In his day, they bothered with May Day and Michaelmas and that's all.'

> "Have you been much to court, dear husband? I fear it must be quite sepulchral with the Queen weltering in her great grief over Prince Albert's death. Gone are the splendid balls we knew, I suppose? I long to hear more of the world. You bring me tidings, Philo."

Clemence laid down her pen. She propped her chin in one hand. She peeped around the curtain again.

The carriage-sweep leading to the road was full of twists and turns, in and out of the wood. That was how they built asylum driveways – to hide the horrid buildings from those on the outside. Actually, Clemence had heard a kind of euphemism for the occupants of an asylum just coming into use: *round the bend.*

> "I must rely on the newspapers for the latest from the world outside. How pleased I am that Italy is to be a united nation at long last, having finally thrown off the Austrian and Bonapartist yoke. I recall the patriot, Signor Garibaldi, visiting London. Ladies took to wearing Garibaldi blousons – it was quite de rigeur that year."

Dwellan was not going to hold her forever, oh, no! Out of here soon she would be. Only a locked cell and the queer, diaphanous barrier of fresh air stopped her.

But it was odd all the same, she thought, that here in Dwellan House's micro-universe warfare did not intrude. Nations did not rise and empires crumble.

> "The world's upheavals pass our tranquil nook by,' Clemence went on in her letter. "It is quite pleasant to sit

with my Aunt Cassandra and the women in the sewing-room, the travails of humankind shut out."

Aunt Cassie. Clemence smiled to herself. Her father's strange sister had been here for almost twenty years. Cassandra lived in a dream-dimension of fairies and magic. Used to walk the mere bank at all hours, and claimed she'd visited Jenny Greenteeth's lair. Believed the dairymaids were plotting to kill her – one of the cows in the dairy herd was sending her messages, so Cassandra said. Prophesied that an elf-prince was coming from the sea to destroy the Somerlees.

Cassie wouldn't ever leave Dwellan House. Nor would she wish to. She'd been here so long it was her home now.

Clemence had been a little girl when they'd put Cassie away. But Clemence loved her aunt and had visited often. How bizarre to now be sharing her incarceration.

> "I don't think they told Cassandra that I'm a patient like her," Clemence wrote. "My poor auntie believes I'm here as her companion! It will be hard on her when they release me.
>
> "Actually, I shall miss quite a few of my friends here. I love the women I talk to in the sewing-room. I tell Betty what it was like nursing soldiers in the Crimea, and Betty tells me what it's like being the Czarina! Oh, and there was one chap who used to say that word 'f**k' in every sentence and swore he could not help it. But Dwellan was short of beds, and the last I heard he was made Ambassador to Belgium.
>
> "Please give my love to Dickon and Mathy when you see them next," she added. The nib gouged deep in the notepaper.

Little could she remember of what had happened three years ago.

She knew she had survived the cholera, which had claimed her beloved brother and sister. While she had lain enfeebled in her sickbed, she and Philoctetes Consett had been married by special licence. She was the Duchess of Ardenne.

Sometime soon after – God knew how long; she had been too befuddled – they had brought her to Dwellan House. A sick woman who needed to be cared for. Who might be a danger to herself and others if not kept behind a locked door. Amathia had even seen to it that Aunt Lysithea was kept away from the asylum and was allowed contact only through correspondence which was vetted first by the superintendent of Dwellan.

And all, Clemence assumed, for the late Juncker von Schwangli's money coffers. Philoctetes was her husband. She had been certified insane. So, her possessions became his. Worse must have been done for lesser fortunes than hers.

And what part in all this had her brother played? He was Amathia's lord and master. He could have done something to thwart her... couldn't he? Yet he hadn't... 'I'm sorry, Clemmie. It's for the best, dearest one...' he had told her, once, sometime. *You toad, Dickon. Under your wife's thumb. And you're making me hate you as much as I do her...*

Clemence drew back the curtain a little further. A few cool sunbeams stole into the attic room.

A team of labourers and male patients was tramping out to the fields for the spring sowing. Two were leading a heavy horse pulling a spike harrow. In the threshing yard, four old-timers were weaving ash stakes and hazel wands into hurdles.

Asylum grounds, tended by professionals and inmates alike, rivalled those of any country house. But there was one conspicuous difference: the gardens were without water features of any sort; Dwellan's needs were met from its water-tower whose pinnacle Clemence could see pointing above the trees. No ornamental lake, reservoir, stream, bridge – nothing except a drinking-fountain or two. Nowhere a patient might be drawn to drown himself.

Behind her, a key was heard grinding in the lock. In bustled a wardress. The woman wore a black gown and white cap. A bunch of jangling keys hung from her girdle. After her followed the superintendent, Dr Warburton.

'Good day to you, Your Grace. And what a fine day it is indeed!'

Was Clemence's cold bath due, maybe? Warburton usually did come in person on such errands to the duchess when he didn't bother with most of Dwellan's inmates. He was a social-climbing yokel. And looked like a prosperous country gentleman. Well, in a way, so he was: must make a profit from the boarding of patients from wealthy families.

'Good afternoon, doctor, Sarah,' said Clemence. 'I have just seen some of my fellows heading into the fields. How content they all looked! I even heard one singing.'

'Ah! Well, you know, Your Grace, we want only what is best for our patients,' Warburton said. 'No-one is here to be punished for their sorry affliction. See the charming gardens, pretty gatehouse, fine trees, peacocks and sheep wandering the grounds? All designed, you see, to induce healing of the soul!'

'Yes... except that few of your patients actually get better, do they, Dr Warburton? My aunt has been here since she was forty years old. She must now be almost sixty.'

'Miss Cassandra was fifty-six last birthday, in fact. Sadly, ailments of the mind are difficult to cure! We can humanely treat the symptoms, but not the underlying causes. And so, Your Grace, how are we feeling today?'

'The same, doctor. A little fatigued perhaps. I am composing a letter to His Grace. I hope I can advise him of the date of my release?' She looked up with a bright smile.

'I will check once I return to my office,' said the doctor with a reassuring nod. She knew what that meant – her warders hadn't set a date. But Clemence would hound them until they did. She was no longer the feeble-wit they had brought here three years ago. She was getting out – preferably by legitimate means.

'I come on other business however, Your Grace,' Warburton continued, 'though no less welcome, I trust. You have a visitor. Lord Fanshawe, no less, is waiting in the parlour.'

'Fanny!'

'He is a friend of you and Sir Richard, I believe?'

'Yes! He was with us in the Crimea.'

'Splendid! Then I'll leave you with Sarah. Let's make you presentable, hey?'

Left alone with the wardress who began to dress her hair, Clemence stared at her dim reflection in the toilet-table mirror. Lord, how the passing seasons were encroaching. When had those silvery strands crept into her hair? She was only twenty-five. Had illness ravaged more than her mind? How sick had she really been? It was, what, seven years since the war ended?

'I am well again, aren't I, Sarah?'

'Better each day, Your Grace,' said the woman as she went to the clothes-press. 'So, let's see you in your prettiest frock for your handsome visitor.'

'He's a family friend! And happily wed. As am I!'

Heaven knew what secrets she might have broadcast, though, during the height of her raving. Maybe the whole of Somerset knew her feelings for Brandon Fanshawe.

Three whole years of her life, the time she had spent here, were beclouded. Minutes stretched to days. Months shrunk to fleeting moments.

Had that really been her… tearing sheets and screaming? Dr Warburton leering over her. He had looked like a snarling ogre with slobbering fangs, stooped back and claws which pawed at her. Well, he was no oil painting anyway… but why had she been so afraid of him? And a harpy-woman in the uniform of a wardress, who was holding Clemence down on the bed as she thrashed to get away?

What was that tiny room they'd shut her in… pink walls, soft as swansdown to the touch, but without windows – just a grill which the harpy's face sometimes glared through?

And the visions and sounds in her mind and head? Screams of dying horses… the precipice of Saupon Hill veering down, down, into the pit of Hell… Lord Lucan with demon's horns grinning up at her… Captain Nolan – a devil jigging through the lava fields towards the River Styx at the head of the valley… and then her fiancé and her lost brother… two dead hussars soothing her brow…

How could it have seemed real? Yet it had, back then. Sebastopol had never fallen, not in her mind.

Clemence fingered her butterfly brooch, turning it over and over and over.

'You're not well, sweetheart. You need to go where you can be looked after…'

Maybe Richard hadn't been wrong. How uneasy that thought made her.

But it was over now, yes, the war was finished – and soon she would be free.

'Lord Fanshawe. How good of you to call! Polly…' She turned to the young maidservant who had escorted her to the visitors' parlour. 'Please bring tea for His Lordship and me.'

When the girl had gone, Brandon turned from looking at the framed landscape hanging over the fireplace, crossed the room, and clasped Clemence's outstretched hand.

'Clemence, my dear.' Brandon raised the hand to his lips. 'How are you?'

'Well enough to wonder why I am still here,' she replied.

The two sat in the fireside chairs, facing each other.

'How are you, Fanny?'

'Oh, never anything wrong with me! I'm in the rudest of health as always.'

'How is Phyllis? Such a beautiful woman.'

'Oh, ravishing still,' Brandon said. 'Though sadly we have not yet been blessed with a family.'

'I am sure God will grant your wish in good time,' she said with her most gracious smile.

Could it be… he was not happy in his marriage? She kept her eyes on the man sitting opposite, searching for anything which might be a sign all was not rosy with him.

Lord – she seized on any morsel and made a starveling's feast of it. The last occasion Brandon had visited, he had mentioned his dislike of the Turkey carpet which Phyllis had chosen for their dressing-room. Clemence had danced to her chamber in the eaves that same evening, glad that all must not be well at Woodmancote. And didn't that mean she must still be mad – more unbalanced than old Jack who had dug up the flowerbeds one night last year and built his version of the Malakoff on Dwellan's lawn, convinced that the Russians were coming?

'Speaking of expectations,' said Brandon, 'Dickon and Mathy have another blessing due in the autumn, you know.'

'Oh, I had not heard! But then, it must have been before Christmas that my brother last visited.'

'You know how awkward it is for him…'

'Oh, don't make excuses for him, Fanny! He is ruled by his wife, and she is the one who put me here.'

'Clemence, my dear… you weren't very well, you must realise that…'

'I'm getting out, though, Brandon… soon I'll be out.'

Clemence rose and went to the window overlooking the parkland. The chestnut boughs were sprouting buds. Cream and yellow daffodils spread across the lawn, rippling in the soft breeze as if an invisible hand had wafted through them. There had been a time when she could not even peep through the glass. Now, at least, she was risking a glimpse or two.

'I cannot remember the last time I went out of doors,' she muttered.

'Why? Why does the outside frighten you so?'

'I don't know!' she said. 'But when I step out, all the world is spinning – closing in as if to smother me, and I cannot breathe...'

'Maybe the air is toxic, then, after all.' Brandon sat back and rested one boot on his other knee.

'But now...' Clemence brightened, 'I want to get out there in the hills again, truly I do! Tomorrow, perhaps, or next week...'

'Well, that's progress.' Brandon propped an elbow on the chair wing, chin cupped in hand, and gazed at her. 'I'm staying at Eardingstowe for a few days,' he told her. 'I managed to coax Caroline out of the nursery. Took her for a sail on the mere.'

'Gosh, Caroline must be almost four now! She won't remember me!'

'Dickon and Amathia cannot tell her where her Aunt Clemmie has gone, of course...'

'If they don't let me out of here soon, Fanny, I'll climb down the ivy and escape!'

'I truly believe you would, Clemence.'

A warder could be seen leading a male patient across the lawn towards the fence which shut off the asylum's fields. Clemence heard chanted lyrics which went something like 'Enjoy yourself! Enjoy yourself! Life is cheery, and our drink is beery!' The patient tapped the warder on the shoulder: 'Don't 'ee get soused on the cider this early, Mr Pennyways, else it'll be the jacket for you, my friend.'

'If you stay a little longer, Brandon,' Clemence said with a smile, 'you'll see the one who insists he's Nelson. He strolls around on the terrace, sweeping the view with a telescope. He's a skinny, little fellow with only one eye and one arm.'

'They've not ill-treated you, have they, Clemence?' Brandon said.

'With my brother the chair of the magistrates' bench which renews Dwellan's licence? I doubt it,' she said.

Yet she frowned. Being locked alone in that strange room. Something vile she was forced to drink. Fastened into something so tight that she could not move arms, legs, or speak? A straightjacket, God forbid. Were these memories… or just fantasies?

'You know,' Brandon said in a low voice, 'Richard suspects the narcotics they give you are hallucinogenic.'

Hmm… now there was a ghastly thought. Were there patients here being fed hallucinogens? So that Warburton could keep them and their fee-paying relatives within his cosy demesne? Would be a nice little earner for him indeed, and none to gainsay him.

Polly came in with the tea tray. Clemence waited until the girl had withdrawn again.

'I'm getting out of here, Fanny! I swear it. They cannot keep me here, not when I'm getting better. And what good will keeping me here do Philo? I'm hardly likely to produce an heir for his precious duchy, am I?'

Brandon fumbled in his pocket and brought out a crumpled note.

'It's from Lizzy.'

Clemence eyed it sadly. She had not seen Lysithea since before they'd brought her to Dwellan. Brandon must have read her thoughts.

'You know she cannot visit, Clemmie. Amathia and Philo gave instructions that she wasn't to be admitted if she was to try.' Brandon handed her the notepaper. 'Lizzy sent it through me so that I could smuggle it in without Warburton seeing it first. So, might be best to burn it when you've read it.'

Clemence scanned the contents. Lysithea was writing from her lands on the continent, from her palace in Pressburg.

'She says she hopes I will be released soon. In the meantime, she will be sending a hamper of treats to Aunt Cassandra. And there will be something for me in the package too. But not to speak a word.'

Clemence lowered the note into her lap and looked up at Brandon.

NINETEEN

The key rattled in the lock. And rattled again. Clemence heard some disgraceful language.

Sarah came in wearing a disgruntled expression. Her first task was to subject the errant lock, which had impeded her ingress, to a savage jab.

'You forgot to lock it again,' Clemence pointed out. 'That's the second time this month. Fortunate, isn't it, that there are three further locked exits between here and freedom, or I could have been wreaking havoc halfway across the county by now.'

'Huh!' snapped the wardress. 'Well, I've come with news for 'ee, Your Grace.'

Clemence had sniffed liquor on the woman's breath not a few times. You never knew – such knowledge could be to Clemence's advantage someday, somehow.

'The panel's finished considering your case.' Sarah drew herself up to her full height, hands clasped before her. 'I'm afraid they've decided you're still too ill to be released. So, it's another year of cold baths for you before they'll again consider letting you out!'

In the hospital grounds, in the shade of the great chestnut, stood an octagonal shelter.

Clemence watched a figure shuffling around the walkway of the freestanding structure, clasping each support as he passed. Old Jack paused, glancing up towards her window. He knew by custom that she was there and observing him; the fellow gave a shy grin and waved. He was settled into a routine which would never change until the not-too-future day when they carried him out of Dwellan in a crate.

So, they were planning to keep her in Dwellan forever too, were they?

Meanwhile, Lysithea it seemed was sending a hamper to Aunt Cassandra… and it would contain something for Clemence too? Not just a nice veal and ham pie, presumably. Something Lysithea couldn't address to Clemence directly through the mail because the superintendent or his staff would see it first. But they'd not bother checking anything sent to Cassie.

The Baronet of Eardingstowe passed among the crowds at the Newmarket races. He spotted Sir Bertrand and stopped to talk.

'You're looking deuced well, old boy,' his friend said. 'Putting on weight where it counts.'

'In the wallet you mean, Bertie.' Richard grinned. He tipped back his top hat with his cane.

'Heard a few rumours about your rising fortunes. This gold mine business, is it?'

'One shouldn't listen to rumours, Bertrand. That's how wars start.' Richard gazed over the shifting sea of racegoers' smart hats: bows, feathers, pins, roses and grey silk. 'What might be these rumours you've heard?'

'Oh, a few acquaintances have been talking about a company called Smoky Mountain. And my nose has traced the source of the scent to you, old fellow. Do tell. What's it all about?'

Richard took Sir Bertrand's arm, and led him to one side.

Both men paused, raising hats as a lady passed close by. Richard spoke into the other man's ear.

'Not to be common knowledge, Bertrand, you understand. In fact, it is indeed a gold mine. One of the richest seams ever found apparently. I'm told Smoky Mountain will be supplying one third of the world's gold needs by 1870!'

'By Jove!' whistled Sir Bertrand. He removed his hat and mopped his brow.

'Well, I'm only telling a select few like yourself. We don't want a rush on shares. Would devalue them.'

'Of course, old boy. Not sure I'd be interested meself. Too much of an old stick-in-the-mud. But, erm… say one did fancy a little flutter, eh?'

'I'm a close associate of the director as it happens. He prefers to keep a low profile. But I suppose I could mention you to him. Mind – it's on the understanding you don't go telling absolutely all the world!'

'Oh, certainly, old boy, certainly! Mum's the word.' Bertrand tapped his nose with a glint in the eye which warmed Richard's heart.

He wandered on through the spectators who were milling near the grandstand. He met an old school friend named Dr Thaxted. The two men raised hats in greeting.

'Fine day, Sir Richard. Had any winnings?'

'Afraid not. Yourself?'

'No. I hear there's a good bet in the three-fifteen, though. The Monster Mirage. Worth a flutter if you want a tip.'

'Thank you,' said Richard. 'Perhaps I shall.'

'I, ahem…' Dr Thaxted hemmed, then peered around to see who might be listening, 'hear you're dealing a few tips yourself lately, Sir Richard?'

'Oh? Where did you hear this whisper?'

'From the Duke of Bedford, in fact. Said you'd sold him

shares in some mining company on the other side of the world, and that they'd returned him a pretty profit. Only, old Bedford said I wasn't to tell anyone. Is there any truth in it, old chap?'

'Well, actually...'

And thus, the afternoon advanced.

Richard admired the gold-tipped cane he'd recently purchased. Four years he'd been the public face of Smoky Mountain – while Cormorant remained in the shadows doing all the real work! And it was a success, by George, it was. Eardingstowe was to have a new wing after all, although he'd put his foot down about having the old hall demolished; Amathia was buying dress after dress after jewelled necklace, and hostessing party after lavish party; his youngest surviving brother, Carswell, was about to join a smart regiment; and Miss Caroline Somerlee would be one of the richest débutantes of her season when she was presented...

So easy to forget, wasn't it, when you were a coming man, that you were a bounder who'd not stood up to your wife and brother-in-law; done nothing to stop your sister being shut away in a nuthouse.

"I hope and pray, Clemmie, that you are found sound of mind as you should be."

The package for her had been hidden in the basket for Cassandra just as Lizzy had said. Clemence read the note in the privacy of her room.

"Please God you are able, therefore, to leave without furtiveness," so wrote Lysithea. *"But if they don't release you, I have furnished you with the means of your escape."*

Escape? Clemence's heart went thumpety-thump. Oh, dear God, she had not seriously thought of that. Only in her dreams.

Was that someone spying on her through the eyehole in the doorway? She listened. No further noise came... the rustling sound must have been mice. She was safe – course, she was – locked in her own cell for the night.

Clemence laid down the letter. Also tucked inside the food hamper had been the parcel which Clemence now turned over and over. A rather large cloth bundle tied with string. It had been snuggled deep inside the crate, beneath hothouse legumes and home-baked starry-gazey pie.

She listened for footfalls on the stone corridors or stairs. No, all was silent. In the grounds an owl hooted; the church bell rang the hour of eleven.

Clemence pulled and pulled at the string, fretting to loosen the knot, and at last set frustrated teeth to it. Of course, they'd not let inmates have anything as convenient as blades in their rooms.

Out from the goody bag tumbled a garment of some sort. Plain, grey homespun cloth. Not one of Lysithea's cast-offs, then.

Clemence unfolded and spread it across the bed. It looked like the uniform of an asylum wardress. Now what the… a girdle and white cap to go with it?

Next, Clemence took out from the package a bottle of diaphanous liquor. She held it up to the light. *No – don't recognise it.*

She slumped onto the mattress, turning the bottle over and over.

How could she escape? She couldn't even get through the front door, let alone shimmy down the ivy. *What are you asking of me, Lysithea?*

She took up her aunt's letter again. *No! This is absurd. I'd be caught before I got to the gatehouse. Oh, Lizzy, how could you ask something so beyond me?* Breathless, she sank her head in her hands.

Someone is coming… sweep this pirate hoard beneath the bed…

No, not footsteps. Only the scurry of mice again.

She laid a hand on her chest until the pounding slowed.

Clemence stared at Lizzy's note for a long moment. It was almost glowing, the words seeming to burn on the page.

"This wardress of whom you have written – Sarah – she of the slack habits and a penchant for a tipple – you should invite her to stay with you one evening after she comes off duty. In the bottle is a Slovakian delicacy called slivovica. Believe me, two glasses of this stuff and Sarah, too, will be out with the fairies.

"You'll be able to relieve her of her ring of keys, won't you, Clemmie? And in your wardress's uniform make your way? Fashion your hair in similar style to hers. Anyone looking on will see Sarah, won't they, on her way home for the evening?

"I have opened an account at Laine and Potterton's bank in Taunton. It is a small country bank, with no previous business with Somerlees, Consetts or Schwanglis. The account is unlikely, therefore, to be traced to either of us. It is in the name of Mary Carswell. The codeword you should use to access the funds which I shall deposit there is 'Greenteeth'.

"You will be a wanted woman, of course – a lunatic at large – and the constabulary will be on the lookout. Ergo, you should draw funds as soon as you are able and purchase new garments.

"You should then travel by train to London. There, in the great, wide metropolis, you can safely disappear.

"I have also opened an account in the same name at Mr Almond's bank on Little Wild Street. On the first of each month, I shall make there a deposit of one hundred pounds. These funds will keep you in board and lodging, until you feel ready to quit the country. Then make your way to my home in Geneva.

"Of course, Clemmie, you cannot go to Somerlee House or to anyone of your acquaintance.

"The next time I hear of you, then, will be either a joyful communication telling me Dr Warburton and his panel have certified you sane and you are getting out legitimately; or else in the newspapers – as the duchess on the run."

'They'll never let me out, will they?' said Clemence. She was sitting in the window-seat, peeping out at the new morning.

'Oh, don't 'ee get upset, Your Grace!' Sarah pinched Clemence's chin. 'You're not well. If Dr Warburton says you'd not be able to cope in the nasty world outside, then he's only thinkin' of your welfare. We want to make 'ee better, dearie, and the doctor thinks you're not, yet.'

'I see.' Yes, Clemence certainly did. Philo must be paying high fees to keep his wife in relative comfort here. 'Sarah – you're my friend, aren't you?'

'Course I am, Your Grace. Here to look after 'ee, you know that.'

Clemence drew in a deep breath.

'You know my aunt, the countess, sent some dainties in a hamper to Miss Cassandra yesterday? There's the most delicious starry-gazey pie and apricot tartlet. How would you like to try a slice or two?' *No going back, then. Let's cross that dratted Rubicon.*

'Ooh, very nice I'm sure, Your Grace. But you know Dr Warburton's rules…'

'Yes, I know,' Clemence purred. 'But how about after you've come off duty?' She parted her lips in the kind of grin shared between conspirators. 'Listen – I know this is probably against your rules too, really… but it really is a very delicious pie, baked by my aunt's French chef?' Sarah looked as if she was about to start salivating. 'Why don't you stop by my room after you come off duty tonight? We can share a little feast! And we can have a good talk too, just the two of us, eh?'

'Well... I'd like to, Your Grace. But we're not supposed to fraternise with patients, you know that...'

'Didn't you say you'd a sister who was struggling to find a place in service? Well, I know of a vacancy at Kingsmede...'

'Well, Your Grace...' The woman cast a nervous look behind her to see if they might be overheard. 'All right then, Your Grace...'

Sarah grunted a few times. Her chin settled onto her chest. She slumped into a snore.

The wardress was sitting upright on her patient's mattress, head lolling on one side as she'd dropped off to sleep.

Clemence crept up close. She checked for signs of lingering alertness. Then she gently lifted the feet and ankles in their spring-heeled boots and eased them up onto the bed. She settled Sarah into a lying-down position.

Sarah curled herself into a contented slumber. She slipped an arm around Clemence's pillow. In her sleep, she licked the last blobs of Lysithea's blackberry jam from her lips. God bless the Slovaks. Not for hours would the woman wake.

Clemence fished out the uniform and white coif from where she'd stashed them behind the cupboard and got dressed.

Would she pass for the wardress – hair gathered beneath the cap, girdle clinking with Sarah's keys? Sarah was older than Clemence, but not so much so that it should be obvious at a distance. And Sarah's colouring was fair, like Clemence's.

But what had not occurred to Lysithea, Clemence thought, was that some – in fact most – females were better padded than her niece.

It's now or never, though.

Clemence peeled back the curtain. A few spots of rain dotted the window glass. Blackness hid the lawns. The great chestnut was just a shadowy shape. She could hear its branches creaking in the wind.

Back to Sarah sleeping on her bed she looked.

The wardress would be found with liquor on her breath, snoozing in the bedroom of a patient who had absconded from under her nose. Whatever the outcome of Clemence's flight, this poor woman faced being bounced from the heights of Will's Neck. A shame – Sarah didn't deserve that. But losers there must sadly be.

'Sleep and dream, Sarah, and thanks for everything!'

Clemence stooped, and kissed the sleeper's brow, before sliding the keys and their ring off her girdle.

Sarah had left the cell door unlocked. Out into the passage Clemence peeped. Empty and quiet.

There were four cells and two washrooms on this floor. It had housed servant accommodation when Dwellan had been a private residence. You couldn't hear the screams from the isolation cells here – best rooms in the building, therefore. The four wealthiest women patients currently in residence occupied them.

Clemence listened at the door of her neighbour Mrs Buxomley, wife of a former mayor of Taunton; she was in colloquy with her dead husband and wouldn't trouble the escapee.

Clemence crept down the winder staircase. Around the bend flickered a nightlight. Looming ahead was the first barred portcullis between her and liberty.

Five keys dangled from the iron ring. No way of knowing which would unbar her way here. Just try each. The first which Clemence tested rattled, and wouldn't go in.

Slow down, ticker, do. Someone will hear you.

The second key she slotted in did it. She pulled back the door she'd unlocked and investigated the corridor on the level below her own. All the cell doors which lined the passage were shut fast.

Clemence carried on down the stairwell. At ground level, the second blockade faced her. Three fumbling attempts with the keys before she could progress.

Here was where she might meet someone. Night warders on the prowl. Domestic staff coming and going from the kitchen and laundry in the basement. What if someone stopped the woman they believed to be Sarah with a 'Oh, Miss Cummings, did 'ee sign the requisition I left for 'ee earlier?' knowledge of whose contents Clemence could not bluff?

Just march bossily should someone emerge from a door and see you.

In the rooms she was now passing the poorest female patients were housed. These souls had no families who could afford to pay fees, and the asylum treated them as such. Definitely don't want to rouse any of them. Clemence walked on the balls of her feet to prevent her heels clacking on the tiles. Many would recognise her, for sure; they had more sense than the staff.

She paused only at Betty's door. There, she whispered a 'God bless, darling.'

Clemence reached the bend in the corridor which led into the entrance hall. The patterned, marble tiles shone with an eerie glow. Potted indoor greenery cast deep shadows. She had not been here alone before, after sundown.

Oh, God... the huge main door. How had she done it the night of the village fire? God knew... but she did recall that she'd roused the whole blessed household in so doing.

Dire necessity must have pricked her out into the vacuum that night; a current zapping through her brain that said 'get your unmentionable rear portions out, woman, or lives will be lost.'

She was passing a curtain which draped a small alcove.

A hand touched her shoulder.

TWENTY

Ah, oh my dear God...
    Her keys fell to the tiles with the loudest clatter in the universe. She clutched her thumping heart.

Not a hand... just had seemed so in her shock. Instead, a small woolly paw.

With trembling fingers, she stroked her discoverer who was behind the curtain, sitting on the sill at shoulder height.

'Sorry, puss, I have nothing for you. No treats. But if you don't give me away, you varmint, I promise I'll send you a whole swordfish from Lake Geneva!'

She stood still and listened. No footsteps were scuttling in the direction of the rattling din. One of the inmates in the passage behind had started shouting, though – thank God. The disturber of the peace should draw away any attention.

Now for that last humungous foe – outdoors.

Holy Heaven, footsteps... coming this way...

The door of the reception room swung open. Forth came a maid bearing a brush and pan. Clemence slipped into the shadow cast by the nearby potted fern.

Not, though, before the girl had caught sight of the other woman. The newcomer halted in surprise.

'Miss Cummings?' she said. 'What's 'ee doin' 'ere so late of an evening?'

Clemence didn't know all the staff who worked here; but this one's name she knew... thank Heavens.

'Trouble on the first floor, Mabel, thas what,' Clemence said in Sarah's Somerset speech. 'Attempted 'anging! 'Ad to stay with the old girl, didn't I! But it don't concern 'ee, my girl, so you be on your way now. And goodnight to 'ee.'

'Night, Miss Cummings.'

The maid went, in the direction of the noisy wall banger.

Just go now, while your heart's still a-thump. Don't think about it. Just go. Think of puss sticking his claws in your backside.

She took up the keys. Fumbled and fumbled. Not that one. That was for the first-floor landing. And this fat silver one she'd already ruled out – had seen Sarah use it to open her own door; must be the master-key for the cells.

That one. Don't recognise that one. Go in, key, go in. You do fit, you do.

The key slotted in... and clicked a revolution. *Please stop shaking, hands. Or I'll not get the key out again.*

The hall clock ticked twenty times or more in the period it took to prise the door ajar. Clemence peered around the barrier. The forecourt veered away into darkness beyond the light shed by the porch lamp.

From between the clouds, a monstrous moon radiated beams which were painful to her eye. Like a phalanx pelting out lethal javelins left, right, above, below. The vast and spectacular outside loomed and trembled.

If she closed her eyes and took a deep breath... the worst would be over.

Clemence was round the first two twists in the drive before she paused, hands on knees, taking jagged breaths. When her breathing slowed, she raised her head.

The great ivy-clad frontage of Dwellan House was behind

her. Ah, the rain. Nothing but a drizzle, in truth. But how long since she'd last felt rainfall on her face?

The moon was now playing grandma's footsteps behind the rack of shower clouds. But it was keeping its cold distance. Not jigging across the heavens or zooming down on her. No seismic upheaval shook the earth below. She was outside, out of doors… free.

Clemence gave a low cry of pleasure. She turned around on the spot. Yes, it was she who was in control. Not the whirligig universe which had always stopped her when she'd tried to go out of doors before.

She looked up at the building. She worked out which her window must be… never seen it from outside, of course – one of the dormers in the roof. The glow from the lamp was as she'd left it. Sarah must be sleeping soundly where she'd left her.

Three other windows had light behind them. The hour was between ten and eleven. Those patients with lights on must be sitting up, reading. Might glance out at any moment and wonder what Sarah Cummings was doing – loitering in the drive, getting soaked like a gormless mommet.

Yes, the rain. Some sort of covering had not occurred in the flash decision to go ahead with her flight. Clemence didn't possess any kind of outdoor wear, for obvious reasons. Did Sarah have a coat or cloak in a closet back in the house? Perhaps the last of the keys gave access.

But Clemence hadn't time. She must put as much distance between herself and Dwellan before her absence was discovered. Chances were that wouldn't be before breakfast. Sarah lived alone – no-one to report her missing. Still, if there really were an attempted topping, or someone else chose this same evening to be on their way, the night warders might inspect the cells.

Clemence cleared the remaining asylum buildings – outhouses where the last of the patient accommodation was found. Once she'd rounded the bend and entered the copse, the final lit window vanished behind her.

On the further side of the trees, the gatehouse stood in darkness. Sam Ruby the gatekeeper went off duty when the main doors of the hospital were sealed for the night.

Already Clemence was shivering. She might have dismissed as luxuries a coat and preferably umbrella too. But all her aunt's carefully-laid plans would come to naught if Clemence took the pneumonia before she reached Taunton.

This last key… might it be worth just a try? The gatekeeper might have something she could use, such as a coat…

The key fit, and the little door let her in. Now why would Sarah need a key to this outhouse? Might she and Sam Ruby have been keeping trysts here? Time for that mystery later.

It also occurred in that moment that with the fat silver master-key in her possession, she could have freed the whole kit and caboodle. Somerset would have been overrun with self-proclaimed Kings of the Netherworld by morning. Moreover, the chaos and confusion would have speeded her own departure undetected. Too late now.

By the intermittent shine of her new ally in the sky, Clemence explored the gatekeeper's small kingdom. The silver shimmers fell on a mahogany bureau. Clemence pulled open a few drawers. She made out some tools, a paper file of some kind, and in the bottom drawer three bottles of cider. Well, well. If her escape failed and she was bustled back to face a spell in the punishment block, at least she now had scope for blackmail.

A second room lay beyond a further door. Clemence went through. A tallboy stood against the far wall. She dragged it open.

There hung a black or navy sinfonia. Clemence ran her fingers over the waterproof silk. She put the coat on over her damp vestments. The garment was masculine and could shelter another person beside herself in its generous folds. But right then it was the loveliest coat in the world.

Once out of the gate and in the lane, Clemence picked up pace. She stumbled over ruts, unseen in the dark, which pitted the track.

Only a minute away from Dwellan House, she stopped at a stile. She set a steadying hand on the damp wood. Her heart was pounding again. And that gave her pause.

The cholera had weakened the vessels of her organ. She'd been warned not to excite or exhaust herself. Likely she had done both, many times, in Dwellan – rebelling against the straightjacket and isolation cell.

But she had not been ill since the cholera. So, did she have something to thank Dwellan for? Had rest, convalescence and wholesome food restored bodily well being whatever it had not done for her sanity?

When her flutters settled, she went on her way.

A wagon trundled up from behind. The driver leaned down to the walking woman.

'I can take 'ee as far as Cothelstone, maidy – '

She peered up at the carter's kindly, moonlit face. No – decline she must. What if he recognised her uniform, and knew Dwellan and its staff?

Where would she sleep? In a barn, she supposed. Wrong time of year for a convenient hayrick. She'd not get all the way to Taunton without at least a few hours' repose. She had no money for a room in an inn; in any case, an innkeeper might be a wee suspicious of a female tramp, wearing a man's coat, whose trajectory of travel led alarmingly back Dwellan House-way. No, must find a barn or shepherd's hut.

Clemence spied through the trees the lights of a homestead or farm. She set her feet that way. Please let there be a lonesome outhouse of some kind. One bark of a hostile dog, however, sent her back to the lane.

The moon had gone entirely now. The rain was growing heavier.
Curses. Slime squelched as her foot sank in a puddle. Clemence hobbled to the hedgerow to drain her footwear.
Voices and a girl's laughter came floating her way from around the hedge. She peeped into the field which lay beyond. She could make out the shape of a great tree. From there came the human sounds. A pair walking-out during an April shower? A smile came to Clemence's lips, only to freeze there.
She was twenty-five and had never known a sweetheart's embrace.
Now she might never – bound to Philoctetes Consett as she was, who had married her for her money. She could not see him again anyway; he'd send her back to the nuthouse. The lowliest of her brother's tenants possessed something she did not... love. And was it not worth more than all Eardingstowe? This country cottar and his sweetheart canoodling as they sheltered beneath the boughs were richer than the duchess.
Her mind went back to the battlefield, and the wounded Cossack. At the time, his injuries had been all that troubled her. But the image pricked her now of peeling back his coatee, her fingertips brushing the bare flesh and downy hair not far from the lacings of his trousers, and the skeletal and muscular contours of the abdomen.
Clemence struggled into her wet shoe.
She picked her way around the slime pool and tramped onward.
Lights clustered in the dip around the next bend. A hamlet was approaching.
Out of the dimness, the shape of a church spire took form. Also, the brighter lights of a tavern. As she drew nearer the

drinking-hole, she could hear a tune piped on accordion and flute. *The Barley Mow* read the swinging, creaking signboard.

Clemence kept to the further side of the road, out of range of the beams of light which reached from the interior. She followed the small hurdle fence of the first homestead in the village. Had she heard the clink of a horse's bridle?

She peered into the blackness ahead.

A horse and wagon stood in the shadows. There was no sign of any human aboard. Closer she crept. On the side of the dray she discerned a legend: *Timothy Maybold, Maltster.* The horse was a heavy draught animal with shaggy hooves. Clemence rubbed his forelock.

'Where's your master, then? Taking the waters in *The Barley Mow* before heading home to a no-doubt long-suffering spouse?'

Clemence stepped back to survey the cart. The malt merchant must have deposited his wares for the day. The rear was empty of all but a few piles of sacking and discarded rope.

Who would suffer if Clemence took the dray? The maltster might have to walk home tonight. But if she abandoned the vehicle in town, it would surely make its way back to him when he reported the loss. It had his name on it. So, he'd not lose his livelihood, would he?

By all that was sacred… what had she done? Where would she go? What could she do… alone out in the terrifying universe? Lizzy was her only friend… But she was a continent away. Fanny… if only she could go to Brandon… No, he was with Dickon and Mathy. There was no-one, no-one, anywhere, who was on Clemmie's side.

Taunton Vale spread before her below the brow. Spectral spires and roofs jutted from the low-lying daybreak mist. Clemence thought of the masts of the dead ships sticking up from the surface in Sebastopol harbour.

Why not just slink back to Dwellan House? There she'd be looked after for the rest of her days. They were kind enough, if you did as you were told.

It wasn't yet fully dawn. The earliest pinkish rays of morning were streaking the sky, bird song just starting to be heard. She had left the tradesman's wagon, horse munching away, by the wayside and meant to go the final half a mile into the township on foot.

What if they had already found her gone at Dwellan? And were scouring the land around about? Full well she knew what befell recaptured escapees… God, don't think of it.

Ahead, crossing her way, glinted the River Tone. Within Taunton, the bells of St Mary Magdalene's church could be heard chiming the hour of five. She could see the castle; last time she had been there was for the Lord Sheriff's Ball four years ago… or was it five? She'd come to the shire town in her finery with Richard and Amathia as a member of one of Somerset's leading families.

She gazed around at the grassy banks, snowdrops and wood anemones growing there. The gentle breeze felt as if it might knock her down. It was so strange.

She was right to fear the outdoors. So many predators waiting to do you harm. On all sides. She could feel them… eyes watching from the hedgerows… She might not be reeling, the world spinning around her, great hands clasping her throat and pressing, pressing, pressing… but right she was to be afraid. So right. *Please let me back indoors, away from the poisonous air…*

But she couldn't return. She knew what they would do to her if she did. And did she want to in her heart…?

The Roman Ram's Horn Bridge came within sight – entrance to Taunton. The skin of Clemence's feet was sore by now. The soles of her indoor shoes must be wearing away. But she broke into an almost-trot.

She sat upon the riverbank. The reflection she could see in the water showed a woman who'd not slept – bruising eye sockets; strands of sweaty hair coming loose from the topknot she'd fastened under her wardress's cap.

Could she take a few hours' sleep in the parkland which surrounded the church? No – cannot risk being taken up by the constabulary for vagrancy after she'd come this far. Just wait until the shops and bank opened. Only a few more hours. Just a few hours more to wait.

Clemence listened to the sounds of the community coming to life. Hooves on cobbles. Clink of a blacksmith's hammer on anvil. Earliest calls of a milkmaid in the street behind the closest houses.

The bells struck seven. Minutes seemed stretched to hours. She was counting. Willing the hour to reach eight, and then nine.

'Is all fair with 'ee, maidy?'

Clemence had been staring into the drifting water. She jumped. The words came from right behind her.

'I was wonderin' if you might be lost, maidy?'

The burly, grizzled figure wore an apron and carried a basket over his arm. He was the muffin man who she'd heard calling his wares around the streets for the last half hour.

'I'm not lost, sir… only waiting for someone,' Clemence said. Calling a tradesman 'sir' indeed; if only Amathia were here to hear it.

'You look as if you've had a rough night, maidy. Here! Let me give 'ee a morsel of my bakery's finest. And no need for payin'. 'Tis only what the Good Lord would have me do.' The man handed her a crusty roll of soft bread.

In Hammet Street she found the tiny bank. Only half an hour to go now before it would open. She paced the thoroughfare from

St Mary Magdalen's to castle and back with a fresh spring in her aching step.

On her third trip up and down the street, she paused outside a rather dingy premise a few doors from Laine and Potterton's. Three globes hung above the shop's entrance. Not surprising she'd never noticed it when she'd been in town before. What in blazes would a Somerlee want with a jerry shop?

Just as the rays of the sun were furling above the crenellated battlements of the castle – a thought struck her. She must do something about her clothes. Back at Dwellan, her flight would be discovered around about now. That servant she'd bumped into would be remembering a woman she'd erroneously believed to be Sarah – wearing a wardress's uniform.

Clemence plucked up the hem of her skirt and took a good look at it. Not much soiling despite the night's adventure. A few mud splashes, and a small rip from when she'd clambered into the maltster's wagon.

In London since the Great Exhibition, there were warehouses where you could buy readymade clothes and all accessories under one roof. But a country town had not caught up. In Taunton, you must still visit the draper first for the material, then the mantuamaker to have the frock made up, milliner and parasol shop separately. She could afford these once she drew funds from Mr Laine and Mr Potterton. And there were many shops which Clemence had never patronised – where she'd not be recognised.

But they'd take a week to make up any dress she ordered. She needed to shed the asylum gear now.

Her eyes went back to the premise with the globes above the door. Yes, whatever ghastly raiment Mr Peabody the Pawnbroker could furnish her with would be *haute couture* as far as Clemence was concerned.

Oh, why won't those minute hands on the church clock turn a little faster?

She paced once more as far as the gates of the church.

The town centre was coming alive now. A flock of geese was honking its way towards the market, drover following. Three elderly women passed Clemence on their way to matins at the church. She was attracting the odd glance or two – stalking the street the way she was.

'Hoy! You! Stop where you are!'

Clemence's heartbeat sped into overdrive. The shout had come from behind her. Warily, she turned around.

A policeman was there – some thirty paces away.

'Don't move!' the constable bellowed. 'I want a word with 'ee!'

A jeweller and his lad, pulling down their awning ready for opening time, stopped what they were doing, and looked. The churchgoers turned Clemence's way, too.

Clemence stood frozen to the spot.

The policeman broke into a run, truncheon raised.

She shut her eyes and prayed to whoever might be listening. A whoosh of air whipped past, knocking her sideways.

Clemence staggered against the pawnbroker's railings. She steadied herself, hand over her poor ticker.

The policeman stopped his dash for one moment, turned to Clemence with a regretful look, touched the rim of his helmet, said 'sorry, madam' to her, and in one instant was back on the chase.

Clemence just caught sight of the cheeky-faced young gonoph disappearing behind the church wall, waving the gentleman's silk fogle he must have pickpocketed.

TWENTY-ONE

Fleet. Farnborough. Deepcut. Names of unknown towns and villages. But each one chugging her nearer the metropolis.

'How much further, ma?'

'About ten more stops, I fink, an' we'll be at Waterloo Bridge, Billy.'

Clemence silently thanked the snot-faced terror who'd asked his parent the question which she, too, had wanted an answer to.

At each halt on the Exeter to Bristol line, her heart had thumped. Would there be lunatic-catchers and police waiting on the platform? Now aboard the Great Western and heading eastwards, each station inched her closer to London's sweet-smelling bowery vale where she ought to be safe.

In Mr Laine's office in Taunton, she'd mumbled 'Greenteeth,' and then prayed. Might he enquire whether she had, perhaps, just escaped from Dwellan House? But no – the banker had at once disappeared, and then returned with a sum of money.

What a brainwave she'd then had: to go by Parliamentary train – the government's budget transport for scumbag third class passengers. She could have afforded fifty shillings for a first-class ticket. But, no… enlightenment moment! She must be under pursuit by now; they'd *expect* Her Grace the Duchess of

Ardenne to travel first class, wouldn't they? Never look for her on the Parliamentary train with the pond-life, would they, oh, no.

Brilliant, Clemmie. *She didn't think.* Now she was stuck in a chug-along without lavatories or upholstery on the seats, which stopped at every piffling country station, sharing a carriage with a snoring chap who looked like a publican, a carter with his family of eight, which included a suckling infant and youngsters who chased each other under the seats, a surly fellow with grimy hands and a smudgy face – possibly a chimneysweep – and, sitting opposite her, a young man wearing a billycock hat who she thought might be an apprentice draughtsman or articled clerk; he'd spoken to the guard in the accent of Bethnal Green which Clemence was used to hearing from street-vendors… and who'd had his smouldering eye on her ever since he'd boarded at Andover.

She should be so censorious. In her grey wool gown from the pawn shop, which had been stitched to clothe a larger dame than herself, side-spring boots, straw hat and patched shawl, the apprentice-type person looked her social superior.

'Down't 'ee disturb that lady and gen'lman, Billy,' the woman warned the little nightmare, who was clambering behind first Clemence's seat then her admirer's.

'I don't mind, ma'am, truly I don't,' Clemence said in her Somerset accent. 'He reminds me of a brother of mine who was a real rascal at that age, always in scrapes. Sadly, I have since lost him. Died at Balaclava fighting Johnny Rusky, he did.'

She'd be worse off if she changed carriages; a pack of larrikins occupied the one on the other side of the corridor. The devil's locomotives had been around for two decades by now, but she knew some older people who'd yet to risk a voyage aboard one; she could see their point.

'Looks as if the rain ain't keepin' orf,' said Bethnal Green, surveying the vista outside. His gaze returned to Clemence.

'Have you a conveyance awaitin' at Waterloo Bridge, ma'am? I should be glad to share mine to where'er it is you is heading.'

Clemence bestowed a gracious nod of the head.

'I am much obliged, sir. But my husband will be waiting with the carriage. Dingy thing it is,' she added with a conspirator's smile. 'I've told him, I have, "Theo, you could have bought us a smart barouche with the prize money you won when you became Middlesex County heavyweight champion." But would he listen? Oh, dear me, no!'

She enjoyed the corridor view a trifle better for that.

What if her husband really was waiting at the station, though? He could be. It must now be eleven or twelve hours since they'd have found her gone from Dwellan.

A constable had been standing on the platform back at Taunton. He had been looking her way... she felt sure he had been. Had he taken a step toward her as she stepped aboard the train? Couldn't be sure... saw no more of him... she'd just huddled in a corner of the compartment all the way to Exeter.

But Philo or Richard could have been telegraphed, couldn't they? And advised that she'd bought a London ticket?

The Brunswick-green locomotive juddered at last into Waterloo Bridge Station, and sat there, hissing.

Clemence let the little tyke and his family scream and bustle their way out first. *Get out in the midst of the company. Less conspicuous. And keep my head down. Slip in between them and Bethnal Green – even if it does mean his pinching my backside.* She might pass along the platform unnoticed then. If there was someone waiting. *Was there?*

Oh, dear sweet God, yes... there *was* a policeman. Clemence could see him... standing beside the barrier at the platform ticket office. He held a truncheon behind his back. It dangled down between his spread legs – to young Billy's amusement.

The policeman's eyes were following the mass who'd got off the train. He *was* looking for someone among the crowd. He was. *Dear Father, what shall I do?*

She kept her face averted. Stared at the track and steaming side of the train. *But he is looking at me! He is – I know it.*

Could she slip her arm through Bethnal Green's? Make like they were man and wife? It was a lone woman Warburton's hounds would be seeking.

But, ah! Over by the arch which led into the central station was a vendor wafting editions of *The Illustrated London News*. Oh, God – the press. Yes, the story of the mad duchess's flight might be in the newspapers by now.

Meanwhile, the splotch of humanity shuffled its way towards the exit. The policeman was only two feet away. His eyes were boring into her. Her heartbeat sounded like the fast, measured clickety-click of wheel-on-track which she could almost still hear inside her skull. *Wasn't* looking at anyone else. No, he was not! Staring straight at *her*. Only her.

She kept her head right down as she drew level with the policeman.

A smacking-kiss kind of noise came her way. Clemence jumped as her left buttock was pinched. But it wasn't Bethnal Green who'd done it... he was busy talking to the ticket collector.

For a few moments she was stupefied... stood there, mouth agape... until dulcet tones somewhere to her rear barked out 'Oy! Get a bleedin' move on, will'yer, missus?'

The ticket-man was holding a palm under her nose – stern expression in his eye.

The policeman had pinched her bottom.

Clemence pushed her way through her fellow passengers, dashed through the arch without glancing at the headline on the newspaper billboard, bumped into someone, mumbled an apology but didn't stop... out through the station entrance into the open.

Why didn't she take his number or something? Grrrr... Just wait until next time she was dining with the Chief Commissioner...

She leaned a hand on the damp, mossy stone of the great doorway arch. Someone collided with her, called her a name... she only remembered later. Right now... she was gasping for breath.

Next time she was dining with... oh, no, Clemmie, there would be no next time. A lunatic at large was she. If she was caught she would never leave Dwellan again – never, ever. As an escapee she'd be deprived even of the small liberties she'd enjoyed before.

She raised her eyes to the wide yonder. Before her lay the expanse of the capital. The Thames glinting with sunlight. St Paul's and the rooftops and chimneystacks of Lambeth.

Even if she *wasn't* apprehended she was scarcely better off... a fugitive. She'd never dine in polite circles again. Cut off she was. Severed from all she had ever known... family, friends... all on the far bank of the river which, for her, no bridge crossed.

She stood up straight... and saw blobs of yellow wetness on the ground beneath her. She'd thrown up? But this couldn't be the outdoor-sickness back... not now, when she'd come so far? That old familiar carousel was not spinning her round and round... *I can breathe. I'm not suffocating. But I'm sweating... sweating... why?*

'You needin' a shove, lady?'

She spun around as the words were spoken right behind her. A spotty youth in a filthy frock coat and stovepipe hat was leering at her.

'I can take you to the cigar-divan where they sells it,' he went on. 'For a farving for me trouble.'

What on earth was the specimen talking about? Better not give her ignorance away, though. He was, presumably, speaking the *lingua franca* of the locale which it might seem suspicious she did not know.

'I don't need a… shove. I'm new in town from the country and I'm a trifle lost.' *Take a gamble? Why not?* 'You know of any lodgin's around 'ere?'

'There's Vaudrey's Nethersken if you likes, missus. Or the spike, of course. Most of us prefers it 'ere, though, 'neaf the railway arches. But if you fancies Vaudrey's… it's threepence a night.'

That was a point, though. Was her money intact? It was all she had to get her to Mr Almond's bank. Might she have been robbed during that squash to get off the platform? She'd hidden her reticule beneath her skirt, dangling from the waistband… thank the Lord, she could feel it there still.

'But I can see you's definitely needing a shove, lady,' said the lad with the unpleasant smile. 'Ain't had one and yer due, ain't yer? Yer sweatin' and divverin', see. Anyone can see that.'

It was as if the sun had flashed out from a cloud.

'I'm not… I ain't an opium fiend, see?'

'All right! All right! Only tryin' to 'elp, Pretty Ellen!'

Thankfully, he backed off.

Dickon thought the medication they gave you…

Oh, my God. I'm not ill at all. Clemence choked, and then laughed. *I'm in withdrawal from whatever it was they were tranquilising me with at Dwellan House.*

So, before she tried to go any further, she must sleep. If she was right about what ailed her, then all she could do was sweat and shiver until Warburton's poison was out of her system.

TWENTY-TWO

Clemence stepped out of Mr Almond's bank into Little Wild Street. She now had, in her reticule, thirty pounds and the address of a lodging-house for respectable single ladies, whose proprietress had been advised to expect Miss Carswell. First call, though, should be to a Marshall and Snelgrove's store to acquire something decent to be wearing when she arrived at Mrs Bonney's.

A fine drizzle was falling. She slipped beneath the boughs of one of the lime trees which lined the street. An envelope had also been waiting for her along with Lysithea's money. She read the note, sheltering it from the rain beneath her shawl.

> 'Miss Carswell. I trust this note finds you well. As I do not know the date you are expected in town, please reply via Mr Almond. I shall call in daily to Almond's bank to see if a response is forthcoming. Would you, pray, meet me at the Harp Tavern in Covent Garden at seven in the evening on the first Tuesday after your arrival? I will bespeak us a private parlour there. Yours in friendship, BF.'

Could she trust him?

Clemence wandered through the pathways of Kensington Gardens. A recent shower had left the grass smelling fresh, a breeze blowing the surface of the Long Water into ripples and wavelets.

For two days she had been mulling and mulling over Fanny's note. Four years of loss and illness had not changed her feelings for him. Except that the ecstasy of realising she loved him had flipped into pain.

But loving someone did not mean they could be trusted. He was Richard's friend before he was hers. Had broken her heart. Could a thoroughly sensible man have misread her so utterly? And it didn't seem to her that he had done aught to thwart Philo and Mathy in having her committed to the asylum – although quite what he might have done escaped her for the moment. Still, could she meet him as he asked?

Yet the only way he could have known about the arrangements with Almond's bank was if Lizzy had taken him into her confidence. So Lysithea must trust him absolutely.

From the walkway of the little bridge, Clemence looked out over the small lake. Water birds were squabbling and yark-yarking as they scudded across the surface. She wished she had crumbs for them.

What if the note was not from Fanny at all – but someone in Amathia's and Philo's employ, and a trap was being laid?

Clemence settled on a bench in the sunken terrace known as the Dutch Garden. Beside her was a bed of daffodils, their nodding heads dripping raindrops. A lady and gentleman ambled by, smiled at her, and the man raised his top hat. She looked respectable again in a plaid cotton dress, chemisette, cape and bonnet. She'd had to flash her money at the smart warehouse in Oxford Street before they'd even serve her.

One reason she was haunting the park was because there was a news vendor's stall close to the gate. She'd not seen a news sheet since her flight. Her adventure must be all over the press by now. For over four days she'd been gone from the asylum.

And what would the headlines say?

Lunatic peeress at large. Public are warned not to approach this woman who is said to be dangerous. If you see her, inform the police at once...

No, that was too unsubtle.

Flight of the Duchess. Beloved wife of one our most distinguished peers of the realm went missing four nights ago from a hospital where she was being treated. "I'm out of my wits worrying about my dear wife's safety," His Grace the Duke of Ardenne said yesterday...

She must at least see what the newspapers were saying. However bad it was. But each time she got up to go to the stand and purchase a broadsheet... her heart failed her, and she sat down again.

Her mind kept dwelling on those worse off than she was. At least she had Lysithea's money to live on for now, and Mrs Bonney's warm roof to sleep under. That first night after she'd gone on the run, she'd spent in a nethersken. Netherskens were the lowest lodging-houses in the meanest of London's rookeries.

She'd learned what a cigar-divan was, though, through listening to the enlightening discourse of her fellow dormitory lodgers: a sort of swell smoking-lounge for gentlemen, which was really a front for a brothel or opium house. The sort of place Philo might frequent. She'd not put it past Richard either.

Then, in the dead of night a ruckus from downstairs had awoken her and drawn her to the head of the dormitory stairs to see.

The doorman had been quarrelling with a sobbing girl. She had been the thinnest creature Clemence had ever seen – two shivering stick arms peeking from her shawl, sunken pools where the eyes should be.

'Please, sir, just let me in out of the rain! I'll get the money tomorrow, I swear.'

'I'll be blessed if you will, you varmint! Spend it on lush, you will, and I'll not see none of it. Rules is rules! If you ain't got threepence you ain't sleepin' 'ere.'

'Oh, please, sir! My baby's sick! I don't fink he'll last much longer in that damp cellar. Just one night in the warmth, sir, please...'

Beneath her skirt, Clemence's reticule had felt as if was burning her flesh. The remaining funds it held would pay for a cabriolet to take her across town to the bank, and a smidgen to eat, perhaps. But she could go without the food, couldn't she?

She had been about to offer to pay the wretch's fee. But – ah... if this lowlife thought she had money on her...

And so Clemence had turned away, the feel of the coins in her reticule biting her thigh a thousand times sorer than ever could the bedbugs. And would remember the blue-lipped girl to her dying day.

Were there homeless and hungry all over the city... the land... the empire? Shivering in the snow beneath the windows of the plump? Who had all attended, along with Clemence, the public readings of Mr Dickens's most harrowing passages, and who thought only what an astonishing performer of his art the devilishly debonair Mr Dickens was? On the Boulle cabinet in her aunt's sitting-room perched a Delft figurine of a stag which Lysithea's late husband had bought for a sum which could have fed and housed all Seven Dials.

What could Clemence do – one frail, sick woman on the run from the law, facing legions of poverty and rampant indifference among her own class?

But... what in blazes could she do, she had cried, for the dead and dying in Balaclava? Yet she had gone on to assist in her own minuscule way. A Christmas dinner for the denizens of that black pit; shoes for all the children... when she thought things through the possibilities were boundless.

A gust of wind rustled through the trees and shrubbery nearby. Clemence clutched at her headwear.

She rose from the bench and paced back and forth. The church bells struck three o'clock. She realised she had eaten nothing since the muffin and cheese she'd had for breakfast at Mrs Bonney's. A coffee stall stood close by. She crept near enough to smell the pea soup which the vendor was ladling into a bowl for a customer.

But suddenly, in her mind, Clemence saw that nethersken girl. The spindly fingers seemed to stretch towards her. Black, empty cavities where the eyes should be. 'Please ma'am... just a bowl of soup for my baby? He'll die...'

Where were that wretch and her child now? Dead in a doorway somewhere? Clemence could have saved them.

She hurried through the park towards the news vendor's stall.

The evening edition had just arrived. She watched as the newsboy unloaded the bundle from his cart. Should she go, then... now? See what it said? Would it be better *not* to know what the press was saying about her? No, she had to know – for better or worse. She took a firm step forward.

Clemence eyed the pile of print. She handed the boy a penny. He cut the newspaper's corner, and then handed it to her. Could not bring herself to read the headline; she blurred her vision.

Across the park she dashed. Her purchase was under her arm, unlooked at. In her haste, she splashed in two puddles.

Back at the bench, as the first lights of late afternoon flickered on behind the Kensington Palace windows, she plucked out her newspaper. All the birds seemed at once to cease their twittering. A yapping dog suddenly shut up.

Clemence peeked at the headline.

Funding Threat to New Underground

She almost swooned. Then began a knuckle-gnawing read.

Palmerston had told an angry Commons that the planned opening of the capital's new underground railway network, currently under construction, might be delayed.

Clemence turned the page. Would the runaway duchess story be on page two, or three, then?

The Union army had defeated the Confederates on the bank of the Tennessee River after a two-day battle at a place called Shiloh. As many as four thousand men on both sides were feared dead.

Her trembling hand turned another page. And another.

The Earl of Elgin had been appointed Governor-General of India. In Lancashire they were rioting over the cotton recession.

Clemence let the journal fall into her lap.

Diddleysquat. Not a word. A duchess escaped from a nuthouse was so un-newsworthy then?

It was an insult… wasn't it?

The group of three settled at an alcove table in Westminster's Strangers' Gallery. Richard sent away the waiter with an order for two cognacs and, for the lady, a syllabub.

Amathia spied around the lounge where, in its discreet bays, MPs dined constituents. Below the hum of conversation and clatter of cutlery came the soft notes of Mendelssohn being played on a piano in one corner. Every Prime Minister Great Britain had ever had was looking on in bust form from all sides of the room. The Duke of Newcastle was frowning from his marble plinth as if he didn't like her.

'Very well, this is what I have been able to glean,' said Richard. 'A wardress named Miss Cummings, who Clemmie was on good terms with, was summoned to my sister's room late on Thursday evening. Finding the space apparently devoid of occupant, Miss Cummings made a frantic search – this, you will understand, is Miss Cummings's own version of events given later, of course.

'While she was looking in the closet, where a frightened patient might find refuge behind the hanging garments, Miss Cummings received a blow to the head. It was the last the brave woman remembered before she woke – to find her keys and uniform gone. Clemence had purloined both.

'Before her spectacular exit from Dwellan, Clemmie also relieved Dr Warburton of the contents of his strongbox.'

'My God!' breathed the Duke of Ardenne. 'Got to admire her spirit, what?'

His sister gave him a sharp tap on the wrist.

'The woman is a menace, Philo, to herself as well as others.'

'I say, Dickon,' said Philo, 'is it true that she also battered the gatekeeper and nicked his coat?'

'Yes, and that poor maltster person left half dead when she stole his horse and trap?' said Amathia.

'She did indeed relieve this worthy tradesman of his transport.'

'How right we were to have her put away!' said Amathia. 'She must be found! Before she kills someone.'

'She'll not get far,' Richard said. 'Why – she has no money once whatever she took from Warburton runs out – and I doubt it's very much. And the dray she stole was found abandoned near Taunton.'

'Given her earlier escapades,' said Philo, 'who is to say she'll not turn corsair on the open highway, and rob some poor traveller of his purse?'

Was Philoctetes enjoying this as much as Amathia suspected Richard was?

'Now!' said Richard. 'I've had to grease a few palms to keep this out of the press.'

'It's more than she deserves!' said Amathia.

'Quite. But would you care to ride Rotten Row, Amathia, and be pointed out as the sister-in-law of an escaped lunatic? Although it might not be our secret any longer, now that the whole of Westminster might have heard it!' Richard glanced around the lounge where other diners had looked their way more than once during the conversation. He steepled his fingers on the tabletop and leaned towards his listeners.

'If Clemence knew she was being pursued – who by, where and how – she would be forewarned. But this newspaper silence means that she cannot, now, acquire this intelligence. Thus, she might grow bold and careless.'

Somehow, somehow, Amathia suspected Lysithea's hand in this. Swooping bat-like from her Galician mountain retreat.

'I say, Mathy!' Her brother laid a hand on her shoulder. 'You look rather pale, dear. Don't take on so. It ain't likely Clemence will really get far, you know.'

Richard smiled, and gave her hand a pat.

'Philo's right, my dear. The police have been sent her description. And when they find her – she'll never, ever, be released after this.'

But Amathia knew that mocking eyebrow of his.

'You don't believe she will be caught, do you, sir? Do you even wish it, I wonder?'

'Now, now, sweet one,' Richard said in cooing tones. 'You really mustn't upset yourself so. Think of your nerves – and our son.' He laid a gentle hand on the small hillock beneath her gown.

Amathia was about to retort… but the waiter arrived with the refreshments, and all three fell quiet.

TWENTY-THREE

The *Harp* Tavern stood in a sidestreet close to Covent Garden. It was early in the evening, a week after she'd come to London. Clemence paused by the nearest lamp and looked up at the place where Brandon Fanshawe had asked to meet her.

A three-storey Georgian building with slender windows, white-stuccoed frontage and jutting tracery and small portico. A cigar-shaped shadow was cast across the cobbled street from a poplar which grew in its tiny front yard. Not very fashionable. She would be unlikely to meet anyone she knew here. But not a disreputable locale either, where a gentleman like Lord Fanshawe might fear for a young lady's safety.

Still time for her to return the way she'd come. Could she be sure it was Fanny who'd asked her out here? Was it a trap?

Eventually, she'd asked Mr Almond to describe the man who'd left her the note. Average build; mid-thirties in age; hair of a reddish-brown colour just beginning to turn silver at the temples. Probably was Brandon, then. Not Dickon or Philo, anyway. Even then… could she trust Brandon Fanshawe? Well, Aunt Lizzy must. He wouldn't have been admitted to the conspiracy otherwise.

She drew the rim of her bonnet down so that most of her face would be hidden and stepped across the threshold. She'd never entered a hostelry alone before. Still, she'd done rather gutsier things in the last few weeks.

A man who looked like the host was there in the front room.

'I believe a gentleman might be expecting me,' Clemence ventured. 'Lord Fanshawe?'

Over by the hearth, a newspaper rustled. Brandon Fanshawe appeared from behind it.

'Thank you, Jobson. I'll take Miss Carswell to the parlour. You may bring us a warm posset. But then we'd prefer not to be disturbed unless we call.'

'Very good, My Lord.'

Brandon got up from his easy chair. He reached out a hand to Clemence in greeting.

'Come, my dear. There's a nice fire waiting in the private room I've bespoke for us.'

'Thank you, Lord Fanshawe,' she said, aware that the publican was still in hearing. 'Lead the way, sir.'

She followed him along a dimly-lit stone corridor. There had been a handful of customers sitting in the bar-room when she'd entered. No-one had taken much of a look at her. She knew what they'd all be thinking, landlord too. A peer's clandestine tryst with his *femme galante*. Amusing thought. No doubt these places catered for such assignations, and it would be kept quiet about in exchange for a greased palm.

'Clemence. You're safe. Thank the Lord!' Brandon said as soon as the parlour door was closed behind them. 'So, you've been living at Mrs Bonney's for a week?'

'Yes. It's quite a decent lodging really. I'm comfortable there, for now.'

'For how long?'

'Until I can leave the country.'

Good, bright flames were prancing in the hearth. And an oil lamp burned on the bureau close by. Golden tapeworms of firelight flickered in Brandon's sideburns. Shadows lay in the curve of his cheekbones, and the edges of his heartbreaking smile.

She turned her eyes away. The window frame had a yellowy-amber glow from the light of the streetlamp which was just out of view. In the sky above the rooftops opposite was a feathery crescent moon.

'Have a seat, my dear, and take off your bonnet and cape.' He went behind one of two leather armchairs which stood either side of the hearth.

Clemence sat and eyed him before striking up talk again.

'Aunt Lizzy wants me to go to her house in Geneva. I assume she'll meet me there.' She eyed him during the following pause as he moved to take up the other seat. 'How did you know how to find me? Did Lysithea take you into her confidence?'

'Yes… it was me who made up the food hamper. You don't imagine that came all the way from Pressburg, perishables and all, do you? Although I don't believe Lizzy really wished to involve me. Doesn't entirely trust me.' Brandon inclined towards her and smiled. 'I get the impression you don't either.'

'Why should I? You're Dickon's friend.'

'I hope I'm yours too!' In the quietness, out in the street a hurdy-gurdy man could be heard playing a barrel-organ. 'I don't believe you deserved to be in Dwellan still. One doesn't have to be an expert on mental disorders to see you're well again. It's scandalous that Warburton vetoed your release. No doubt on Mathy's and Philo's request. There – does that satisfy you?'

Clemence averted her eyes, to take in instead the brassware gleaming on the fireplace. 'You didn't stop them sending me there in the first place, Fanny. They got their pet doctor to certify me insane. Haven't you a family doctor of your own who could have put in a word for me?'

'Clemmie,' Brandon said. 'I don't think you appreciate that you were ill. Really ill. Not now. You're well again now. I see that. But you were very sick, my dear. Maybe the way Amathia went about having you certified was a bit underhand…'

Clemence made a sound of annoyance. Trouble was… those very dark thoughts had occurred to her also. So, he wasn't really in the wrong.

'How do you propose to quit the country?' Brandon asked.

'I'm not going to fly, am I? How do you imagine?'

'Your description has been sent to every police force in the land. They're watching all the main ports.'

So, they were on her trail after all, despite the newspaper silence.

'You're not wanted just for escaping from the asylum. Warburton says you coshed a wardress named Miss Cummings senseless and robbed his strongbox.'

'I see!' said Clemence. How flattering that he thought she'd know how to. 'Well, I didn't, Fanny. My only income comes from the account at Almond's which my aunt set up. I have a bank account in the name of Clemence Somerlee, but of course I cannot access it just now.'

So, how was she going to get out of the country? Could she sail in a fishing vessel from some remote harbour which was unlikely to be under surveillance? It would only make her more conspicuous. And probably that was the way fugitives usually fled abroad. If she was a fisherman… she'd wonder whether the reward on this woman's head might be more valuable than whatever sum she was offering for her passage to France.

Brandon sat back, making the leather creak, and crossed his limbs. She looked down at the black cambric reticule lying in her lap.

'Where did you spend your first night before you arrived at Mrs Bonney's?'

'Seven Dials,' Clemence replied. 'I don't suppose you've heard of it, have you?'

'On the contrary! But how did you end up in that bijou neighbourhood?'

She sighed and told him what she believed had happened.

'Dickon was right when he said he thought they were giving me narcotics of some sort at Dwellan. I suffered withdrawal symptoms, Fanny. Sweating… feverish. Only reason I know about such things is because we once had a footman who was on that stuff – opium. I saw what it did to him, miserable fellow.

'Well, I must have stumbled through the lanes and courts, possibly for miles, with no idea where I was going – in a state because I hadn't had my "shove." And finished up in Holborn. Seven Dials to be precise. I'd heard of it because a clergyman named it once when he came collecting for charity! I paid three pence for a squalid berth in a nethersken. I'd no idea such places existed!'

Brandon gave a quick laugh.

'I've had my concerns about slum districts – rookeries, they're called you know – like Seven Dials for years.' He leaned his elbow on the wing of the chair, propped his cheek against it, and went on looking at her. 'So, go on – your plans to quit the country?'

'Perhaps I could go in disguise?' A moment's gazing at the moon while she thought it through. 'You know how I might pass incognito, Fanny? If I wasn't alone – part of a group. In the train of a family, say… as a servant of some kind. Abigails, linen maids, valets – they pass unnoticed among the luggage.'

Brandon gave a wry chuckle.

'You tried your dainty hand at nursing. Now you think you can become a lady's maid as glibly?'

'Look! I've lived with servants all my life. I know what they do, for heaven's sake! Good Lord – I used to think I could do a better job with the mending than our linen maid Rosanna.'

'What do you want me to do? Write your character to land you your new situation? Of course – you know what they'll think?'

'That I'm some doxy of yours you're doing a favour for? Fiddlesticks, Brandon Fanshawe. You think I'd care after what I've been through?'

But she'd thought it through now, anyway. Finding a well-to-do household which just happened to be tootling off to Marienbad to take the waters in the next fortnight or so, all their servants in tow, and who didn't happen to know the Somerlees or Consetts? And wouldn't therefore recognise their new maid? Oh, yes, lillibolero bullen a la!

Should she try her luck on a fishing vessel, then? Or just lie low for six months? She could stay at Mrs Bonney's, living off the income Lysithea sent her… and after so long those watching the ports might have lost their keenness, and have melted away to more pressing business.

'I could help,' Brandon said.

'What, you mean keep an ear out for someone travelling abroad, who is also seeking a new maid?'

'No, dear.' He kept his eye on her during a pause. 'I mean… I could hire a vessel and take you over to France. It would only need the co-operation of a captain who could be trusted. No-one else need be involved.'

'Gosh…!'

'I suggest we sail from a small place like Seaford. I know it, and there's a decent hostelry called the *Old Harvester* where you'd be safe to stay the night before. They'd not be watching such a place.'

'I couldn't ask it of you, Fanny! What about your friendship with Dickon?'

'You objected that I didn't help you when they locked you away!'

'Yes, yes!' She gave it all some thought. 'What about Phyllis? Would she have to know?'

He hadn't needed such an out-of-the-way place as the *Harp* for his assignation with Clemence. She'd have been safe enough going cloaked, at night, to his townhouse. No-one would be watching to see or recognise her. So, *did he not trust his wife?*

'No need for Phyllis to be troubled with this, Clemence. I can say I've been dispatched on some commission on behalf of the Lords, and I'll only be gone a day at most. And Clemence – Richard is more on your side than you imagine. He's very worried about you! But, yes, I do agree that you are probably safer out of England right now. But… ah!' Brandon cocked an ear towards the sound of footsteps approaching along the passage. 'That sounds like mine host with the warm beverage I ordered!'

TWENTY-FOUR

Amathia and her brother sat at a table in a coffee-shop overlooking Waterloo Bridge. Richard had said he'd meet them at noon. It was ten minutes past according to the nearby clockface on the tower of St Clement's.

'Well, he cannot have good news,' she said after a lengthy silence. 'Otherwise he'd have come straight here! Of course, he might just have stopped off at a parasol-shop with his light-o-love and that's what's keeping him!'

'Hmmm,' said Philoctetes Consett. 'More coffee, dear?'

'I shouldn't be fretting like this, Philo,' she said as he poured from the pot. 'Not in my condition. And the rain isn't keeping off,' she added. 'If I miscarry the precious Somerlee son and heir, really, it will all be Dickon's own fault for putting me through such discomfort.'

Richard was to meet with the Chief Commissioner of the Metropolitan Police later that afternoon. Would learn the latest in the hunt for Clemence. Did he even want her caught, though? Did Philo? Amathia had her doubts. An embarrassment Clemence was, who had made the Somerlees gossiped about, and therefore the Consetts too by association.

'Well now,' said the Duke of Ardenne. 'Supposing it is bad news. And Clemmie has escaped across the sea or something of that ilk. What are we going to do, Amathia?'

'We, Philo?'

'Well, I cannot stay tied to the woman forever, can I? Either we have the marriage annulled on grounds of my wife being a certified lunatic – and lose her inheritance with it – or we must agree to her release. It don't bother me if I don't leave an heir, you know – I'll not be here to care – but the hassle I get from the sisters and old aunts! Prefer a bit of peace, sissy.'

Amathia turned her eyes to the view outside. St Paul's dome wore a half-hearted rainbow like a jaunty hair comb. The cupolas and towers of Southwark on the further shore of the river gave off a violet and greenly glow in the sunlit rain. Garlands hanging from the boughs in Temple Gardens billowed and tore at their fastenings in a fierce wind.

When she'd had Clemence put away three years ago, it was in the belief that Lysithea was at death's door, and the inheritance would be coming Philo's way pretty quick. That had turned out not to be so.

What else should you do, pray, with a relation who sat on the stairs on the night of the Sebastopol ball, showing her drawers to the assembled county set, screaming that she'd seen her deceased brother Aubrey out by the lake – except see she was dispatched to a place where, for decent fees, she would be softly treated?

Little doubt had Amathia, though, that Richard hated his wife for what she'd done to his sister, however justified Amathia believed she'd been. She saw it in his eyes when he was what was laughingly called making love to her.

Should she agree to let Clemmie out, then?

'Jumpy, ain't you, miss?' the serving girl said as she poured Clemence coffee at her corner table.

'Weather looks a bit threatening, Susannah,' Clemence said. 'We mayn't be able to sail this afternoon.'

'Be anuvver boat tomorrow, won't there, miss?'

'Yes... but my aunt is expecting me in France tonight.'

After days of pacing, trying to decide what to do, she was taking a chance on Brandon Fanshawe. Lizzy trusted him... apparently. There was no love lost between him and Amathia. And however she tried to flee the country she was up against the odds. Might as well take Fanny up on his offer. As much risk, trusting him, as going any other way.

Clemence sipped her coffee. She looked out from the *Harvester's* front parlour. A pear tree was tapping its blossomy bough against the glass. She watched a sparrow in the branches, tweeting as she went about her construction work. Happy little homebody building your nest – you may just fly away.

She could make out one edge of Seaford's marina. Four yachts bobbed there at anchor.

Clemence glanced at the timepiece which stood on the mantelpiece. Ten minutes past the noon hour. Willing those hands to move faster, just as she had in Taunton the morning after her escape – waiting for the bank to open. Fanny had told her to be at the marina at one-thirty. A private boat called the *Pyramus* would be waiting there. She should board. Fanny would be there. They would sail at once. And be in Calais by nightfall.

Out on the marine parade she could see one policeman on patrol. Maybe the waterfront was just his regular beat. Clemence had dyed her hair black. But she couldn't alter her age or build.

Could her hostelry be under surveillance? Such a small place Seaford was – why Fanny had chosen it. But how could they know for sure?

Some eight or so other people were taking luncheon at the *Harvester*. No-one was looking her way, though. No innocent bystander parked on the garden wall, seeming to be reading a newspaper, but eyeing the wayfarers' halt where Clemence was lodged. No flash of sunlight came from a window opposite to give away a watcher there with a telescope trained.

She relaxed, however, as the lawman went out of sight.

'I was thinkin' of the last time I was down 'ere on the south coast,' she told the serving girl next time she stopped by. 'During the last war. We sailed from Portsmouth. My sweet'eart was a soldier. And my brother. I went out east with 'em. They died. Both.'

'How very sad for you, miss. You must miss 'em.'

'Yes. Yes, I do. Very much.'

'Was you scared, miss?' the girl asked. 'Travellin' into a war?'

'No. No, not scared. Back then I was a Judy O'Grady – a soldier's woman,' Clemence said. 'I 'ad a document called a passport. It means that when you goes abroad into foreign parts, you're still under 'Er Majesty's protection. I'm more scared now,' she said, smiling up at the girl. 'No such protection for me this time. Couldn't afford a passport.'

For what Her Majesty's protection is worth she thought, as the girl went about her business.

What o'clock now? Twenty-five minutes to one.

Just how chancy was this – trusting Brandon Fanshawe?

Suddenly, the outer door swung open. A sea-breeze blew in. A heavyset man with a greying moustache stood there. He wore a Chesterfield coat and deerstalker hat. His eye swept the tavern's interior.

Clemence's heart gave a lurch. Not a Customs official. Nor a sailor. Too well-dressed to be the sort of holidaymaker who frequented a lowly establishment like this – he looked as if he could afford to stay at the railway's Grand Hotel which overlooked the seafront at Dover.

The man ducked under the low lintel. He ambled through the dining-tables, scanning the faces around him. He had a word with the serving-girl, Susannah. *Who turned and looked towards the corner table where Clemence was seated.* The man looked too. Susannah appeared to point her out to him.

A long-suffering organ had gone from lurch to pained thump. *He was coming over. And yes – his eye was for sure focused on Clemence. Not the old sailor sitting at the next table. Her.*

'Might I have a word please, madam?' the stranger said.

Clemence hid her trembling hands inside her cape. The man, meanwhile, took an identity card from the pocket of his overcoat.

'I'm Detective McCready from the Sussex Constabulary.'

'I'm seeing the Commissioner at four,' Richard told his relatives as he joined them at table. 'Oh, miss! Fresh coffee and teacakes, please.'

'Three hours to fill, then,' Philoctetes pointed out. 'What shall we do in the meantime?'

'Well,' Richard said. 'How do you fancy an anti-slavery debate in Exeter Hall? You pair can proudly tell the audience about your grandsire.'

'Actually, Dickon,' said Amathia, 'I believe the Sacred Harmonic Society is giving a concert this afternoon. Or why don't we go to St Clement Danes? There's a performance of Hässler's Grand Gigue in D minor.'

'And we're missing it? Oh, boo-hoo!' said Philo. 'How about the cider-cellars in Maiden Lane? Now – that's my idea of my entertainment.'

'Oh, how deplorable you are, Philo!' said his sister.

'What about a stroll then? I hear there's a magnificent view of the city from Waterloo Bridge. St Paul's looks rather heavenly, they say. How much do they charge to take a walk on the bridge?'

'Halfpenny, Philo,' his brother-in-law replied. 'Each.'

'Damned highway robbery if you ask me,' the Duke of Ardenne muttered. 'Pay the blackguard gatekeeper, Dickon. I'll pay you back when I've seen my bank manager!'

'Oh, how absurd!' hissed Amathia. 'I cannot go out in the open air in my condition!' Actually, she wasn't showing that much yet. So, she could still decently appear in public for now. But it was a good excuse.

'You obviously don't have the salt blood of the sea in your veins, my dear wife,' said Richard. He swelled out his chest as he looked out at the river. 'One of my ancestors served in Drake's navy, you know.'

'You have mentioned it once or twice, I believe, Dickon,' snapped Amathia.

Great families all decline eventually, she thought. A little further along the Strand lay Savoy Street, site of John of Gaunt's stupendous palace of that name. The ruins had been cleared to construct this bridge. In her dreams, she saw Eardingstowe crumble too, and go tumbling over Kilve Cliff. And Kingsmede rule supreme in its stead.

The girl arrived with the refreshments. She set fresh china before the three of them, coffee and a plate of warm teacakes.

Of course, the demise of the Somerlees was naught but a fantasy. Amathia was bound to Richard, like it or no. If he fell, so did she. And her children.

At times, she felt as enslaved as the wretches her grandfather had bound in chains and dispatched across the Atlantic. Richard and his siblings had never known the dread of poverty as had she. Her father the old duke had been teetering on the brink all through her childhood. Next knock on Kingsmede's great door might have been the creditors to take all away and cast the Consett children adrift on the chancy ocean. And that was a fear which never quite freed you.

Dickon had assured her he was doing fine. Something about shares in a mine he was acting as a broker for. And for sure he was not stinting on her pin-money. Expense was no bar whenever she wished to entertain at Eardingstowe. There was even talk of a royal visit.

Amathia spooned her sugar into her cup.

She just wished she had means of her own for once in her life. Even if an aunt like Lysithea or an uncle like George bequeathed a tidy nest egg to her, by law it would be Richard's. Anything a woman owned became her husband's.

'What do you suppose Clemence is doing now?' asked the duke. 'I'll roll a dice if she's not having more fun than are we.'

'She might be in danger, you know,' Richard snapped.

'Clemmie? Oh, I very much doubt it. She's a survivor, that one. Now if it was you, Mathy…' Philoctetes said. 'Can't imagine you climbing down the ivy, love.'

'Clemence did not escape that way either! She was in one of those "I'll throw a tantrum if you make me go outside" hissy phases of hers. So, she couldn't have got out alone. Someone assisted her! I wouldn't be at all surprised if it turned out to be either of you pair.'

'Only wish I'd thought of it,' Philo mused, buttering a teacake. 'Do you realise I've celebrated my third wedding anniversary? I must be the world's loneliest bridegroom! And she's rather winsome, is Clemence.'

'She isn't what is usually counted handsome,' Amathia said.

'On the contrary! I think she's lovely… in a fairy princess kind of way. Not as charming as you of course, sissy.'

'The woman is sick, Philoctetes – sick in the head! And a danger to decent people. Yes, a danger!'

'You should be careful, Amathia,' said Richard. 'You're beginning to sound hysterical when you talk about Clemmie. Who knows… maybe I'll recommend my unbalanced wife to the excellent ministrations of Dr Warburton and his staff.'

'You'd not dare, husband. What if I were to tell the world where the demon in the chamber is?'

'I beg your pardon?'

'We all have our demons,' Amathia said. 'Shut away in the chamber of our minds. You have your secrets, Richard, same as any man. And you'd prefer me to keep my mouth shut about them, I daresay.'

'Men are simpler than you think, my dear. I've been a Member of Parliament since 1848, and like any politician I've had my enemies who would have dished up dirt on me if they could.'

'Oh, you can be infuriating, Dickon!' Actually, she knew very little about his private business, so if he was up to anything scandalous or illegal, she wouldn't know. And he was right, damn him. He could get *her* committed as she had Clemmie if it suited him. It was unbearably easy to do. 'Well, we never settled our earlier argument, did we? I'm going to listen to the Grand Gigue. Alone. I don't need either of you boobies making exhibitions of yourselves by falling asleep and snoring through it.'

'Tol-lol, sissy dear,' Philoctetes said, and took a bite of teacake.

'Would you mind telling me your name, madam?'

The plain-clothes policeman loomed over her corner table, blocking out the light. Clemence felt the eyes of the serving-girl, Susannah, and some of the other diners darting her way, and ears straining to listen.

Should Clemence bother trying not to look scared? Who wouldn't be – under the pitted red nose of a blooming great crusher?

'Miss Mary Carswell, officer,' she said. 'I'm goin' over to France to visit my auntie. I've not done nothin' wrong – I swear on me mother's soul!'

Officer McCready looked taken-aback.

'No-one's said you have, young woman.' He blinked several times in surprise. 'How have you paid for your coffee this morning might I ask?'

'With a few coins I had in my pocket,' said Clemence, also surprised.

'I thought so. Haven't missed this yet, have you?'

The man produced a black cambric reticule from the pocket of his Chesterfield. He dangled it before her on its ribbon.

Clemence let out a small gasp.

'May I?' he asked. He laid a hand on the second chair at her table, and then accepted his own invitation to sit down.

'Jeremiah Fishbone was picked up this morning,' he told Clemence. 'Had on him three wallets from the Grand at Dover, as well as one or two pieces from this here establishment. Must have been into your room while you slept, love. Lucky your notebook's got your name writ in the front, isn't it, miss, and the address of the *Harvester*, so's I could trace you – else you'd not have been going anywhere today.'

Clemence began to weep. She extended a hand towards her pilfered property. She opened the little bag. Drew out her notebook where she'd been scribbling train and steamboat times and ticket prices as she'd ruminated on her best means of escape, and most of the rest of her money drawn from Almond's.

'Thank you, officer,' she squeaked. 'Thank you so much.'

'Not at all, miss.' He raised his hat. 'We've been hoping to catch Fishbone red-handed for months. A good long trip to Australia is on the cards for him now, I think. I'd ask you to give a full statement at the station, miss – but I see from your notes,' he nodded to the notebook, 'that you are due to sail in just under an hour.'

She wiped both eyes.

'Yes… yes I am,' Clemence stammered.

1870

Eight years later

TWENTY-FIVE

In the lounge of the Carlton one afternoon, two dozen club members read their newspapers, chatted, or just dozed in the late spring sunshine which slunk through the half-closed drapes. A whiff of manure wafted through the open casements, and you could hear the hoof-beats and wheels grinding by outside in Pall Mall.

Many had been discussing the battle clouds gathering across the Channel. The King of Prussia and Emperor Louis Bonaparte had been at fuming loggerheads all year. War was on the way, for sure. Should Britain stay out of it?

One stout, middle-aged gentleman-politician, however, was engrossed in a broadsheet, and his mind seemed to be elsewhere.

The Baronet of Eardingstowe looked up from the print, gave his reading spectacles a wipe, and tried to compose his thoughts. After an interval, he began reading once more.

RETURN FROM THE VALLEY OF DEATH!
A war hero, lost in action during the Charge of the Light Brigade, has been found alive.

Cornet Aubrey Somerlee of the Eleventh Hussars, assumed dead, has been discovered wandering in confusion around Vienna. It transpires that the brave soldier had lost his memory. Barbarous Serbian captors, he has claimed, had held him prisoner for many years in a castle.

Naturally, there will be those who might question the authenticity of a man claiming to be the long-lost cavalryman. Let any doubters heed the words of the hussar's own sister: "I'm absolutely convinced he is my lost brother Aubrey," Lady Isabella Markham told this newspaper last night. "He remembered the name of my pet rat, Bickerstaff."

Well, really! Wasn't that just typical of Bella! Richard slapped down the newspaper. He gulped his brandy. When the butler called, Richard asked him to leave the bottle.

After a further swig from his drinking glass, he took up the story again.

Aubrey Somerlee was taken prisoner at Balaclava sixteen years ago during that battle of illustrious fame.

It has now emerged that the missing officer was, in fact, first located three years ago. His former colonel, the late Earl of Cardigan, was visiting Vienna when he stumbled across a man without a memory.

The unfortunate soul was being cared for by the holy brothers at Klosterneuburg Priory. Where he had come from, no-one knew. But the earl, who led the cavalry charge which Lord Tennyson immortalised in verse, noted that the gentleman unknown possessed a sword which bore the inscription of the Eleventh Hussars.

"He did not know his own name or where he belonged, nor did he know me," Lord Cardigan reported in private correspondence which this publication has seen, "but I was sure he was Cornet Somerlee, and the sword was certainly genuine. Perhaps I scared the poor fellow, however, for when I returned – in great excitement – sadly, he had vanished again."

It seems His Lordship decided not to inform the cornet's family immediately for fear of raising their hopes unnecessarily. Then the earl's untimely death in a riding accident two years ago left his discovery unreported until now.

Cornet Somerlee is now in the care of Vienna's City Hospital. He has been able to advise that he sustained a severe blow to the head when he fell from his horse in the infamous Valley of Death. Only after many years did memories gradually return.

"I remembered my horse was named Sparkle. My home was Eardingstowe in Somerset. I even recalled the green man carving on the hall clock..."

My, my, Richard scoffed; *have we done ourselves proud with the detail in our guidebooks!*

"I remembered the storm that was blowing when my dear little sister Margaret was born. And how my brother Carswell didn't like the cook's Potage à la Parmentier and would pour it into the mere..."

No wonder Jenny Greenteeth hates us! Richard took a long drink. *And I might be on the lookout for a new chef when I return to Eardingstowe!*

Richard had yet to meet this man claiming to be Aubrey. Of course, the person was an impostor, but that was beside the point. If someone wished to claim kinship with the renegades and lunatics the Somerlees had spawned over the centuries, he was welcome as far as Richard was concerned. But Uncle

George's legacy, and the two thousand a year which their pater had left to each of his younger offspring... Ah, now that was more of a tricky-woo; Richard had been spending Aubrey's portion with glee for the last sixteen years.

Of course, thanks to the bounty of Smoky Mountain Richard was now one of the wealthiest men in the land... wasn't as if he couldn't pay the fellow back, for pity's sake. Still, would be jolly awkward if it got out that the public face of Smoky Mountain had snaffled his unfortunate sibling's inheritance.

> *And what does this restored hero recollect of that fateful day in October, 1854?*
>
> "I remember Lord Cardigan calling out the order to advance. I was riding into the valley in the second line. And I saw Captain Nolan trying to stop the charge.
>
> "I remember a hail of cannonballs from every side. We were racing as fast as the wind, right through the enfilade, heading straight into the firing range of the Don Cossack battery. Men were screaming and falling dead all around me. A bullet tore out some of Sparkle's mane. He whinnied but gritted his teeth and galloped on.
>
> All I could hear was the gunfire and hammering of the hooves. Just imagine it... zing, zing, before my eyes, behind my head, everywhere. One shot after another, and the roar of the cannons in the battery coming ever closer."

Oh my, Richard chuckled to himself, *been reading his Tennyson, hasn't he, in preparation for this fraud of his.*

For a long time, Richard had been anticipating some trickster trying to impersonate Aubrey. It had seemed almost inevitable. Only surprising one hadn't come forward before this. Well, Aubrey was a monied man in his own right, leave alone his blood-tie with the fabulously rich Baronet of Eardingstowe.

Egads, you might do it just for the glory, never mind the inheritance!

Richard went on reading, starting to smile a little.

"My messmate, Captain Mortlake, was riding alongside me. When we got to the battery, we ducked under the limbers and spiked two of the guns with rocks.

"Then the Cossack cavalry rode down on us. They surrounded us, snarling, pitiless brutes that they were. We fought hand to hand. I struck swords with a Cossack. I can picture his vicious, scarred face as he bloodied me in the arm, and nearly knocked me from the saddle. But Mortlake raced up behind, sliced through the chap's neck, and he tumbled lifeless.

"Mortlake and I helped drag away one of the guns our chaps had caught.

"I can still smell the sulphur, hear the cries of the wounded. I recall a dragoon lying across our way, his bloody head split open. I had to jump Sparkle over him – so disrespectful.

"Then a troop of Polacks appeared right before us. I thought we were about to die! 'Heaven help us!' I called out! But, by George, the Polish captain waved us past! The Polacks have no love for their Russian masters you know! Mortlake saluted, and shouted 'Viva Polska!'

"Mortlake and I were at school together. I used to call him 'Applejohn'. Lord knows why…

"Then four massive shells exploded overhead. The whole valley vanished in whiteness. I remember falling, terrible pain filling my head. And that is where my memory falters…"

This Mortlake character had survived the charge, was a major now, and would doubtless confirm all this had occurred as told. And his silly schoolboy sobriquet which only the real Aubrey would have known, and so on, and so on… *Of course, this chancer's going to set about proving his identity with rubbish only Aubrey and the family could know. Dashed awkward if he remembers publicly what I used to do in the rotunda…*

'I say! Rum business this, what?' Richard looked up as someone spoke to him. 'I hear your lost brother's been found, Dickon!'

Richard sighed to himself. He set the newspaper aside. This story was going to be massive and outshine even the warring Fritz and Frenchies. Richard and the Somerlees were going to be exposed to national, maybe global attention.

'Will you even recognise him after being gone for so long?'

'I don't know, Bertie. Do join me. Collins, another glass for Sir Bertrand please. How is dear Lady Grace?' Richard made a feeble attempt to change the subject.

'Oh, fine, fine… but your brother, Dickon! Must be devilish exciting to have him back after all these years? Scary, too, perhaps? Bit like a spectre from the grave, what? Well, I daresay you've been mourning him as dead. How many years is it?'

'Sixteen. He disappeared during the Battle of Balaclava. We heard he was taken prisoner by some Serbs. Then… nothing. Until now. Yes, Bertrand, I have been mourning him as dead.'

'Heavens, heavens!' His friend shook his silver head. 'How do you truly feel about his return, old boy? Well – he'll be a stranger to you!'

'Indeed, he will.'

Richard thought back over the years. He remembered a boy with black hair, nine or ten years younger than himself. Adored his big brother Dickon and toddled around after him. But because of the age gap Richard and Aubrey had not been close. One was away at school when the other was in the nursery. One went into Parliament, the other the army.

Richard could call to mind few moments of togetherness with Aubrey. Mannerisms? A particular way of waving his hand or tossing back his head? Words or phrases which were uniquely his? No, nothing that Richard could recall. The sound of Aubrey's laughter, his voice? No – it was gone.

'Suppose you'll recognise him?'

'What do you think? A man changes with age! Now just take me if you will,' Richard said, raising a brow. 'Sixteen years ago I was dashing, I daresay. Now I'm forty-five, about two stones heavier, gammy-eyed, more silver than gold in my hair these days, ruddy face... will Aubrey recognise me is more to the point?'

'Oh, come, come!' Sir Bertrand said, and chuckled. 'I've a decade on you, and you're in fine fettle, sir, fine fettle! And you know – I've heard the Jewish upstart is thinking of a cabinet post for you.'

'I heard Derby was too, but it never materialised.'

'Ah, well.' Richard's friend sighed. 'What's Lady Amathia think of this... well... *upheaval* in your lives?'

'I haven't been home since I had the news Aubrey had been found.' Richard stared into his glass. 'We are expecting another little blessing, you know,' he said. 'Could have done without something like this upsetting her nerves at such a time.'

'Well... you've done well in that department, my good fellow! Four is it so far?'

'Yes. Girls. Not banking on anything different this time.' He sincerely hoped it would be a son, though: because then he would never have to sleep with her again.

'I say, Dickon!' A pair of new voices joined the discussion. 'We've just heard the news about your brother. Incredible, what? Home from Balaclava after all these years! Found in a monastery? Lost his memory? Amazing! What do you feel about it, old man? Think you'll recognise him after all this time?'

Over an hour passed before Richard was left alone. The butler brought him a fresh decanter of brandy. He asked if Sir Richard would be dining in this fine evening.

'I think not. I'll take myself for a stroll I think, Collins. I'm returning to Somerset upon the morrow and shall relish my last night in town.'

Donning his top hat, cape and cane, out into Pall Mall he stepped. He hailed a cabriolet and set off for the Haymarket. A night of felicity before a return to morbid domesticity. Ghastly thought.

He lay awake for a long while after his lovemaking.

The night-house's chic boudoir was roofed with a ceiling of mirrors. Reflected lamplight, crimson and magenta in colour, glowed down on him. He glanced at the oriental features of the young lady whose head lay on the pillow beside him. Richard must have transported her to another world with his passion. She was asleep.

Convivial noises reached his ears from the Café Royale's salon downstairs. There, clients and girls mingled before repairing to the chambers above.

Richard had paid for one of the establishment's most superior rooms. Drapes of scarlet Indian silk swathed the four-poster's canopy, windows and dressing-chamber. A half-empty bottle of Moselle stood in the ice-bucket.

He reached for his coat which lay sprawled across the seat of the divan. From the breast pocket, he took the things which had been troubling him all day.

One was a watercolour miniature of Aubrey set in an oval frame. Richard remembered the sitting. A local artist had taken all the Somerlee children's portraits on the occasion of their parents' twentieth wedding anniversary.

The subject was pictured in half-profile. He would have

been, what, about nine? Peachy-fair complexion. Midnight-dark curls. Eyes as blue as sapphires. Little Master Perfect. No spot or blackhead had dared come near him. Pater's favourite. Mater's sweetest cherub. No, he was never coming back. Never.

Richard laid the little likeness down.

He turned up the lamp. Then unfolded the letter which he had also been carrying. He had to hold it close to the light, so poor now was his eyesight.

'My dearest Dickon, from your ever-loving Clemmie. Despite your continued silence when I write, brother, I shall not despair of mending our fractured relationship somehow.'

Richard slapped his feet out of bed. He paced to the window and plucked back the curtain.

The hour was about two in the morning, but Leicester Square was still vibrant and wideawake. Patrons from the Café Royale swaggered about below and splashed in the puddles. One top-hatted chap seemed to be taking his be-feathered Judy home with him. The establishment boasted a liquor licence, and even a policeman standing guard at the discreet entrance – tipping his helmet to the politicians, noblemen, foreign diplomats, admirals and colonels on their way in or out.

On the other side of the square, the Alhambra Palace and Burford's Panorama remained open through much of the night. What a marvel the Panorama was – like a magic lantern show on a giant-sized scale; onto the screen were projected photographs of a horse, say, in each stage of galloping up to and leaping a fence, or a bird furling out its wings and taking off into flight; the series of frames zapped across so fast it was like watching a real horse or bird in action. One day we'll have real moving pictures, you'll see, Richard had been told.

The world was changing so speedily you felt dizzy. Even the current fashion fad of putting frilly skirts on furniture got on Richard's wick. Amathia had done it to a perfectly nice pier table in the Eardingstowe Great Drawing-Room.

'People one hundred years from now will think we're such prudes we want to hide their legs!' he had snapped.

He put the letter before his face again. The streetlamp below the window gave illumination. But he'd read it so many times the words read themselves.

'I pray, Dickon, that you can forgive what I did. The dreadful deception. The terrible worry I gave you. I can live with the disapproval of society. My estrangement from my husband troubles me not, for Philoctetes is nothing to me. But that you have cut me out of your life, Dickon, is a daily sorrow.'

He laid down Clemence's note.

He doubted he would be able to sleep if he returned to his bed. Should he join the revelry downstairs? No thank you; he might bump into a Party whipper-in wanting to know why he hadn't responded to Monday's protocol. One night lately, he had encountered a senior member of the Colonial Office wearing frilly drawers, emerging from one of the private parlours, who had asked him if he knew how to fasten garters. Yes, you could get Mary-Annes here too if you fancied that kind of thing.

He flopped onto the divan and laid back his head.

Clemmie and Lizzy had returned to England five years ago. They'd set up home at the Schwangli house in Mayfair. Moreover, Clemence had come with her head held high. Three doctors had declared her sane. Not just any doctors, either. That was Lysithea's doing. She was a friend of the Austrian Emperor. Well, not *friend* exactly. Franz Josef didn't have any. But she was the nearest thing; her Swiss husband was said to have saved the young Franz from an assassination attempt and had been rewarded for his trouble. As had his widow.

One of Franz Josef's court physicians, and two from Vienna's Narrenturm Asylum – the most progressive institution for the mentally deranged on the blooming planet – had examined the countess's niece. She was a little highly strung, perhaps, but sane.

Richard could have told them that for half the fee. Nor could he blame Clemmie for her flight. Even admired her for it. Everyone tacitly did – a gutsy young Grace Darling. And did that prickle? If he was honest – yes. She'd made him seem a fool. Cruel, even.

The tops of the Quantocks peeped above the passing hedgerows, shimmering from behind a curtain of heat-haze. The slopes were coloured mauve and buttery-yellow with flowering heather and gorse.

The Somerlee brougham rattled homewards through cider-country. Through the open carriage window drifted the scent of new-mown grass and ripening hay. Overhead, a bird-arrow was heading towards a feathery daytime moon. Hazel, blackthorn, dogwood and elder were all in full leaf. White butterflies hovering in the roadside foliage caught Richard's eye. But his mind was elsewhere.

He hadn't seen much of Clemmie since her return from the continent. A few times their eyes had met across a busy public room. Enough to nod – but not so far smile or speak.

Hellfire – she'd even made her peace with Dwellan House. Written to apologise. *Apologise*, would you have it? And offered to pay for a spanking new shelter for its garden. At which that infernal snob Warburton had gushed his gratitude. Even announced publicly that he'd been mistaken about Her Grace robbing him.

So, now Clemence was chirpily visiting Aunt Cassandra and the other lifelong friends she'd made as if naught had happened. Sickening.

The carriage swayed over a narrow bridge which crossed a sluggish waterway, and on through villages where forelocks were tugged, and caps doffed at sight of the Yew and Quatrefoil coat-of-arms. A column of geese waddled across the lane, bringing Richard's transport to a brief standstill.

He took out Aubrey's framed miniature once more. Whatever headaches this epiphany was going to cause Richard – as much would it affect Clemence. A smile curled the baronet's lip. Just the trauma, eh, to send her fragile mind into meltdown again?

Most of the household was in the forecourt to greet him when he arrived. The domestic staff was ranged in tiers up the colonnade steps, the line bobbing up and down in bows and curtseys like a draught-wafted curtain as his presence passed. Tall, handsome footmen. Petite, pretty housemaids. Weather-beaten outdoor staff. Nice to know the estate could afford them.

As he glanced from face to face – most of them unknown to him since they rarely crossed paths – he was weighing up how many might remember young master Aubrey. Not many. Flitcroft of course. He'd been at Eardingstowe longer than anyone. Mrs Dean. They were the only ones as far as he could tell. Frampton the gamekeeper, who had taught the Somerlee boys to shoot, was long dead. So too Nanny Jude.

'Flitcroft,' he said as the staff began to disperse, 'is Her Ladyship at home?'

'Yes, sir, in the sitting-room, keenly awaiting your homecoming.'

'Yes... I'm expecting my man-at-law, so admit him to my office when he arrives,' he said, making a cowardly retreat on a day when the Light Brigade had been much in people's thoughts.

He was not looking forward to hearing what she'd have to say about this Aubrey business.

In his study he sat, tugging and twisting his cravat. Only the butler and a few dust-clearing and grate-cleaning servants were trusted to enter this sanctum. None had access to the drawers in the chiffonier whose only key remained with the master when he was away from home.

He took a bottle of laudanum from the cache and drank… and drank…

Richard watched as the shaking hands on the desk before him settled. Had the autumnal mist lifted from his mind? How the dog days did start to whine when he was without this nectar.

Presently, the solicitor arrived.

'Brandy, Mr Boscawen?'

'No thank you, sir.'

Richard cast the man a suspicious look. Did those around him think he drank too heavily?

'Well, Mr Boscawen!' Richard perched on the edge of the desk. 'What are your thoughts on this person purporting to be Aubrey? If you won't have a drink, have yourself a puff or two of good, clean tobacco.' He offered the box and lit the cigar Boscawen picked.

The solicitor peered at the baronet through his first exhalation.

'You are convinced the person is a fraud, then, before you meet him?'

'Of course! If the Serbs had him all along – why no ransom demand or anything? He'd have been no use to 'em.'

'Well, if he had no memory, sir, they'd not have known who he was!'

'Wouldn't have been difficult to find out. Hussar uniform. Distinctive enough. So, you'd think they'd enquire were there any hussars in the charge unaccounted for. Not hard, surely?'

'We don't know for sure what happened to him,' said Boscawen. 'He might have escaped the Serbs for all we know.'

'Hmm.' Richard narrowed his eyes. 'Clearly, you're enchanted like everyone else, Mr Boscawen. Even my daft sister Lady Markham has been out to Vienna to meet him and is waxing lyrical about it. A long-lost wanderer returns. Does have a certain appeal to the romantic sense.'

'Why are you so hostile?'

Richard went behind the desk and, with a sigh, eased his aching backside onto his cushion. He felt as if he'd been shitting bricks. If it wasn't constipation these days, it was piles. Didn't some blasted doctor warn him once that overuse of laudanum could do this kind of thing to you…?

'He's an impostor, Mr Boscawen! I just know it. I don't have to meet him and have him remember what we had for dinner one evening in March 1848 to decide this. I don't want him here; do you understand me?'

'As you wish, sir. I assume you intend to take the matter to court?'

Yes, that would be less humiliating than repaying the Aubrey impersonator what he was owed.

And what if the man really was Aubrey…?

Richard's look went to the miniature of his father, the elder Sir Richard Somerlee, which stood on the desk. The eyes glared right out at him. Displeased with everything Dickon ever did or thought. And young Aubrey? *You* make a pater proud, my boy. Please God he should be watching and weeping…

TWENTY-SIX

As Richard was sitting down to a luncheon of rabbit fricassée and a glass of Marbuzet, just over two hundred miles away in Shoreditch a cripple with a crutch was shuffling along on one and a half limbs. A scruffy pig snuffled in a heap of rotting fish. The infirm elder took no notice. He peered through the glass of one property where a sign hung.

Inside the unremarkable office, a lady was sitting at a desk, writing away. From her garments and appearance, she might have been a schoolmistress or governess. Her fair hair was worn in a topknot. Her muslin gown was a dove-grey colour. A plain, silver quatrefoil hung from a chain around her throat. In the fingers she was not writing with, this charm she twisted around and around.

'Help an old sweat?' The fellow gave her a hopeful beam as he limped through the door. 'Veteran of Inkerman. Seventeenth Lancers.'

The lady looked up from her correspondence. A freezing smile was on her face.

'Lost your wits as well, did you? Cavalry weren't at Inkerman. How did you really lose your leg? In a dock fight?'

'Yeah, madam, summink like that...'

The lady sighed and looked him over.

'The credibility of my agency depends on reputation, I am afraid. I cannot offer you employment.'

She glanced outside. Rain clouds were gathering. London's dregs were stooping towards the workhouse. Legless-one would be joining them no doubt when she turned him away. She went on, in a softer voice:

'Go through to the kitchen. Take a bowl of broth and be on your way.'

The woman leaned her brow on one hand and went on working.

'What time you want to close, Your Grace?'

Clemence looked up from her escritoire as her assistant put the question to her.

'Perhaps when the daylight is gone, Meg, as long as there is no-one waiting. Or sooner, maybe. I am tired… Toiling beyond what a body can stand is bad! I learned to my cost once before.'

The employment agency was her own creation, the premises and small staff she'd hired paid for out of the allowance her father had left her. What would her money be spent on otherwise? Prettifying her senescent figure in fripperies and furbelows?

She had started with a dining-hall for the poor of East London. But as she'd dished a ladleful of good things into a bowl, the customer had sniffed and remarked to the next in line: 'Ain't as good as the Whitechapel soup kitchen. They do chops there.' Anyway, filling bellies of indigent souls was dropping pebbles into a well.

Yet she could find those who had come upon hard times employment! A situation in service, even scouring dishes, was a step out of the vicious circle of destitution. A fallen woman with bastard issue, a Crimean veteran minus a body part – who would employ them? Snobs would, if the Duchess of Ardenne recommended them. And so Clemence had set up her agency, shamelessly exploiting her connections.

Even so, she had to be steely. Those she wrote her characters and letters of introduction for must be of integrity; she would lose the goodwill of her social-climbing and titled employers should she supply ne'er-do-wells or persons in liquor.

Her aunt had been against her scheme. But was it a knife in the ribs in the savage courts of Bethnal Green which Lysithea feared? Or that Clemence was in danger of overwork and another breakdown?

'I'm not china, Aunt,' she had snapped. 'Sixteen years ago, I was barely out of pantalettes, and I'd just lost the man I loved!'

'Here, take your testimonial.' Clemence handed the document she had been composing to a woman who had come through the connecting door which led from the soup kitchen. 'With this, Lady Percival should take you on.'

'Thank'ee, Your Grace!' The child-bundle under the woman's coat also bawled its thanks.

Clemence watched the shabby mother crossing to the street door. Who was the blessed and who the unfortunate? This woman had no home, no means of income apart from prostitution – until Clemence had secured her a situation as a scullery-maid, lowest of the low in the servant hierarchy. But she had a child. Something Clemence did not.

The poor wives of the East End cried over where the rent was to come from; Clemence wept into her feather pillow for what most women took for granted. A child of her own. To Clemence, these flowers in life's garden became more remote with every season plunging her deeper into barren middle-age.

Where was Philo these days? Clemence's husband called sometimes when his dwindling coffers dictated. If only he'd divorce her.

What if Clemence was free of him? She was thirty-three last birthday. Still tolerably charming, and wealthy enough to be married for her money if naught else.

But she had spent three years in an asylum. Who would take a bride with insanity in her family? Well, Albert of Saxe-Coburg did it for a crown…

Yes, her prospects. Exit the Duke of Ardenne from Clemence's life and another more unscrupulous still might take his place. The new groom would wed her, bed her, and report his fears over her renewed mental instability. Clemence would be locked away again, this time for life, and her spouse left to enjoy Lysithea's inheritance unchallenged for the rest of his undeserving days. Strange to say therefore, but Philoctetes Consett was the best protection Clemence currently had.

Brandon Fanshawe was seldom far from Clemence's thoughts. How rarely had she seen him, though, since he'd helped get her out of Dwellan House. Society functions where they might have met were rare territory for outcasts like Clemence Somerlee.

Now and then, Aunt Lysithea might remark something like 'Oh! I saw Lady Fanshawe at the Marlboroughs' dinner-party last night. Looking pale, poor creature, since the pneumonia laid her low last winter.' Or 'His Grace was telling me Fanny Fanshawe was in the Lords for the debate on Monday. Why, we haven't seen him for years, have we, chicken? Perhaps we might invite him and Phyllis to dinner…'

But Lysithea never did. And the spectral sightings continued to dot Clemence's landscape.

She'd heard once, the previous year, that Brandon was going to be at Viscount Van Schalten's wedding, which she and Lysithea had also received invitations to.

'I think we should go, Aunt Lizzy. The Viscount's such an old friend of the family.' Occasional acquaintance of Dickon more like. But it was worth a try.

'Oh, I don't think so, Clem. You've nothing decent to wear, dearest!'

And thus, Clemence had got the message.

One thing her aunt had *not* reported was seeing the Fanshawes together at some occasion. Might it really not be a happy union, then? They had no family.

Clemence sighed and went to fetch her outdoor cloak and bonnet.

'What is it?' she asked the woman she employed to help run the agency, who was waiting to say something.

'Beg pardon, madam, but I'll not be back next week. Got a place in the match factory I have. Pays better, madam, with respect to you.'

'Aye. Well, I wish you well, Meg, and I trust you'll not be back in the soup queue when they've laid you off with phossy-jaw! Here, take the wage you're owed.'

A light spring shower was in the evening air when Clemence went out into the street.

On the corner, a bespectacled socialist with an East European accent was bawling. His shrill voice competed with the boozy ruckus which was issuing from the *Duke of Cambridge* tavern behind him. A sailor and his chuckling, buxom Nancy were rodgering on the steps.

Three men who wore the pearly coats and flat caps of costermongers were performing something Mr Blake was unlikely to have composed as they staggered Clemence's way.

'Whassa matter, girl?' one said, seeing Clemence looking. 'Shockin' you, are we?' and burped.

'I've been more soused than you on the chef's sherry!' Clemence retorted. She'd surprised herself – and Lysithea – with the coarseness she had brought back from the Crimea.

She caught sight of a young woman shivering by the railings and stepped over.

'Do you need the fee for the nethersken?' Clemence asked. She would hand over the three pennies with pleasure. But what good would it really do? Such an outcast might as well die of cold this night as the next. The workhouse – the spike as it was commonly known – would have closed its doors for the evening by now. Clemence asked her name. 'Well, Martha, do you think you could work for me?' she told the surprised girl. 'Aye, I mean it.'

Clemence sat beside her in the doorway. The socialist's shriek grew as he began to speak of the destruction of the ruling classes.

'I've lost a worker today and I need someone to replace her. If I give you money for the nethersken for tonight would you come to my agency tomorrow? You'll be sweeping up, serving in the soup kitchen, running errands. I will pay you enough to find regular lodgings. Then we can look out for a better position for you.'

Martha was just mumbling something, when a rattling sound made both women jump. They looked up to see a policeman looming over them.

'You've been told once!' he barked at Martha. 'You ain't soliciting outside this here pub! And you,' to Clemence, 'ain't seen you before, but we'll not have Judies on this beat. Go ply your trade down the docks.'

'And if Martha and I refuse to move, what then?' said Clemence.

'Well! Let's see if a night in Bishopgate Police Station gives you a civil tongue!' He shook his rattle again. A policeman's rattle was meant to summon a colleague to his aid.

Instead, the wheels of a vehicle clattered into the court. A barouche appeared. On its door was the coat-of-arms of the Juncker von Schwangli. A liveried coachman halted a pair of horses with their noses in the air.

The policeman's chops dropped open.

'Just one moment, Archer,' Clemence told the driver. 'I wish to see this young lady settled in her lodgings.'

'Very good, Your Grace.'

'Here, Martha.' Clemence took a shilling from her reticule. 'Try Nettle's nethersken. I hear it's not so bad. And if you want the job – be here tomorrow bright and early.'

When she'd sent Martha on her way, she returned to the sumptuous equipage which so did not belong here. Archer handed her inside.

She leaned out to speak to the speechless officer, who had possibly just ruined his career.

'My aunt, the Countess of Schwangli, will be dining with the Chief Commissioner next week. I am sure she will mention you.'

Lysithea was waiting for her.

'In the sitting-room, Your Grace,' the maid told Clemence. 'Mistress said you was to see her soon as you returned.'

'Oh, really? I can't imagine what I've done now, Gates,' Clemence said. The maid took Clemence's cloak. 'Aunt doesn't approve of my grubbing in the slums, but I fancied she was used to it by now.'

Lysithea rarely took her into society. Clemence was too wont to turn a drawing-room conversation onto what should be done about the spindly living shacks of Limehouse whose walls oozed dampness like they had pustules, and their starving occupants. There would be an awkward rattle of saucers by way of response.

All day, Clemence had been working up to: 'Aunt, do you think we might spend the summer with Philo at Kingsmede this year?' *where we might get invited to the Fanshawes' over at Woodmancote sometime.* Now she might not get chance to ask if Lizzy was preoccupied with something else.

'Your sister was here, Your Grace, until about an hour ago,' the maid went on. 'Lady Markham was waiting for you, she was, but got bored and left. But she looked real excited, Your Grace, when Mr Pickford let her in.'

'Well I never!' Clemence muttered. The only thing she and Isabella had in common was estrangement from Dickon and Eardingstowe and the enmity of their sister-in-law.

'What did Bella want?' Clemence said as she entered the sitting-room.

The countess was facing the hearth. She swung around. Her look was ashen.

'Aunt Lizzy? What is it?'

'Clem!' Lysithea crossed the room as swiftly as her rheumatic pains would allow and took Clemence's hands in hers.

'Sit down, dearest. I have something to tell you.'

Her aunt eased her onto the ottoman and sat beside her. Lysithea heaved a massive sigh.

'Be prepared for a tremendous shock.'

TWENTY-SEVEN

The candle-flames in the two branched, ormolu candelabra were the only heat-source at the dining-table. The atmosphere between the two diners was frigid. Three footmen were also present, so the baronet and his lady had to be polite to each other. Somerlee ancestors in ruffed, Tudor costume were looking on from within their picture frames.

'Better send felicitations on the meal,' Richard said after his first taste from the dish of compote of orange, 'after that gaffe about Mrs Dean in the newspaper. I trust you were able to placate her, my dear, and persuade her to stay?'

'With difficulty,' Amathia replied.

Richard downed a few more mouthfuls. He must remember for his own future use brother Carswell's bright solution for the disposal of Mrs Dean's less successful offerings.

'Might I enquire what business kept you in your study all afternoon?' his wife asked.

'Mr Boscawen, my notary, detained me. He can be a dreadful pettifogger when he chooses. I didn't think I'd get away in time to dress for dinner.'

The entrée finished, Richard watched as the white-gloved footmen removed the plates to the pier table.

'So! How are you, my dear?' he asked, dabbing his lips with a napkin.

'Suffering all the usual tribulations which a woman's lot are,' she replied, referring to her pregnancy. 'We have received invitations to the Duchess of Manchester's ball,' she told him, 'and Princess Louisa's wedding.'

'Splendid. Plenty to look forward to then! And how are the girls?' He did not take in most of her reply. Her interest in their daughters, he knew, was as flimsy as his own.

'How was Parliament since we last saw you?' Amathia said.

'Interesting. You'll know about the new Reform Bill?'

'Of course! Where will it end I wonder?' Amathia shook her head as the footmen served the baked turbot. 'I gather the outcome will be the enfranchisement of every artisan and coal scuttler in the land? Madness.'

'Quite. And not only working men,' Richard said. 'Do you know there's talk of the vote for women too? And this isn't merely the fancy of bluestocking spinsters. Some perfectly sane, scholarly men are in favour of female enfranchisement.'

'Well! At least we women get to understand these things by proxy. We hear enough politics from our menfolk! But giving working *men* the vote… that's unthinkable.'

'Oh? How so?'

'Really, Dickon! What can a hedge-mender know of politics? So how can he be trusted to vote in the best interests of the country? *And* it would make him forget his place.'

'Hmm… revolution, eh? And the ruling classes pitchforked into the ditches! I doubt our legislation will take things so far, Amathia, so don't practise kneeling on the block just yet.'

Richard took a long sip of claret. He peered at her through the cut glass of his drinking vessel. With candles and a silver table centre separating the diners, and the chandelier twinkling over them, quirky physics distorted her image into a spotty goblin with flaming eyes and a billhook nose.

Some evenings, dining with her like this, he bethought of slipping something into her wine. The inkling set his mind on fire.

Then the thoughts – in this order – of some Liberal-supporting pathologist from the Home Office easily detecting Richard's unsophisticated crime, the socialists' jamboree when one of the landed gentry was hanged for murder, and the disappointment of his easy-going God, deflated the fantasy like a burst balloon making a rude noise.

He set down his glass with a thud. He narrowed his eyes as he gazed at her.

'I suppose we must discuss the homecoming of our wandering Odysseus.' Richard sat back and cupped his hands over his middle. 'You know, I can barely picture Aubrey's face any longer. I seem to remember his gleaming sword and cherry breeches rather better!'

The main course of jugged hare arrived. As the footmen served, Amathia gave him a withering look.

'Has it not occurred to you that this person is most likely a fraudster after your brother's money?'

Richard stabbed the hare with his fork, chewed, and finally looked up.

'Isabella believes him. She's the only one of us who's met him so far.'

'But he could have discovered what he knows about the family and Eardingstowe from guidebooks!'

Richard raised a brow.

'I don't believe Mr Baedeker mentions Bella's rodent.'

'Some dismissed servant, then, would be privy to this kind of information!' Amathia snapped.

'I appreciate what you say, my dear,' said the baronet. 'Quite right you are, of course. As a matter of fact – that was the gist of my long conversation with Boscawen. I'm thinking of taking out a lawsuit.'

His listener gazed in surprise, and then looked pleased.

'Bravo, sir!' Amathia said. 'Of course, this person's a fake! I've no time for Isabella. Sometimes I think she's as mad as Clemence. Indeed, let's see a lawyer on the case!'

Yet suppose he's for real? The silent words made the meat in Richard's mouth taste rather uncooked. *After all he's suffered – his own family shuns him!* And really – there was nothing implausible in memory loss after a blow on the head, was there?

'Are we sure this is Aubrey?' Clemence asked at last. 'I mean… he will have changed so.'

'Bella's convinced of it,' the countess said. 'She's met him. I suppose she learned first because her husband's with the diplomatic corps. Bella's been to see him at the hospital in Vienna.'

'So, what happened to him?'

'He'd lost his memory. Now his memory has come back.'

Clemence twisted the quatrefoil charm on her pendant around and around. Could she picture Aubrey's face after so long away?

She heard her own stunned voice asking where had he been?

'A captive in some kind of gaol. He didn't know his own name, poor soul. Imagine the terror!'

'I've thought he was dead all these years!' Clemence turned her eyes to her aunt. 'It'll be like meeting a phantom.'

How had she felt during that old tragedy? Heaven knew. The war and its aftermath had gone dim, and good riddance to most of it; blasted, she supposed, when Dwellan House turned her mind to mush. Could not remember what Sebastopol looked like, what colours this or that regiment wore, what famous people who she knew she'd met like Lord Raglan, Captain Nolan or

Florence Nightingale had ever said to her. It was all a wasteland like what a dust-whirling tornado would leave behind.

Only... now it appeared it was all going to be raked up again.

'What does Dickon think?'

'It remains to be seen, chicken.' A merrily wicked look came into Lysithea's eye. 'But Richard has Aubrey's inheritance now, remember? This is going to be very awkward for him.'

'If the man even is Aubrey.'

'What do you mean?' Lysithea demanded.

'He could be a fraud... All the world's heard of Aubrey Somerlee, the dashing hussar who never returned from the Valley of Death. And all the world knows he'd be worth a lot of money if he resurfaced.'

That night, Clemence had difficulty sleeping. Flipping one way on the mattress, and then the other. Sitting up. Thumping the pillow.

The brass inkstand and Tompion clock on the davenport desk, frilled rim of the toilet-table, oriental fan in the fireplace, and silk swag draping the mantelpiece... all gave off a yellowy glow from the light of the lamp below the window. The hour was close to midnight, but from the roadway there came an unstopping rattle of wheels, hooves and coachmen's cries.

Even after a decade of living in the metropolis with her aunt, still she missed the lullaby of the owls, watery moonbeams shimmering through the branches of the yew. Clemence had not seen her birthplace for many years. Visiting the dotty relation in Dwellan House was her only contact with her native shire.

Immersed in her work among London's poor, she was forgetting.

Until this shattering news had come. Aubrey not dead. Something worse. A lonely prisoner without friends, loved ones, even a name all those years. It was ghastlier than the most gruesome of battlefield slaughters she'd conjured in her nightmares.

Meanwhile, she had to face him soon. Where would she find the courage to meet this spectre? *Or trust that he was who he said he was?*

The butler came in and bowed.

'A visitor, Your Grace.'

Already? Clemence's drawing-room calls were not due to start until the afternoon, and many would they be. Stacks of cards had been left in recent days – callers wanting mainly to jabber and drool over the wonder of the season. The return of Cornet Somerlee had pricked the attention of even the morose widow of Windsor: Lysithea had been invited to court so that the Queen might hear the news in person.

'Who is it, Pickford?'

'His Grace, Your Grace.'

Clemence soothed a hand over her eyes. She laid down her pen.

'Good day to you, Philo.'

The Duke of Ardenne poked his head around the morning-room door, beamed at her, strode across the carpet, swept up her hand, and embraced it.

'You're looking well, m'dear.'

'Any reason I shouldn't?'

'Well, I am a tad relieved, Clemence, to see you radiant!' Philoctetes Consett stood beside the escritoire, her hand clasped within both of his. 'Heard you'd been consorting with some rough sorts down the East End. Feared I might find you smoking a pipe and singing sea-shanties!'

He took himself to an easy chair, sank into it, and crossed his legs.

'Don't mind if I smoke, do you, Clemence?'

'Lysithea does...'

Philoctetes lit a cigar and began puffing away.

'Really – it is good to see you blooming, Clemmie!'

'Yes. Not in your interest, is it, that I should go before Aunt Lizzy? Then you'd not see her inheritance.'

'Now, now, Clemence! So cynical you can be!'

'Philo – you and your sister shut me away in a nuthouse. How cynical should that make me?'

'Come, Clemmie! You know that was sissy's doing, not mine. And you were genuinely in a state, you know...'

'So I was.'

She found her eyes trailing the coils of cigar-smoke, and making dragon-patterns out of them, as she tried to think back to a lost time. Her month or so of marriage-tide, before they'd taken her to Dwellan, was obscured in the dreaminess of her illness. One scant remembrance she had was her bridegroom parading about the boudoir in a quilted dressing-robe and tasselled nightcap.

'Well... you can't do me much harm now I don't suppose, Philo... except give me the clap, perhaps. But what brings you here?'

'Just a social call! I say – ' The duke leaned towards her. 'That brother of yours what went missing. Dash it – I've heard he's turned up again!'

'Oh... I see... you've heard the news.'

'Sure he's the real thing, are you? Well, I mean, he could be an impostor you know.'

'As I haven't met him I cannot say!'

She invited him to stay to luncheon so that he could hear all about Aubrey. He could then regale his courtesans with the tale, and his path need not cross hers again for the foreseeable future. Since he was here, though...

'Philo... are you intending to spend the summer at Kingsmede this year? Only reason I ask... Lizzy and I quite fancy a country sojourn.'

'Sorry, old thing. Bluebely Baxter and I are heading off to Biarritz. But you're the Duchess of Ardenne, damn it. Your home as much as it's mine, old girl. Shall I tell the staff to expect the both of you?'

'I'll... I'll have to discuss it with Lizzy,' Clemence uttered. Probably she wouldn't dare; Lizzy might wonder at her ulterior motive.

'So, Clemence, I hear his regiment are bringing Aubrey over right now...?'

TWENTY-EIGHT

She stared up at the soaring, blond façade of Dorchester House – one of the city's most elegant residences. The twin turrets glowed in the light of flambeaux which jutted over the street. It was a blustery evening so the flames flickered and darted. Orchestra music floated from within. That polka – didn't she once dance to it with James?

Lysithea, meanwhile, had mounted the wide, marble steps. She was giving her name to the footman, while Clemence held back. She didn't really want to attend a ball, did she? And prance and stuff herself while half of London starved and shivered in the rotting tenements? She'd rather be in Seven Dials among the beggars, thieves, whores and cut-throats... wouldn't she?

Stuff and nonsense – she was no saint, really.

'Well, Aunt, I'll come for your sake. Because they'll all be twittering about Aubrey. I'll not leave you to face the clacking tongues alone,' she'd said, or something like it. But in her secret thoughts? *It's a ball... I may wear my prettiest dress again...and you-know-who will probably be there...*

'My dear, dear Countess! What's this we hear about your nephew, the wandering cavalryman?'

Three feathered headdresses and two evening suits with sky-blue sashes zoomed down upon them the instant the Somerlee women stepped into the entrance-hall.

'Is it true Aubrey's been found alive?'

'Why! My dear Duchess!'

Lady Percival swept across the vestibule, manoeuvred through the horde, and then thrust her arm through Clemence's.

'All the town is talking about the news! Your brother – that brave hussar who disappeared – coming home at last? How thrilled you must be! But apprehensive, too, perhaps?'

'What a tremendous shock for you, eh, Duchess?' Sir George Rutherford appeared on her other side. 'Have you met the chappie yet? Convinced he's really Aubrey and not some impostor, are you?'

'He'll be much thinner, I daresay, after being kept a prisoner in that castle all those years,' said a second chortling gentleman. 'Feed him up, Duchess, feed him up!'

Clemence had never lost her fear of crowds and wide-open spaces. No man of medicine she had consulted seemed to understand her malady... just another symptom of hysteria. So very usual in females who had no husbands, or who lived apart from them in her case. And she didn't wish to be sent back to hospital now, did she?

Normally these days she could confront and overcome this bugbear.

This swarm of beings in the entrance-hall of Dorchester House, however, felt as if it was going to suffocate her. Separated from her aunt in the crush, Clemence mumbled an apology – then flitted away. Creatures... so many *creatures*... A splotch of social-climbers, place-seekers, fortune-hunters... Like a swarm of insects. Buzzing every unknown tongue in the galaxy. *Sucking all the air, suffocating!*

Up the grand staircase to the saloon where the music was she hurried.

She found a seat with the other matrons at the edge of the dance-floor. No sign of Philo as far as she could see. That was a relief. Otherwise she'd be obliged to partner him in a waltz or two.

'Your Grace!'

She looked up to see a rather charming beau standing in front of her. He made a polite little bow.

'Are you otherwise engaged?'

He was requesting her hand for a dance? The fellow couldn't be more than twenty-two! Heartbeat quickening, she glanced to either side to be sure it was no mistake, and he hadn't meant to address some youthful beauty sitting nearby. No... only dames even older than herself flanked her. Fancy... she was a girl again in her first season – going all fluttery when asked onto the floor.

'Thing is, Your Grace,' the young man went on, 'I was wondering whether you would...' He hesitated, diffidently. 'Well, Your Grace... my sire's the proprietor of the *Daily Globe*. We were wondering about the possibility of an interview with you and your aunt. About this person claiming to be your brother Cornet Somerlee...'

'Oh! Ah, yes, of course!' She snapped open her fan to hide her blush.

'Is he truly Cornet Somerlee, Your Grace? Can you be certain of his identity?'

'As I haven't met the man yet, I cannot say. Please put your request for an interview to my aunt in writing. We shall consider it,' she said.

What had she been thinking? Even the gouty oldsters weren't likely to ask a dowdy duchess to dance. She was a married matron... kept forgetting that somehow. What a scandal her tripping a measure with this young cavalier would have been... the thought rather cheered her up.

Her eyes followed each dancing pair which came by. Green silk Polonaise gown. Black velvet embroidered Swiss belt. Dress uniform of the Royal Welch Fusiliers. A triple loop of pearls with a diamond pendant. A pearl-studded *cachepeigne* with a lace net. Over by Sir Robert Holford's magnificent fireplace, meanwhile, Aunt Lysithea was talking with an elderly, be-medalled, military gentleman.

Presently, Clemence's sister, Lady Markham, swept into the saloon. She was at once beleaguered as Clemence had been – and didn't Bella just adore it.

'Lady Markham!' Clemence heard someone exclaiming. 'Do, do tell us about seeing your poor brother in Vienna. Pray, how has his ordeal altered the poor fellow?'

Isabella might see Clemence any moment and bring her retinue over. So Clemence stood and slipped away.

Artificial greenery in a Grecian urn partly covered the doorway. The leaves obscured the people who were gathered on the balcony beyond.

'Heaven forefend!' came a female voice. 'What can have persuaded the countess to bring her? What is the creature wearing, I ask you? That garment must have been gathering mothballs since 1858!'

'Oh, dear me yes, Janet dear,' said a different woman. 'I daresay flounced gowns were high fashion in her girlhood in the fifties. But this is 1870! Hasn't she heard of the bustle the poor thing?'

'And, oh, that hairstyle, Clarinda! Ha-ha! No doubt she hasn't heard of the chignon either! Ringlets belong to the day Sebastopol fell! The day, I suppose, that Clemence Somerlee's mind stopped.'

Clemence's knuckles, which were clenched around her fan, turned white.

'No wonder the dear duke wouldn't be seen dead in her company! Poor Aubrey will head back to Austria in horror when he glimpses her, ha-ha!'

'Mad as the moon, like all the Somerlees! You know the unbalanced creature actually visits the very worst parts of the city? Bringing home heaven knows what rampant diseases.'

'Probably came straight to the ball without changing or taking a bath, ha-ha!'

Clemence swept into view.

'Good evening, Mrs Marchelsea, Mrs Wriothesley,' she said with a welcoming smile. 'A wonderful soirée Sir Robert is giving as usual, do you not think? And how remarkably clean he keeps Dorchester House! No rampant diseases anywhere.'

Clemence went on her way, leaving the fragments of shattered social careers trembling on the airwaves behind her.

Scurrying downstairs, she brushed past someone just mounting. She sprang to one side.

'Your Grace!'

'Lord Fanshawe!'

Her voice had come out as a squeak. She snatched at her silver quatrefoil and twisted it around her fingers.

'Is the ballroom on fire?'

Oh, yes, Fanny, it sure is. She turned her eyes away from him.

'Are you here with the duke?'

'Good Lord, no! With Aunt Lizzy. And you… you are here with Lady Fanshawe?'

'Regrettably not. My wife is indisposed with a seasonal ailment.'

'Ah! They can be such a trial.'

'But you, I trust, are in good fettle?'

'Very rude health, thank you, My Lord. I've barely had a day's sickness since the cholera almost bore me off.'

The dance ended. A new waltz begun. She'd not heard it before. Might it be that new piece the world was talking about? *The Blue Danube.* Mr Strauss, wasn't it? In Vienna. Vienna… her thoughts came back to Aubrey.

'Lord Fanshawe, have you heard that Aubrey has been found? Yes, he has been alive all these years. A prisoner, it seems. He'd suffered memory loss.'

'Your Grace... I do read the newspapers...'

'Everyone is talking about it. Talking, talking all the time! Asking me what I think, what I'm going to do about it...'

'Your Grace!' His tone was sharp. 'Clemence,' he went on, gently. 'Please don't talk about it if it upsets you.'

'You've as much right to ask as any! You were with us when he vanished.' She flapped her fan so hard the breeze ruffled the locks of hair which had strayed loose from her ringlets.

'Clemmie!' He caught hold of her hand and halted the flapping. 'Look at me, Clemence.'

She focussed, blood flooding her cheeks as she did.

Green-flecked grey eyes. She'd once thought they were like the sea – deep, deep, deep and changeable. Sometimes, in the fastness of her bedtime, she thought of Phyllis receiving an anonymous warning that there was an assassin out to get her. Or being able to spy on Fanny in disguise without his knowing.

'Clemmie.' He smiled suddenly and bowed his head to her. 'May I have the pleasure of the next dance if you are not already engaged?'

Clemence found her way out onto the terrace. She could still hear the music despite the walls in between.

She needed air, Clemence had told Brandon after their dance, and hurried out here alone. She breathed in the earthy, grassy scents of a damp garden.

One dance with Fanny and all the pain of losing him – dull after so long – had burst like an ulcer. She'd never got over him. Just shut a flimsy door on the wailing waif. And fantasising about hurting him, or Phyllis and therefore him? What kind of a beast was gestating inside her?

She puffed out her cheeks. Pressed a warm forehead against a marble urn full of flowering hollyhocks.

Across the flagstones zigzagged the moonlit trail of a night creature which had lately scuttled by. Past the steps lay the lawns. Chinese lanterns lit the walkways. A lady and gentleman ambled arm-in-arm beneath blossomy cherry boughs. The glow from the city's lights made a milky canopy over the grounds.

A soft footfall paused a few feet behind her. Had Brandon pursued her after all? Would he make her his lover here on the terrace of Dorchester House, with Sir Robert's party guests looking on? What a rainbow Armageddon that would be.

'Clemence? You are Clemence, are you not?'

But it was an unfamiliar, male voice. Something about the sound made her shiver.

'I almost wouldn't have recognised you! Why – you were only seventeen last time I saw you.'

She could feel her heart hammering like an old fruitcake she'd known back at Dwellan shut up in isolation and banging thump-thump with his fists on the door for hours on end.

'Aren't you going to greet me, Clemmie? I thought Bella might have told you she was bringing me here tonight.'

Her unsteady legs would not support her. *Where was the bench...?* She fumbled her way along the wall and crumpled onto the seat.

Slowly, she raised her eyes. Couldn't look into his face... stared instead into the beams of a lantern which hung beside the French windows... all she saw in her side vision was a blurry, smiling, masculine figure in evening dress, scarlet sash, and dark hair shiny with oil.

'You are Aubrey?' She heard the piping of her own voice.

'Aye, Clemmie. Lost all these years! Back from the dead.'

He took a step closer. She leaped up from the bench. Stumbled behind it so that it shielded her from the apparition.

'Oh, my sweet sister!' He stretched out his arms towards her. 'The last time we spoke, you and I, was the night before the Light Brigade charged. We ate the fruit of the strawberry tree together, do you recall, on the cliff top overlooking the bay? And we could hear the bells of Sebastopol.'

Clemence backed a further pace away from him.

'I was scared, remember? You were the only one I could admit that to,' the stranger said. 'Recollect what we said to each other that night, Clemmie? I said I was afraid I might be riding to my death. You said… "All that loss of life, Aubrey. Those poor, dead men… English, Russian… and the wives grieving at home. But maybe it will mean there will be no more wars. Wouldn't that be worth dying for?" Then you gave me the locket which Mater gave you on your confirmation day – the one with the engraving of St Anne and the Virgin. And I carried it with me into battle.'

Around her the garden, the house, everything went whirling. He dashed and caught her in his arms.

TWENTY-NINE

Cramped between the corner of King Street, and the church of St Katharine Cree, Somerlee House's only elegance was a colonnaded porch. The baronet's residence in town was four narrow storeys of smoky brick and Georgian-era windows. Leadenhall Street was not terribly fashionable; the family rarely entertained here.

'Do you know there are some exquisite, *modern* establishments for sale in Berkeley Square and Regent Street?' Amathia said one day. The parlour where she was looking out from overlooked the office of a maritime insurance company. Wagons carrying fruit and vegetables to Covent Garden market were lumbering along, and drovers chivvying soon-to-be-eatable-meat. You could see stray dogs and sots, too, using the historic Aldgate pump as a public convenience. 'Eardingstowe has its faults, but it does possess a certain quaint charm.'

Richard looked up at his wife who was perched in the window-seat. Her shape was very *enceinte*. From it, any month soon, the next baronet should pop. Or just another daughter. The way Richard's luck was going right now, what were the chances?

'Do you realise we've had a property around this site for as long as we've had Eardingstowe?' he asked.

'Oh, that does not surprise me, Dickon. No doubt they are original drains, too.' Amathia wrinkled her nose.

'I wouldn't have thought so. The original drains probably didn't survive the Great Fire. But some of the stonework has! Once, when I was very young, one of our longest-serving retainers took Ivo and me, with Aubrey toddling along after us, right down into the deepest reaches of the basement! We saw some very old bricks with black fire stains. But this wasn't from that piffling mishap of 1666, no, this was from Boudicca's conflagration. That's how long the Somerlees have lived here, Amathia, so tell me again you prefer more refined neighbourhoods!'

'Boudicca tried to burn this place down, did she? Good for her!'

But he wasn't listening any longer.

'Are you coming with me to Westminster Hall?'

'I most certainly am. Never mind how unsightly I am in this condition. I'll go to the witness-stand if necessary to tell the world this upstart's an impostor.'

'Well, it's comforting to know that at least I have your support, Amathia! Although not everyone believes this man's a charlatan, you know. Isabella's convinced he's genuine,' he said – to himself.

He got up from the sofa and sauntered over to look out. A cart jolting its way along the street shed a cabbage which plumped into the gutter. An urchin dashed to scoop up the bounty.

'And I made up my mind to take out the lawsuit before I met him,' he finished.

'Richard! You've seen the fellow. Spoken to him. You'd know your own brother for heaven's sake however many years he'd been away!'

'Yes! Absurd. Of course, I would.'

Truth be told, his memories of Aubrey weren't especially endearing. He pictured the juvenile Aubrey climbing the

Eardingstowe yew tree... doing gymnastic fancy stuff while swinging from the lower branches, something the young Richard had been too plump to do well. Aubrey braving the legend to wade into the mere waist-deep. Aubrey tumbling a farm-girl in a hayrick when he was barely out of school.

So what? Richard had everything else – house, land, title, cut-glass wife, a politician's power to send men to their deaths on a remote peninsula, flunkeys to wipe his backside if he wished.

And then he had met the man claiming to be Aubrey. Those eyes, that smile... By George, they were remarkably similar, weren't they...? Stirred some feeling in him, somewhere...

'Ivo believes in the fellow too,' Richard went on, troubled. 'Ivo's told me, in no uncertain terms, he thinks I'm quite callous....'

Oh, let this bothersome person just be a fortune-hunting impostor. It would make everything so much easier.

Lysithea faced the drawing-room door as the butler brought in the visitor. Clemence was seated beside the hearth, feeling antsy.

'Your Grace, My Lady... Mr Aubrey Somerlee Esquire,' Pickford announced. How to designate the man was debateable in fact. Technically he had never left his regiment and Cornet Somerlee was still correct.

The man stood for a moment on the threshold, surveying the room. A smile melted his features. He stepped forward, lifted Lysithea's hand and kissed it.

'Aunt Lizzy! Clemmie!' he said as he bowed to each in turn. 'Tea by the fire, just the three of us! *Quel* cosy delight!'

Middling height. High cheekbones. Slim to medium build. Cavalryman's moustache. Softly curling hair between black and dark brown in shade, gleaming with Makassar oil. Bright eyes of an autumn-sky blue. A nonpareil of manly beauty, indeed. A well-spoken beau in checked, nankeen trousers, morning coat and embroidered, piqué waistcoat. An urbane officer... Everything Aubrey had once been. Yes, he could be Aubrey. But he could be plenty of men who you'd chance to meet in the park.

Quel... yes, Aubrey used to say that, though...

'My dear nephew!' Lysithea took a deep breath. 'How pleasant to see you restored to us!' She hesitated before laying a cautious hand on his upper arm.

'Aunt Lizzy.' Aubrey smiled, and kissed her on both cheeks. He held her at arm's length, studying her face. 'You have barely aged at all!'

Well, that was a brazen fib for a start. The countess's once-raven hair was claymore-grey, and she'd taken, this year, to walking with the aid of a stick.

'Do sit down, Aubrey. Would you care for some tea?'

'Yes please, Aunt.' He perched on the ottoman, crossing one leg over the other. The countess sat opposite, tea-table between them. 'I see you no longer have that Chinese carpet with the yellow and mauve lotus flower pattern,' the newcomer said, espying around. 'I never forgave myself for spilling tea on it that time. Do you recall? Mind you, little Peking, your dog, loved it remember? He was lapping it up.'

'Yes! Yes...' Lysithea's words came out in an awkward squeak.

Clemence twisted her quatrefoil around and around. *What is he trying to do? Prove he's Aubrey by remembering things only the real Aubrey could have known?* And who could blame him after the aspersions the press had cast? And Richard taking him to court to expose him as a fake? Well, Dickon and his wife would, wouldn't they? They were the ones who had most to lose by Aubrey's return.

But what if Richard is right? Could this courtly swain taking tea with us be a cheap conman after Uncle George's legacy?

The countess handed him a cup. Clemence stared... and caught a flash of gold as his lips parted to thank Lysithea. *The* tooth Aubrey'd broken, tumbling from the hayloft one merry harvest-time.

'So! You have endured a great ordeal, Aubrey,' said Lysithea.

'Mercifully, Aunt Lizzy, I recall very little from those lost, dark years. My captors told me I was an Englishman. But that I think I perhaps knew. I mean, isn't it in the blood, being an Englishman?' Aubrey smiled. He sipped his tea and his look turned to Clemence. 'Do you know what became of Dora, Clemmie?'

Dora? Who on earth was she? Oh, yes...

'Your sweetheart before you went away? Well, I believe she married a merchant seaman. Her eldest must be at Charterhouse by now.'

Aubrey nodded.

'Yes... couldn't expect her to have waited really I don't suppose...' He drank some more, then turned to the countess. 'And how is dear Aunt Cassie?'

'Still at Dwellan, Aubrey.'

'Ah, that is sad to hear. She was the most loving lady I knew – so kind, and gentle.' He gave a wistful smile.

'I was a patient in the madhouse too, Aubrey, for some time after the war,' said Clemence. He looked up, startled. 'Did they tell you? I was ill, you see...seeing strange things, hearing voices...'

'A scone, Aubrey?' Lysithea handed him a plate.

'However many years you were gone, Clemence,' he said, 'you cannot imagine the decades of loss which I endured. Do you realise I did not even know who I was? No name, home, history, nothing.'

'And how did you come to remember?' Lysithea asked.

'My memory started to come back. My own version of your voices and pictures, Clemence, you might say. Images that meant nothing at the time. The violet bushes in the parterre which you and I helped plant, Clemmie. Then one day my name came back too.'

He munched a scone.

'Thank you for looking after my faithful Sparkle,' he said to Clemence.

'Sparkle?' Clemence replied. 'Yes, he was found wandering loose after the charge. Most of the horses were killed. You saw their great, fallen shapes all over the valley. Like boulders left over from a battle of gods and titans! But Sparkle survived. Richard kept him at Eardingstowe until he died.'

'Richard has his last shoe in fact... had it silver-painted,' said Lysithea. 'It's hanging in the gunroom. By rights it ought to come to you, Aubrey.'

'No. Leave it be! It can be a curiosity to show future visitors. The shoe of a horse who rode in the Charge of the Light Brigade.' He finished his cup of tea. 'You must miss Eardingstowe,' Aubrey said to Clemence. 'Why did you leave?'

Clemence gazed beyond him towards the light shining in through the window.

'I don't believe I would have... if it had been up to me.'

'Have you been home to Somerset yet?' said Lysithea.

'No, no I haven't, not yet.' He smiled as he looked away for a moment. 'So many memories coming back now like old friends! Clemmie, do you call to mind that time you and I ran away together to Dowsborough?'

Clemence pictured the deserted, windblown banks and ditches of the Iron Age hill-fort high in the Quantocks.

'There's a legend about that place. No Somerlee is welcome there,' she frowned to herself. 'So, two arrogant little Somerlees wanted to defy the curse,' she went on with a half-smile. 'I suppose we Somerlees must have done something unspeakable there once.'

'Which we've fortunately now forgotten!' Aubrey said.

'Well, you and I thought to spend the night there, remember? But we got hungry for our tea and scurried back to Eardingstowe—'

'—before the shadows got us,' said Clemence.

'—and we found when we got back they'd shut the main door! Flitcroft let us in, though, through the garden door.'

'So he did…'

'A young footman he was then, and a kind heart to be sure.'

The stranger downed another mouthful of scone. He looked up at the countess.

'I believe you've lost Uncle George while I've been away? Killed during the Indian Mutiny, I understand? My condolences, Aunt Lysithea. He was your favourite brother, I know.' Aubrey laid down his plate. He sat back, an arm resting on the back of the sofa. 'Dash it, I was fond of George too, Aunt Lizzy. Recall how he used to visit us children in the nursery and tell us about Waterloo? I used to ride that old rocking-horse remember, and pretend I was there in the cavalry charge in Flanders. Pegasus…'

'Yes, well… I think we've had enough reminiscences now, Aubrey!' said Lysithea. She rose and rang the bell. 'I've had a room prepared for you.'

'Well, I'm quite comfortable at the Carlton, Aunt Lizzy.'

'Oh, we've years of catching up to do, Nephew. And we'll begin over dinner.'

Was there a glint in Lysithea's eye, Clemence wondered? Did she, too, suspect him a fraud?

THIRTY

'So! You have no recollection of leaving the battlefield at Balaclava?' Sir Berkeley Mountjoy Q.C. boomed into a hushed courtroom in Westminster Hall.

'No, sir,' mumbled the man on the witness-stand. 'There is much, still, I don't remember. The headaches come and go.'

'And yet you claim you are Aubrey Somerlee of Eardingstowe, Cornet 7460 of the Eleventh Hussars, last seen on October the twenty-fifth, 1854! Remarkable memory, really, wouldn't you say?'

Press and public benches were so crammed they looked like overcooked sausages bursting at the sides – Somerlee versus Somerlee was the must-see event of the season.

Could the stranger really be the vanished cavalryman, returned from the Valley of Death after sixteen years? Or was his brother Sir Richard right and he was an impostor?

How uneasy Richard seemed. And who could marvel? The world knew the baronet had declared Aubrey legally dead – and had been gaily spending his not inconsiderable fortune. How very awkward. How very *unbrotherly*.

Richard could hardly bear to look at his fellow litigant. He focussed instead on Mr Justice Porteous's quill scratching away as he made notes. Gazed at Sir Berkeley's wig. At the clerestory windows. At dust particles floating in the ochre-coloured light which beamed down from them. All around the grand courthouse where England's justice creaked and crept like a glacier gouging valleys and raising mountain ranges. Studied his wife's wedding ring as she showed her solidarity with him, laying a hand over his and squeezing. That plump, pale appendage had done nothing more strenuous in its life than throw erring servants into vats of boiling oil.

Tiny bits of silver threaded the fellow's dark side-whiskers; just a very few lines beginning to make inroads on his brow. So – about the right age. Aubrey would have been thirty-five. The right height, too. But so were half the men in the courtroom. Lean. Consistent with a man who'd withstood a hard life in captivity. Even the way he'd swaggered a little as he'd climbed the steps to the witness-stand… it stirred something in Richard's memory.

None of the Somerlee children had been photographed, more was the pity. The pater had been something of a fogy. He'd never ridden on a train. And he'd not had his or his children's photographs taken. Only the miniature watercolour of Aubrey existed – and it had been painted when he was still in Eton jackets and caps.

But Aubrey's gold tooth? One of the young cornet's few distinguishing features which those close to him could summon up. Of course, someone out to impersonate the missing Somerlee for the money would affect all Aubrey's idiosyncrasies as part of his grand scheme, including deliberately disfiguring his gnashers for authenticity.

'He's not Aubrey, Amathia!' Richard whispered. 'I'm sure… certain – yes, absolutely certain. Beyond a shadow of a doubt. Yes!'

Sir Berkeley Mountjoy Q.C. had been questioning Aubrey all morning.

'When did your memory begin to return?'

The litigant put a hand to his brow. He claimed he suffered from mal-à-têtes – a symptom one supposed of his catastrophic head injury. His eyes rose to meet Sir Berkeley's.

'About a year ago… I believe… I was in hospital. But I don't know how or when I got there.'

'This was the hospital in Vienna, loveliest of cities. What do you remember of Vienna?'

Aubrey shook his head.

'Nothing. Only the hospital. A little.'

'And how did your memory start to come back?'

'It began with images… visions… which meant nothing, then. I had dreams of a tall, thin lady with bluey-grey hair, wearing an apron with a daisy-motif on the left breast. I know her now. Nanny Jude. And I saw people – working people – dancing around an old yew tree. One of the girls wore a kind of medieval tabard. May Day at Eardingstowe… the girl was dressed as St Laurey.'

Noon came and went. The sun shone at its highest and brightest in the brilliant, stained-glass window in Westminster Hall, sank and faded into amber. The questioning continued.

'Think back, if you would, Mr Somerlee.' Sir Berkeley had an indulgent smile on his face. 'What was the name of your first nursemaid?'

Aubrey frowned; was he searching deep in a damaged memory for an answer?

'Sally Dacres, sir. Her father was carpenter on the estate.' He smiled. 'When she came up to the nursery each day, she used to bring plums and sparrow-grass from the kitchen-garden, and always left the largest plum for herself.'

'And Reverend Brookes, who was vicar of St Laurey's for most of your childhood. Sir Richard had a particularly revolting nickname for the poor fellow.'

'Indeed.' Aubrey smirked. 'I shall write it down, sir, and show you in private so that the gentlemen of the press remain oblivious.'

'Where were you held captive, Mr Somerlee?'

'In a castle. My captors were Serbs. I speak Serbo-Croat. Must have learned it from them, I suppose.'

'Yes, we have established this,' Sir Berkeley said. 'Mr Visnijic from the Austro-Hungarian Embassy has already testified to this court that you do indeed have a reasonable command of this tongue.'

'My gaolers used to talk about a free land for the Serbs.' Aubrey looked distant. 'And assassinating the Sultan of Turkey.'

'How and when did you come to leave this anarchistic fortress?'

Aubrey hung his head, looking lost.

'I don't remember. I only remember the gentleman from the British Embassy coming to me in the hospital in Vienna. He asked me my name. Suddenly I remembered it was Aubrey Somerlee.'

'Quite remarkable,' said Sir Berkeley. 'I don't believe I can recollect so much detail about my earliest nursemaid.' He sniffed, shaking his head and sipped his water.

Richard had been engrossed throughout the exchange. He leaned over the bench and whispered to his solicitor.

'We did right paying for the best, Mr Boscawen. Berkeley's making a nonsense of his story.'

'Tell me, Mr Somerlee,' Richard's lawyer went on, 'when was the summerhouse built in the grounds at Eardingstowe?'

Aubrey looked lost again; how bewildered must a man be – journeying back from the Valley of Death? He brightened, smiling.

'There is no summerhouse! But we have a rotunda in the Paradise Garden. I don't know when it was built…'

'Heaven forbid,' muttered the baronet. The end of the session was nigh, and the impostor had not so far been caught out. True – he had been unable to tell the court whereabouts in Eardingstowe the portrait of Pretty-boy Somerlee hung, but then, to be fair, Richard did not believe he could either. Thankfully, the Aubrey-fellow's counsel looked a paltry cove – having waived his fee no doubt, because the high profile Somerlee case was an opportunity to get his insignificant name in the newspapers.

'And there's a stone circle and prehistoric cursus,' Aubrey went on. 'Up on the hill on the northern shore of the mere.' He looked faraway as if picturing these treasured mementoes. 'And a Temple of Victory by the ha-ha. It was built to commemorate the end of the Seven Years' War.'

Richard took a swift glance at the itchy, eager scribbling of the pressmen in their notebooks. The story had gripped the nation's and world's imagination. The Queen and Prince of Wales were said to be following the drama unfolding at the Court of Common Pleas. President Grant was reading about the Aubrey Somerlee case in the newspaper over breakfast in the White House. On ranches in Brazil they had heard the name Somerlee. And family dirty linen would be aired in Ultima Thule.

Dear Lord... had Richard done the right thing? Maybe it would have been less damaging just to accept the Aubrey-fellow.

On the following day, Aubrey's witnesses gave evidence. Among them was a hussar captain named Radlett.

'On the evening before the Charge of the Light Brigade,' he told the court, 'I had a private conversation with Cornet Somerlee. We discussed death and the afterlife. We knew – as soldiers do, you see – that it might be our last night on earth. We were alone when we had this talk, he and I. There was not a soul near us. I am positive I have never spoken of this conversation with anyone. Yet this man,' glancing at the litigant, 'knew what Cornet Somerlee and I discussed that night.'

Sir Berkeley rose to cross-question.

'Captain Radlett. You say this discourse was conducted in total privacy.'

'Absolutely. I have never breathed a word.'

'I'm quite sure,' said the lawyer with a smile. 'At what time in the evening was the conversation? Before or after dinner?'

'Before.'

'And where was Cornet Somerlee during and after dinner?'

'I'm afraid I'm not sure…'

'No indeed, Captain. Just because *you* have not breathed a word of this encounter, does not mean Cornet Somerlee did not! In fact, he had about ten hours between your conversation and the mustering of the troops next morning when he could have told the whole of Balaclava for all you know. Hah! He could have sent a telegram!'

Sir Berkeley flapped out his gown and sat down.

Throughout the day, Sir Berkeley went on to cut a swath through the cream of the British cavalry.

Major Mortlake moved the court to tears recounting the last time he'd seen Aubrey. The final certain sighting of him, in fact. The duo had been riding close by the Causeway on the return from the Don Cossack battery when a cluster of shells had gone off. Aubrey had vanished in the sulphuric residue which smothered the scene.

The major was adamant that this fellow could not possibly have known about their meeting with the rebel Polacks unless he'd been there that day; but Berkeley established that Mortlake had told God-knew-how many people of the anecdote to the extent that the Czar himself had likely heard it by now.

As the sun set and the close of the day beckoned, Aubrey's counsel summoned his final witness.

'I call Lady Markham.'

Richard drew in a sharp breath as his sister swept into court. Isabella spared him a brief glance only as she approached the witness-stand.

During the court's noonday recess two days later, Richard took a walk along the Embankment. He thought he might go insane sitting in that stifling chamber – so many eyes watching his every move, his every nuance. Amathia had returned home to Somerset yesterday, unable to bear any longer the double discomforts of pregnancy and public scrutiny.

He watched the passing river-traffic as he sauntered. Great steamers and little wherries were churning water before them which glittered with sunshine. A different watercourse was this since Mr Bazalgette had built his sewer-system. Only a decade had passed since the Great Stink. Refuse, animal corpses, rotted foodstuffs, night-soil, government protocols… anything which could ming had found its way into the poor Thames. Westminster had ponged so even the politicians could not stand it and vacated the seat of government until something was done about it. Well, Richard smiled to himself, maybe London never would be fragrant like spring roses. But compared to what it had been before Mr Bazalgette's engineering feat…

He tipped his top hat to other strollers he passed on the breezy waterside. 'Why, that's the bad baronet!' he just caught a gentleman whispering to his lady companion.

Yes, doubtless in the drawing-rooms of the ton they were all gossiping about the maleficent Sir Dickon, eulogising Aubrey in middle-class parlours, and cocking a snook in low gin-palaces. Aubrey was a hero and an underdog; Somerlee the bounder who had snaffled the rightful inheritance of his brave kinsman who'd survived the Charge of the Light Brigade.

And there was his public face at stake, God damn it! Not just his parliamentary career... but Smoky Mountain. He'd sold thousands upon thousands of pounds' worth of shares in that faraway fount of plenty... Without Richard's discreet networking among the moneyed classes, investment in the mine might cease and the gold nuggets stay where they were. He was Roger Cormorant's figurehead – upstanding, spotless, dependable...

Yes, he wished he'd never brought the lawsuit. He should have tacitly accepted the stranger. If he was the real Aubrey, wouldn't he have been so relieved to be home among loved ones again that the small matter of the legacy could have waited? And, let's face it... what harm, really, could a pseudo-Aubrey have done?

Too late it was now. Richard had ridden into the Valley of Death and had no way back.

THIRTY-ONE

Clemence galloped across a heath and wetlands which were buzzing with arthropodal life. Weeks of grinding legal argument in Somerlee versus Somerlee had left her yearning for the breezes of Somerset. She'd got away from London before facing the wham of the judge's decision.

She rode over bronzed countryside still in flower despite the approach of autumn. Waysides and riverbanks were flecked with the lace, blush, lemon and ultramarine of cow parsley, ragged robin, silverweed and speedwell. The waterways were bubbling and vocal from recent rain.

Through a small gate she walked her horse and onto a twisting dirt-track. The path climbed the outlying slopes of the Quantocks. She remembered the way from her girlhood. The sangaree-coloured hackney she was riding was a local hireling and knew the route too.

She came out from the woodland onto a blustery hillside of flaxen gorse, bracken and heather, dotted pink with meadow saffron. The shifting air current tossed the leaves and rocked the branches of the few elderberry bushes which grew here. Pristine cloud raced overhead like the sails of superyachts. The keening of skylarks, stonechats, pipits and buzzards filled the warm air.

Will's Neck rose ahead of her against the sky – zenith of the Quantocks and Eardingstowe demesne.

Will's Neck. What an odd name. As a child, she had once asked the oldest tenant then living on Eardingstowe land who Will was. *Wealas,* he had told her, it truly was. The old Britons, then, the proto-landowners of hereabouts – and these uplands saw their last stand against the usurpers. Blood must once have darkened these brooks and winterbournes. It was as if the feathered airborne were the spirits of those slain cawing their jubilation at her misfortunes.

Clemence dismounted and tied her horse to the branch of an isolated rowan tree. She stepped onto a rock to look over the landscape. A scent of moss was in the wind. Her cloak was billowing westward. A beclouded sun beamed a violet and amber fan onto the dark ridge of Exmoor's heights on the far skyline.

Holy Heaven, she wasn't afraid any longer. Horizons as far as the eye could see – and she could ride and ride and ride. So, were her own demons dead at last – cast into the firmament with abandon? Blossoms sprouting again in the trampled soil of the Crimean battlefields?

She remounted and walked her cob around the summit path.

Sixteen years ago, Clemence had prayed and prayed for her brother's return. Now, she almost wished this man was not Aubrey. If he was… what fresh pain must he be suffering as his loved ones denied him?

Every twist and turn of both sides' cases she had followed. The man's knowledge of the family and Eardingstowe. Things only a Somerlee could know. Or could they? Was there really anything he could not have learned from a former servant, say? Who knew what intimacies might be lying dormant in her father's yellowing correspondence, which pretty-well anyone could get hold of if they knew where to look?

What about the reception which Aubrey's brother-hussar, Captain Radlett's testimony had received? How could anyone but the real Cornet Somerlee have known about this private discourse between two soldiers on the eve of the battle, demanded the newspapers?

But Clemence had. The last time she'd spoken to Aubrey that evening, he had told her what he and Radlett had said to each other. Even so, who might Clemence in turn have told? Few indeed, surely?

She approached a ring of rowan and thorn trees. The wind was so fierce on the most exposed face of the hillside they were swaying their limbs like pagan priests worshipping at an altar. Three Quantock deer shied back into the woods as the horsewoman drew near.

All those prayers answered at last. He was back. He was safe. She should fling her arms around him; clutch him so that he could never go away again.

But if he isn't Aubrey? What if Dickon is right and he is committing a fraud against me, against all of us? Is he Aubrey? I don't know. He was nineteen when I saw him last. His hair is dark like Aubrey's was. He has bright, blue eyes...

Heaven knew what Lysithea thought of him. She wouldn't say. But she'd seemed at ease in his company, laughing with him. And Isabella? Oh, Bella's belief in him could have won him his case.

'The pale blue *poult de soie chinée* parasol with the guipure fringe which I received for my fourteenth birthday? How could anyone but the real Aubrey have remembered this?' Isabella had asked the Court of Common Pleas.

No. He cannot be Aubrey! The Aubrey I remember would not be so cavalier as to dredge up our past just to prove who he is. "Did you ever own up to Nanny Jude that it was you, not little John, who snaffled her currant buns that time, Carrie?" *Honestly!*

Yet if he is Aubrey... and I don't make up for the love he has missed all these years? Can I take that chance?

Dear God, what if he is Cassandra's elf-prince come to destroy the Somerlees?

Mr Horace Boscawen hurried out of the courtroom. Leaning against the brass-studded door behind him, the baronet's solicitor took a few heavy breaths.

Richard had dashed off to Somerset the day before to attend the birth of his hoped-for son and heir... and as Lady Amathia had retired into her chamber, so His Honour Mr Justice Porteous had retired to his.

Boscawen waddled along the corridor formed by the screens which shut off the other law courts. He sought out a clerk.

'I must send a telegram to Sir Richard urgently!'

Richard turned a page of a book he was not really reading. He eyed the clock in the Eardingstowe library.

'Oh, my! How ghastly all this is,' he said.

The sounds lately coming from the direction of the mistress's boudoir had made him uneasy. He'd heard somewhere that females made that ruckus because the agony of childbirth was the Lord's punishment for the first woman's sin; men hadn't got off much lighter; they had to live through the dreadful melodrama. Surely it couldn't bode well? Or maybe she was doing it on purpose to scare him?

'Thought for one frightful moment it was my playing you were objecting to!' his friend Brandon Fanshawe ventured. 'It's a new piece I've not played before. Unpractised, see...' He was sitting at the grand piano, proud centrepiece of the reading room.

'No, you go on playing, Fanny. It's a pleasant distraction. I was talking about this hateful business – begetting an heir!'

Richard went on. 'Wish we didn't have to. But,' he intoned on a deep sigh, 'Somerlees there've been at Eardingstowe since before the Roman occupation, and the ancestors will never forgive a fellow who lets the line die out.'

Brandon put his head down and picked out a few more bars. Curses… Richard had gone and put his foot in it. Brandon Fanshawe had been widowed two weeks ago and had no children at all. At least Richard had the girls, which were better than nothing.

Brandon ceased playing as the sound of hurrying footsteps approached along the corridor. Both men turned to look.

'Congratulations, Sir Richard!' The midwife bustled in, still wiping her hands. 'You've a healthy son. Hear him, bawling furiously!'

Sure enough, they could.

'Ah, thank you, Mrs Birtles! The best news a man could hear.'

'And Her Ladyship's in fine fettle too, or as fine as might be expected after the ordeal.'

'I am pleased to hear it. Please convey my intention to call on Her Ladyship as soon as she wishes.'

The woman departed. Richard breathed a long-drawn-out sigh.

'My congratulations too, Dickon!' Brandon said with a smile in his eye.

'Thank you, Fanny. Amathia and I have decided on naming our first-born son Edmund, after my grandfather. We'll make that Edmund Brandon if you'd care to be godfather, old friend?'

'My pleasure. I think Beethoven's Ode to Joy might be in order. May I?'

'By all means, Fanny! Never so sweet will it have sounded!'

Brandon turned back to the keyboard.

Richard crossed to the bay-window. The slopes of the hills were blazing with flowering gorse. He could make out a pack of wild ponies. They looked as if they were racing the rolling sun-shadows towards the fold of the combe.

'So, the Somerlees go on for one generation more, eh?' he said. 'I was getting worried! Might have seen the old place in the grubby hands of that impostor otherwise.'

'Oh, Dickon, why can't you just accept Aubrey? Everyone else does. It would make all our lives easier, you know.'

'I suppose you were converted because he remembered how you once took him fly-fishing, were you?'

'No! It's simpler than that. I just like the man. He seems so genuine. So very plausible. So *likeable*, Dickon!'

'He can steal the silver now if that's what he came for, Fanny, for all I care,' Richard said with a beam. 'Well, I've announcements to make! Edmund Brandon Somerlee, born the twenty-ninth of September, 1870. Grand new entry for the family bible! Ring the bell would you and ask Flitcroft to fetch us a bottle of the best champagne,' he said as he was already heading for the door. 'And let them have a jug of cider or something downstairs...'

As the sun set on Edmund's first day in the world, the baronet took a walk on the northern bank of the mere where the tree cover was densest. Squirrels hoarding their contraband were heard scurrying up the nearest boles as the human tread crunched through the undergrowth.

Richard paused on the shore where tiny wavelets lapped up to his feet. He breathed in the pondweed smell of the water. So refreshing to be away from the city. Ah, the tang of whortleberry, heather and bracken – all damp after a brief shower in the afternoon. Soon he should do the decent and go and see his wife and infant.

Richard frowned, and calculated: fifteen years he'd been enduring arctic couplings with that woman and doing his damnedest to render them life-engendering. His endeavours had been rewarded until now with four little girls and a stillborn boy.

Now, at last, a living son. Very alive in fact: from the south stairs Richard had been able to hear the little monster howling.

Meanwhile, he could now tell Amathia what he had long rehearsed in his dreams – amuse yourself with whichever of the footmen takes your fancy from now on, and I'll trouble you no more.

But one shouldn't be complaisant, however; children sometimes died young; the memory of little Margaret and John saddened him still. And age had advanced early on the onetime beauty Amathia. Her fecundity might well be done sooner rather than later. Perhaps he ought to do his marital duty for a few years yet.

His eyes swept the estate as far as he could see. Just over the brow of the further bank stood the prehistoric monuments. By Heaven, the enormity of the legacy! The ha-ha followed the course of the medieval inner bailey, which in turn followed the boundary of the Iron Age enclosure.

Well, it seems you have a new guardian when I'm gone. The birth of young Ned meant that the bloodline which stretched back to that proto-Somerlee who'd planted the yew was unbroken for one generation more.

After dinner, he paid his calls. Exchanged politeness with Amathia, lying weak in her birthing chamber. Proceeded into the nursery to see the new Somerlee.

Well, the wriggling youngling was noisy, fat and fleshy, thank the Lord. Jerky hands already trying to grab things.

Two of Richard's girls were present too, and they were thrilled.

'We'll be having a christening feast for all the tenants won't we, Pater?'

'Whatever you like, Feodora dear.' Richard continued to gaze at the new-born. The hours-old creature seemed to catch his eye and return his stare. Amathia's grey-green eyes, not Richard's blue ones.

The nursemaid lifted Edmund out of the crib. She offered him to the master to hold. Richard flinched.

'Don't you want to nurse him, Pater? I've held him. He's beautiful.'

'Ah, but you have steadier hands than an old crock like me, Beatrice.' But to satisfy them… with a dopey smile, he stroked the baby's wispy, fair hair.

A sizzle from the hearth. The warm day had become a cool evening, and the nursery faced away from the afternoon sun. The spout of the kettle on the mantelpiece was dripping a little. A drop into the fire sent a funnel of flame hissing into the flue, there to etherealise.

Two days later saw the new father puffing his unfit way into Westminster Hall. Richard's solicitor was waiting on the steps beneath the great, arched stained-glass window in the St Stephen's end of the building, visibly fretting.

'I've taken the night-train to get here as quickly as I could, Mr Boscawen. I assume this is important enough to merit it?'

'Yes, sir. His honour returned to court an hour ago, sir.'

'Oh! And…?'

THIRTY-TWO

Mr Boscawen loosened his cravat.

'He's found in Aubrey's favour.'

Richard leaned against the arch to steady himself. He covered his eyes so that multicoloured supernovae spotted the blackness.

Still wheezing from his one-hundred-yard dash from the cab, he peeped through a gap in his fingers. Beyond Mr Boscawen's shoulder, he saw newsmen scrambling for the exit to file their stories. They were not shy of elbowing each other. In the rush, a passing clerk got mishandled. His upset pile of legal papers went fluttering and hammock-rocking on the disturbed airwaves. Boscawen, meanwhile, was babbling something about an appeal…

'No!' Richard rubbed a moist brow. He hung his head for a moment, and then straightened. 'No, Mr Boscawen. I'm sick to Heaven of this ghastly business. I'd rather just graciously acknowledge defeat.'

'Oh… fair enough, Sir Richard. By the way. Congratulations, sir, on your new arrival.'

Richard grimaced his thanks. With slow and heavy tread, he made his way along the arcade which ran around the law courts. The notary went too.

'You believed in him, didn't you?' Richard said as they drew near the outdoor egress where the pressmen had headed.

'I just do your bidding, sir, you know that.'

Outside in Palace Yard, Aubrey was already beleaguered.

'Please...' he was saying to the reporters. 'Don't crowd me!'

'But you must be delighted at the verdict, Cornet Somerlee?'

'How do you feel about your brother now, Cornet Somerlee?'

'Do you think Sir Richard treated you cruelly?'

'Do you intend to rejoin your regiment or live at Eardingstowe?'

'What was it actually like to be in the heart of that famous battle? Did you see the death of Captain Nolan? Lord Cardigan deserting the field?'

'Please,' Aubrey murmured, 'I'm tired... and I can hardly take it in.'

The baronet stepped forward. A hush dropped upon the pack. All eyes turned to him. Traffic down on the river and in Whitehall seemed to have halted. Even the crows and pigeons who haunted the site seemed to have fallen silent.

Richard laid a hand upon Aubrey's shoulder.

'You heard my brother. He has been through a terrible ordeal and desires privacy, as do I. Please do us that courtesy.' He steered the bemused man towards Whitehall where there were cabriolets waiting, baying bloodhounds still in pursuit notwithstanding his plea.

'We can talk here. Lost in the crowd,' Richard said. 'The Gardens are one of the attractions of the season.'

Richard and Aubrey alighted from the ferry at Cremorne Pier. Ahead of them, the pleasure garden's famed illumination display was in progress. A phantasmagoria of light was sweeping the grounds and treetops.

The two men joined the swarm of bustles, feathered chapeaux, billycock hats, bobbing balloons and little sailor suits, hurdy-gurdy men and organ-grinders funnelling through the gates. Viennese music came floating over the flowerbeds. You could smell fried periwinkles, onions and dog-mess everywhere.

From a stall, Richard purchased Yarmouth bloaters on forks, and glasses of hot sassafras.

'I imagine your palate is not refined, Aubrey,' he said, handing the other man his food. 'I don't suppose the Serbs fed you like a Christmas goose?'

'Not as mean as the army,' Aubrey replied.

The two men joined the crowd heading along the avenue towards the heart of the park.

'They're selling something pretty adventurous at that stall over there if you're in the mood,' Richard said, pointing with his cane. 'It's called a "cock tail." Something brought over from America, I believe. Got whiskey in it. Have you falling over before you reach the Crystal Platform.'

'I don't think so, thanks all the same,' Aubrey replied. 'We Somerlees have never been ones for moving on with the times, you must agree. Shan't try to change the habit of a millennium,' he added, and took a bite from the bloater.

'As you wish…'

The pair stood among the oohing spectators who were watching the zooming light beams. For one shining moment they all inhabited a fantasy-world of gold trees, indigo humanoids and grassy-green heavens. As he ate, Richard eyed the man who stood beside him. *We Somerlees*, indeed! Who was this sprite, this hobgoblin, who had brought such turmoil into his life?

'Recollect Cremorne, do you?' Richard said. 'The Gardens were here, as I recall, in the summer before the war.'

'Yes…' Aubrey drawled, frowning as if struggling to remember.

'I believe so…' Was his mosaic memory still troubling him, Richard wondered? Or was it all part of his impostor's act? 'I came to Cremorne with some chaps from the mess. I believe Charlie Radlett was among them…'

'This might be new to you, though.' Richard waved towards the far side of the field. 'The world has moved on since 1854.'

A balloon was preparing to take off. As the two men watched, it began to rise, carrying a basketful of earthlings-no-longer, squealing as they left the ground for which their Maker had intended them.

'Quite thrilling, that,' Richard said. 'Went up myself when I was last at the Gardens. You can see most of London laid out like a model-town. Tiny trees. The river looking like a little ribbon with toy boats on it. But I suppose you've already had all the excitement one can expect in a lifetime?'

Aubrey was still gazing at the flying-machine. His eyes and hair kept changing colour from the lights.

'How are you feeling, old man?' Richard said. 'You looked pale – back there, facing the press. The Cossacks were nothing in comparison, I'm sure.'

'Why did you rescue me from the reporters?' Aubrey turned puzzled eyes on him.

'You looked as if you were about to pass out.'

'But you don't believe I'm your brother.'

Richard and Aubrey stared at each other. Sapphire-blue eyes holding midnight-blue ones. Neither flinched. Richard was the first to look away.

'I don't know what to believe anymore. You're a stranger, whoever you are. But I don't wish to go on fighting you. You've a home at Eardingstowe if you want it.'

'Eardingstowe!' Aubrey murmured. 'Somehow, I knew, even when I didn't know who I was, that I didn't belong in that cold castle. I knew I had a true home somewhere.'

'As I say, you're welcome.'

Defeat wasn't easy to accept. But the world could not call him an unfeeling landowner if he put his arm around this lost waif and took him home.

On the far side of the trees, the orchestra could be heard playing 'Lorelei.' Richard strolled on in the direction of the music. On every side you brushed shoulders with the well-to-do and merchant classes out for an evening's jaunt. A kid with a whip-and-top made the damn thing spin right through an upended bowl of plum duff so that the mess spread right across the walkway just in time for Richard to tread in.

'I suppose you won't know much family news?' he said. 'My wife's name is Amathia, daughter of the late Duke of Ardenne. We have five children – Caroline, Clara, Feodora, Beatrice and baby Edmund.'

'Yes, I remember Mathy Consett. She came out with Clemmie. I recall you danced with her quite a few times, and we all thought you made a handsome couple. I look forward to meeting your lady, Dickon, and my nieces and nephew.'

'And, indeed, they are all so looking forward to meeting you!' Richard said. Hardly surprising; even in Eardingstowe's turbulent history there could not have been many dead men to dinner. 'Ivo's a vicar now, bless the dull fellow, and has a dull wife. Carswell's in the army. A cornet like you, in the Buffs. Bella I believe you're already well acquainted with. I'm afraid we lost little Margaret and John in the cholera outbreak of '59.'

Aubrey touched his brow and shut his eyes for a moment.

'Please be patient, Dickon. I have difficulty remembering things even now.'

'I'll be as patient as you wish, Aubrey! Eardingstowe's thriving,' Richard went on. 'We can afford more these days. We've a Brueghel hanging in the saloon. Entertain more too. Amathia's made our soirées the most sought-after of the season.

There was talk of a royal stay. But since Prince Albert snuffed it, the old girl don't get out so much. Pity.'

'You did not mention Clemmie,' said Aubrey.

Richard turned away for a moment. On the small lawn in-between the flowerbeds, a travelling band of German musicians in Bavarian costume was playing flute and oboe. They said 'Ta, chuck' to those who tossed them coins.

'I'm afraid Clemmie and I are not really speaking.' Richard felt warm under the collar. The other man's look was boring into him. 'She's a duchess, you know. Married Amathia's brother. Not that we see much of either of them,' he said, pretending to smile.

'How is your parliamentary career these days, Dickon?' Aubrey said. 'I hear Disraeli thinks highly of you.'

'Well, that's as maybe!' Richard gave a wry laugh. 'Not that it matters much in the wilderness! Gladstone and the Liberals are in power, of course.'

'Well, let's hope the Tories supplant them soon. The Tory Party,' Aubrey added, musingly. 'You know – it's odd. In Ireland the word 'Tory' means a rebel. Yet here – the political party most closely associated with the landowning class. Don't you find that strange?'

'I suppose so. But I've not heard it before.' Richard eyed him. 'How do you know this, Aubrey? You've never been to Ireland. None of us has.'

'Oh, one third of the army is Irishers.' Aubrey laughed. 'Tommy, Sandy and Mick, you know. Must have heard it in the mess sometime.'

'Talking of Ireland... we have some land there,' Richard said. 'Not worth all that much. But there's a house I believe... some paying tenants. Little place named Kilara or somesuch... Damned nuisance it is in truth! Spend most of my time evicting the bothersome tenants when they default on their rent! But land is land. Perhaps you'd like it, old chap? Don't suppose you'd want to live there...' Richard shuddered. 'But it'll take you away from me... I mean, give you independence.'

'Kilara, eh?' Aubrey's outlook turned inward. 'I'll give it some thought, Dickon.'

The two men had reached the Crystal Platform in their walk and stood gazing up in wondering delight. The three-tiered structure, like a thirty-foot high wedding-cake, was swimming in radiance as evening fell. The music you could hear all over the pleasure gardens issued from the middle floor where an orchestra played, while at ground level dancers swirled through the light of gas jets and cut-glass lustres. Cables twined around with flowers and hung with Chinese lanterns splayed from the uppermost tier to ground level like outsized maypole ribbons.

'Why won't you accept me, Dickon?' Aubrey asked softly. 'Bella has. So has Ivo, and Carrie, Clemmie and Aunt Lizzy.'

'Frankly, old chap, whether you are Aubrey or not is not the issue! It's just damned uncomfortable – a stranger coming back from the dead...'

'I understand. There's the question of the money too, I guess,' Aubrey added, observing Richard. 'I don't blame you for believing I was dead and claiming Uncle George's legacy... anyone would have.'

Richard waved a dismissive hand.

'As I told you, I'm quite wealthy now so it makes small difference. We'll meet with Horace Boscawen, my man-at-law, anytime you like to discuss particulars.'

Aubrey sipped his sassafras. He peered at his companion over the glass.

'Might there be any chance of making up with Clemence?' Richard's face darkened as Aubrey pressed on. 'I don't profess to understand your quarrel, Dickon. I know only that I have two siblings I love who aren't talking, and that makes me sad.'

Had the old Aubrey been such a busybody? Aubrey or not… Richard was growing to hate this man.

'It wasn't a quarrel in the ordinary sense. Quarrels, as you say, can be mended. Clemmie very nearly went the way of our poor aunt Cassie. Had some kind of breakdown at the time you went missing. She was playing at being a nurse in that ghastly hospital with that harpy Nightingale. What with the worry over you as well… drive anyone moon-mad. Never went as bad as Cassandra, thank God… recovered well enough… but my wife wouldn't have her at Eardingstowe lest there be a relapse.'

'Dear, dear! Have to admit instability runs in the family. Didn't that brother of Grandpater's try to throw himself into the Cheddar Gorge?'

'Yes…' A mischievous thought pricked Richard. *Let's see just how determined an impostor this fellow really is.* 'I say, you really ought to visit Aunt Cassie now you're home.' Ah yes indeed – he perceived the oh-so-very-brief recoil in the other man's eyes. You'd have to want Aubrey's money very badly to go play the part of dutiful nephew in a nuthouse. 'Nothing to fear, old chap. A hussar who charged the Russian guns can face a dotty old dear. And I say – if Cassie accepts you as Aubrey then that truly will settle it. Isn't it the blind who see best and the mad who reason? Oedipus, you know…'

'She might not know me, Dickon.'

'True. So maybe someone should explain to her that the devilish handsome cove who comes a-calling is her nephew! God knows we're inbred enough already. Likely where the insanity came from.'

'Well, you are quite right though, Dickon. I really should call on Aunt Cassie. Clemence said she was visiting sometime next week. I'll go along.'

The duo wandered on, towards the North Gate away from the music.

'Whistler's painted this view, you know,' Richard said, gazing back along the avenue towards the Crystal Platform. But Aubrey's attention was on the balloon as it began its descent.

'The light display… it reminds me of something…' Aubrey said with a faraway look. 'Something's coming back. The shellfire over Balaclava? No, not just that. Something nicer… warm…' He frowned, and then opened his eyes wide. 'Dickon!' He gripped Richard's arm. 'The magic-lantern show in the Great Drawing-Room! The light beams on the wall and the moving pictures in them! You were there, I think. I guess I must have been about thirteen, fourteen, maybe? It must have been Midsummer Eve. I remember there was a fire on the hill, and birch leaves and lilies around the door… Clemmie was there, and Bella… and another girl… I think her name was Janet… She sang "Lovely is the Summer Moon" while those strange images were marching across the wall.'

'Good Lord!' Richard came to an abrupt halt. 'Janet Wilkes-Rodney. She was a friend of Bella's.' He stared at the other man. 'I had forgotten… but now I remember.'

'Yes! Magic-lantern show…' Aubrey's eyes grew distant. 'To us it truly was magical. We'd never seen the like. I mind something you said, Dickon. You said…' he narrowed his eyes in thought, 'you said our whole lives were like a magic-lantern show: false, dancing images projected onto a wall.'

Richard stumbled… and gripped the latticed ironwork of the gate.

Clemence wandered through Dwellan House's parkland.

In the fields beyond the gate, the stalks of wheat rippled as the breeze blew through. An odour of burning drifted from the heath. It must be the swaling of old heather – first hint of the season on the turn towards winter.

The drone of machinery grew louder. The harvest team was

rumbling Clemence's way. This must be one of those mechanised reaper-binders she'd heard of – a thoughtless, bloodless creature which did the work of fifty men. In her youth, a battalion of labourers used to slice their way across Eardingstowe land, sunlight glancing from scythes.

She turned to the ivy-clad house which had been her prison for three years. She could remember which had been her room – up there in the dormers, with the light shining on the glass. Even though she came only as a visitor these days, and a welcome one as she had become a benefactress, she loathed the place because of its memories.

Aunt Cassandra's first meeting with Aubrey had passed as well as Clemence might have hoped.

'Look, Auntie, it's Aubrey back from the war at last.'

'Would you like to know the news from the war, Auntie?' Aubrey had cooed. 'Sebastopol has fallen. The city held out for almost a year. But eventually we captured the Malakhoff and the city fell. The Czar surrendered.'

'That was fifteen bloody years ago, you fool! Are you a madman?'

After two hours of humouring a twelve-year old in a sexagenarian's form, Clemence had left Aubrey to his private thoughts. She could see him still, ambling around the other side of the garden, taking a good look at the chestnut and the shelter.

What was worse than a brother's disappearance? The homecoming of a stranger she could not recognise, know… *or love*. Smiles she gave him were assumed, embraces so perfunctory they made her ache for shame. Shared, obscure memories he insisted on coming up with only irritated. The wisest judge in the land believed he was Aubrey. Why was there no response in her… *why*?

Aubrey returned to her side.

'How can you bear to come here as often as you do?' he asked.

'Because I love my auntie dearly.'

'Our auntie.'

'Oh! Yes… of course, Aubrey… I'm sorry. Just a slip of the tongue…' Clemence summoned a smile. She bent and observed a Painted Lady which was resting, quivering, on a yellow pimpernel, until the butterfly took flight.

'Somehow, I imagined the patients would be walled-in,' Aubrey said. 'But all they've got are a few wattle fences, hedges and that big chestnut tree.'

'There's no need,' she answered him. 'They watch all the time. Up there, see.' You couldn't see behind any of the windows, which either had the light shining on them, or were shuttered. But she knew from her own time here… 'If an inmate strays beyond the hedge, they are down at once.'

'Were you really a patient here, Clemmie?'

'Yes! You'd not believe the weird things I saw and heard. I saw you, Aubrey, many times – a lost soul on the bank of the mere, trying to get our attention and we couldn't hear you. It was heartbreaking.'

'Ah, that was the grief of loss, Clemmie, not madness.'

'Well, it was Amathia and Philoctetes who had me put away – with some assistance from Florence Nightingale. So they could get their fingers on Lysithea's legacy.'

'Clemence, this is terrible! It's criminal that you were sent here!'

'I'm not so sure, Aubrey. Even now, people who recall the night of the Apsley ball give me odd looks.'

'As I heard, you just got a bit potted! That hardly makes you mad. You aren't the Clemmie I remember, though. Always laughing and happy.'

'The war changed me, Aubrey – likely not for the better.'

'I don't suppose I'm the brother you knew, am I?' Aubrey smiled suddenly.

Little as she'd wanted to say it, it was true. Sometimes she thought – that smile, yes, that was how Aubrey smiled; or the way he flicked the dandelion clocks which caught in his hair – she was sure she'd once seen the old Aubrey do the same.

But am I really? Or am I just hoping? Seeing what I want to see?

THIRTY-THREE

Richard was walking his horse along Rotten Row in Hyde Park. The still, warm air was fragrant with the scent of roses in the last bloom of autumn. As he went along, he exchanged greetings with the great and good who one met on this, the capital's most fashionable bridle path.

'Ah! Lady Carbury. Is this your charming daughter? What a sporting bonnet.'

'Thank you, Sir Richard. And will you put in a word with the Party whippers-in about dear Lord Carbury's recent spot of trouble?'

'Certainly, ma'am. Would you excuse me? I see an old friend waiting.' He touched the brim of his hat and rode on.

Mounted on a handsome grey opposite Wellington's statue was Roger Cormorant.

By mutual consent, Richard and his shadowy business partner did not see much of each other. Hundreds had invested in the gold mine over the previous decade, each passing what he trusted was an exclusive whisper to family and cronies… and Richard was laughing all the way to the bank.

'Sir Roger!' Richard drew up beside the other man.

'Good day to you, Sir Richard,' Cormorant said. 'How are you by the by?'

'Fine, sir, fine!'

Richard eyed him with a degree of caution. What would his associate make of Richard's recent rather high-profile humiliation?

'Shocking business over in France, what?' said Cormorant. 'The French Emperor captured! Battle of Sedan was a catastrophic defeat for the Frenchies, eh? Can't see them fighting on with half their army wiped out, Bonaparte in the Prussian King's hands – '

'Or the *Kaiser* as he now likes to style himself,' said Richard. 'As for that Prime Minister of his – dangerous knave, that. Heard Bismarck wants to unite all the German States under Prussian rule. A German Empire? Makes me shudder!'

'Indeed, sir! And now I hear the Prussian army is marching on Paris. Gloomy days again on the continent, Sir Richard. Hope we keep out of it, don't you? Still, at least we're enjoying dashed warm weather, what?'

'So we are, sir.'

Richard kept an eye on the well-to-do riding to and fro along the path. Top hats being raised in greeting everywhere you looked. Ladies in velvet riding habits. Careers could be made or dashed here on the avenues of Hyde Park. The jangling sound of the horse bit could be the clink of coin on coin.

So, Cormorant was not vexed, was he, by all that bad baronet business? *Quel* relief, as Aubrey would say.

'On Friday I'll be going down to Eardingstowe to see my wife and new son,' Richard continued. 'And there's the Exmoor Hunt, too. And then, as you may know, I've a new brother to introduce to Somerset society!'

'Ah yes, I was following the case in the 'paper,' Cormorant said. 'Must say I thought the blackguard an impostor. Had every sympathy with you, old boy.'

'Yes, well, impostor or not, I'm bound to accept him by order of the court.'

'Perhaps you might persuade him to invest in the mine, sir?' Cormorant was smiling mildly.

Yes, that was an idea, wasn't it? Get back some of what that deceiver had stolen from him? In the meantime, Richard had a few notable kills to report to impress Cormorant with.

'I've just come from a meeting with Prince Karl of Romania. He's bought one thousand pounds worth of shares. And Viscount Van Schalten's made a profit of five hundred pounds on his first purchase. He's in the process of spreading the word, ever so discreetly, among his fellows at Boodles.'

'Excellent, Sir Richard.'

'And I've at last persuaded my closest friend Fanny Fanshawe to invest.'

'The Fanshawes of Woodmancote, eh? Very old family! I'm delighted, Sir Richard.'

'So far he's shied from the subject whenever I've raised it. But Brandon recently lost his wife, so I thought a little good fortune would buck up his spirits. And the value of his estate has been falling every year since 1865, you know. So, I assured him that if he could find a hundred pounds in his coffers, he'd be building new hunting stables with his returns by Christmas.'

'You really are invaluable to me, Sir Richard, invaluable!'

'Thank you, Sir Roger.'

'The best thing which ever happened to me was running into you at the opera that night. You more than anyone, Sir Richard, have made Smoky Mountain the global success it is.'

Windsor Castle's soaring Waterloo Chamber this evening in November was ablaze in amber brilliance. Around all four walls one hundred gasoliers were alight. A rainbow merry-go-round of waltzing pairs went by. Diamonds, rubies, amethysts and pearls all shining in the light.

Richard ambled around the edge of the dance-floor. He nodded to the Count of Flanders, greeted the Duke of Cambridge, and paused to pass a few words with Baron Hampton.

Always fascinating to see who had and who had not graced a state ball. Who was in favour and who out? Beside the Prince of Wales and his infirm, half-crippled Princess danced the French Ambassador; but Richard looked in vain for his Prussian counterpart. And here – the ovine features of the Anglophile Jew who led Richard's party; but maverick Prime Minister Mr Gladstone was absent.

A torchère lit with flames stood close by the minstrels' gallery. There Richard halted.

Among the dancers he spotted his brother cutting one hell of a dash in the regimental dress of the Eleventh Hussars. Aubrey was a celebrity wherever he went these days.

Tonight, he had claimed the Queen's daughter, Princess Helena, among his conquests. Her fingerless glove rested on his shoulder; his arm circled her waist above the bustle. Richard observed Aubrey whisper in her ear, and Helena laugh.

So, Aubrey could even make a matronly princess look starry-eyed and dreamy like an unstable schoolgirl. The world danced with him – and sniggered at Dickon. No Cossack who struck Aubrey from his horse, or Serb who shackled him, could hate Aubrey as did Richard. *Oh, how can I make you disappear again?*

'Dickon, m'boy!' said someone, giving him a jolting tap on the shoulder.

Richard pulled himself together. He turned to see an elderly High Court judge at his side. The man had been at college with the first Sir Richard Somerlee.

'Good to see you here, Sir Mervyn.'

'Even the gout won't keep me from a state ball,' the judge chuckled. 'Heard the latest from the war, old chap? You know Fritzy's got Paris under siege? A rumour spreading, you know, that the Parisians are starving! One story I've heard... they're shooting the elephants in the city zoo for food. And using those balloon things to get food in and people out. But the Prussians shot 'em down, the dirty swine! Dreadful business.'

'Yes, indeed,' Richard said.

'Napoleon's dynasty has fallen at last, eh? To that at least I can drink!'

'Ah, don't speak so soon, Mervyn! With all the German states in Bismarck's iron grip, we might be sorry the Bonapartes are no more.'

'Quite... quite... by the way, my boy, what's this I've been hearing about you and some sort of mine, Smoky something...?'

Richard forgot his other cares for a moment. What had come over him? Jealous of a shallow-headed fool like Aubrey just because he looked good on the dance-floor? Richard had shares in Smoky Mountain to sell, and there were dozens of likely buyers at a grand occasion such as this. Ere long, Sir Mervyn was parting from him, yet another satisfied customer.

Half an hour later, the Duke of Sutherland joined him.

'Evening, Sir Richard. Ghastly affair over in France, eh? I've heard Bismarck's even proposing to bombard Paris and all those starving civilians. Frightful! Don't see how we can do business with a fellow like that, do you?'

'No, Your Grace, I don't.'

The duke cleared his throat.

'Thing is, Sir Richard... I was speaking with Lord Pendlebury recently. He was saying you'd tipped him about some shares. Said it was all hush-hush and I mustn't mention it. But just between the two of us... what's it all about, old chap?'

Richard smiled to himself.

'Well... if you can promise to keep it quiet, Your Grace... it's a mining company... gold seeping out of the seams apparently... but not too well known about yet. Marvellous opportunity if you're interested. And if you are interested, sir, my advice is buy now, before too many others winkle it out and get in on the act.'

'Oh, I can be discreet, Sir Richard!' Sutherland said on a chortle.

'The director and I are bosom bows,' Richard went on. 'I could put in a word if you're wanting to buy.'

'Absolutely! Absolutely! Perhaps we might meet next week to discuss it further, Sir Richard?'

Richard agreed. The two shook hands, sharing conspirators' smiles.

The duke looked back to the dance-floor.

'That's your brother, isn't it, Sir Richard, dancing with Princess Helena? The one you took to court. Still think he's an impostor, do you? Handsome devil, ain't he! Suppose he makes you wish you'd looked after your looks and figure, what?'

Richard muttered an excuse to get away.

An archway festooned with floral garlands led through to St George's Hall. Fewer people were here. Richard might sulk undisturbed.

Here, the supper table was set for the five hundred guests. It stretched from one end of the chamber to the other. Seven huge candelabra were spaced along its length.

Richard sent a footman to fetch him a drink. When the man returned with the brandy, Richard was gazing out over the Middle Ward and Round Tower. It was a night cold enough for breath to steam. Six flambeaux lit the courtyard. You could make out frost glinting on the stones.

Richard heard footsteps approaching from behind him. They were on the heavy side, but their sound was muted by the Persian silk carpet. A very large shape eased in beside him at the window. A miasma of cigar fumes blew his way. Who the devil was intruding on his solitude now? He turned... and leaped to attention.

'Your Highness!'

Prince Albert Edward, heir to the throne, chuckled as if to forgive the unwelcoming expression which had been on the Baronet of Eardingstowe's face.

'Enjoying an early stiffener, eh, Sir Richard? Think I might join you out here in the cool. Getting stuffy in there. Anyway, I don't have a partner for the quadrille. The Princess of Wales is soliciting the hand of that rogue of a brother of yours after my sister has finished with him.' The Prince of Wales rumbled with laughter. 'Must be damned frustrating for you, what? A brother who gets all the girls?'

Well! Richard thought. *At least my wife can't stand him!*

'Quite a pleasant, dry evening,' observed the prince who was known to one and all as Bertie. 'A bit of a nip in the air. But nothing to stop one taking a stroll on the North Terrace. Care to join me, Sir Richard?'

Whether Richard would or wouldn't, Queen Victoria's son and heir steered him towards the State Entrance. The pair passed a column of bowing footmen, and then out into the chill.

'So, Sir Richard,' Bertie said. The two men crossed the courtyard to the Lancaster Tower and went beneath the arch of the King George Gate where the flames of two more flambeaux pranced in the wind. 'You're a veteran at Westminster, aren't you?'

'I suppose so, sir,' Richard replied. 'I've been in Parliament since I was twenty-three. And little to show for it, I fear.'

'Scandalous that a man of your distinction has not been recognised ere now. Quite scandalous! You deserve better, my good chap. The fortitude you showed when you lost that court case was quite praiseworthy. If some jack-a-napes turned up claiming to be my sainted sire who we all believe went to his rest in 1861... well, I doubt I'd welcome him with open arms...'

What could Bertie want with him? If the whiskery, over-sexed, not-overly-endowed-with-brains fatty took an interest in a fellow, it was usually because he fancied his wife. If he was after Amathia he was welcome and good luck to him.

'Yours is an old family is it not, Sir Richard?'

'Yes, sir.' *Older than yours for a start!* 'Geoffrey de Somelay came over with the Conquest.'

'Never been in the nobility, though. Great pity… And there's a vacancy for a new Knight of the Garter, too.'

A tingly feeling ran through Richard – usually a warning that he needed his laudanum dose. A ball he had not been enjoying suddenly looked more promising. How dreamy looked the Brunswick Tower – from each turret and window slit, gay lanterns hanging.

'Listen, Sir Richard…' Future king turned to future subject as they reached the terrace. 'I'd like to see a man like you in the Lords.'

'You do me great honour, sir!'

'Well… thing is, Sir Richard…' Bertie scratched his pudgy ear in a vague kind of way, 'my good friend Harty-Tarty mentioned you to me. Said you'd sold him shares in some sort of mine…'

The old lady turned her eyes up to the frontage of the building as she made her way across the gravelled forecourt. A dry wind was blowing the ivy yellow-side up. Dead, fallen leaves skittered across her path.

Not weather for outdoor rambling was this. But after an hour in the carriage, Lysithea wanted the stretch in the fresh air before going in to visit her sister. Leaning on her walking-stick, she descended the three steps to Dwellan House's garden.

In her maidenhood, Lizzy had taken her morning rides before the Eardingstowe staff had stopped yawning. But these days her knees and fingers seemed to be seizing up; one day she would wake and find they'd locked, and she'd have to resign herself to spending her remaining days indoors.

She passed a patient who was tending a small bed of winter heliotrope. This character was so far gone in his madness he thought working men should have the vote and said 'how do' to the Countess of Schwangli instead of tugging his forelock or whatever. Nevertheless, Lysithea admired his growing things. If you didn't know what this place was, Dwellan House and its park would look a little paradise.

But a woman could be heard sobbing in one of the nearest airing courts. An unsettling sound.

Clemence hadn't spoken volumes about her time here – partly because great wodges of her memory were missing. But Lizzy had heard enough asides to make her fear Dwellan and worry for her sister Cassandra here too. Imagine that great door swinging shut behind you. And knowing you were likely never coming out again.

Hard by the boundary hedge ran a winterbourne. The water of the little brook was driving along leaves. In the far distance the mist became one with the phantasmal Quantocks. The countess watched an arrow-head of birds heading that way. Wouldn't be many more before the snow came down.

When you got to her age, you started to look back over your misspent youth. Not so much your sins. Oh dear no, they were too much fun. But your follies… ah, yes.

Like getting separated from her father's baggage train on the trek through the hills around Salamanca and getting captured by a French patrol. What a riot going with her parent, General Sir Edmund Somerlee, to the Peninsula would be she'd thought – just like her niece during the very next war.

Only – Lysithea's captors had taken her to Marshal Marmont. Who, on discovering she was the offspring of one of Wellington's commanders, had dispatched her under guard to the Supreme One himself to make use of as he saw fit.

What had passed between him and Lizzy Somerlee, prettiest

débutante of 1811, in the seclusion of his tent remained her secret and Bonaparte's.

She had been gossiped about ever since. She would in due course become another Eardingstowe legend. Future generations would tell of her alongside Laurey, Jenny Greenteeth and the demon in the chamber.

The cries of the woman-patient Lysithea could hear brought her back to the here and now. They were sounding more desperate. What gruesome punishment had been threatened? Lizzy knew they sometimes fastened patients into straight-jackets, although that practice was regarded as Georgian these days. She also knew about the isolation cells where Clemmie had been confined during the height of her raving.

Lysithea hobbled on her walking-stick away from the noise, crossing the lawn in the direction of the shelter.

Cassandra was one of the regrets in Lizzy's life. Her fey little sister had been found one morning on the path of the mere, her nightdress soaked and pondweed-bedraggled, claiming she'd visited Jenny's lair. And sagely warning of an elf-prince who was coming to destroy the Somerlees.

Right, that was it, had said their brother the elder Sir Richard Somerlee. She's out of here. She's been upsetting the servants for years. But now this…

We could have looked after her at Eardingstowe, Lizzy had raged at him. Engaged a discreet minder and kept her in an out-of-the-way room.

Oh yes, and have her set fire to the place when we've guests one night?

And that was final.

Lysithea had never quite forgiven her brother. Or herself for not standing up to him. He'd been dead now for years. Often, she'd considered bringing Cassie out of Dwellan, and seeing her cared for at one of the remoter Schwangli continental properties.

But after all this time Dwellan was where Cassie belonged. She'd be afraid to leave. And those family members like Clemmie and Ivo who came often to visit Cassie would no longer be able to. Overall, Dwellan was the least bad option.

A sudden gust of wind sounding just like the sigh Lizzy felt like letting out rustled the leaves which were still clinging to the chestnut's branches.

She turned her steps towards the great front door of Dwellan House.

Maybe Aubrey was Cassandra's elf-prince. He was causing enough trouble.

Lysithea had long given up wondering whether he was who he said he was. Could he have known about this or that if he wasn't the real Aubrey? Could he have learned such-and-such a private anecdote from someone who'd lived on the estate? Quite frankly – pooh!

The stark truth was – Lizzy didn't like him. He had shown no familial tenderness towards Dickon, Clemmie, Ivo or anyone; caring only, Lizzy thought, for convincing them all he was genuine by dredging up sometimes painful Apocrypha. The point being that only the real Aubrey could have known about Flitcroft's duodenal ulcer say, regardless of how Flitcroft felt about this being broadcast in *The Times*.

Aubrey seemed to think less about being restored to the bosom of loving kinfolk, and rather more about his inheritance. And by Jupiter – was he sure enjoying his celebrity.

That Lizzy didn't like him didn't mean he wasn't the man she'd known since she'd held him in his christening robes. Only that his fiery trial... years of loneliness, loss of self, imprisonment... had warped him.

The superintendent of the asylum entered the visitors' parlour where the Countess of Schwangli was waiting.

'My dear, dear Countess! How lovely to see you again.'

'Dr Warburton,' Lysithea said.

'You are here to call on Miss Cassandra, My Lady? A moment, ma'am, while I ring for some tea.' Dr Warburton headed for the bell-pull. 'If only all our patients had such a devoted family to keep an eye on them.'

'Well, I remember my little Cassie as she was growing up,' Lysithea said. 'She was such a loving sister. If there's anything I can do for her…'

'Of course, My Lady.'

Warburton returned, and took a seat.

'The best we can do for Miss Cassandra, ma'am, is ease her remaining years with kindness.'

'I'm sure you and your staff do your utmost, doctor.'

'I hope so, My Lady. I sincerely hope so. You know we have some dedicated staff.'

And a few who like a tipple Lysithea thought, but kept quiet.

'We don't tolerate cruelty at Dwellan, My Lady,' Warburton went on. 'Any attendant who mistreats a patient – paying or pauper – faces summary dismissal. Ah,' Dr Warburton smiled to himself, and sighed. 'We had one attendant, an Irishwoman named Thady. She left us at the end of last year. What a treasure! The best female attendant we ever had. So good with the patients – and particularly with Cassandra. Miss Cassandra really took to her. Used to fair bloom when Thady was looking after her! How disappointed I was when Thady left. And so was poor Miss Cassie.'

Lord, what kind of mood would Cassandra be in today, Lysithea wondered? She might not know Lizzy any more, poor soul, and fly at her with cat-claws.

'Well, I can bring Cassie the good news that young Edmund continues to thrive,' Lysithea said. 'She was so thrilled to learn she's a great-auntie again, now that my nephew the baronet has a son at last. A big, healthy boy from what I've heard.'

'Ah, that will cheer Miss Cassie!' Warburton said. 'She does so love to hear of Eardingstowe – it's home to her still, after all these years. Thady used to get her prattling about the family, and she wouldn't stop! Chatter, chatter, chatter... ah, such a shame Thady left.'

'Really?' said Lysithea. She glanced at the mantle clock.

'Thady could calm Miss Cassie just by asking about Eardingstowe,' the superintendent continued. 'And Cassie would tell her about, say, the family of stoats in the mere. Ah, here's tea.'

A maid brought in the tray and poured. Lysithea took a few sips from her cup.

'Cassie once,' Warburton said with a light laugh, 'told Thady about Mr Carswell pouring Mrs Dean's soup into the mere.'

Lysithea's cup gave a rattle. She had been about to lift it, only to let it fall back into the saucer. Her eyes snapped up to the man sitting opposite.

'What? What did you just say?'

THIRTY-FOUR

'My dear Countess! I merely said…'

'Yes, I heard you!'

Lysithea set her cup and saucer down again. She took up her walking-stick and got to her feet. She paced a few steps towards the window. Her breath was coming fast.

She turned back to face him.

'What else did my sister tell this woman – Thady?'

'My dear lady, I'm not sure I can recall…'

'Think, man. This is important!'

Lysithea gave him a kindlier look. She returned to the sofa and spoke in softer tones.

'Miss Clemence – Her Grace the Duchess – comes to visit more than most of us. She talks to Cassie about my missing nephew Aubrey a lot. Did Cassie ever, perhaps, tell this wardress of a conversation Aubrey had had with a certain Captain Radlett the night before he vanished?'

'Yes… yes I believe she did…'

'And I'm guessing she also mentioned our poor butler's duodenal ulcer?'

'Err…'

Lysithea slowly sat back. She stared at Warburton for a long moment.

'I wonder if you could tell me where I might find this Thady?' Warburton looked unco-operative. Lysithea smiled. 'It sounds as if she did a lot of good for my sister. I would like to thank her in person. At least, maybe,' she persisted as Warburton opened his mouth to object, 'you might let me know her surname.'

Golden and violet polar brilliance spread across the snowdrifts. The wind was blowing powdery crystals sparkling in the sunshine into whorls and dragon-tails. Aubrey shielded his vision.

The snowfall was so deep that dwellers in remote spots of the Somerset countryside might be cut off and go hungry. God, they'd never know real hunger though. And anyway, spare a thought for the folk of Paris who were creeping like sewer-rats, seeking morsels to eat and splinters to burn. They were hoping Bismarck would shell their city, so they could get out.

Aubrey trudged along the lane through the snow. On either side of him stalks and leaves of wayside knapweed, ox-tongue, wild carrot and rest-harrow stood stiff and crusted with ice like skeletons of little, frozen men. He kept well huddled inside a hooded cloak.

Inside the doorway of the final hovel of the village which he passed, a bevy of fishermen's wives was sitting around a brazier. The women were twisting mistletoe and rowan branches into kissing boughs, and ribbon-binding the crowns for Christmas. The oldest dame called out 'Good day to 'ee, Mast' Aubrey' as he went by.

'Good day, Mistress Roswitha!' Aubrey grinned, and blew a kiss. 'You know – it hardly seems yesterday that I was a bairn – sitting outside this same cottage, listening to your tales of the sea. Remember that bouquet of sea-pinks and samphire I brought you that time? So in love with you, I was! And, you know – I think I still am, just a little!'

He continued on his way, flattered cackles following after.

The man passed through a gate at the end of the path. He emerged onto the exposed headland above Kilve beach. A torrent was surging down through a break in the cliff into the sea. Oystercatchers, gulls, dunlins, godwits and guillemots were circling, swooping and shrieking above him.

Aubrey, Aubrey… Christ. He was almost coming to believe Aubrey was his real name. When he'd set out to take his revenge on the hated Somerlees by impersonating their lost kinsman, he'd not thought the deception might run so deep that he'd be in danger of fooling himself too.

He spotted the woman who was also here on the cliff top. Clemence Somerlee – waiting for him as they'd agreed. She was leaning against the trunk of a birch tree, looking out over the water. Strands of hair peeped from beneath her hood and fluttered in the wind. As he drew near, he could see snow-dust sprinkling her pale fringe. The crystals glinted with rainbow colours as a quick shaft of sunlight shone out from behind the cloud.

His eyes narrowed to slits as his hatred seized hold of him.

So! The Somerlees did something atrocious in the hill-fort, did they? To the Celtic tribe who flourished there no doubt. Well, after pent-up, brooding centuries – here he was to pay them back.

She and he were alone save for the watery fellows of the deep. Thoughts of what he could do to her flashed through his mind. He was hardly a large man, but he could get the better of a puny thing like that. Could take her, bloodily, in the cliff top bracken. It would be like blistering her with a branding-iron – just like a shepherd marking ownership of a sheep. Charge roaring into the valley with thundering hooves, bulletproof blade thrust before him – slashing up enemies in volcanoes of spouting gore.

When can their glory fade? O the wild charge they made! All the world wonder'd.

In her morning-room, Lysithea opened the package with a feeling of dread. Her aching, arthritic fingers trembled at what she might find inside.

The correspondence which she unfolded was from the private investigator she'd hired to trace the woman, Thady, from the asylum. Lysithea speedily read it through.

The woman's full name turned out to be Thady McFarland, born Thady Horan. What was of most interest to the detective, however, was that she was the niece of a character named William Kidney.

A Dubliner, this man was a career malefactor with untold convictions for fraud and deception. He had spent seven years in the Australian penal colony after a fight which left the other man without use of an eye. Kidney had almost lost his too and had a permanent scar to show for it. He was so successful at his dishonest craft, wrote the private detective, because he was 'able to affect the manners and speech of a gentleman.'

Will Kidney's multiple recorded aliases were then listed. One leaped from the page.

Roger Cormorant.

Lysithea drew in a sharp breath. The Earl of Bedingfield had not long ago tried to interest her in buying shares in a gold mine called Smoky Mountain. 'The director's an elusive fellow called Sir Roger Cormorant who no-one ever seems quite able to track down. Nevertheless, it's a marvellous investment opportunity, Countess...'

But she hadn't been interested. It had sounded a bit fishy. In any case, Bedingfield had wanted a share of her profits in exchange for the introduction. Goodness, how right had she been.

Lysithea set the detective's report aside, feeling very shaken.

Also enclosed was a copy of Thady's marriage certificate. Her wedding had taken place in June 1857, in St Brigid's

Catholic Church, Ancoats, Manchester. The bride's father had been deceased. She had been given away by her uncle, William Kidney.

Lysithea looked up. Ancoats. Why was that name familiar? Oh, yes... she grimaced. Carswell's Mill.

Her brother, the late baronet, had married the mill-master's daughter. Somerlee fortunes had been on the wane at the time, and the elder Richard had needed Joshua Carswell's wallet. Sir Richard Somerlee Bart. of Eardingstowe, and Miss Leonora Carswell of Ancoats, Manchester. Not the daintiest engagement announcement ever in the society columns. Caused some sniggering at the family's expense. Still, Leonora had been a pretty blonde; and her daughters Isabella and Clemence both favoured her in looks.

Lysithea turned back to the marriage document in her hands. One Father Cassidy had conducted the service. Thady Horan had been united in matrimony with a cotton-spinner from Carswell's Mill by the name of Michael McFarland, formerly of Kilara in the County of Limerick.

Lysithea frowned. She thought she'd heard both those names, McFarland and Kilara, sometime, too.

The bridegroom, Michael McFarland, had been twenty-two years of age at the date of his wedding... born therefore, Lysithea quickly calculated, around 1835. The same year as Aubrey...

...a young footman he was then, and a kind heart, he was, to be sure...

'Begod and saints prasarve us!' muttered the countess.

'The times we ran along those cliff tops together as children!' Clemence said. 'Escaping from Dickon, pushing Bella into the rock-pools...'

'Remember the bathing-machine?' Michael stood beside her, one arm leaning against the bole of the tree. 'We were supposed to be the first family in Somerset to acquire one. Green with pink stripes, remember? We couldn't get the pater in it, though, any more than in a railway carriage.'

'Remember how we used to take the sled to fetch in the sticks for the ashen faggot?'

'Ah, yes,' Michael said, 'brought in on Christmas Eve, and burning until Twelfth Night. Bustard and partridge to fill the pie, and, ah! the hot cider, spices and roasted apples of the Lamb's Wool… I remember returning from Holford Wood with the faggot one year… Ivo suddenly goes "Goodness! I do believe I spy some fossils which might date from the Cretaceous period!" So, he leaps off the sled and goes poking about in the rocks. You and I were sitting there, getting cold, and bored, and eventually we set off back home without him. Ivo comes bounding after us. Then his glasses blew off, and we spent another hour searching in the snow.'

'Yes, I remember now you mention it…'

He stared at the woman. The wind had tugged an untidy ringlet free from her hood.

A moment ago, he had pictured those itsy-bitsy girly bosoms torn and bleeding. But he couldn't… couldn't grope this woman as he had the gagging mill-sluts in three sordid, soughing minutes beneath an Ancoats canal bridge. Or just tumble in the bracken.

Why? Because she'd been in the asylum once – chased butterflies, wore yesteryear's fashions, was still living in 1854… and he had *scruples* over that? No… Because it would undo all he had worked for. To get Eardingstowe. Destroy Dickon and all his kin. Pay back every crime the Somerlees had done since the world was young. And mistress Clemence was still worth more to him whole.

'Look! It's starting to get dark and we hadn't noticed, we've been so busy reminiscing, Aubrey. The quire's setting out.' Clemence indicated inland, away from the headland. In the distance, a mass of bobbing lantern-lights could be seen gathering.

Michael peered over his shoulder. Fluty toots and trombone honks could be heard playing *The Boar's Head Carol*. Hedgers, drovers, carters, cowmen, keepers, ploughmen and the landlord of the *White Swan* who made up the bucolic orchestra would soon be trudging in procession along the lane towards the village.

'They'll be calling at each homestead, and finish up at Eardingstowe,' Clemence said. 'You should be there for the welcome in the great hall, Aubrey.'

'I wish you were coming, Clemmie...'

'Aubrey, I haven't set foot in Eardingstowe for over ten years! You know how Dickon and Mathy feel about me. A room at the *White Swan* is the closest I may go.'

With a creak of leather glove, he reached up to stroke her cheek.

Lizzy's first glimpse of Cotton City came as her train crested the moors to the east.

It made her think of Sebastopol after the sack – brooding beneath a cloud of smoke. Mill chimneys looked like prehistoric beasts bathing in the steamy marsh – gangling necks popping up here, there, near and far; the bellowing noises they made could be male chimneys' mating calls to females.

A carbuncle on England's fair, green face was Manchester. The Romans had abandoned it, sensible fellows, and no-one in their senses had settled here since – until the cotton-masters had moved in.

The city's back-ways were only just wide enough for a vehicle to pass; and a sleety blizzard was blowing, which made progress still more hazardous.

From behind the window blind, the shocked passenger peeped out. *People lived in these leaning shacks?* Of course, they did. Their toil made the lucre which bought Richard his silk ties, waistcoats, braces and gold-tipped canes.

The façade of Carswell's Mill when they reached it couldn't have been much less in length than that of Buckingham Palace or Apsley House. Three storeys of oblong window after window after window. Bricks stained from fire. Major source of her brother's and nephew's prosperity these fifty years.

It sounded as if it was in ulcerated agony as a thousand power-looms whirred inside its belly. Its oesophagus was a two-hundred-foot-high chimney puking out sickness into the snowstorm. Any bird which ventured to fly over Manchester would go down in avian history as intrepid an explorer as Dr Livingstone. No volcano could aspire to this in its ash-cloud dreams.

Lysithea dropped the blind, and kept it drawn. She did not care to attract attention. Her carriage was plain black and unmarked.

'Drive on please,' Lysithea called to the coachman in a shuddering voice. 'I want St Brigid's Church.'

'I'm guessin' you're an Anglican, My Lady,' the elderly, stooped man said with a chuckle as he led his guest into his parlour. 'So, I'll be giving you tea not whiskey to drink.'

Father Cassidy shuffled back in with a pot of tea.

Lysithea sat opposite as he poured. She'd have offered to do it; but her sore hands were even less reliable than his dithering ones.

She took a look around instead. A crucifix hung on one wall. In one niche, a statue of Christ was pointing to an exposed heart. And there was a framed, rather gruesome print of some martyr or other, pricked with more arrows than were necessary surely to kill him.

She studied the Man of God's vigorous, aged face.

'You've been in charge of St Brigid's parish for many years, Father Cassidy?'

'Aye, My Lady – a quarter of a century. Since I first come to Manchester during the famine.'

'I wonder… could you think back to 1857 for me? You married a couple named Thady Horan and Michael McFarland.'

Lysithea was not really hopeful. The fellow must have joined hundreds of couples in matrimony.

But no, Father Cassidy was settling into his armchair with his cup of tea, and nodding.

'Aye! I knew Mickey well, and his family. He worked at yer mill over yonder – Carswell's.'

Lysithea's heartbeat began to race.

'Was he a regular worshipper here? Is that how you knew him?'

'Faith, not he!' the priest chuckled. 'Rarely come for mass or confession. Come to read my newspapers, so he did, and learn about money things, if you can swallow the irony – Our Lord whipped the moneylenders out of the temple, if you recall!'

'Money things?'

'Aye. The stock market, things like that.'

Lysithea nodded to herself. She took out an envelope from her reticule.

'This is a photograph, Father. It was taken recently at a royal drawing-room at Marlborough House. Take a look at the gentleman in the centre of the group. The lady whose hand he is kissing is the Princess of Wales, Alexandra of Denmark. The elderly lady also vying for his attention is the Countess of Beaconsfield, Mary Anne Disraeli, wife of the Tory leader.'

Incredulity spread across the clergyman's face.

'Holy Jesus, it can't be!'

'Is that Michael McFarland, Father?'

'Aye! Though he's years older, of course, since I last saw him.'

Lysithea took the photograph back. She stared at the familiar face in the picture.

'He's been passing himself off as my nephew, Aubrey Somerlee, who we believed perished in the Crimea. Perhaps you read about the recent court case?'

'Aye, I did. But I never thought of Mickey! There was a good reason why I did not.'

'Oh?' said Lysithea.

'Aye!' Father Cassidy crossed himself. 'Yer Ladyship, I thought he was dead, I did! Well, that was what I heard…' He shook his head to gather his wits.

'Thady and Mickey left town after they wed. I knew no more of them. Until we heard Mickey had gone to Americay during the war, joined the Irish Brigade, and fought for the Union against the Rebs. We heard he was killed at Gettysburg.

'Wouldn't you know now! The night I heard of his death, I warned the Lord in me prayers to watch out, 'cos he'd cheat his way out of hell where he belongs, that one, playing card-tricks on Old Nick!

'Ah, so he's been to Marlborough House now? Puttin' poison in the Prince of Wales's dishes no doubt!'

'What do you mean, Father? Is he a Fenian?'

Father Cassidy gave her a wary look. Lysithea urged him to go on.

'If you'll forgive me now, I'd say the McFarlands hate the Somerlees more than the English.' He paused again. 'Well, the McFarlands come from a village named Kilara, see. The Somerlees are landlords there.'

'My God…' Lysithea breathed. Suddenly, the voice of her dead brother came echoing down the years.

O'Briens? Not paid rent for six months – out! Flanagans? Not paid for four – out! McFarlands… they're the worst of the lot, damn their hides! Turf them out, out, out! And get tenants in their place who can pay, damn it! What's that you say? Well, I don't believe they are starving! Just their excuse to swindle their landlord, that's what it is!'

'Mickey and his family were thrown out of their cottage,' Father Cassidy went on. 'I think it was at the time of the famine. Mickey talked about it so much. A festering obsession, it was. Wouldn't listen to reason. Swore he'd get even with the Somerlees, somehow, someday.

'T'was the reason he come to Manchester in the first place. Because someone had told him the Somerlees owned a mill here. He had a firewood round – used to trudge the alleys hawkin' his bundles, sure he'd one day knock on a door and find the Somerlees behind it. My Lady? Are ye all right?'

Lysithea buried her face in shaking hands.

THIRTY-FIVE

"SMOKY MOUNTAIN"
GOLD MINE FRAUD EXPOSED

The newspaper print swam before Michael's eyes.

"Thousands of investors are today facing huge losses after a massive and audacious financial fraud… Some facing bankruptcy…

"The so-called "Smoky Mountain" has been exposed as a hoax…

"Decent people bought shares in good faith in what they believed was a sound venture, a profitable gold mine in South Africa… But it now emerges that no such mine has ever existed…

"Many of the duped are members of some of our noblest titled families… Marlborough House spokesperson refusing to comment on rumours the Prince of Wales has lost money in the scam…

"Police confirmed they wish to question the Baronet of Eardingstowe, Sir Richard Somerlee, M.P.…

"Meanwhile, who is the mysterious 'Sir Roger Cormorant'…?

Michael laid the newspaper down.

His mind slipped back over the years. A torrential autumn day in 1849. That's probably when it all began – the day the Somerlee agent came a-calling to evict Michael and his family. Two years his ma had been dead, then. Of the famine-fever. Not even a wake for Bridey McFarland. No-one left to do the burying in the mud.

Michael had left Kilara along the Limerick road. His bare feet dangling from the rear of Seamus McFarland's cart. Nothing but a hood to keep out the rain. It had seemed to Michael that flames had shrivelled up every one of Kilara's hundred hillside streams and watercourses.

He'd not have done all this without Will. Faith, he still called to mind the first time he saw him back in Manchester. Will Kidney, the most notorious swindler and all-round conman in the East End. On the run from three police forces, it was said. Michael was just one of many awed moons in orbit around the gas giant as he told his stories in the *Cotton Tree* pub.

'So Lanegan don't believe Fogarty's been to Americay and come back, of course. "Speak some Yankee lingo, then, Fogarty!" Lanegan says. "Okay," Fogarty replies. "O'Kay?" says Lanegan. "You've seen Paddy O'Kay in America, then? Still owes me a farthing, so he does!"'

'How do you run a betting lay, then?' Michael had asked when he'd at last got the great man alone. Kidney was older than Michael by about twenty years.

'I had me what's called a list shop.' Will's voice was languorous. 'Classy premises. Discreet back room with a girl or two. Gents what came in placed their bets with me. I offered better odds, see, than they'd get at the racecourse. Then I had me a few cronies in the racing world. They'd be nobbling the favourite. And I'd be tipping the high and mighty.

'But I had to leave the Smoke. Too hot down there for me, it was. So, I set me feet on the road to see where they'd take me – and find meself in Manchester.'

'How did you get the English nobs to trust you?' Michael asked.

'Well, my dear fellow, they supposed I was one of their own – a gentleman, sir!'

'Where'd you come by that plummy accent?' Michael laughed.

'I could teach you if you want. I knew a priest in the Old Country what had his learning at some lah-di-dah school in England. I just practised talkin' like him.'

'Faith, what we learn from priests! It was Father Cassidy taught me what I know about the stock market. Listen—' Michael slipped into deep and grave thought. 'Could you do somethin' similar with stocks and shares?'

Will Kidney gazed at him, impressed.

'Aye... You could run a lay on the stock market.'

'What I was thinking,' Michael said, 'is a fancy company what don't really exist, selling shares in somethin'... diamonds... oil... anythin' really. A fairyland out there in the golden sands. Everyone buys your shares. You get rich. But they've bought naught but dreams and empty air.'

'Aye!' Kidney said. 'You'd have to be quick, though. Investors'd be looking to see their returns before you've finished selling to your other clients – and gettin' impatient!'

'How about this,' said Michael. 'Let's say my first investor is Mr Smith. I then sell shares to Mr Jones. I pay Mr Smith with some of the money I take from Mr Jones, and as far as Mr Smith's concerned – it's returns on his investment! Then I pay Mr Jones with some of the money what Mr Wilson invests.'

Kidney nodded.

'Take more than theory to make it work, though.'

'How do you mean?'

'Ah, you don't think city investors are going to buy shares from an Irish yahoo from the slums of Manchester? Why, sir,' Will went back into his drawl, 'they deal with gentlemen, sir. One of their own whom they can trust... went to the right school. And it's not only your investors you've to fool. It's your brokers too. And they're a canny lot.'

'Could you, with your fancy English voice, convince 'em?'

'By Jove, sir, I should surely like to try! What have I to lose? Only another seven years in an Aussie swamp!'

'I was in the Working Men's Institute. They have a library there. There's a book called *Extraordinary Popular Delusions and the Madness of Crowds* by a man named Mackay.' A smile crept across Michael's face. 'Now, your one smart man, you see, ain't likely to fall for a lay on his own. He's too clever. Knows a fraud when he sees one. But if all his friends and foes believe it's real, so does he. And they all go charging in. Like the Light Brigade. The madness of crowds.'

Kidney lit his pipe, deep in thought.

'You're wantin' to do this real bad, ain't you, lad?'

'Aye. I'm real excited, Will. But I need you in with me.'

'You'll need false statements to convince your investors. And company reports for your brokers.'

'Aye. I know.'

'And you're looking to me now, I take it?' Kidney exhaled a few puffs of smoke. 'Well, I did a bit of screeving work – forging wills, that kind of thing. Grander scale, this... Makes a bit more sense, though, than that hare-brained scheme of yours to impersonate the Vamoosing Hussar! I mean – supposing the real Aubrey comes home while you're at dinner with the family? Ah, nonsense it is! Do somethin' else with your life, Mickey McFarland!'

But Mickey never had. The idea had grown and grown and become a monster. It was as if he'd nurtured a tiddy bud until it grew into a humungous, blood-redheaded hibiscus blocking out all sunlight.

He called to mind the miniature paintings of Somerlees and their lovely house on display in Carswell's Mill butty shop where the mill-hands took their lunch-breaks. That was when the thought had first come to him. The missing cornet's hair had been blacky-brown, his eyes bright blue... just like Michael's. And if Aubrey was a younger brother of the present baronet and a soldier in the Crimean War, he must be around Mickey's age...

Michael would need to learn to ride a horse. Bit difficult to convince anyone he was a cavalryman otherwise. And just knowing Aubrey Somerlee had been born on the twenty-whatever of March, and Sir So-and-so Somerlee had been King Knut's lifeguard would not be enough, no. No! The argot, or notions, used by Winchester schoolboys might not be difficult to find out – but what about the closet words Aubrey had had with his siblings, pranks he'd played on the gardener, what he'd said to his messmates on the eve of the cavalry charge...?

And then Michael had come to hear the rumours about Cassandra Somerlee... the mad aunt in the attic...

An old bat in a nuthouse would chatter... and chatter... Aubrey's pets, his toys, his young loves and wet dreams. Nanny's birthday. What kind of cakes they had for tea while the Irish were starving. Anecdotes only the family could know. Like the time Flitcroft tripped over the dog while serving dinner and spilled the cauliflower cheese over the Countess of Portland. All Michael had needed was access to Dwellan House...

'And then I guess I had my own dollops of Irish luck, Will,' he finished his reminisce. 'Lucky it was that Sparkle was no longer with them. No-one would have been harder to convince I was Aubrey!'

He raised his eyes to the man who was facing him across the beer-sloshed boards of a dockside tavern table. Close by, a pianist was playing, and a band of sailors was singing *Stormalong*.

'Faith, and where is Sir Roger Cormorant now?'

'Sir Roger Cormorant's vanished into the vapour of Smoky Mountain,' said Will. An oil lamp was dangling from the roof beam. In its light, the old scar on the man's cheek looked like a silvery tapeworm. 'Just like I'll be doing next ship out of port.'

'A genius you are, Will Kidney.'

'I've the luck of the Irish, Mickey, is all. 'Twas lucky I found a screever who had a printing press. He'd forged banknotes with it. And lucky, too, that the Carlton Club was hiring casual staff, and I had me the opportunity to leave Sir Dickon his substitute copies of *The Times*.

'Sir Dickon's networking worked, as I knew it would,' Kidney said. 'Each one passing the word, secret-like, onto his own particular pals – and Smoky Mountain's fame spread! The Duke o' Westminster! The Duke o' Sutherland! Duke of Argyll! Mr Disraeli! Princess Vicky's husband, the Prussian Crown Prince, had a flutter too. And the Czar's brother, Grand Duke Konstantin Nikolayevich. Hundreds and hundreds of 'em.

'But poor Sir Dickon's startin' to realise something's badly wrong – he cannot find the cormorant anywhere. The address I gave don't exist. "This fellow who sold you shares in Smoky Mountain," Sir Dickon says to Lord Spuffington. "What do you know about him?" "Smoky Mountain?" says His Lordship. "Dash it all, Somerlee, I'd never heard of it until you started your blethering!"

'And now they know it was all a con, and how much they've lost. "Thanks to you, Somerlee – you blithering dunderhead – I've lost sixteen thousand pounds on this damned-fool escapade! I've a good mind to horsewhip you, sir!"' Will gave a crooked half-smile. 'And there's some who've lost so much, they're ruined. Sir Dickon's brother-in-law, the Duke of Ardenne, put a gun in his mouth two nights ago.'

Michael turned his eyes away.

'I've sailed a few choppy waters since I left the Old Country,' he said. 'Paying an impoverished Serb to teach me his language… fighting the Yankees' war for 'em… well, truth be told, I caught sight of the Rebs on the Gettysburg horizon, did a fast one into the trees, sneaked back to the battlefield after dark, and planted some of me personal effects on a likely-lookin' corpse. So almost everyone who'd known Michael McFarland believes him dead.'

'You carrying on as Aubrey, then?'

'I ain't made plans yet, Will.'

'What do you suppose happened to the real Aubrey Somerlee?'

'Who knows?' Michael gave a slow shake of the head. 'Maybe he did what I did at Gettysburg – an about-turn and head for safety, and he's too ashamed to show hisself.'

He leaned across the board. A hush came into his tone.

'You know Eardingstowe's fallin' to its knees, Will? Yesterday, Flitcroft clutched his heart and tumbled down the grand staircase, his silver tray clattering after him.

'Dickon's youngest brother Carswell came home two weeks ago on furlough, and he went strolling by the mere. He'd downed a fair glass or two of cider. Well, he stumbled and fell in. They ain't found the body yet. There's a kitchen-maid and two labourers on the estate say they were lookin' out as he fell. They say they saw two arms, wreathed all about with fronds of weed, reachin' up out of the water, grabbed a hold of him, and pulled him down never to be seen again.'

Michael sat back. He gazed into the rafters for a moment.

'Ah… let's not be thinking sorrowful thoughts, lad!' Will Kidney said. 'Let me be filling your cup.' He summoned over the serving-girl.

'Do you know the Prince of Wales bought shares in Smoky Mountain?' Kidney said as the girl refilled both their cups with jacky. The sailors singing around the piano had moved on to *Haul away, Joe*. 'Somerlee knows Harty-Tarty, see, the Prince's best friend. And Lord Hartington t'was who passed the word to the future King.'

'Will…' Michael said as a slow-burning grin spread over his face, 'we've done more to bring down the English, us two between us, than all the Fenians. Half the aristocracy is toppling in the bankruptcy courts.'

'Well now, we all know our brave countryman, Captain Nolan, deliberately led the Light Brigade to its death because he secretly wanted the Russkies to win.'

Michael tossed back his head and laughed into the rafters.

'"Not tho' the soldier knew someone had blundered: Into the Valley of Death rode the Six Hundred."'

'It won't be long before the law'll be treadin' a path to Eardingstowe and Sir Dickon. When they do, Sir Roger Cormorant'll be nowhere to be seen.'

'It's been a pleasure workin' with you, Will. And not just for the money. Hey, but can the money be traced to either of us?' said Michael.

'Course not. Your share is in your bank account, mine… waitin' for me in Americay.' So that was where Will was heading then? 'Aye. I'm past fifty, Mickey. Aussie swamp fever weakened these old bones. I'm getting out while I'm on top, and I'll see me days out peaceful.'

'Tell me, though, Will?' Michael leaned across the table. 'How much are we worth?'

'Give or take a penny or two?' Kidney smacked his lips dry with the back of his hand. 'About two hundred thousand!'

A spillage sloshed from Michael's mug onto the board. He gulped five mouthfuls and dribbled. The two guffawing men got up and threw their arms around each other.

THIRTY-SIX

A shuffling retainer led the visitor through the vestibule and into the great hall. Clemence could hear her own footsteps echoing emptily.

A lantern dangled from the ancient butler's skeletal hand. It dribbled fingers of yellowy light up the banister and cast blacker-barred shadows. Gasoliers jutted from the walls, but they were dead – like most of the interior, it seemed to Clemence.

The lantern's jigging beam lit up a chair-shaped, white dust-cover in one corner. Then a picture-sized darker patch of wall-panelling, which said 'something of value must have hung here, until recently sold.' This old-timer who had answered the front door to her was, she guessed, born on the Woodmancote estate, devoted to the Fanshawes, and had stayed when all the rest had flitted away.

They came across Lord Brandon Fanshawe sitting by the hearth in the morning-room, huddled inside a coverlet. A high colour in cheeks and nose told of a winter ailment. He'd not been expecting Clemence but looked up without surprise when she was announced.

'May I take your cloak, Your Grace?' said the butler, suddenly remembering what should already have been asked.

'I'll keep it on, Kincaid,' she replied. Brandon's must be one of the few fires alight anywhere in the house. 'I'd welcome something warming inside me, if you could stretch to a glass of sherry? And something for my suffering coachman who I had to leave outside?' She looked hopefully from master to servant.

Brandon nodded to the butler, who hobbled away.

'Sherry...' Brandon mused. 'Yes, I'm sure we can still reach to a tipple or two. Gone are the days when Woodmancote entertained royally, though.'

Clemence moved from the doorway to stand by his side. His eyes looked bloodshot and watery. She'd not seen him wearing spectacles before. You could see mini-fires flitting in the round lenses.

'I was sorry to hear of your loss,' Clemence began.

'Thank you, Clemence. A short illness – an influenza in the late summer. Phyllis didn't suffer much.'

In the pause, Clemence took the chance to look about her. A seventeenth-century tapestry covered one wall, the trumpet banners of an ancestor who had been High Sheriff of the Shire hung opposite, a leather-bound travelling chest with brass knobs stood in one corner, and on the mantelpiece was a gilt and ebony eight-day clock. She pictured these things disappearing one-by-one like the painting which had gone from the hall. He must dream of displeased forbears who had garnered these treasures.

'Yes, I know – place is going to ruin,' he said as if reading her thoughts. 'How could it have come to this? Well, unlike the Somerlees we Fanshawes have not oiled our fingers on the cotton looms. And the value of land has been falling and falling. And Phyllis liked her dresses and jewels. Then bailing her three ne'er-do-well brothers out of debt took its toll.'

Clemence eyed the fretful hand which was poking from his blanket.

'And buying shares in Smoky Mountain? At least you can blame the Somerlees for that.'

'Ah, no, Clemmie. I bought the shares. I didn't have to listen to Dickon.' A smile was struggling to break through. Like a beclouded sun shining out and vanishing again. 'You know, Clemmie, I've heard appalling rumours about conditions in the workhouses. Is this an opportunity, I wonder, to undertake a fact-finding mission since I might end up there myself before 1872 comes around? Well... in debtors' prison at the very least.'

'Oh, Fanny, surely it's not as bad as that?'

'Woodmancote is mortgaged to the rafters, Clemmie. It won't be long before the bank'll be foreclosing.'

Clemence wandered to the window as he rambled on.

'Maybe Dickon will take me in as a dependent? He owes me as much, I daresay. And I'm Amathia's cousin.'

'There is not room at Eardingstowe to house all the bankrupts Richard owes!' Clemence said.

'No, I fancy not! Besides – I might have no money, but I've not lost my pride.'

The window where Clemence looked out from was in one of the wings. She could see most of the neat Carolinian mansion's frontage and gardens. Really – from outdoors, Woodmancote looked in better fettle than Eardingstowe. What would in summer be luscious roses climbed the porticoed great chamber, and a brass sundial hung above the porch. A rill ran through the grounds. It passed so close to the edge of the house that Clemence could hear the tinkling of the water.

A ruby sun peeped through the dip in the Sussex downs. The ice clinging to the rose-stems, lawn, hedges and orchard trees glowed with a modest blush. A mistle thrush hovered, and plumped onto a branch, making a shower of powdery whiteness. A corn dolly tied to a post flapped in the wind – the harvesters' offering to the goddess of the land so that rebirth should come. Bossy life was breaking out from wintry death.

'Fanny... You know why I said yes to James Swynton when he asked me to marry him? Because Dickon wanted me to marry you.' She turned around to face him. 'I was sixteen and a rebel. Didn't care to be pushed about by a big brother.'

Brandon stretched out a hand.

'Come here, Clemence.'

She crossed the room and stood beside him.

'I courted Phyllis because you'd chosen someone else,' Brandon said. 'Even after James was killed. I assumed that was what made you ill – losing a man you loved so much. Didn't think I could compete with a love, even a dead love, like that.'

'Fanny... I didn't come here today just to pour out my heart to you...'

The inefficient tread of Fanshawe's man was heard approaching. She waited while he shuffled in, laid down a tray, mopped up the spillage he caused in so doing, sniffed, blew his nose, and poured out the refreshments.

When he'd pottered out again, Clemence perched on the wing of Brandon's chair. She downed gulps of sherry until a warm glow spread through her.

'I've come with news you have likely not heard – cooped up here as you are. Half of Burke's Peerage invested in Smoky Mountain, you know. You are in some exalted company.'

'I daresay. But it don't help me knowing that, does it, Clemmie?'

'Philo was one of the biggest losers. Even Richard didn't realise just how many shares Philo bought. The Bank of England has seized Kingsmede. Ardenne treasures, such as they are, will soon be going under the hammer at Christie's and the Dorotheum.'

Brandon gave a short laugh.

'The Consetts have been going to the dickens for years. We knew that, however much they tried to keep it quiet. What Philo's lost on that cursed gold mine, he likely did not have in the first place. More mess for Dickon, I fear. But the Consetts will come out smiling. They always do.'

'Not this time. Philo's put a gun in his mouth.'

'What…?'

'A housemaid found him two days ago – in the Kingsmede drawing-room, in a pool of blood. Amathia is quite inconsolable. The carpet was rather valuable it seems.' Fanny looked as if he wasn't quite taking it in. Couldn't he work it out? 'Your father was the former duke's next eldest brother, I believe, who married the Fanshawe heiress and took her name? Deary me – I never could keep up with the genealogies one has to listen to at dinner-parties. But I believe I got that right?'

'Yes. So, I'm Duke of Ardenne, it seems.' Brandon gave an unfunny laugh, and then sank his head in his hands. Another bankrupt estate and a disgraced title? Oh, that was just what he needed right now.

'That's partly why I've come – to break the news before the Ardenne lawyers get here. But there's another reason too.'

Clemence stared into the flames for a few moments.

'Look. My aunt did not invest in Smoky Mountain. Not for want of an offer. The Earl of Bedingfield tried to interest her – said he'd wield his influence on her behalf with someone right at the heart of Smoky Mountain. Dickon, probably, with hindsight. But Lysithea thought it sounded suspicious.'

'Of course. One of the smartest people I know is Lizzy.'

'She would settle your debts, though, Brandon. All of them. Pay off your mortgage, I feel sure.'

'And why should the Countess of Schwangli offer me such charity?'

'Because it is what I want, Fanny! We'll sort out it all out, Lizzy and me. In exchange for something.' She slipped her fingers into his. 'You see… I actually quite liked being Duchess of Ardenne…'

Amathia peered around the study door.

Her husband sat slumped there, head in hands. A cider bottle lay on its side on the bureau before him, dripping its lees onto the carpet.

'Dickon?' Amathia spoke softly.

She repeated it, louder. Two blotchy, watery eyes rose to meet hers.

Amathia crossed to his side. He wore no jacket or waistcoat – only shirt and braces. The button of his trouser waistband, unable to cope with the burden, gaped guiltily.

'You were not at breakfast. Or luncheon, Dickon.'

'Skipping meals won't harm me.' Richard gave his belly a pat.

'But this will.'

He suddenly sat up.

'For heaven's sake, woman! Fanny and I drank each other under the table as undergraduates! I can take my liquor.'

'I didn't mean the cider.' Amathia nodded towards the chiffonier which stood to the side of his desk and which no-one but him had access to. 'I know you have a supply of laudanum in there, Dickon. The servants all think it's where you keep the key to the demon chamber. Suppose they're right in a way.'

Amathia settled on the wing of the chair. She slipped an arm around his shoulder.

'Dickon, you need help…'

'Oh yes, Amathia, I do indeed!' Richard let out a tragic laugh. He shifted his seat to ease his cursed rear-end pain. As if calamity was not enough – his haemorrhoids were back.

'Will hiding in a fug of laudanum put your world to rights?'

He stared at his wife for a moment, and then ran a hand through his hair.

'No. No, it won't. I'm a coward as well as a dunderhead.'

'You're no coward, Dickon. If you were, you would have shot yourself like Philo.'

'I still might.'

He looked past her to the window. Somewhere on the mere, bitterns could be heard calling yutter-yutter-yark. But could not be seen because fast snow was sweeping across the parkland. The marsh-lights could be made out though, glowing then vanishing.

His poor brother Carrie was out there still. They'd likely never find the body. If a Somerlee went missing in the mere, he was unlikely to be found. A new plaything for Jenny in her reedy realm.

'Look at that brooding old tree, Amathia. Withstanding one more winter storm. How many must it have survived?'

'Hundreds,' said Amathia. 'No, thousands. And the Somerlees are still here.'

'Not for much longer. The yew is going to topple soon, and I'll be the Somerlee to watch it fall... the Somerlee who brought about Eardingstowe's ruin.'

A canine padded across from beside the fireless hearth, laid her head in his lap, and whined. He fondled her furry ears.

'At least I haven't let you down, old girl,' he said to the dog.

'But, Dickon, if you've lost money it's hardly the end of the family. Think what disasters that old yew must have seen over the centuries – and we're still here!'

'Amathia!' Richard sagged forwards, brow in hand. 'If only losing money was all it was!'

'Tell me, Dickon,' said Amathia, 'how much, exactly, have you lost?'

'Oh, we could survive. If I sold Gainsborough's Black Beauty, it might keep you in frocks for a twelvemonth. But the money isn't the issue, really. It's the disgrace which will ruin me... us.'

'What then, Dickon? What have you done?' Amathia demanded.

'Amathia – I've been selling shares in a company I thought I was part owner of. Smoky Mountain. A gold mine.' He eased himself upright and reached for her hand. 'But it was a fraud! And I had no inkling! Never smelt a whiff of suspicion! And now the crook who flimped me has disappeared without trace – and I'm left to face the angry victims!'

Amathia's eyes grew wide. Her lips parted.

'I heard of this gold mine, you know. Lady Wycherley was gushing about the profit she'd made. She'd invested half her late husband's estate.'

'She and about a thousand others, Amathia. I was taken in by a rogue. But all the hundreds of fooled investors who've lost money – life savings! – won't believe that.

'And think of all the others who will suffer along with them. It's as if an earthquake has struck and Smoky Mountain has collapsed into rubble! And the climbers on its precipice are pulling others into its maw – all those roped to them. Servants might lose livelihoods, tenants their homes.'

Richard righted the bottle, and downed whatever drops were left.

'Tempestibus hiemis defendimus…' he mumbled and began to cry.

'God, he even convinced me he was a Wykehamist!' he sobbed into clasped, trembling fingers. 'The hollering horde'll soon be beating on Eardingstowe's door, and unlike the cormorant I cannot fly away to sea.'

Amathia pressed her lips to the top of his head in a light kiss.

Richard eyed her through his tears.

'Why the concern for me, dearest one? Aren't you glad to see me in dire straits?'

'You know, husband – I hated you so much when I was younger, I used to fanaticise about something like this happening to you. If you succumbed to some winter chill tomorrow, of course all this would be mine... Eardingstowe, the estate, Carswell's Mill... mine, all mine... at least until Edmund comes of age, which won't be until 1891.'

'Hmm... how tempting for you!'

'Except that now I see it isn't going to work out that way, if you're in trouble with the law, Dickon.'

'Yes. I'm not sure whether fraud is still a hanging offence.'

'Even if not... you're ruined, aren't you? You'll lose Eardingstowe, your title, everything, won't you? The estate will be forfeit.'

'I expect so, yes.'

'So, the children and I would be destitute! We'd have to depend on the goodwill of some distant, well-wishing relation taking us in out of charity.'

'Quite. Makes me realise why some women want the vote!'

'How long has this been going on, Dickon?'

'Years...' he sighed.

'Dickon,' Amathia fondled his hand, 'everything started going wrong for us when Aubrey came home, didn't it? So... maybe... if he went away again, things might be good once more.'

Richard stared at her.

'What do you mean?'

His lady waved a graceful hand.

'We cannot wipe out the disgrace of Smoky Mountain. And you'll always have the reputation of a fool, come what may. But Aubrey could save your neck.'

'Just what are you suggesting, Amathia?'

Amathia cupped Richard's face in both hands. She looked deep into his eyes.

'We could fashion evidence, couldn't we, that Aubrey mired himself in debt over Smoky Mountain? And even that he was the one behind Smoky Mountain and duped you! Years ago, if need be, before he went away to war. You always said he had the reputation of a spendthrift, didn't you?

'Suppose Aubrey was to meet with an accident at Kilve Cliff… well, you are Justice of the Peace for these parts, Richard. Who would gainsay a verdict of suicide? We might have to buy off persons like Boscawen maybe…' she finished on a shrug.

Suddenly, a rattling and squeaking rent the air outside the window. Amathia let out a startled gasp. Her look shot towards the source of the disruption.

The letter-carrier could be made out through the blizzard. He was approaching along the carriage-sweep – pedalling a contraption. The large wheel at the front churned the snow like butter.

'Goodness! What on earth is that?' Amathia cried.

The silent Richard stirred himself to look.

'It's called a "bicycle", Amathia. Don't it look ridiculous? Doesn't go faster than a horse and takes a lot more effort to ride, although I suppose it eats less hay. The world's a crazy place today.'

She smiled weakly.

'When there's no way out, and you've no option but to continue onwards, whatever lies ahead and whate'er the cost… *"Cannon to right of them, Dickon. Cannon to left of them. Cannon in front of them…"*'

'"*Into the mouth of Hell rode the six hundred!*"'

She smoothed away sweaty strands of hair from his brow.

'Why don't you come with me to the nursery, Dickon? The nursemaid Kate tells me Ned rolled himself over for the first time this morning. Another three months and he'll be crawling. Our little prodigy is going to have a great future, Richard, and I shan't let anyone stop him.'

'Clemmie, do you recall that old fisherman who used to live in the shack at the foot of the cliff? Warned us children to stay away because at high tide the water came almost to the threshold – and Jenny Greenteeth had been seen there sometimes.'

'Ah, yes! But you and I were curious, as always, Aubrey… snuck in one night… and found the old rogue counting his smuggler contraband!'

Clemence ambled her way around the Somerlees' beach cottage, flicking at months' worth of dust. The little retreat was not far from the path to Kilve. In summer, the family came for fishing and boating trips or picnics on the cliffs, even an adventurous night or two out.

In the dark months of the year, though, the property stood unused. A seaweed smell hung in the musty air. Clemence gave the cushion on the seat in the oriel window a sturdy brush. There she settled, looking out over the waves.

Michael lit the candle in the lamp. Amber light furled into the corners and chased away the shadows. Earthenware, pots and kettles gleamed on shelf and mantelpiece. Upon one wall hung an anchor.

'I thought to bring along a supply of flints to get the stove going. And some clean goblets! And cider. I knew there'd not be much of a welcome here at this time of year.'

'That sounds good, Aubrey.'

'It's a good place for us to meet though, Clemmie. Away from Eardingstowe, and Dickon and Mathy.'

Michael softly crossed the rug and bare floorboards to where the Somerlee woman sat. He handed her cider which he'd heated up.

She began to drink. He stood over her as she did. The warm liquid began to colour up her cheek. One Saxon-gold ringlet dangled against a sinewy, breakable neck.

Her eyes flickered shut and open, and shut again. She must be slipping away into drowsiness.

Michael fingered her hand – so lightly that a dozer would believe it no more than a dust mote. His touch slid up her wrist. Leaning close, he was about to brush an airy kiss on the side of her face.

Seabirds shrieked around the chimneystacks. Seawater battered the glass as a mega-wave crashed upon the rocks.

But Clemence wasn't asleep. She dashed for the fireplace. Up swept the poker – aimed at his heart.

'I'll use this poker – I swear I will – if you lay another finger on me. We know who you are… Michael McFarland!'

Michael sank into the window-seat she'd vacated.

'Aunt Lizzy's met with Father Cassidy. He's identified you from a recent photograph. And he's willing to sign an affidavit. We know you faked your own death after you ran away blubbering from the battle of Gettysburg. We could get you hanged for desertion and cowardice if nothing else. And we know it was you behind Smoky Mountain!'

For a long while, he stared at the termagant with the pointy weapon.

He began to laugh.

'All right, then. Game's up!' He set his head on one side, studying her. 'Is that what you're going to do then, you and Lizzy? See me hanged?'

Clemence relaxed and lowered her weapon.

'Funnily enough… Michael!… no. For what it's worth… most of those who've lost money in your little fraud probably deserve it. And that includes Dickon.' She took a step towards him. 'And what was done to you and your family back in Ireland was terrible. I'm very ashamed… Michael! Listen! If you want to go on being Aubrey, and enjoying your fame and fortune, then Lizzy and I are willing to turn a blind eye. We'll say nothing. Just as long as you don't hurt any member of the family any more than they have been already. Does that sound fair?'

Michael sat back in the seat.

'Have you asked yourself why you doubted for so long that I was Aubrey? Was it because you fancied me that you realised I couldn't be your brother? Ah, Clemence – deep down, did you?'

'No...' she replied, thoughtfully. 'I'm such a fool I think I did believe in you – or at least I was in turmoil over it for many, many months. My aunt searched high and low for my brother, even spoke with the Russian high command. If Aubrey'd been a prisoner we'd have found him. I think he died – the Serbs murdered him and disposed of his body somewhere that he would never be found to shame them.'

She stepped to the centre of the rug to look hard at him.

'We've always thought Isabella was the scatterbrain of the family, but on this occasion she showed more wit than Richard or me. She saw through you straight away, you know. As soon as she saw you in Vienna. She knew you weren't Aubrey.'

'Yes... that I gathered. Fancied me something rotten, though. Playing along with my deception was her way of getting inside my breeches.'

'Quite! You know, I don't believe it was your so-called memories that made me and Dickon and the others so uncertain. I think it was the fact that Bella seemed so convinced – that's what persuaded the rest of us.'

'The madness of crowds...' Michael muttered, and smiled.

'But now Bella has come to Aunt Lizzy and me in tears. Because she's with child. Everyone knows it can't be Lord Markham's – not while his taste runs for young men rather than his wife.'

'So, what do you expect me to do about it? Even if Markham divorces her, I can hardly marry a woman the world thinks is my sister.'

'No... no, I realise that.'

The two stared at each other for a long interval.

'Isabella has been an awful flirt for years. You aren't the first to get her in the family way, you know. There were two others. Lord Markham isn't foolish enough to imagine he could pass them off as his own. So, he spirited her away to some remote estate of his, then paid a tenant whose wife was expecting to pretend they'd had twins.'

Michael slowly got to his feet. He collected his overcoat.

'All right. I'm on my way, Clemence.'

'We've copied one good idea you had, Michael McFarland,' Clemence said. 'Aunt Lizzy has her own spy placed in Dwellan House now. Gathering intelligence on Warburton and his staff to expose their mistreatment of Cassie and the other patients.'

'It's been nice knowing you, Clemmie.' A slow, dragging smile came to Michael's face, and he laughed. 'And for what it's worth… you I really wanted.' He crossed to the exit. There – he paused, hand on the open door, and looked back.

'There's just one thing I'd like to tell you,' he said. 'When the story was first in the newspapers last summer… Cornet Somerlee found after all these years… one newspaper mentioned the Earl of Cardigan. Said Cardigan had been to Vienna a year or two ago and found the man with no name being cared for at Klosterneuburg Priory. And Cardigan was convinced this man was Cornet Somerlee… said he had Cornet Somerlee's sword.

'Well… I never saw Cardigan. I was never in Klosterneuburg. And I didn't claim to have Aubrey's sword – I figured he'd have been robbed of his valuables, see! Whoever it was Cardigan saw in the priory… it wasn't me, Clemmie.'

Michael smiled a final farewell, went out and shut the door.

She rode at a gallop over the headland and through the lanes to Eardingstowe – desperate to see Dickon.

But a tweenie Clemence did not know answered the door.

How far Eardingstowe must have sunk that a between-maid was doing the butler's job. Sir Richard and Lady Amathia were not at home, the girl said. Clemence might leave her card if she wished.

'Please! You must tell Sir Richard to see me or the countess as soon as possible. It's urgent!'

But that was the most she could manage.

She returned to the road. There would be snow soon, she thought, looking up at the darkening sky. A sense of dread was also falling.

And what more calamities could descend, hey? Her brother Carrie had drowned in the Eardingstowe mere, Richard's life was in tatters, the Somerlees in disgrace the length of the land – even Lysithea had not been invited to Marlborough House the Christmastide just gone.

Philo was horribly dead; and Clemence found she had cared for him – in a way. Enough to miss never bantering with him again… *laughing* with him, damn it. Liking being with him… as much as she did Fanny, truth be told.

The beautiful city of Paris was starving, France facing ruination at the hands of the vengeful Prussians. Now 1871 to come would see Clemence's sister bring a half-Irish bastard into the world.

Clemence looked up at sound of clumsy hoof beats heading her way.

Mr Shankly passed her, hurrying his pony along the lane in the direction of Kilve. She waved and called out to him.

'Miss Clemmie!' he said as he looked back and saw her.

She smiled to herself. At least someone didn't call her "Your Grace" – he'd known her as Miss Clemmie all her life.

He must be one of the last parish constables in England since Sir Robert Peel had introduced the police force. Lived above the Eardingstowe lock-up where poachers, thieves and other wrongdoers were kept before being handed over to the baronet. The constable's ornate truncheon hung above the lintel.

But Mr Shankly was eighty-three; after him, Clemence guessed, there would be no more of his ilk.

'Is the Taunton road still open, Mr Shankly? I'm staying at Dwellan House overnight, and it looks like snow.'

'Still open, Miss Clemmie. But 'ee'd best get going, m'dear. Tis late, see. I'd come part way with 'ee… see you safe on your road. But I'm summoned to the cliff top. Been an accident, so I'm told.' He looked that way with a worried frown.

'Well, I'll not keep you, Mr Shankly.'

Clemence watched after the constable until he disappeared behind the wall of St Laurey's.

She walked her mount through the gate in the lane which led into the Taunton road, and began to ride the bridle path. The Quantocks were bruise-coloured shadows in the cloudy distance.

The Earl of Cardigan, who had known Aubrey well, believed he had met him? Didn't wish to tell the Somerlees for fear of raising their hopes?

"He did not know his own name or where he had come from, nor did he know me," Lord Cardigan reported, *"but I was sure he was Cornet Somerlee, and the sword was certainly genuine. But maybe I scared him, for when I returned – in great excitement – sadly, he had vanished again."*

And now Cardigan was dead, and his knowledge with him.

But whoever it was Cardigan saw was not the impostor McFarland?

Was this that cruel trickster's final vengeance on the woman who rejected his loving charms? *Or was it true?*

The first snowflakes began to fall. She drew her cloak tighter and shielded her face. Soon there were more and more snowflakes until she could barely see her way ahead.

And now McFarland, too, had vanished into the blizzard.

Gone, then, just like Aubrey. And maybe he, too, would one day come back.

Lightning Source UK Ltd.
Milton Keynes UK
UKHW02f2002131018
330382UK00006B/123/P